Black Mulberries

CAITLIN DAVIES

POCKET
BOOKS

LONDON • NEW YORK • TORONTO • SYDNEY

First published in Great Britain by Simon & Schuster, 2007
This edition first published by Pocket Books, 2008
An imprint of Simon & Schuster UK
A CBS COMPANY

1 3 5 7 9 10 8 6 4 2

Simon & Schuster UK Ltd
1st Floor
222 Gray's Inn Road
London WC1X 8HB

www.simonandschuster.co.uk

Simon & Schuster Australia
Sydney

A CIP catalogue record for this book is available from the British Library

ISBN: 978-1-4165-2254-6

This book is a work of fiction. Names, characters, places and incidents are
either a product of the author's imagination or are used fictitiously. Any resemblance
to actual people living or dead, events or locales is entirely coincidental.

Typeset by Rowland Phototypesetting Ltd, Bury St Edmunds, Suffolk

Printed and bound in Great Britain by
CPI Antony Rowe, Chippenham and Eastbourne

To Mum and Dad,
for first taking me on safari

Prologue

Night comes quickly to the Okavango Delta. At six pm the sky turns the colour of a milky peach and the fronds of the palm trees on the watery islands become silhouetted against the sky like black knitting needles. Within thirty minutes, the light will be gone and the sky the colour of a raisin.

It was the time of evening when the African Mourning Dove gave its last sad sunset call, its yellow eyes dimming in the dusk. It was the time when the safari guides tied up the mekoro, roping the canoes firmly to the rows of wooden posts lining the jetty that stretched out over the waters of the Khwai River, swollen from the recent rains.

With the mekoro secured, the men threw down their poles and the wooden mophane sticks clattered dully against the sides of the canoes. The sound echoed in the flat land so that up in the wooded area of the camp even the chambermaids heard it as they turned down the guests' bed sheets and placed chocolates as delicate as shells on the pillows.

Leapile Muyendi was the oldest of the guides and so the others hung back, allowing him to lead them back to the camp. His boots were wet and scuffed, the laces that wound up around his ankles tied in knots where they had repeatedly been broken and repaired. He had spent some hours clearing one of the river channels of papyrus, so the tourists would have an uninterrupted view of the nearby lagoon when they went out the next morning. As he worked a pair of Swamp Boubous had watched from the reed bed, one whistling, the other replying with a rattling sound.

Leapile Muyendi always wore his boots when he stood in the waters; he believed they protected him. For twelve years he had worked for Wilderness Camp – he had been the first to be hired and he was the longest serving safari guide. One of his former colleagues had been killed by a hippopotamus while out clearing a river channel; another had been taken by a lion in the bush. But Leapile was still here.

He didn't speak as he led the way back to the camp; he was a man not much taken with talking. If he were asked a question then he preferred to use his eyebrows to respond. That was another reason he had been here so long: he didn't take part in the camp gossip. Unlike his first-born son Electricity, he refused to be drawn into the politics of the place.

Leapile reached the end of the jetty, his boots shielding him from the wooden slats which were still hot from the heat of the day. He turned left, his posture relaxing slightly as his boots found the grass. He heard the spark of a match and smelt the sudden flash of sulphur in the air. Two of the guides were sharing a cigarette.

'There's going to be meat tomorrow,' said one.

Leapile coughed warningly. Of course there would be meat the next day; Isaac Muyendi was arriving. But there was no need to make an announcement of it; conversation should be reserved for things that were important to say. And Leapile felt a little defensive for he was Isaac's cousin, the son of Isaac's father's eldest brother, the late Nkapa Muyendi. But then Leapile knew that many people regarded themselves as Isaac's cousin, or his uncle, or his nephew, or any relation at all that would enable them to stake a claim to such a successful man. For like a Chief, Isaac Muyendi provided for those who were beneath him, and if you were his relative then he ensured you were well cared for.

As the safari guides walked on they could see, in the distance to their right, the outdoor dining area and the clump of marula trees whose leaves were still green. Leapile could smell the scent of roasting chicken and rosemary and, behind that, a sticky chocolate smell. The tourists would be returning from their evening game drive, their dinner was being prepared. The guide who had been anticipating meat began grumbling about the night before; he had gone into the bush to urinate and nearly stumbled over a snake.

The guides separated, each making their way through to the back of the camp on the meandering, well-worn series of pathways. The pathways were fashioned from sand, the surrounding bush held back by short wooden poles laid horizontally end-to-end. The sand bore evidence of the passage of the day, of the footprints of the women carrying laundry from the tourists' tents in the morning, the weaving smudge of a puff adder crossing the sand to seek shade in the undergrowth at midday, the flecked toe prints of a hornbill which had strutted down the path as the air began to cool, the large bootmarks of the tourists setting off on their evening drive.

Leapile passed by the supplies tent to ask for a bowl of sour milk for his youngest son who had been sick that morning. His wife said sour milk would revive the boy. If the fever continued then they would have to ask for help, but for now neither Leapile nor his wife wanted anyone to know the boy was there. His wife was on duty now, laying the table for supper, and from the dining tent he could hear the muffled clang of the heavy silver cutlery being placed upon the table. The kitchen woman told Leapile to come back later; she would have some sour milk for him then. He took off his boots, arranging them carefully on the grass dampened by the camp's sprinkler system, and sat down to wait.

Tim Loveless stood by the fireplace, legs apart, his hands held firmly behind his back. His right foot rested on a pile of wood and he thought the sole of his open-toed sandal looked vulnerable somehow against the thick chunk of mophane. Tim could feel the heat of the fire; see the blond hairs on his leg lit up by the flickering flames. The fire was stoked each evening at seven pm and Tim always stood in the same place, waiting for his guests. This was the part of the job he liked the best, the end of the day when things began to wind down, when the tourists wanted nothing better than to sit outside and share their stories, to eat their fill, and eventually to retire to bed.

The camp was full, it was the beginning of both the hunting and the tourist season, and the camp had re-opened after a break of two months. Tim had just taken eight of the guests on a driving safari: a German couple, an American family with a young girl, two Italians, an elderly British man. Most of the guests were from South Africa and Namibia, so it was an unusual mix tonight. On the whole Tim liked the Germans best, for while they craved a constant programme of events, they were generous with their tips and with their praise. The Americans wanted only to see the big game, the Italians appeared to think they were on a fashion shoot, the British were notorious complainers.

'Ah, here you are!' Tim called as the German couple emerged from the porch of their tent, one of six erected to the east of the camp beneath a group of sycamore fig and fever berry trees. The couple strode across the lawn to the fireplace and Tim could see, even from a distance, that they had showered and changed. Their faces shone in the semi-darkness, he could see the daggers of freshly ironed creases in their clothes.

Tim had changed as well, dressing in his evening clothes: a blue shirt, a pair of khaki shorts, a crocodile skin belt around his stomach to which was attached his Leatherman penknife and the strap of his walkie-talkie. He had shaved too, and applied gel to his hair so that it gleamed now like a wet Secretary bird. Tim took his right foot off the woodpile and in a practised gesture brought his left hand forward, holding it out in welcome.

The Germans looked expectant. Tim knew they would

want to talk about the leopard they had seen draped gracefully on the branches of an acacia tree an hour earlier. He took personal pride in having found it and had immediately radioed two other camps in the area, alerting three guides who, like Tim, were roaming the area in safari vehicles. Tim enjoyed the bantering, competitive relationship he had with Craig, the manager at one of the lodges on Chief's Island, and he had scored a point by finding the leopard. It was the end of the wet season, the game were not as dense or as visible as they had been during the dry months. Tim knew it was all a question of luck.

He pulled out one of the chairs, a wooden camping chair with a green canvas back that he thought was the sort a Hollywood film director might use on set. The German woman looked at her husband as if for permission and he nodded, so she took the chair and eased herself down. As she sat a tumble of bats came flying out of the eaves of the thatched bar area behind the fire. The bats fluttered, criss crossing each other, disappearing into the night.

'The real Africa,' sighed the German man, Klaus, pulling out a chair for himself.

'Ah yes,' Tim nodded enthusiastically and rubbed his hands in front of the fire. This was what the guests paid for, this was why they came, and this was what Wilderness Camp had to offer. It was one of the oldest and most successful of the camps that had sprung up, in the past twenty years, on the outer reaches, on the inland islands, and on the waterways of the Okavango Delta.

Tim pulled out another chair as the American couple arrived, without their daughter.

'She's sleeping,' said the mother, a nervous, pale skinned woman. 'She is, like, OK in a tent on her own, isn't she?'

'Of course,' said Tim. He smiled and the creases around his eyes that came with years of squinting into the African sun deepened. He waited until the American woman had sat down and then he rested his hand on the back of her chair in what he believed was a protective manner.

A waitress came bearing a tray, offering bottles of beer and chilled glasses of almond coloured wine that had been flown up from South Africa on the company plane that morning.

'Last week we were in Etosha,' said Klaus, settling back on his chair. 'It was like going on safari in a zoo!'

Tim sighed in weary agreement. 'Namibia is getting totally overrun. It's heading the way of Zim, a basket case of a country if ever there was one.' He stopped and gave a short laugh. 'If you want to see game, this is where you come. It's not for nothing we're known as the predator capital of Africa.' Tim took his hand from the American woman's chair and held out his arms, waving them in the evening air. 'Look at this, it's totally pristine. We're talking over *two thousand* square miles of swamp. There are no fences in Moremi Game Reserve. No guards ...'

'And tourism is very important for your country?' asked Klaus.

Tim smiled; he did not say it was not his country.

'Tourism creates ten thousand jobs in Botswana. And it was the tribe itself that created Moremi.'

'The real Africa,' said Klaus again. 'But we have not seen any crocodiles,' he added a little petulantly. He took out a well-worn guidebook, flicking through until he found a checklist of animals, and began to read aloud. 'Lion, yes. Elephant, yes. Hippo, yes.'

'Sable antelope,' added his wife.

'Sable antelope, yes. Crocodile, no.'

'No,' agreed Tim smoothly. 'But we will tomorrow.'

'And are there many?' asked Klaus's wife. The wine had brought a flush to her face and she was relaxing now, growing talkative.

'In these parts? There's been sightings of some monster Nile Crocodiles, four metres plus. Even in Maun, where you arrived, there are plenty. Only last week a man shot a three-metre one in his garden.'

'He shot it?' asked Klaus.

'Yes. It had eaten his dog.'

'That seems rather harsh.'

'Absolutely,' said Tim. 'The whole point is, Africa is wild. That's why we got you guys to sign indemnity forms. Only kidding,' he said to the American woman who looked alarmed. 'If you go around shooting game because they killed your dog then what's going to be left?'

'For us to see,' said Klaus.

'For you to see,' agreed Tim. 'And that is why,' he added, his voice rising a little so that the people around the fire turned towards him, 'and that is why this is the place many call the last of the Old Africa.'

The conversation paused and, in a moment of silence, the guests surveyed their surroundings: the lawn that led down to the jetty, the clumps of dark papyrus that fringed the water, the fan palm trees situated on the open grassland on the other side of the river, the sliver of moon that had taken up position in the blackened sky. But the silence didn't last long for soon there was a party of sounds, a clackering and a whistling, a bouncing and a trembling, as birds and bats and frogs called out to each other in the darkness.

'Where is the nearest village?' asked Klaus's wife, putting down her glass.

'Village?' queried Tim. 'We're in the wilderness here!'

'There are no people?' asked Klaus.

'There are no people,' agreed Tim. He felt safe in saying this, for the lodges were careful to take their guests in a long loop around the village of Khwai, long enough that they never saw a village was there. 'This is one of the last areas of pristine wilderness in Africa. It gives you the feeling, doesn't it, that you have the place all to yourself?'

'Oh!' said the German woman. 'We were hoping to see some traditional dance.'

'My wife is a great exponent of cultural tourism,' said Klaus.

'Is that so?' Tim responded politely. 'Have you visited our curio shop? Plenty of cultural items, baskets, leather goods . . .'

'Locally made?' inquired Klaus's wife.

'But of course,' said Tim.

The guests watched as a man walked slowly down the pathway that led from the fireplace, stooping every few metres to light candles that bobbed in individual bowls of water. In the distance, far off in the darkness, the air was broken by a trembling laugh and then a high-pitched whoop. Wuwu-we! Wuwu-we!

'Hyena,' said Klaus.

Tim nodded.

'Ugly scavengers, I think,' said Klaus.

'Ah yes.' Tim spoke carefully, not wanting to contradict a guest. 'Although they do of course also hunt.'

'Of course.'

'Amazing jaws,' Tim mused, glancing at the German woman who seemed to have a smirk on her face. 'You should see the way they crack open bones.'

'The Masai,' said Klaus authoritatively, 'put their dead out for hyenas to dispose of.'

Tim smiled politely. 'We had a sighting last year, twenty hyenas cleared a site of a two-hundred kg zebra *and* its foal in less than half an hour. After killing both.' He wondered whether to explain the traditional hyena greeting, the way clan members licked each other's genitals. He decided not, picking up his beer and taking a single sip. Isaac Muyendi was arriving tomorrow; it wouldn't do to have a hangover. Things were always tense when Isaac came to camp. Tim far preferred dealing with Lenny Krause; they spoke the same language, and it was Lenny who'd got him the job, not Isaac.

'And for tomorrow, what is the plan?' asked Klaus.

'I think we have you down for a sunrise game walk?'

'And will you be armed?' asked Klaus's wife.

'I will,' Tim said. He didn't feel it necessary to explain that he didn't have a licence for a gun, that guns were not allowed in a national park anyway. He loved the feeling of leading the tourists out of camp at sunrise with a weapon in his arms. He never told them it wasn't loaded.

By eight pm the twelve guests were all seated comfortably at the dining tent, arranged around a long wooden table carved from mukwa and covered with a white tablecloth. It was cosy in the tent; the canvas walls were open at one end allowing a view down to the jetty and to the river, a view that was now lit with dozens of flickering candles. The kitchen women cleared the table, taking away the large white ceramic plates, removing the traces of chicken and rosemary, of ostrich fillets and peppercorn, of beef with monkey gland sauce. The women moved quietly, their black plimsolls pattering softly on the sand floor of the tent, the light from the two candelabras on the table making dancing patterns on the chequered cloth of their full-length aprons. The women kept their eyes down, except to glance occasionally at Tim or his assistant Julie, an Australian woman from Melbourne with a shiny red nose and a butterfly clip in her hair.

Tim was standing, about to pour the American woman another glass of wine, when the first shriek came.

'What was that?' the American woman shivered.

'Hyena,' said Klaus.

Tim frowned. For a second he thought it was a baboon. The baboons had become troublesome recently, running through the camp, raiding food from the supplies tent, knocking over the dustbins. The American woman looked at him, waiting. He smiled and was about to speak, to offer reassurance, when the people around the table heard the second shriek. Tim put the bottle down hurriedly, too hurriedly for it spilled and the red wine began to soak into the starched tablecloth, disappearing into the cloth like water into sand.

'It sounds like a child!' Klaus said, and the American woman stood, her face panicked as she turned to the camp manager. But Tim had left the dining area and was racing along the stone path that led to the toilet. From here the path passed the supplies tent, then a thatched gazebo with wicker chairs and footstools, and then it forked into two. One path led right to the tourists' tents, the other wove west through the camp to where the staff lived. Eventually all the paths joined at the entrance to the camp, marked with a sign burnt into a slab of leadwood, left leaning on the whitened remains of a hippo skull.

As Tim reached the supplies tent Leapile emerged from the shadows to join him, his naked feet moving silently on the sand.

'What the fuck ...' Tim said into the darkness. He could distinguish two sounds now: the scream of a child and the mocking squeal of a hyena.

Now Leapile was running too and as the two men ran the screams intensified until they could hear a whole pack of hyenas, long drawn out calls that got higher and higher, more and more hysterical. The squeals pierced the night like drunken laughter. Then suddenly they stopped and were replaced with giggles and whines.

Leapile reached the tent first. It was Leapile who saw the hyena come galloping out, who recognised at once the beige skin splattered with dark brown markings. He noted the way the animal's ears were cocked, its long tail arched forward over its back, the crest of the caramel coloured hair on its neck erect.

Tim reached for his walkie-talkie, fumbling as he took it off his belt. 'Craig,' he said, his voice a mixture of urgency and relief, 'we have a kill. Over.'

BOOK ONE
Candy

Chapter One

I'm sitting on the floor opposite my grandmother and the floor is cool and holds me in place. My grandmother is on the two-seater sofa and her legs are set apart because the shiny black material of her new cycling shorts is beginning to bother her. My mother gave her the shorts yesterday after failing to find underwear big enough to fit my grandmother, who is very disappointed that the shops don't sell bloomers anymore. Not even our general trading store sells bloomers, just silky nylon panties in every colour of the rainbow. My grandmother wants something to wear under her clothes because she is anxious that when the wind blows someone may be able to see up her dress, even though the wind never blows around here.

'Hey it is hot,' she says.

I stifle a smile because I am still looking at my grandmother's cycling shorts and they make her legs look like a beetle's.

'Candy, my child, isn't it hot?'

'*Ee*,' I say obediently, 'it is too hot.'

'*Batho ba modimo*,' she declares, fanning her face with her hand. She shuffles her bottom on the two-seater sofa and sighs as if nothing good ever happens around here.

I stretch my legs out on the floor and see how dry my

skin is because I'm still in my nightie and I haven't washed my body and I haven't put on any cream. If I could I would stay like this all day every day, inside the house wearing a nightie that smells of my body when it has been asleep.

'They aren't trousers, these things, are they?' says my grandmother, picking at her cycling shorts with trembly fingers.

'No, *Mma*, they are not trousers.'

My grandmother nods and a little bit of sun from outside catches the big square lenses of her glasses so that all I can see is reflection and not her eyes. My grandmother doesn't like women wearing trousers, and when the Headman sent the white woman home from the Kgotla meeting this morning because she was wearing trousers my grandmother knew this was the right thing to do. The woman is a newspaper reporter and she said she had never heard of such a rule in her life. But she was not given much sympathy because people knew the Headman was simply enforcing tradition and that was what my grandmother said. Even though we know the woman, for it was Petra Krause. Petra Krause has hair like fire, like the really hot yellow part of a fire, and sometimes I dream that I do too. Mma Ramotswe asked what is Petra Krause doing back here and my grandmother said she didn't know but that she would soon find out. My grandmother knows everything that happens here in Sehuba. Sometimes she knows even before the Headman does.

But my grandmother doesn't know I have a pair of

trousers myself, tucked away in the cupboard I share with my brother Bulldog. My mother doesn't know about these either, but then there are a lot of things my mother doesn't know about, and sometimes I think I am the only one who knows everything. My father says I spy too much and that I should join the police force and go around poking my nose into other people's business and get paid for it and then he can retire and sit around drinking tea all day like my grandmother.

'Where's the tea?' my grandmother shouts as if she has suddenly remembered something, and she begins waving her stick in the direction of the kitchen outside. Her lips are puffed up with annoyance, they are puffed up so much that she could easily hold a pencil between her top lip and her nose.

I smile, thinking about my grandmother wearing a pencil. Pencil is what my father was called at school. It was a nickname, a nasty, mean nickname, because in those days he was very thin. It's not right that people should call each other names.

I look away from my grandmother's cycling shorts and my eyes focus on her chest for she is wearing a shirt that looks like a basket, like the patterns on a basket in which the strands of grass have been dyed maroon and white with a weave that is so tight it makes your eyes dance. I sold a basket like this a week ago to a tourist at our general trading store; it was a basket with the pattern of an antelope running and the man patted me on the head and gave me one pula. My grandmother has agreed to sell baskets at the store, although she says they are not as good quality as they used to be because these days they are made for selling, not for using. And these days you have to travel a long, long way to find the right things to make a basket properly.

'Where is the *tea*?' shouts my grandmother. '*Hela*!' she shouts, and rolls her eyes.

The maid comes to the doorway.

'And the biscuits!' my grandmother says, still shouting, although the maid is right in front of her. The maid is a small girl just like me and she comes from a village near Chobe, and sometimes she cries at night because her family are far away.

I hang my head down between my legs, waiting, for we always seem to be waiting in this house and one of the things we are waiting for is for the house to be finished. My grandfather Rweendo Muyendi built this house many, many years ago and it was to be the biggest house in the village, after the Headman's. It is round, in the traditional style, but big enough that as small children Bulldog and me could play hide and seek for hours. He always liked to hide in my father's bedroom, in a wooden trunk where my father keeps his papers. I always chose to squeeze myself behind something, like the room divider with its faded pictures from old magazines pasted with thick white syrupy glue on the rectangular panels, or the two-door refrigerator that stands against the living room wall and which has never been used. There is still a tiny shiny key hanging in the lock.

I like looking at the women in the pictures from the magazines because they look powerful and they are wearing nice clothes and it is as if they are saying, 'Look at me!' I was the one who glued two pictures of my Aunty Kazi on the room divider; I glued them right down at the bottom so that my grandmother and my father wouldn't see. I found them in an envelope my father threw out and I rescued them because she looks so pretty. In one she is wearing a black hat which I think is made from leather and the lip of the cap is at an angle across her forehead so that one of her eyes is almost hidden. She isn't smiling; instead she looks a bit sulky. And she isn't really wearing any clothes, just a small piece of material around her neck that I think is a leopard print. Of course the picture ends just there, so perhaps she is wearing some other clothes and I can't see them. In the second picture you can see her whole body; she is kneeling with her legs apart, something like sitting on a donkey, and her arms are held down in her lap. I can't see her face so well in this one, but I can see her clothes and they are golden and very wonderful.

I'm glad we have such a big room that we need a room divider, and that's because of my grandfather Rweendo Muyendi. But although my grandfather built this house he never finished it and after his death my father took over the house and he hasn't finished it either. In the middle of the house is a large room which always seems to be dusty no matter how many times it is cleaned. The light from outside never quite reaches this room and the air always feels damp and heavy as if it is a late afternoon in the rainy season. Around this room is a corridor of sorts sectioned off into separate rooms like the pie charts we are told to draw at school. But while the house is grand and still larger than all our neighbours', it is not finished. It has no door, either at the front or at the back, so that snakes and other creatures find welcome spaces inside when the sun or the rains become too much. And when a snake does come in then we know it is a bad sign, my grandmother and I.

But the really strange thing about this house is the room at the top, the attic which is reached by some wooden stairs, stairs I am not supposed to climb. My grandmother is wary of me climbing the stairs because she thinks I will fall. I don't know anyone else who has an attic and I don't really know what it is for. My Aunty Kazi used to sleep there but now it is used only by the bats. It was in the attic that the first fire started. I was standing there, just looking round, when the mattress on the floor popped into flames. I felt the heat from those flames very quickly, even on my head, which had just been shaved because that was the day I became a woman.

The reason I was in the attic was because of the spirit we had seen at the window, my friend Mary and me. There is a very small window, high up on the wall, and my mother covered it long ago with some thin white cloth that may have once been a bed sheet. Mary and me were in the attic one day when the cloth suddenly moved; it billowed out quickly like a sheet drying in the wind, except there was no wind at all that day. So we said that as there was no wind, it was a spirit instead and we cried '*Mme we!*' the way you do at school when the teacher gets a switch and slaps you on the leg. We gave the spirit a name and came up to visit her sometimes, which was what I had done the day the first fire started and when Mary was still my friend.

I didn't tell anyone about the spirit except for my grandmother because I know she likes these sorts of things and won't ever laugh at me. Once I told her when I saw a ghost in the toilet outside, an elderly man with a hat on sitting on a chair. My grandmother said, 'Oh, that must have been Uncle Mogotsi. Was he very tall, with a hat on you say?' I told her no, it was a short man and he had a big scar on his face just above the eyes. So my grandmother said, 'Oh, then that must have been your father's grandfather. Did you ask him what he wanted?' But I hadn't spoken to the ghost at all, I hadn't even thought about asking him what he wanted, only my grandmother would have thought of that.

The room where we are sitting now has uneven red flagstones on the floor and when I rub my toes up and down on the stones I can smell candle wax, paraffin and plastic bags. I was the one who prepared the mixture, melting a whole box of long white candles over the fire outside, then two plastic bags which shrank quickly and smelt bad, and then adding the paraffin and stirring it all until it was a paste for the floor. That has always been my job, to do the floor, and although I last did it two months ago, if I rub my toes then the smell starts all over again as if it were fresh.

There is not much to look at in here except for my grandmother, the floor, my grandfather Rweendo Muyendi's wooden chair that no one is allowed to sit on, and the naked doorway that leads straight to the porch. If

I turn my head to the right I can see the giant sycamore fig and behind that the black mulberry tree. We have all used that mulberry tree; my father used to hide there to avoid a beating. But my Aunty Kazi used the mulberry tree to escape, climbing out of the attic room and down into the safety of the branches. Then she would run off to picnics in the village and to bars where she was not allowed because she was very naughty. But I only know this from overhearing the adults, for no one talks to me about Aunty Kazi very much and I know for a fact she has not been told about the party we are having today. I wonder, if she knew about the party, then would she come and get in a plane and fly all the way to see us?

My brother Bulldog has used the tree as well and last month he fell out of it and sprained his ankle. But no one told him off; he can do whatever he wants. There is one other thing about the mulberry tree, and that is something that happens only when the flowers begin to swell. And it is something that only my grandmother and me have ever seen and I am not to talk about that.

My grandmother knows more about that tree than anyone else and she tells me that it is not correct to call the fruit a berry, for it is a collective fruit made up of different parts like a family. It is not one fruit, but many tiny swollen flowers, and that is why it is so difficult to pick the fruit because you have to squeeze the berries to get them off the tree and when you do they collapse. But if you get some berries and put them in your mouth then there are two tastes at once: it is sweet like sugar and dusty like a flower. My grandmother loves that tree;

she says it is drought-resistant and wind-resistant, just like her. And she will not allow anyone to prune that tree because if they do then the tree will bleed where it is cut and those cuts do not heal.

The maid brings the tea and biscuits and my grandmother cheers up. I stop looking at the tree and I smile at my grandmother because I know she loves me best. Of everyone in the family, she loves me best. But she doesn't return my smile; she has her head cocked to one side listening for my father and so I hang my head again. This party we are waiting for makes me nervous. I just want to sit here in my nightie and watch my grandmother drink her tea and crumble her biscuit.

'What's going on here? Where is everyone?' My father is at the doorway laughing. He always laughs when he arrives somewhere; it's his way of announcing that he has come and his laugh is so warm and deep it makes me feel that everything is all right after all.

He stays in the doorway, looking round the room, though he can see only my grandmother and me are here. My father is a very important person and he goes to a lot of meetings where there are lots of people, even government people, even white people. His face is smooth and he has just trimmed his moustache which is as black as a brand-new pot bought from our general trading store. His stomach is so big that it is further inside the room than the rest of him and I want to run to him and hide in his stomach and smell his sweet bubble gum smell. That is why my father is so handsome because he can eat whatever food he wants and now he is big and soft and all the women like him. When my father laughs his eyes shine and his cheeks fill up like a baby.

A small hoopoe bird swoops down from where it has been sitting in the branches of the mulberry tree and flies straight at the window, its beak hammering against the rusty metal frame of the mosquito net. It's a silly-looking bird, the crown of its head is all puffed up like it just had a big surprise, and its beak is long like the tweezers my father uses sometimes to pull hairs from his nose.

My father frowns and moves as if to wave the hoopoe bird away, but his hand bangs the nail on which I have fixed a string of coloured light bulbs for the party and the string sags and falls so the light bulbs are left hanging in the doorway over my father's head.

I tuck my nightie between my legs and stand up. The fallen light bulbs are not a good sign.

'Candy, Candy, you are looking very sweet today!' my father says in English, laughing at his own joke.

I smile and slide my feet up and down the floor and bask in my father's laughter like lizards do in the sun.

'Get your father a chair!' my grandmother urges. 'My son, come in, come in! Where is your wife?'

'Grace?' asks my father, as if he has several wives, as if he is not sure which one my grandmother is referring to. 'You know women!'

My grandmother nods her agreement; she thinks my mother takes too long about doing things and that is why she is always late.

'What time is it?' my father asks.

'*Hela*!' My grandmother rolls her eyes, but my father

is teasing her, he knows she can only tell the time by the sun.

My father stumbles at the doorway as my brother comes running in from outside. He grabs Bulldog by the arm. 'Hey, *monna*, where are you running to?'

My brother replies in gibberish, he speaks fast like a cartoon character on the videos he is always watching at his friend Neo's house. He thinks he is speaking English but he's not because he doesn't know English like I know English. My brother has a cheeky face, his hair is tufty like a chicken and there is a big gap in his mouth where his two front teeth used to be so when he talks his cartoon talk you can't understand a word because he is lisping as well.

'Go and change, don't you know the party is starting?' asks my father. '*Tsamaya!*' My brother pulls away from him, slipping out of his grasp and running right through the house and out the other side.

'And you?' my father asks.

I don't dare run off like my brother, but I know my father wants me to leave the room so he and my grandmother can talk and it is something important because my father is rattling his car keys in his pocket. But I already know what has happened at Wilderness Camp, everyone has heard what has happened. It was on the radio news at lunchtime and I know what people are saying for it is not normal for a hyena to behave like that; people are saying it is bewitchment.

But we are not allowed to ask, we are to wait and behave as if we know nothing. This is what we are

27

supposed to do every time an animal takes a person. But I know something; I know that when a hyena takes you it takes you by the face and sometimes in dreams it has happened to me.

I wonder if my father will go to the camp as he had planned tomorrow, or whether he will leave right now, and I wish he would take me with him for I have never been to his camp. People pay a lot of money to come to his camp because they want to see our beautiful country and have a nice, peaceful time. But my grandmother says I can't go, she says things in the bush are too dangerous these days.

I get up and head to the kitchen outside where the women are and they are sweating too, sweating with the effort of preparing the food. The small stone room is hot, so hot that I am careful not to brush against the walls. I keep my head down, for above me the rafters are crowded with hanging pots and pans and whisks and knives and drying meat. It is like a workshop in here, a great busy workshop.

I push my way to the sink and lean my stomach up against the cool ribbed metal and the coolness holds me in place and makes me feel that I won't just float up into the sky and be gone. I stare out of the window in front of me and through the smudgy glass I can see my mother in the yard. I know that I can't be seen.

My mother is wearing the dress she always wears; she has three of them and when one is dirty then she wears another one. It is brown and white with a brown trim around the bottom and also around the neck, and a piece of the same material is wrapped around her head. I want to tell her that there is a tear in her stockings and that the heel of the shoe on her right foot is soon going to fall off. But she won't hear me because I am inside and she is not.

She is holding my brother's hand and she looks as if she has just caught him this very second by the fingers, she looks as if she is telling him off and there is a deep line in my mother's forehead which she gets when she frowns. But I can see Bulldog's cheeky face and it is smiling because that is what happens; Bulldog doesn't get told off, and if he does then he just smiles.

I see him as he runs away again and the chickens in the yard scatter, rushing one way and then another as if they can't quite make up their minds, as if they don't quite know from which direction the danger is coming. Chickens are very stupid animals. I wish our ostriches hadn't died, for they were intelligent birds and I dreamt of them becoming friendlier until one day they would allow me to get on their backs and ride. But first one died, and then the other.

I walk down the table in the middle of the room inspecting the bowls. I'm looking for something sweet, something with sugar that will make me feel good. I would take a biscuit, I would take a mango, I would do anything for a *koeksister* the way the Afrikaners make them with the syrup-soaked sponge twisted into a single spiral that squirts sweetness down your throat when you bite it. But nothing here is sweet. There is a cold baked bean salad sprinkled with chilli powder like red sand, three metal bowls of white cabbage sliced in thick crunchy pieces, several piles of skinned potatoes that are still warm and steaming and waiting to be cut up into cubes and dunked in mayonnaise. I take a potato and bite off a chunk. No one will tell me off, I am Isaac Muyendi's daughter.

But one of the women, Precious, hands me a knife and tells me to get chopping, and I think about telling her that my grandmother doesn't let me handle knives; she thinks I will cut myself. But there is an air of urgency in the kitchen; the women need all the help they can get. I take the knife reluctantly, no one will come until this evening, we have all the rest of the day to get the food ready. I wish my Aunty Kazi were coming to the party, even though my grandmother says as far as she is concerned she does not even have a daughter any more and please don't talk about it because it aches her heart. My grandmother says Aunty Kazi will never come back from England because she has forsaken her. My grandmother says Aunty Kazi is deadwood.

Chapter Two

It's dark now, it's so dark that it's past dark, but our house is like an island of light. I've been working with the women, bringing the food out to the trestle tables on the sand, and especially to the table by the mulberry tree which is for the important people and has a tablecloth which is red and shiny so that if anyone spills anything it won't matter, it will just slip off.

There are lights in all the trees, even right up high in the mulberry branches, so high I don't know how anyone got them there. At the edge of the sand where the land dips down to the river there are little tins with wicks dipped in paraffin standing on poles. My father says they use these at the camps and they are good because they are wavering like stars. Everything is moving, the light bulbs are moving and the flames are moving and people are arriving from all around the house. The air smells of coals and soon the meat will be cooked and turned this way and that until it is ready and as brown as chocolate.

Our driveway is full of cars and I have never seen it so full before. The cars are even parked at the back of our yard, on the opposite side from the river where the sand is fine and white and where the only trees are tall and thin with canopies you can see straight through. One person has driven on top of the trunk of a dead tree, which is white and smooth and lies on the ground like the elephant tusks I once saw in the back of a Land Rover in our yard. One moment they were there and one moment they were not, but as for that tree trunk, it has been here since before I even existed. It is deadwood, just like the people the President has been getting rid of in the government because their time has passed and they are useless.

My mother is hurrying across the sand from the kitchen. I can hear the DJ playing Stiger; he has set a table and speakers right next to the mulberry tree and his generator makes the sand tremble. I see my mother stop for a second because Stiger is singing 'Mamalodi' and I know my mother loves this song. But she's frowning because she is too busy, she has too much to do and everything should have been done and finished a long time ago.

My father is standing on the steps of our house greeting people. He is wearing my favourite shirt; it is black and it moves like water and it has a round collar and two pockets at the bottom, only they aren't real pockets because they are sewn shut. MaNeo has spent a long time being greeted, she has shaken my father's hand and admired the yard and said is it correct that three goats have been slaughtered for tonight? And she is still standing there, waving her gold earrings, even though he has other people to greet now.

'Candy we!' MaNeo calls to me. '*Tla kwano!*'

I sidle up and I already know what she is going to do. She is going to look at my titties and say, 'You are growing!'

32

My father laughs and pats me on the head. '*Ee*. We've been watering her every day.'

MaNeo laughs so much that she pretends she has to lean against my father in order to recover and even put a hand up against his chest where her fingers slide along his black shirt. I think she looks like a *mealie* in her dress, like a big wrapped up stick of corn. MaNeo is only paying me attention because she wants to keep my father's attention. When I see her in the village she doesn't pay me any attention at all unless she is telling me off.

'This is so nice, this is an excellent party,' says MaNeo, and she is speaking carefully, she isn't speaking the way she normally does. 'And is your sister here?'

My father chews on his cheek because he doesn't like people asking him about Aunty Kazi and I think MaNeo knows that because everyone else does.

He doesn't answer her, instead he calls 'MaBoipuso!' with a wide smile as a woman as short as an old candle comes round the side of the house.

'I've heard she is very rich,' MaNeo continues before MaBoipuso can say a word. 'She's a model, is that right, in the UK? A very famous model?'

'Yes, so we have heard,' my father says and his jaw muscles clench so I know his teeth are gritted together and they seem to be gritted together so hard I expect to hear them crunch. My Aunty Kazi has had a very easy life ever since she was a baby, that is what my father says. It is OK for her to jet off to the UK but someone has to stay and provide for the family.

MaNeo pats my father on the chest. 'Isn't it lovely

that our sister is doing so well over there in the UK?'

But now the headmaster is here and my father is talking to him and I wonder who has the softer stomach, for they are both very big even though the headmaster is much taller than my father. And now the doctor is here and his head is shiny like clean buttocks and I see the glint of his big thick watch as he pumps my father's hand up and down like he is drawing water at an empty standpipe. Only the doctor doesn't ever have to draw water because he has his own taps at home: he has them in his yard and he has two inside his house as well. And now I know the Headman is coming too because I can hear the noise of the men who always travel ahead of the Headman and check that everyone else has arrived before he does. If you are important then you don't want to arrive at an empty party.

I begin to walk away, pulling on my party dress that is tight on my body for it is new and from our general trading store. The clothes are kept at the back of the store behind a curtain and some are wrapped in plastic that is so soft it sticks to your fingers when you touch it. When I became a woman, after I was allowed to go out of the house, I was taken to choose one of those dresses, and for this party I was allowed to choose another.

I can see Mary and her friends standing near the DJ begging for a song and I can see that behind her back Mary has a can of Fanta and who said she could take that? Someone should give her a thrashing for that. I used to be friends with Mary but that was when I was at school and I haven't been to school for a long time because my grandmother likes me to help her at home. My father says he didn't learn anything at school and anyway, I can work for him. But not at the camp, my grandmother says, there are too many animals in the bush and she wants me at home. Mary waves to me and I feel important because I am Isaac Muyendi's daughter and this is our party.

'Your grandmother is asking for you,' my father calls after me. My grandmother always asks for me, not Bulldog, because I am her favourite and also because I am a girl so I know how to help. She never tells Bulldog to do girl things because he's a boy and he won't be able to do them. So I walk back to the tables on the sand.

I can see my grandmother seated in the middle of the head table where there are red plastic roses in white baskets and her elbows push down on the red shiny table-cloth. She has been complaining of a headache, but she looks happy now. She is wearing a white two-piece suit and the top has ziggy zaggy blue embroidery all around the square-shaped neck and all the way down the front where the gold buttons are.

There are many bottles on the table and thin tall glasses, as thin and tall as lily flowers but without being curled at the top. There is a row of people waiting to greet my grandmother and she calls them forward one by one so she can grasp their hands and draw them right into the light and look at what they are wearing and then we can talk about it later.

'*Ke mang yo?*' she asks, peering at a woman who has just come up behind her. The woman comes forward and introduces herself and my grandmother grasps her and looks up into her face to see who she is. The woman says she is from Khwai and that is near the place that we used to come from.

It is my grandmother's birthday and even though she says she doesn't know the day when she was born and that birthdays are a thing white people do, I can see she likes having a party all to herself. She says this is just like the old days when there was plenty of food and my grandmother very much likes telling me about the old days when the living was good.

And my father is happy too because I know he has signed the lease, that the people near Khwai where we used to come from have agreed he is the best person to work with. That means he can keep the camp and he's happy about that. He says the year 2000 will be a good year and although it's not right that Batswana have to tender for sites in their own land, it's better now people can choose who they work with and they have chosen my father because he is one of them. They haven't chosen the white people who have all the other camps, they have chosen him and he gave them a lot of drink and food and took them to the place they voted because it was too far to walk.

'Candy!' my grandmother calls loudly, although I haven't moved and I am still here next to her. '*Tlisa metsi!*'

I go to the table and pour my grandmother some water from the big glass jug that is right in front of her.

'*Nnyaa!*' She changes her mind. '*Tlisa* Coke!' she says and she laughs naughtily.

So I take a can of Coke from one of the baths under

the table that is packed with ice and I open it and hand it to her and she picks it up and takes one long drink and she doesn't put that can down until it is completely finished. If my father sees this he will be annoyed because my grandmother has high blood and the doctor has said she shouldn't drink Coke anymore.

'Ah!' My grandmother smiles and slaps her lips together. I can see her eyes are sparkling now; the Coke is making them sparkle. She pulls me closer and whispers in my ear, 'Look at Mr *Englishman* there.'

I look around and I know who she is talking about because I can see Norman Ntshinogang leaning against the mulberry tree entertaining three women. He is wearing tight trousers and white trainers and a t-shirt with 'Oxford' on the front. The women look very nice and bright. One has thin braids swept high and wrapped in a puff, another has her hair straightened and sleeked back behind her ears, and the third has a lick of hair styled over her eye and also it is dyed a bronze colour like money. Norman Ntshinogang has a briefcase in his hand and when he speaks it sounds like he is talking through his nose: twing twing twing. That is the way we used to talk when we wanted to imitate a white person.

'Hey, that Norman!' says my grandmother and she pronounces his name in a funny way because that's what he calls himself now – *Nor*-man – ever since he went away to England and came back acting like a big somebody. When the women take the cellophane off the bowls of salad and when the rest of the food comes later I know that Norman Ntshinogang will ask for a knife and fork.

'You see that girl he is with?' my grandmother whispers.

'Which one?'

'The one with the hair like a goat. That is his girlfriend. And you see that one?'

'Which one?'

'The one with the child's clothes on so short you can almost see her child-bearing organs? That is his girlfriend as well. And what do you think is in that briefcase?'

'Money?' I whisper back.

'There is nothing in that briefcase at all!' My grandmother giggles. Then she straightens up and the people waiting to greet her look around and I turn as well because there is a feeling that everyone is turning. And it is Lenny Krause. Lenny Krause moves like a rhino, his head is down and his shoulders are powerful so that even though he really is a normal size person, people move away as if he might run them over. He is wearing shorts the colour of an anthill and his legs are like uncooked sausages, the really fat sausages the Afrikaners eat. There is something wrong with one of his legs which makes him walk in a strange way, and some people say that a lion ate that leg and some other people say it is a white man's disease that when you drink too much it destroys your leg.

I think about hiding somewhere out of the lights but then I see who is walking behind him and I'm excited because it's the white woman with the hair like fire. And I can feel other people are interested too, but they are not saying anything, they will wait until Lenny Krause and his daughter pass them and then they will speak. The daughter stops to say something to MaNeo. From where I am standing beside my grandmother I can see my father on my right still on the steps of our house and Lenny Krause on my left coming towards the table. It is like that game where you have to get ball bearings into a hole and Lenny Krause and my father are the ball bearings and my grandmother and me are the hole. I'm afraid of Lenny Krause, everyone is afraid of Lenny Krause.

My father is talking to the Headman but I know that he knows Lenny Krause is here and suddenly he turns as if he has just realised this and he raises his hand and shouts, 'Lenny!' Other people laugh now, to hear the white man being shouted at with his first name. But Lenny Krause has been our neighbour for many years and we don't even notice that we live next door to a white man anymore.

Lenny Krause waits for my father to come nearer and then he slaps him on the back and says '*Kgosi*!' in his grumbly voice that is so loud I can hear it easily. That's what he always calls my father, Kgosi, just as if he were a Chief.

'Lenny!' says my father again. 'What will you take?' and he waves at my grandmother's maid to come over.

'Whisky,' says Lenny Krause and my father gestures that the girl run and get a whisky.

'Just a family affair, is it?' Lenny Krause asks, looking around.

My father laughs modestly. 'You know what we Batswana are like, why have a party if you can't invite everyone?'

The people nearby who have been listening go back to

their business now. My father lowers his voice a little and he and Lenny Krause both bow their heads as if they are examining something small on the ground like a beetle. But I can hear what they are saying because I'm listening really hard. 'I sent the lease over this morning. I've already signed it, so if you can get it signed too, then I can pick it up tomorrow on my way to camp ...'

'*Ag*, the camp!' says Lenny Krause. He takes the glass of whisky and it is one of the special ones that is very thick with little bubbles of glass around the side and he holds it up and jiggles it around.

My father frowns. 'I'm going there tomorrow, I was going to anyway. I was all set to go when, well, you know what ... I still haven't heard the details and I've not yet spoken with Leapile.' My father puts out his hand as if to draw Lenny Krause away.

'Ah!' says Lenny Krause because he has finished drinking his whisky now and I think it might have burnt him because he's got his mouth wide open. 'Leapile. Can't ever get a word out of him.'

'He'll know everything,' says my father. 'Obviously.'

Lenny Krause nods but he's not looking at my father, he's looking up at the sky. Then he snorts and says, 'They're making a meal of it in Maun.'

'Are they?'

'Man, they've nothing better to talk about.'

My body shivers because now I know what they are talking about: they are talking about the boy who was attacked by the hyena.

'Van Heerden says it's going to do some damage,' says

Lenny Krause. '*Ag*, man, I told him, don't talk kak. What difference will it make to the tourists; some picanin's been chomped? The bloody tourists know fokol anyway.'

My father stares at Lenny Krause and I can see his jaw muscle twitching.

'Look, Van Heerden, I said, it isn't a bloody cartoon. It's Africa. If the tourists can't stand the heat, then get out of the kitchen! Sis, man,' and Lenny Krause spits on the sand.

My father doesn't say anything and I feel where he is looking; he is looking back at the woman, at Lenny Krause's daughter Petra, the one who the Headman sent away from the Kgotla. At first I'm confused because she's not wearing trousers, she's wearing a green skirt and a green top like the people who work for my father. In the pocket of her skirt I can see the outline of something small and square and I think it might be a tape recorder.

Mma Ramotswe has told my grandmother that this is what Petra Krause is doing, she is going around recording people speaking and in particular she is asking people to talk about the safari camps. Her hair is wrapped up and on top of her head is a pair of sunglasses. I see her look sharply to one side, as if checking who is watching, and I see that if you draw a line from the top of her forehead to the end of her nose you will get exactly the letter 'C'.

I wait for her to turn back and see my father. Then I think if I watch too much someone might notice so I pick up the jug of water and I begin to pour it into the thin tall glasses even though I know these glasses are for wine.

'Candy we,' my grandmother croons and she puts out a

hand and pulls me to her. 'I am going to tell you a story. If this is my birthday then I am going to tell you about my birth and all about our life in the old days.' She settles herself happily on her chair and continues. 'Your grandfather, Rweendo Muyendi, may he rest in peace, I am going to tell you all about him because he was a fine, hardworking man, not like these layabouts we get in the village these days. And your great-great aunty, the one who was a mother to me, and your great grandfather and the village where we used to . . .'

I'm standing right next to my grandmother when she leans forward and shoots out her hand and I think she is taking some water in order to soothe her voice so she can talk some more about the old days, but her hand is nowhere near the water and instead she knocks the jug over. She looks at me and her face looks puzzled and then as I look back at her I see her right eyelid just droop over like a petal. I wonder how she manages to droop one eyelid and not the other and I am amazed she is able to do this. Then she staggers back in her chair. She just throws her head back and her eyes roll right up and I see her like that all frozen. Someone screams *Jeso!* and people rush to the table and I am pushed out of the way so I can't even see what is happening. A woman begins wailing, another shouts that someone should bring pills. I hear a man saying she has fainted and I hear another asking if she is dead.

Now my grandmother is on the ground and I am so happy that her skirt is staying down and people can't see her cycling shorts and her legs that look like beetles.

42

I look at the people and my heart is beating too fast and I wonder who can have done this. I look at the people and it's like a bad dream when witches are coming after you.

The adults are going crazy now, my father is shouting that the ambulance must come; the doctor is on his knees lifting up my grandmother's arms and telling people to stand back. Norman Ntshinogang and the three women are standing in a row, their backs against the mulberry tree and their mouths open.

Even when the ambulance comes I can't get near enough to my grandmother to see, but I am desperate and I push and I squeeze myself and I make myself small. They mustn't take her away from me because she protects me and makes me safe. My grandmother makes sure I don't have to see bad things but now the bad thing has happened to her and I'm right here seeing it. And I am here when they put her on that bed and then they lift that bed and slide it into the back of the ambulance. And I see my grandmother's eyes looking out and they are not her eyes, they are not human eyes, they are the tiny little brown eyes of an animal which doesn't know where it is. Then my heart starts beating fast again because one thing I know as they shut those doors is that my father will have to call my Aunty Kazi now, he will have to call her home.

BOOK TWO
Nanthewa

Chapter Three

'What is your name?'

A woman in a blue uniform has her face hovering above mine. She seems to be upside down.

'What – is – your – name?'

She is asking me as if I am a stupid somebody. And she is a foreigner; her Setswana is funny. There are foreigners all over the place now.

'Keep her talking,' comes a man's voice.

'Can you say what day it is? What – day – is – it?'

What does it matter what day it is? Stop asking me silly questions. I want to lick my lips, they are so very dry. But someone has glued my mouth shut.

'Mrs Muyendi? Can you . . .'

So she knows my name! She asks my name when she already knows it! She can't live in Sehuba and not know the Muyendi name.

She is just like those census people who came and asked the questions they already had an answer for. When was that? Isaac wasn't here or he would have dealt with them. They wanted to know what year I was born and so I told them, I was born the year the locusts dimmed the sunlight. 'Do you mean 1940?' they asked. 'I mean the year the locusts dimmed the sunlight,' I told them. So they looked me up and down as if they were

47

buying a goat, and said in their city voices, 'Yes, I would say 1940.' So I asked if they wanted to know when my parents were born because that was the year of the flu, which was also the year the first war ended. And did they want to know when my grandparents were born, because that was the time the BaHerero fled to Ngamiland? As for my husband Rweendo Muyendi, I can tell you when he was born because that was between two great events: he was born just before the floods and just after the earthquake. May he rest in peace. But I myself, I was born the year of the locusts. So write that down, I told them, write that down and put it in that book of yours and stop bothering your elders.

'Mrs Muyendi, can you hear me?'

Of course I can hear you, although I can't see you very well if you move your face away like that because someone has stolen my glasses. It started the year Isaac was married, when I began to have to flutter my eyes together to see things well. For a while I didn't think much of it, but that was because I was waiting for my eyes to become sharp again. And then I realised they never would, that I could only go forward and not back.

This bed, this thing I am lying on, is sloping back. It is like a trolley with one end lower than the other. How can they put a person on something like this?

That was a good time, when I was a child. That was the time of *Mmamosadinyana* and there weren't many people then, not like there are today. And during the time of the English Queen there were no laws, like you can live here or not live here, you can hunt this animal or not that animal, you can hunt here but not over there, you can hunt today but not tomorrow.

It wasn't like when my parents were young. That was the time of starvation and people had to tie themselves with a belt to hold their stomachs in. When I was a child it was a time of wealth, a time when we ate all manner of things, when we lived in Xuku in the Okavango Delta, a country so full of rivers that there is no one who can count them.

There was a river just near Xuku with plenty of water and plenty of fish, and we lived in a clearing lined with tsaro trees that were always rustling no matter how timid the wind was. It was a perfect place to live, it was a protected place, it was only once you left that you became aware of the swamps outside.

Around the houses the grass was cleared, which was a constant job in the rainy season, and when it did rain then outside the village the grass became as high as an adult's waist. When you walked in that grass you had no idea what you would meet, but even though I was afraid of the snakes I liked the grass because as a child it seemed to tickle the skin.

There was no tsetse fly at Xuku, although tsetse was bothering a lot of people then; it was pushing them out of the delta because they were afraid of sleeping sickness. At Xuku the livelihood was good; there was food for everyone, we had our ploughing fields there and in the winter the men hunted. It was said later that our people, the Bayeyi, had no fixed place in Moremi, but that was not the case. If you are ploughing somewhere, then you are fixed.

The Bugakhwe were there first, but we got along fine and we were like cousins to them. The Bayeyi were not as well regarded as hunters as the Bugakhwe, who were very skilled. They didn't hunt the big animals like elephants and they didn't hunt predators like lion because they respected them too much, and while they ate most animals, they would not eat baboons or hyenas.

But although the Bayeyi were not as well regarded as hunters, in my family it was different because my father's family had always been hunters. When my great-great grandparents were young then that was the time of ivory and everyone knew the best elephants were to be found up in Ngamiland. My grandparents hunted elephants too, although by then they had to go further and further afield to find them. And my father was a hunter too; it was in his blood. Sometimes he would travel days in order to hunt a hippopotamus.

My father was a big buffalo of a man and even from a young age his hair was frosted with white, like dust from a burnt out fire. His eyebrows were big too, and very furrowed, and when he was displeased he had a way of looking at you, with those eyebrows of his, that told you to keep your mouth shut and not argue with him. My mother was not a Moyeyi, she was not dark skinned like a Moyeyi, and she came from somewhere to the west. Some said she was a Bushman from the desert. She died soon after I was born and my father was grief stricken and not much use to anyone for a while. It was my aunty who raised my sisters and my brothers and me, and it was she who taught us the meaning of hard work.

Hela, my aunty was a fierce woman. When it was time for ploughing she would wake you up, early, early in the morning before the sun had appeared. And when you arrived at the field if she found the francolins had already arrived and eaten the seeds then she would beat you. If she found you not doing a good job she would grab a hoe and beat you. That was so that you should be as strong as her and so that tomorrow you should not live on the spoils of other people.

My aunty spoke Shiyeyi and she also spoke some Setswana, and later we all learnt to speak Setswana too, especially the proverbs. *Motho ke motho ka motho ya mongwe.* A person is a person because of another person. That was what she would tell me, that was what she was teaching me. And she knew it was best to train a child when that child was still young and tender because if you want to bend a stick then you do so while it's still wet. She also taught us the Shiyeyi proverbs and when she recited these ones then she licked her lips as if she liked the taste of them. *Inkasi yeya ku wuso yati kara ku ldiqo, ya ku ldiqo yi kite ku wiso.* Those in the front will be someday at the back, and the other way round. Remember that, my aunty said, when you are a successful somebody.

It is said a person doesn't remember much from when they are very small but that is not true because I certainly can. I can feel myself standing by the doorway to the reeds that my aunty erected around our house in Xuku. I am standing just to the side of the doorway so that behind me is the light and the warmth of the fire, the sound of adults laughing and telling a story, the pop of an ember. And in front of me is the silent darkness and the outline of the vast termite mound that was shaped, in part, like a running elephant. It must have been winter because I know I was cold, that I was looking forward to the sleeping mat waiting for me in the house, but more than that I was looking forward to my father. And there was no one out there in the darkness at all until suddenly he appeared dragging an antelope. Why he was bringing home an antelope at night I don't know, perhaps it wasn't night, perhaps it was very, very early in the morning. He pulled the animal behind him, he had shot it with a spear, and I could see the shadows of light which played on its long ribbed horns like the grooves a person might make on a stick. Then the adults knew he had recovered from my mother's death and everyone was happy to see him hunting again.

By the time I was a young girl I had plenty of work. I was an obedient child. I did what I was told and everyone admired me for that. Every morning we would rise in the darkness and wash our faces with water that was so clean it was like a slap. And all day we would work, clearing the ashes from the fire, preparing the porridge, sweeping, carrying the pots to the river for water, stamping the corn. There was always work to be done. You could never sit still with my aunty. If she saw you sitting still then she sent you with a job to do. And you were only given food if you had done your job, that was the way it was. If you hadn't done your job then you stayed at the periphery of the fire and you watched everyone else eating.

Who has put me in this thing? Who is the one who has done this to me? They should close that door properly so that it doesn't rattle so much. We are travelling too fast.

My aunty was strong and she ploughed in the traditional way, not with animals but with ordinary hoes. She farmed pumpkin and tobacco and peanuts and beans and sorghum and watermelon. All the people who hadn't ploughed would come and pay money to buy these things and this money was just kept in a tin. It was even there when she died, this hoard of money.

I have money now because of Isaac who is a hard worker, just like me and my aunty, and now we are able to buy all manner of things. Only some of those things don't exist anymore, like bloomers and chamber pots.

Where is my son? I want to get out of here; I don't know what I'm doing bumping up and down like this.

'Shshs,' says the nurse.

My father was a hard worker too, just like my aunty, once he had recovered from my mother's death. At times he hunted on the land, but at other times he did his work on the river. He was a true Moyeyi and he loved his mokoro as if it was his friend, as if the canoe was a part of him. There was one mokoro that served him for many, many years. He carved it from a moporota tree, because that's a strong tree and doesn't split easily, and it took him a long, long time to cut it down. Then it had to be left for some time to dry, before my father could begin to shape it. He was very careful when it came to preparing that tree, he burnt it all inside with hot coals until the wood smoked, for this made it easier to work on and also prevented cracks. And then he hollowed out the trunk with his axe. It had to be perfect for when he was on a trip into the delta then that mokoro was his home. He built a small fire in it at night, moored it behind a bank of reeds, and there he slept. It was safer than on the shore, he said, where a snake or a lion could get you.

As well as digging out canoes, my father made fishing nets and he came up with a device for harvesting waterlily roots in areas where the water was quite high. These days you only see women harvesting *tswii*, but back then my father did it too. He devised a pole and he dug out the waterlily roots from underneath while he was still sitting in the mokoro. He also had a net out there and he would go to the net, pull out the fish and pile it in the mokoro. Fish this side, *tswii* this side, fish this side, *tswii* this side; in those days food was plentiful beyond words. When my aunty came in the evening from where she had worked, maybe in the fields, she would prepare the fish and the *tswii*. *Hela!* All the children were nice and plump from eating nice food. So it was funny that I was such a thin child, and that was why they named me Nanthewa, the mother of thinness.

I am hungry myself. My stomach is growling. Why have they taken me from the party when I haven't even eaten?

And why isn't Candy here? She is weak, that child, she needs looking after. She is not like the way we used to be when we were young. At that time not only were the children plump, but when a child was born then the traditional doctor was called and the baby strengthened against all the harmful things that could happen. The doctors of those days were really good at treating people; we had no need of hospitals then. They would be called even when people were not ill, because that is when you bring a doctor to make sure someone stays well. In the past everyone had a doctor in the family and that doctor specialised in some area. My father's brother was a doctor who specialised in blood diseases and if he were still here today then he would know what to do with me.

And then of course there were the doctors you called when someone was bewitched. The doctor would do rituals and then you would find a person going round the village saying, 'Oh, that's right, yes, I did this but I didn't really mean it.' They would own up after the doctor had been called, they would just own up and say what they had tried to do. Today these doctors who would strengthen you against evildoers have all passed away and all that's left is witches.

I try to get up, to see where I am and where I am going. If this is my last journey then I want to know whom I'm going to meet when I get there. And if it's Rweendo then what am I going to say to him?

Chapter Four

The day I found out that I was to be given in marriage to Rweendo Muyendi started out a normal day, as such days do. It was a day so hot even the butterflies were lazy. I was sitting under a mogotlho tree, shading myself from the midday sun, while our families made the final marriage agreement. The tree was in flower and the bright soft balls with their dusting of yellow gave a sweet, perfumed smell. It was a smell that made me lazy too. Harvest had finished and work had eased for a while. I could hear the thwack thwack sound of my elder brother chopping wood and behind that the sound of someone drumming. From where I sat I could see my aunty's house, the dappled shadows of tree branches dancing on the roof, so deep and dark they rested the eyes from the clear lemon light around me. I was just sitting there dreaming when they came and told me the news.

'It's all arranged,' my aunty said. That was the way she spoke, always as if making an important pronouncement.

I was a young woman by then and Rweendo Muyendi's mother had been asking the same question for a while: 'How about my son as the future husband for your child?' I don't know why she chose me, except for the fact I was a hard worker and liked by everyone. They didn't mind about my colour, that I was of a pale complexion like my mother and her people, nor that I was such a thin girl. They just wanted me for their son.

That was what you did, you were a child and you were given in marriage. Neither my aunty nor my father thought much about school. School was there, the teachers migrated, holding sessions under trees, but it wasn't something people thought much about. Two of my brothers went to school for a while, but my aunty thought school taught prostitution and as there was no one explaining what it was for, I never went.

Rweendo Muyendi was well known in Xuku, he was the son of one of the Chief's advisers and he was a skilled tracker and hunter. Of course he was much older than me and so he knew a lot more. In particular he knew about hunting; he knew which animal had passed, the direction it had come from, where it was going and where it had spent the night. He just looked at grass that had been flattened and he could tell you the size of that animal, and whether it was male or female, and if it was female then whether it was pregnant or not. And as well as being a hunter and anticipating an animal's whereabouts, he also had to ensure that he didn't become the prey himself.

Everyone knew and liked Rweendo Muyendi. He was well named, my husband, for Rweendo means journey and Muyendi means traveller. And for many years he had travelled all over the place. He had been to Francistown and seen a cinema that was taken from place to place in a truck; he had been around Maun and worked on killing the tsetse fly and for a time he had been employed by the Elephant Control Unit; he had been north and cleared the Taoghe River; he had been west and seen people die from the plague.

When my father and my aunty and uncle told me the news about the marriage I was not in a position to say no. And of course I would not have said no, even if anyone had asked me.

As it was, I liked Rweendo Muyendi very much. I had seen him around the village, he had been a visitor to my aunty's house, he was always present at weddings and funerals, he was always called upon when the animals were skinned. And when he visited he would bring us gifts, baskets of wild fruits or watermelons as big as my father's head.

Rweendo was a tall man, uncommonly tall, with a lean chest and strong forearms. And although he was tall he was well proportioned and he never slouched; when he sat down his back was always straight. In his face he was delicate looking, with very pointed ears, thin pretty eyes and a long face. He was always ready with a smile and sometimes all he had to do was to raise his long thin eyebrows and any children in the vicinity would just start to giggle.

Rweendo Muyendi smelt of coffee, he was the first person I knew who drank coffee and it was a warm smell that lingered on his breath. He was also the first person I knew to read a newspaper, he had a whole pile of *Naledi Ya Batswana* in his home and when he read he kept his forefinger travelling along the words. He was a busy man, a very sociable man, and since he had returned to Xuku from his travels he was always playing an important role in our village. And that meant I would play an important role too because now I would be his wife. And his travelling gave him an authority and as a result many people consulted him when they had a problem they needed to solve. Then he would sit on his wooden chair, sometimes by the fire, sometimes not, and he would listen. He would listen to everything someone had to say and then he would trace a stick in the sand, slowly, so that your eyes were drawn to the patterns, and then he would reply. And whatever he said, that was what people would do, for he was regarded as a man with a good mind and strong morals.

Once the marriage was agreed, Rweendo Muyendi's mother came to fetch me and take me to my new home and there she became like a mother to me for now I was her *ngwetsi*. She was a nervous woman, always wanting to know what other people thought so that she could agree with them. If she laughed then she looked around to see if other people were laughing too. She was happy to have me, for her daughters had passed away while still young. She needed a daughter to help her and I was a good one.

The day we married I received my first blanket; any blanket I had used before then had been used first by somebody else. Rweendo's elder brother, Nkapa, who was something of a layabout, brought it with him from South Africa. Nkapa was not a nice-looking man; he was badly scarred from the smallpox and his skin looked as if a woodpecker had been at work. He had been some years in the Rand Mines, but although he had a job he never sent anything home to his wife or to his family in Xuku.

We heard word that he had been seen in a *shebeen* in Johannesburg drinking all his money away. He came home when his first child, Leapile, was born, but then he absconded again. There weren't many paid jobs in Ngamiland so if the rains were bad then some men were lured to those mines in South Africa, just as Nkapa was. And the men complained; they said when the company paid you, first they gave you your money and then they took it back again because they said the men owed them for travel and accommodation. But still, other men did manage to save money, just not Nkapa. The only thing he brought back with him was a rifle.

When the marriage was arranged, Rweendo sent his brother some money and requested that he buy his new wife a blanket. And that blanket was something special. It was woven with a red I had never seen before; I didn't even want to ever wash it for fear it would turn out a cheap dye and be washed away. It was not the red of the sun, nor of blood, nor of fire, it was the sort of red you see in your mind when your heart is full.

At night, when it was cold, I would wrap myself in that blanket and cover my head like a caterpillar. Of course most of the time we shared that blanket. In those years my insides were itching for him and Rweendo knew that, he was the one who made me feel that way. He was not like some men who told their wives, 'I have paid for you, and you have a duty to share the blanket.' My aunty had advised me that I should not refuse, that I was not to disgrace the family, but there was nothing to refuse. That first night we were together I was shivering a little and

60

I was shy and Rweendo was upset about this; he came walking across the floor with his long toes, patter-patter, patter-patter. 'Are you cold?' he asked. And I shook my head, because now I was not cold at all and I felt special because he had chosen me.

After our marriage we continued to live in Xuku and there we built a life for ourselves. The skin trade then was a very good one: whatever was killed could be sold. Sometimes we gave the skins to the river men who went down to Maun with their goods. Even a jackal skin would give you two shillings, and a leopard skin was enough to buy everything a family needed, salt and sugar and soap and maybe a knife.

It was shortly after my marriage that I saw a white person for the first time, when a man came to the village to buy skins. He was wearing Western clothes and as children we had always been warned against those wearing Western clothes because they could kidnap you and make you their servant. I knew that in Maun there were more white people because my father had told me this; they were traders and they had shops where they sold sugar and so forth. We even heard about a white woman living in a camp near Maun; she and her husband had lion cubs which lived with them as if they were cats. She didn't even kill the lion cub that attacked her own son; she just tied her wrist to her son's wrist at night so that if he wandered then she would feel the pull and wake.

Our life was peaceful at Xuku. I tended the house, worked in the fields when it was time, and obeyed my new mother. Meanwhile Rweendo and the other men would go and do their hunting: kudu, antelope, wildebeest, elephant, hippo and buffalo. Game was plentiful beyond words. Then they would come back and we would cut the animal up and send the meat to this place and that, while the skins were prepared and sold. But certain animals were royal animals and people like us were not allowed to kill them. One day two Bugakhwe men in the village were jailed for killing a giraffe. Someone told the police in Maun and they arrested them and took them away and the families were deeply shamed.

For although the livelihood was good, as a people we were sat upon by others and the Batawana in Ngamiland thought they were our lords. The Batawana had come from some land down south and found the Bayeyi who were always a good-natured people and they came in and sat on top of us. But Rweendo said if it weren't for the Bayeyi then the Batawana would all have been slaughtered by the Matabele.

Rweendo was very concerned about this and sometimes he said we should fight for our rights. But because the Bayeyi are a peaceful people, there was never that much real talk about fighting. And if anyone had ever asked me whether it was a good idea to fight or not then I would have replied that I was unsure. What I already knew was this: God will always give us a chance to improve our lives and we are the ones who have to take that chance.

I knew I was pregnant at once. I felt a burning sensation, like a stabbing down inside me. But I didn't tell anyone what I knew because that is the time you can be bewitched and lose the baby. But after some months then other people noticed, women saw my complexion had darkened a little and that my breasts were heavy and that now I had some meat on my bones. When the time came I returned to my aunty's home and that whole night she sat outside the house, checking on me all night long to see how it was going. She had spread dry cow dung on the floor so that when the baby came the blood would be absorbed.

Inside the house I sat against the wall, holding my legs apart as she had told me to do. I had drunk the medicine, the medicine that would help the baby to rush out. But still I stayed like that all night along. Sometimes my aunty came in and held her arms around me from the back and rocked my body to and fro as if she was trying to pull up a stubborn weed.

And at last that baby was ripped out of me and my aunty came in and she tied the cord and washed the baby and laid him on a skin. And I looked at the baby and I was glad he was dark skinned like his father because people favoured dark skinned babies and found them more beautiful. This was my first child and I thanked the ancestors that now I was a woman. We called him Isaac because there was a white trader of that name, and he was a man who had lots of money and bought plenty of skins. And everything was good in Xuku; everything was good until it all fell apart.

63

Chapter Five

It happened around a year after Isaac was born, when Rweendo began to become preoccupied with something that worried him immensely. For we had heard word that something was to be done with the land on which we lived, that the Batawana elders wanted to make a reserve for animals and stop all the hunting inside. We heard that in Maun, first one meeting was held and then another. But the Batawana elders didn't bother to consult the Bayeyi even though there were so many of us. And the Bayeyi loved the Batawana like a mouse loves a cat; if the Batawana wanted something then the Bayeyi did not.

Then one night some Batawana men from Maun lost their way. They had been out on a hunting party and they had got confused and had stumbled across our village of Xuku. My husband and some other men were sitting round the fire, while I was inside the house feeding Isaac. That baby could feed all day and all night and he was growing fat and I was so proud of him. I felt powerful, being able to make this child grow like that.

'*Ko ko,*' a man called at the edge of our compound.

I was alarmed, for people did not usually visit at night, but I heard my husband reply.

'*Ee,*' he called back, replying in a casual voice. But I was at the doorway, looking out into the yard, and I saw him take his knobkerrie and hold it close to his lap where he was sitting on his wooden chair.

The men came in; there were three of them and they were dusty from travelling and from having lost their way. One was a particularly short man with a large nose and lips that pulled down like the handle of a cup. He walked in quick little steps, as if the ground beneath were hot.

My husband and the others made room for the men at the fire. They could see the men were tired, and it was cold that night so they gave them a chance to warm themselves. Eventually the men explained how they had come to be lost and my husband said they could stay for the night rather than approach the Chief, as it was too late to seek his permission now.

And one reason Rweendo was keen for these men to stay with us was that they were from Maun and my husband was so concerned about what was happening with this idea of a game reserve. After the men had rested and been fed, Rweendo asked them about the reserve. And while the men talked my husband's face showed no reaction. But I could see, when I peeped out, that one hand was in his lap, the other was still on the knobkerrie.

He waited for the men to finish and as he did he looked into the fire very intently. 'Yes, everything you've said is what I've heard,' said my husband, raking a stick through the sand. 'We've heard that some people are suggesting this area should be preserved for animals. It's not a bad idea because after all we know that if all the animals are killed then there will be nothing left, and we don't want nothing to be left for our children.' My husband's voice was so much sweeter than those of other men and had the quality of a song about it so that when you heard him you stopped where you were and listened. And when he spoke he always spoke logic, as if he had everything prepared beforehand up there in that head of his. He paused between his words and he never spoke for too long; that way people really concentrated on what he said.

The men from Maun were smiling and nodding their heads. They thought Rweendo was praising them. I watched from the doorway, surprised at the way my husband had spoken. He sounded very agreeable. But then I thought of what my aunty said, *Ldi ku yembe, ldi ku lde.* Use sweet language in order to kill.

'It is kind of you to explain to us what's being discussed in Maun about this reserve,' said my husband. 'We've heard about the meetings that you and your friend Rra Tau have had.'

The men from Maun looked irritated, perhaps because they did not want to be seen as friends of Rra Tau. For Rra Tau was the white man who had a camp near Maun, where he and his wife kept their lion cubs. It was Rra Tau's wife who tied her wrist to that of her son in case the lions roamed at night.

'I understand your friend has proposed this game reserve because his cubs are getting troublesome and he wants somewhere to release them?' chuckled my husband.

'*Ao!*' one of the men from Maun objected. 'That's ridiculous!'

'I believe the reserve will be right here,' continued my husband, and quite suddenly he stomped that knobkerrie so hard that the sand by his feet trembled.

'Well not *there* exactly,' said the short man with the big nose, and he attempted to laugh.

'No, not here, *exactly*,' said my husband, and he thumped that knobkerrie again. 'It will be all over here, is that right?' And he swept his arm out, indicating the village all around us. 'You see, my friends, the reason we're interested in this plan for a reserve is because, as you can see, we live here and hunting is our custom, it is our right. If there is anyone who knows about hunting then it's us.'

'*Ee*! Wild animals are our food!' cut in Haldjimbo, a silly man who always hung around my husband and was always chattering too much.

'This is our life,' said my husband, silencing his companion. 'So obviously, as hunters ourselves, as people who rely on wild animals to feed our families, we agree that we need to preserve them.'

The visitors nodded their heads, looking relieved.

'So there is only one question,' said my husband, and he leant forward then so that his face was lit by the fire. 'There is only one thing that is troubling me about this. Perhaps you can explain it to me? We're not educated people up here, we're not educated like you people in Maun. But this is the thing: we've never had any problem hunting here; there have always been animals. So who is it that is shooting all the game? What's gone wrong that now we have to preserve the animals and stop the hunting?'

The men stiffened, I could see that they didn't want a debate. They knew whom my husband was referring to, the crazy white people who were coming up to the swamps from South Africa. They were holidaymakers, my husband said, they came and shot as many animals as they could and then they left. They didn't even eat many of those animals, but instead they cut off a part of the body, usually the head but sometimes a foot as well, and took that back with them to where they came from.

'We kill for the pot, and we kill to support our families,' said my husband, and his voice was warmer now. 'What these people do is they go to the DC, they say, "Ah, Mr District Commissioner, we're coming in July and we want to hunt in such and such a place." And so the DC tells your Chief to give the go ahead! But they don't follow the rules, they are not proper hunters. What a normal hunter does is this: he kills one animal; he makes sure it is dead, and then he takes it away. We don't stand in a motor vehicle with a gun shooting – bang, bang! – this way and that. We don't kill so much that we have to leave it behind because we have no idea what to do with it. We don't kill females with babies ...'

'That's the idea of the reserve,' objected the short man who had walked into our yard as if stepping on fire. 'The idea is to protect the animals from illegal hunting parties. What would you rather? Would you rather that we preserve the land ourselves, that we keep it for our children, or would it be better that the British take this land for masafari, for Safari South and the other companies, and start building hotels and such like?'

My husband laughed. He could see what the Batawana men were doing, they were making it seem that this idea of the game reserve would unite us all against the British. For if the Batawana sat upon the Bayeyi, it was the British who sat even higher. They had taken the land long before I was born and although we didn't see them, it was they who were in charge. I didn't mind about Mmamosa-dinyana – when I saw her face on a coin I thought she looked powerful and my aunty loved her very much – but Rweendo could be very rude about the British Queen and about her District Commissioner who stayed in Maun with his police and so forth. The British and the Batawana were always quarrelling about something. When the Batawana were not fighting each other over who their Chief should be, then they were arguing with the British over who their Chief should be, or they argued over who was allowed to give land to the whites.

'What would I rather?' my husband asked. 'You give me the option of preserving the land *for ourselves* or letting the British take it and give it to masafari? But we're here on this land and you haven't asked for our opinion. Yet I think you could say we know this land; we do not, for instance, often get lost on it.'

The men from Maun looked furious. They were being made to look like fools and there was nothing they could do, because they needed somewhere to stay.

I thought then of the way my husband hunted in the river, the way he balanced in a mokoro and then used a harpoon to get an antelope or another animal. He balanced and held that animal down while his fellow hunters attacked it with spears and arrows. That was what he had done with the men from Maun. He had lured them at first with his sweet words and now he had attacked them.

Once Rweendo had finished speaking, Haldjimbo and the others suddenly got busy, one walked away from the fire as if in search of something, another picked up an axe and started to sharpen it. And their busyness made the men from Maun nervous, as if they were trapped, as if they should have seen something coming before it came up and bit them.

And the men from Maun looked nervous all that night and they patted the sand all around them before they laid down, and even then the short one with the big nose kept one eye open. I know because still I stood at the doorway to our house listening, waiting to hear if anything else was to be said.

'It is not true that you haven't been consulted,' mumbled the man with the big nose, beginning the discussion again. 'Many Bayeyi spoke up during the debates on the reserve.'

'Many?' asked my husband.

'They spoke up,' insisted the man from Maun. 'And the Bugakhwe have been consulted as well and they have agreed to move.'

'Have you tried telling the Bugakhwe they can't hunt anymore?' asked my husband.

'Ah, those people,' said the man with the big nose. 'They are roamers, they just move around, they don't have a particular area, there is nothing permanent.'

'Is that so?' snapped my husband. 'You think they don't have permanent places? What is permanent? Look around you, look around you at this village you have stumbled into, are people not living their lives here? What we are talking about is manipulation. You are being manipulated by Rra Tau and the DC and the British, and we are being manipulated by you.'

'*Ee*!' chirped up that silly man Haldjimbo. 'Wild animals are our gold mine!'

Then I was too tired to listen and I had not been invited to listen anyway, this was talk for men. So I settled Isaac down in my big red blanket and left the men to argue among themselves at the fire.

Now I don't have any blanket at all. Hey, I am cold. Don't these people have anything for a person to cover themselves with? And where is my bed, who has made off with my bed?

'Shshs,' the nurse says.

'Where am I?' I lick my lips.

'You are at the clinic, Mrs Muyendi.'

'At the clinic? Why?'

She raises her eyebrows as if she can't believe her ears. 'Because you are ill.'

Chapter Six

They came at daybreak to burn Xuku down. We were told to take our things and stand on the periphery of the village, but my husband set out at once for the bush, he couldn't bear to watch. I stood there with Isaac, my water pots and my cooking pots, a sack of mealie, my precious red blanket and my husband's wooden chair. And as they torched the first house some people made as if to intervene. As the reeds began to flame and to crackle and to spark some of the women jerked forward, for there is a moment when a fire starts that it can still be put out, when there is still a chance to pour sand and water on the flames. And there was plenty of sand, and we were not far from the river. But the chief game warden held us back.

Then the wind came and we watched as first one house and then another burnt up before our eyes. That was our home that was burning and as it collapsed it was as if all our thoughts, all our hopes and our discussions, all our nights and our days, were leaving that home and evaporating up into the sky.

Isaac wriggled on my hip, he wanted to get down but it was too hot for that, it was so hot that our houses shimmered and the air became black.

'Mama!' Isaac said in his sweet baby voice and he

looked at me and I could see in his eyes he had a question, he wanted to know why they were burning down our homes.

Then it was all over and everything was done.

The British had won, that is what my husband said. The Batawana had agreed among themselves to form a game reserve to preserve the animals from overhunting. But even before the meetings and the consultations the British had already signed agreements with the safari companies. They had already handed out those hunting areas to masafari and now those safari companies had booked their clients and soon they would build base camps here.

When this came into the open the District Commissioner called another Kgotla meeting in Maun. And at that Kgotla thirty men stood up and they were so offended that they went to the fence of the kraal and they got out their private parts and they urinated right there to show their displeasure. But the agreements the British had made stood as they were.

The reserve had been approved, only the safari companies would be allowed to hunt and now they were fixing boundaries and putting No Shooting signs on concrete posts. The Bayeyi were supposed to assist with this, but my husband refused. And he said it seemed that the Batawana thought this was their hunting ground now, for the reserve was to be called Moremi after their Chief.

People said the Bayeyi Chief had not understood the negotiations surrounding the reserve, he had agreed to his people being moved from the land because he thought it was law and he was scared of the law. He was promised that we would have new jobs in the reserve, but he hadn't realised we would be moved out altogether.

And now there was a game warden and he had come to burn down our home and to threaten us if we dared to cross the boundaries and move back in. We were not wild animals, so we were not allowed in the game reserve anymore. We were travellers and we had to move.

We moved that very day. Some of the people moved to the north bank of Khwai, including my aunty and my father, some went on trucks to Segagame, but my husband said if we had lost our home then we must start a new one in a place of our choice. He thought we should be nearer to Maun because that was the Batawana capital and anyone could see Maun was growing. So we moved to the village of Sehuba where my husband had some distant relatives and where people knew of us and were willing to let us stay.

The journey was long; we had to walk all day with our possessions on our heads. Isaac fretted as I put him on my back and I walked just like that, like a donkey. Rweendo led the way, he had his wooden chair folded and hung over his right shoulder, and in his hand he held a rifle that his brother Nkapa had given him. That night we slept in the bush and we heard the lions, we felt their sound vibrating the land on which we slept.

The next day we arrived at Sehuba, just a small village populated mainly by Batawana. It lay to the east of Chief's Island and on a track that led south to Maun and north to Moremi and the place they were to call South Gate. Here

Rweendo asked permission for a plot not far from the river and away from the main settlement. The Headman gave us a plot without any argument, he knew we were desperate. It was a large, beautiful plot, though very over-grown with forest and the grass was full with snakes because no one had lived here for a very long time and there were no immediate neighbours. And although it was not that different from what we were used to, there was this one tree that none of us had seen before. It was a spindly little thing, still young, with a trunk no taller than a child and we were told it was a black mulberry tree. It had a scattering of thin green leaves, some shaped like a glove, and they were rough on top like a cow's tongue but underneath they were soft and moist. Where it had come from no one could tell us, though the Headman's wife said a white man had planted the tree right there in a space of full sunlight during a time he was camping in the area some years back looking for ivory.

It was shortly after we moved that I lost my second-born. I was already so far along that I could feel that baby begin to nudge me inside. Then one morning I went to the bush for firewood and the pains found me right there. They were terrible pains, as if I had eaten something that didn't agree with me, as if I had eaten a monster that was fighting with my insides.

I had gathered only a little firewood; I had only just begun on my task when I was forced to crouch on the ground. I could no longer stand up, I could only crouch as the blood came down and soaked my dress. And then I could feel that something was there, that something that had been inside had now come out, and when I touched myself I felt a finger and then a hand, hanging out of me just like that. The hand was warm and wet like that of a chicken.

I looked up then, to see if anyone was around, and the air was very still all of a sudden and the land was silver and shimmering all around me.

Eventually I dug a hole and I buried my child and as I did I could feel vomit like lumps of flesh in my throat.

I remained there for most of the day, without anyone to help. I don't know who I could have asked for help anyway, as I didn't know the people in Sehuba and many of them treated us like the outsiders that we were. They were Setswana speakers and some of them looked down upon those that spoke Shiyeyi like my husband. They were very happy the day a certain Moyeyi from Gumare was arrested for writing down Shiyeyi and putting it into a dictionary. He had just got started with this job and was on his way back from South Africa after consulting with a professor there when he was arrested. The man was handcuffed and tied to a bed for days and his family was not allowed to see him. Then he was sent to Maun and imprisoned there. Things like that made a person nervous to speak Shiyeyi, especially in a village of Setswana speakers.

And some of the people in Sehuba had strange habits, like the ones who smoked dagga before working in the fields. They smoked it in a horn with a reed inside, smoking it in the morning and then setting off to do some hoeing. By the time the sun was coming down they were still working intensively. They claimed that if they smoked then they could go on all day; they said dagga gave them energy and they could go on and on.

My husband never smoked dagga, but he did work hard. But for that first year things weren't easy. I lost much of my energy after that day in the bush and my blood became weak. I could not find anything to smile about; I could only feel loss. And sometimes it seemed that Isaac was stronger than me, a little boy stronger than his own mother. Many times he tried to lift things that were far bigger than him, or carry things that were too heavy for him, because he could see it was difficult for me. The pain of losing my child made me weak and slow and ached my heart. When I looked at Isaac I thought, where is the brother or sister you were expecting? Someone had bewitched me and I didn't know who.

But I knew I had to make the best of my life and so I tried to encourage and support my husband in our new place. Rweendo attended Kgotla meetings, and he made visits and received visits. He began to clear a field, but this was hard to do alone. He went hunting, but his old hunting companions were not around and he wasn't as successful as he had been in Xuku. He was beginning to wonder what to do, how to support his family and to better his life. He didn't sit as straight anymore, his shoulders began to sag when he sat on his chair and it pained me to see this.

The people who had been moved out of Xuku had now been told to move again because the reserve was made bigger and the boundaries extended. Then they were moved again until now they had crossed the Khwai River and lost everything in the park that used to be their home.

One morning I was in the yard fixing a reed fence around our new home when I heard a rumble in the distance. It was towards the end of the wet season, we had cleared the fields and repaired what needed repairing. As I worked I ate from a basket of marula fruits which I had collected earlier. I had been eyeing these fruits on the tree for some time, waiting until the green skin changed to yellow, until they were ready. Now I ate them slowly, putting a single one in my mouth, chewing around the white shiny pulp until I reached the smoothness of the stone and spat it out. They made me thirsty, those marula fruits, so thirsty that the only thing that was good enough to do was to eat another one.

The sound of the approaching motor vehicle made me nervous. Our plot was a little elevated so as well as hearing the rumble I could see a cloud of sand travelling closer and closer.

'Mama!' Isaac called and he went running out of that yard before I could stop him. He was always running, he simply went from standing to walking just like that.

'*Hela*!' I shouted after him. 'Where do you think you are going? It will run you over, come back here!' But the motor vehicle had stopped and Isaac was standing right there when the two white men climbed out.

'Whose *picanin* is this?' asked one of the men. He was

tall and he had to unbend himself out of that vehicle and shake his legs a little before he was upright again. His face had very bad skin, like something was erupting from underneath.

'Good morning!' Isaac told the men.

The tall man laughed. 'Nice bit of English!' he said. 'Nice bit of English!' and he patted my son on the head.

I was smiling to hear Isaac with his English, for his father had taught him some few words. But I didn't like the white man patting my son on the head; I didn't want a stranger touching him.

'*Dumela Mma*,' said the tall man when he looked up and saw me at the fence.

'*Ee*,' I said, speaking carefully, watching.

Then the white man spoke in English and I had no idea what he was saying and that panicked me. I didn't know where these men had come from and I didn't like the way they had walked in, it was as if they thought they belonged when they did not. I tugged at my dress and I could feel the money where I had tucked it under the strap. It reassured me that the money was still there, that I could feel it and that the men did not know. My husband had given me the money, he had sold a skin and I was to buy provisions. I shouted at Isaac to come, he was touching the motor vehicle and I worried that he would soon climb on board. Then Rweendo appeared and I went back to building the fence.

'They offered me work,' he said later, setting out his chair after the white men had gone. 'They said there is plenty of guide work with their company.'

I sucked my teeth, I didn't like companies. It was companies that had made us lose our home. And I knew that masafari had been bribing the new game guards, offering them a pound if they informed the company when they saw a lion spoor leaving the reserve so that they could go and hunt it. And one man in South Africa had even said he would like the whole of the reserve for himself, he'd asked to hire it for the winter so that he could bring his family and friends up and have a good time.

'I would travel with them and their clients,' said my husband. 'They want someone who knows the area. I would get a sleeping blanket, my food, some tobacco.'

I waited.

'And that is all.'

I held my tongue; I could see the disappointment on his face. It was a job for a youngster, not a married man with a child.

'So I said no. I want something better for my wife and our children. Now we have the reserve there will be even more whites coming here, there will be masafari everywhere. And they're going to need fuel for their trucks, they'll need other supplies, they'll need food for the clients, cooking pots. The people they hire will need things too; the guides will need food, tobacco, pills for when they are sick. The base camps need equipment, tools and building supplies. At the moment there's no one selling these things, but look at us; we're not far from the road and one day that road will be built properly. So first we'll build a small shop, a *semausu* at the edge of our plot, there by the fence, near the road. You can sell while I'm in the bush. We don't need much to build a *semausu*, some wood, some tin maybe, and a serving hatch that we can close at night. Then when the *semausu* is successful we'll get another plot nearer to the centre of the village, a commercial one, and use that plot just for a store, a general trading store.'

I smiled to myself to hear him speak. And I watched while he took a stick and began to map out his plans on the sand, forgetting for a moment, just for a moment, about my lost child and instead beginning to look towards the future. I could see myself in that *semausu*, I could see just how I could arrange the goods on the shelves and I knew exactly the sort of box I would keep the money in, a tin one with a nice strong lock.

'And then we'll build a new house,' said my husband. 'The one we have now will be a storeroom; I want a brick house here. It will be round but it will have a room at the top.'

I opened my eyes wide; I didn't know where he got these ideas.

'And this house we're going to have here, it will be the best in the village.'

Isaac laughed with delight and threw himself on top of his father, his chest on his father's back, his little chubby hands grasping at his father's hair.

And later that day my friend Wanga came by. She was my first friend in Sehuba, I had met her on a pathway near our home one day, she had been carrying water and had fallen and I had helped her up. And ever since then we had been friends. Wanga was a Moyeyi too, but she had lived in Sehuba for some years with her husband, a fat little man with skin like butter, and her two small girls. Wanga had a tight little body and long arms which she swung when she walked as if she were marching. That was how she had fallen over that day, she was so busy marching along she hadn't looked down to notice the log on the path until her feet had found it and she had fallen.

Now she came around to see me most every day; she was a very talkative woman and liked nothing better than to drink tea and tell me about things she knew. When she arrived that day, after the safari men had gone, I told her that she was welcome to sit and stay but that I was busy. My husband was to build a store, I said, so I needed to begin on the bricks and hey, how I smiled when I said that.

'And will you give me credit at this store of yours?' Wanga asked.

And I laughed and said of course I would.

By the time I was pregnant with my third child two harvests had passed in Sehuba. Our yard was cleared now, the snakes had left. We had the *semausu* at the corner of the plot selling candles and matches, single cigarettes, soap and sugar, corned beef in thick metal tins.

The mulberry tree we had left where it was, in the full sun, and it grew very fast with fat buds and sturdy twigs and plenty of fruit. While most of the berries were still green, some were turning a watery pink and soon I would shake the fruit down. As I sat one day bundling reeds together I looked up to see a curl of smoke emitting from those swelling berries. The smoke was not there all the time, just now and then. I couldn't tell where the smoke was coming from, from the flowers or from the berries. I thought perhaps it was a type of powder for it only lasted a few seconds and then it evaporated into the air. I told my husband about this and he said perhaps it was a type of fungus and that as it was growing into a bush it was time to train that tree. He also told me that the tree was more useful than we had thought, for people in other parts were said to boil the juice of the fruits until it was thick like honey and they used it as a treatment for throat pain.

I told my friend Wanga about the smoke but she just laughed. I was the only one to see that smoke. I sat and patted my stomach and I didn't know if I could see that smoke because I was special or because I was mad.

Chapter Seven

There is nothing like a ripe mulberry, when the berries are so large and so soft that they fall right into your fingers. But you have to be careful. They look so firm up there on the tree but once you pick them and collect them then you see they are so delicate that one can easily bruise another just by being pressed against it.

The first fruits were ready when my third child Kazi was born. My aunty came to Sehuba to help me and this time the birth was easier than it had been with Isaac, but when I looked at that newborn I was shocked. She was white; she was so pale that I could see the veins under her skin and in the darkness of the room her body glowed like milk. And I knew at once how people would talk; asking how a dark skinned man like Rweendo could have an ugly white baby like this. But you never know what colour a baby will take and this baby Kazi took after my mother. I called her Kazi because that is a name for a lady and I thought perhaps it would help her in life.

At first I did worry what my husband would think, if he would listen to the gossip in Sehuba, the gossip that came on the rare occasions that a woman had a white baby. And people in Sehuba did gossip about us because now we were becoming successful and now they were becoming jealous.

Just as Rweendo had predicted, development was on its way. New roads were being made and the trucks belonging to the safari companies were passing through most every month on the way north and to Moremi. Our fortunes had changed. The *semausu* we had built on the pathway by our house did well and we hired a young girl to serve there, and we quickly built another one on the main road into the village. Rweendo applied for a commercial plot and then he set about building a general trading store.

The day the store opened I brewed many kegs of beer and Rweendo slaughtered a goat and people came from all over Sehuba to celebrate with us. I was a good hostess by that time, anyone who came to our yard was welcomed in and fed with meat and treated as a visitor should. It didn't matter that they were a gossip or not, they were treated the same. And it improved my husband's life, that his wife was such a good hostess. He didn't listen to the gossip about Kazi, and our daughter's complexion darkened a little and there were no arguments between us. And it was then that I began to help other women with their babies, to help them through birth like my aunty had with me, until I became much sought after as a midwife in Sehuba.

The village was expanding now, as well as our general trading store there was a butcher's, a small bottle store and bar, and a new church hall built by some American missionaries.

Our house was being built too, and it was brick just as Rweendo had promised. He said it was to be a combination of the old and the new; the round shape was the old and the bricks were the new. He even made a little room at the top of the house that was reached by a set of stairs. When you went up there it was like being in a tree.

The year that Kazi was born, the year we finished our store, that was also the year we saw independence from Britain. I know that year, it was 1966. Now the government told us we were to have schools and clinics and all manner of things we hadn't had before and so there would be more employment opportunities too. And my husband told me about the diamonds, the diamonds that had been discovered in Orapa that the British had known nothing about and he chuckled when he told me this. God had blessed our country, that is what we felt; we knew that we had been blessed. We had lost our first home but now we had another. I had lost my baby, now I had another.

That first Independence Day wasn't celebrated in every village, but it was in Sehuba, and Rweendo was the one who helped organise the events. He had a good position in the village now; he may have been seen by some as an outsider, but he was also contributing to the village's development. When a man is successful then he draws other people to him, because they want to share in the spoils of his wealth. But some men, when they are successful, that's when they start to squander it all away.

That night of Independence Day was the first time it happened. It was a moonless night and especially dark. The children were asleep and I was lying still awake on my mattress, a flat pad of a thing that we had begun to

86

sell in our general trading store. I was worried because Rweendo had not come home and I thought if I just lay there very still then he would come back from the Independence Day party and everything would be all right. It was too dark to go out and look for him.

Then I heard him outside, I heard the clang of a metal lid as it was knocked off the pot by the fire.

'Who is it?' I called out.

'It is I!' he called back and he was laughing. 'He he he.'

I sat up on the mattress.

'Where is the meat?' he called.

'There is none,' I said quietly. I didn't want to wake the children and I didn't know why he was speaking so loud.

'What do you mean, there is none?' He stood in the doorway now and there was something odd about the way he stood, as if a wind were blowing him. 'What we beer drinkers need is something a little salty,' he muttered to himself as he went back outside.

So that was it. My husband was drunk. I was shocked beyond belief

'Papa!' Isaac shouted. He was awake suddenly and sitting up on the mattress and his face was as fresh as if it were morning. He fumbled around the mattress and I knew what he was looking for. 'Where is it?' Isaac asked, his little boy voice sounding so indignant. 'Where is *my* money?' That was the way he spoke: where is *my* food? where is *my* mother? as if he could claim everything around him as his own. And then he found it, he found the few coins where he had laid them under the mattress, and he stood up with the coins in his hand and he shouted 'Papa!' again.

Kazi stirred and I moved quickly to soothe her before she woke as well. Unlike Isaac she was a fretful baby. She didn't sleep easily and she didn't eat easily. After she was born I tried so hard to feed that child and she just refused. I had never heard of a baby who refused the breast before, but she did. Unlike Isaac she was not a fat little baby, instead she was thin like me.

'Sshs,' I whispered to Isaac. 'You'll wake your sister.'

'But I want to show Papa the money!' he cried.

Isaac was so proud of his money, the money the white hunters had given him that afternoon. He had been at the general trading store when they had passed, they were asking the whereabouts of a very large crocodile that was known in the area. Isaac told them where it was. But first, before he told them, he asked them for money. And they gave him four shillings. Then they went off to find that crocodile and I don't know if they killed it or if they took it alive, for it was said that a zoo in South Africa wanted crocodiles to show people who hadn't seen one before.

I watched anxiously as Isaac went out into the darkness, for my husband had never been drunk before and I didn't know what would happen. But Isaac showed his father the money and his father was pleased and eventually they both went to sleep.

My husband said it would never happen again, the drunkenness. He was very mournful the next morning. But it did happen again because once again things were changing. The first time it happened he was celebrating,

88

but shortly after that there was nothing left to celebrate. The drought came, the cattle were wiped out, the crops failed, the white man built the other general trading store in Sehuba. And the hunting was bad too; I don't know why but the animals were not as easy to hunt anymore. And Rweendo became a very angry person. It seemed that everything irritated him, even his children.

He didn't much care about our daughter. Kazi's behaviour didn't bother him, it was like he didn't even see her sometimes. If she cried, and she cried a lot, he just walked off somewhere else. But with Isaac it was different and my husband was very concerned about his son; he wanted him brought up in the right manner. If he found Isaac was disrespectful then he sent him off to the mulberry tree to break off a switch so that he could beat him. And sometimes Isaac just hid in that tree, climbing up so far that his father couldn't reach him.

And Rweendo spent too much time drawing out designs on the sand, thinking up new business plans. That was when he began on the mausoleum.

'I have been at the plot where I've suggested we build a cemetery,' he said one evening after the food was eaten and the pots cleaned.

'A cemetery?'

'*Ee*,' he nodded. 'Like they have in Gaborone. And I have an idea. People elsewhere are starting to build cemeteries and graves, but the graves they are using won't last long.'

'*Rra*?' I didn't know what he was talking about; I didn't follow the way his mind was working.

'Graves like that aren't going to last very long. For my grave I want a proper structure, something out of cement perhaps. And it can go like this,' and he took out a stick and began to draw on the sand. 'Instead of putting the body in the ground, you put it above the ground so it's protected.'

'Above the ground?' I objected. 'But what about animals? What about the jackals and hyenas that will sniff the body out?'

'As I said,' continued my husband, 'the body is put above the ground, but it is in a structure, like a house. No animals can get in there. It's much better than trying to dig in rocky ground like we have around here. This is like the pyramids.'

I stared at him, speechless.

'The pyramids we Africans built, the ones for Kings. It can be big enough that several people can stay in there, a family group for instance. That's what I'm going to build.'

I shivered to hear my husband talking so casually about graves; I thought it was bad luck. 'We don't need to be worrying about graves,' I said.

'I'm not worrying about it, woman, I'm saying that if someone builds a cement structure like this then it will last a long time. So I will be the first to build one. It will be something for the future, for our children and our children's children.'

And for the next few months that was all my husband did. He went to where the cemetery would be, he chose a space and he hired men to help, promising to pay them when the work was done. Then he took some cement and some stone from our general trading store and he began to build his mausoleum. And he checked on it endlessly, like a hungry farmer who has just planted a seedling and already wants to harvest it.

Rweendo liked working in that place, he said it made him feel closer to God. For now my husband started praying like you wouldn't believe. He would say that we should rely on God and wherever we may be we should come to a tree, kneel down and pray to God. He began to attend the London church, the UCSSA. This church didn't heal, they just prayed. There was no healing at the London church, you just went there and told your sins. This London church had been around for many, many years and it had even been there when my great grand-parents were born, for that was the time the missionaries sent two Batswana evangelists to Ngamiland. One was called Mogodi and he had a lot of arguments with the Batawana Chief about tobacco and brandy. He told the Kgosi not to smoke and the Kgosi refused so Mogodi refused too, he refused to preach. Instead he returned to his old job trading ivory and after some more arguments with the Kgosi, he was sent away. My husband used to laugh a lot about Mogodi and the Batawana Chief, but now he didn't find the London church funny anymore, he was a real convert.

And that got me worried and I thought that perhaps I too should believe in God, just in case.

'Where is the meat?' Rweendo demanded one night when he had come back from the cemetery plot. 'Woman, where is the meat?'

91

'There is none,' I said. When there was no money then there was no meat.

And that is when the violence started. Rweendo hit me first because there was no meat; he slapped me about the head just like that. Then it was because I had allowed the fire to go out, then that I had allowed a male visitor to hold my hand when I was a married woman, then because the *bogobe* wasn't ready when he wanted to eat. The blows did not leave any marks at first, he did not slap me in the face or anywhere that was soft because men know that, they know not to leave any evidence of what they have done.

And I knew to keep quiet. This was nobody's business but our own; I knew I was not to mention our problems outside the house. I didn't have my family near; I didn't know whom to turn to. I was too ashamed to tell my friend Wanga, I thought it would cause her to look down on me. I was supposed to appeal to Rweendo's family, but they too were far away and everyone knew Rweendo's father had beaten his mother for many, many years, which was why she was such a nervous woman. And if I had gone to them then I know what they would have said, they would have told me to return to my husband. So I just kept on waiting for it to get better and I tried very hard to make that marriage work.

My husband left Kazi alone, he didn't care for her whatever she did. He began to reject her; he began to question why he had such a light skinned child. But Isaac made him angry, and so did I.

One day my husband came home with a sign, a plaque that would go on the mausoleum. I had my head down that day, I was injured. But he brought that plaque right up to my eyes. It was shaped in a round fashion, only long, and around it was a circle of feathers. In the middle of the feathers was where you wrote the name of the person who was deceased.

'*Dumela, tsala ya me!*'

I put the lid on the pot of tea I was brewing. I didn't have to look up to know who it was, it was my friend Wanga. So I just stirred those leaves in the pot and waited while she hurried into our yard, her arms marching as she went. It was a winter afternoon and she wore a thick cardigan which she had bought from our general trading store. I had given her a good discount because we were selling off our stock now, we didn't have money to buy anything new. The other store was doing well, but we were not. And Rweendo seemed to have forgotten about his earlier business plans, now all he was interested in was the mausoleum.

I thought perhaps Wanga had smelt the small piece of chicken that was stewing on the fire, for if there was food around then she always appeared. She was pregnant with her fourth child and I could tell at once just by looking at her that it would be another girl.

Wanga came into the yard, shouting a greeting to Isaac who was struggling with a car he had built, a car made from wire with a big handle that he turned this way and that, and she called out a greeting to Kazi who was dozing by the mulberry tree, for as usual she hadn't slept during the night.

'*Dumela, tsala ya me*!' said Wanga again.

I hadn't seen my friend for a long time, she had been away visiting in the south, and I smiled as she walked into our yard for her pregnant stomach was unbalancing her and she swayed back and forth and from side to side. I wished the piece of chicken we had was bigger, it was the first meat we had had for a long time and it was intended for my husband that night.

'You're back,' I said, making room for her on the blanket where I sat.

'Hey I am so tired,' Wanga said, heaving herself down. 'I have been travelling for days.' She took a cup of tea and she began to add the sugar. 'Are you well?'

I ducked my head for a second, keeping my eyes away from hers because I didn't want her to know my husband had beaten me again. 'How is everyone down south?' I asked.

'They're fine.' Wanga smiled and began to stroke up and down on her legs which were very swollen and painful. 'My brother has three children now, all boys. And he's got twenty cattle.' She stopped to let that piece of news sink in. Sometimes Wanga was a very competitive somebody, she liked to boast about what her relations had even though I had told her that this was dangerous, people don't like those who boast. 'So we did a lot of eating,' said Wanga. 'We went to church, we even went to a beauty contest.'

I stopped with my tea halfway up to my lips. 'What's that?'

Wanga smiled to have my attention. She liked to tell me things I didn't know about. 'Well, in a beauty contest you get all these people to enter and compare them to see who's the best. People pay to watch, just some few pula, but then when a winner is chosen the money goes to develop the village.'

Wanga thought this was a very good idea and she was excited about it and wanted to hold a beauty contest in Sehuba. She said we could even organise one for children, to see who was the most beautiful.

'*Ee*,' I agreed. 'I can enter Isaac.'

She laughed and slapped me on the arm. 'It's not for boys!'

'Then I will enter Kazi.' I said it a little stubbornly, and I felt my friend looking at me sideways.

'Fine,' she said, and she smoothed out the lap of her dress.

I got up, irritated. Just because my baby looked like a white, it didn't mean she couldn't enter a beauty contest.

Eventually Wanga left but I didn't walk her halfway home as usual, I walked her only to the edge of our yard I was so annoyed.

And then Haldjimbo, my husband's silly talkative friend who had recently followed us to Sehuba and built a house nearby, came into the yard bouncing on the heels of his feet. Haldjimbo had developed a new habit whereby when he wanted to scratch his right ear, instead of doing so with his right hand he loped his left arm right

95

the way around the back of his head and used this one instead. It irritated me, this habit, because it suggested my husband's friend always took the most complicated approach. So when I saw him arriving I wasn't happy at all and I wished my husband were here to deal with him.

I was reluctant when Haldjimbo took my elbow and led me back towards the house, stopping by the mulberry tree. I thought he was going to ask for something, perhaps even money.

'MaIsaac,' he said, calling me after my first-born child as was proper. Then he started clearing his throat. 'MaIsaac,' he said again. He was still holding onto my elbow and I was about to move away.

'What is it?' I asked, for I sensed now that something was wrong.

'It's Rweendo,' said Haldjimbo at last. 'We were at the cemetery this morning, as you know he was keen to finish . . .'

'Yes?' I interrupted.

'He fell in.'

'He fell in?' I laughed in relief. I had been afraid something terrible had happened and it had not. Then I saw Haldjimbo's expression and as quick as anything I put my hand to my mouth and I covered it as if I could force that laugh back in.

'He has been killed.'

'I don't understand what you are telling me,' I said. I was standing there, completely still, right beside the mulberry tree. I looked around, at the empty teacups, at the place where Wanga and me had been chatting and talking about the beauty contest.

'Well, it was this morning and I left the cemetery to check on something and when I came back I saw Rweendo had . . .'

'No, I mean I don't understand.' And I didn't. It was impossible. Rweendo had left home that morning once the sun was up and he would be back once the sun was down. It was not supposed to be this way. People need warning when someone is about to die. If it happens like that then you don't know what to do, you don't even know what to tell your children.

'Who else was there?'

'*Mma*?' asked Haldjimbo.

'Who else was there?' I lowered my voice. 'At the cemetery.'

'Only me. We were alone, I was the one who found him.'

'Only you?'

'*Ee*, only me.'

'So he fell in?'

'*Ee*. He must have hit his head, but it's strange because he also has a wound here.' My husband's silly friend grasped his right shoulder. 'Perhaps he fell on his side, on a post or something. Because when I rolled him over it was as if something had pierced him, on the side in the shoulder.'

And I thought, what will people say? Why would my husband die in such a silly fashion, and what about my children?

'Then you have told me,' I said. 'That is all you need to do. If people ask, you can refer them to me.' As I spoke I could hear myself as if I were looking down upon my body standing there in our yard and I could hear that my voice sounded just like my aunty's.

The day was windy, the day we buried Rweendo, the day we took the coffin to the cemetery on the sledge. I could hear the wind howling, I could hear it tearing angrily around the trees. There was sand everywhere; it had even blown inside the mausoleum. And the people of Sehuba all stood around and watched and the women wailed and several threw themselves onto the ground. I didn't like that; I didn't like the way some women always made a drama from a serious business. They shouldn't have wailed when the burial was just beginning.

And I expected Rweendo to jump out of that box he was in and say, 'I'm here, don't hide me away in this thing. I never meant any of those things I did. I should never have beaten you, I should have been a better husband to you, let me try again.'

But he didn't and now he would never have the chance for things to be better. And I thought I should jump on the box and stop what was going to happen and pull him out before it did. But of course I didn't, because that's not what you do at a funeral. At a funeral you bury the past.

It had been hard moving the body after the accident. We had taken it from the cemetery, my husband's silly friend and me, in a wheelbarrow covered up so no one would see. I had not looked at my late husband, except to check the wound was where Haldjimbo had said it was. Other than that, I didn't look. I closed my mind from what I was doing in order that I could do it. I told myself I was simply moving some particularly heavy firewood.

We took the body right into the bush, hurrying quickly, afraid of the hyenas we could hear in the distance, and there it had stayed for some few days. Then I reported that my husband was missing and then the men went into the bush, discovered the body and came to inform me.

I watched while the men put the coffin inside the mausoleum; it was like a little white box with thick stone walls and a square black hole in the middle. And because they didn't know what a mausoleum was, they began to shovel on the sand and the soil and the stones. The men shovelled and shovelled until the soil and the stones were in a big pile on top of that mausoleum so that no one would have even known there was a mausoleum underneath. It looked like a sleeping hippopotamus. I watched the mound grow and I wondered when the soil would be eroded until the mausoleum would be seen again. The mausoleum that my husband had worked so hard to build. The mausoleum that had killed him.

The people came to me and touched my shoulders and took my hands. People in Sehuba had been kinder to me since our business and our crops had failed and they didn't gossip so much. And they said my husband had been a honourable man. They said he had been a brave man, that he was sure to have fought that buffalo that had got him like that, all alone out in the bush. For that was what they suspected had happened and I confirmed that the last time I had seen my husband he'd been setting off to the bush to hunt buffalo, and Haldjimbo backed me up on this. No one doubted what had happened; everyone knew what buffalos were like. Perhaps a white hunter had shot one and missed, perhaps it was a wounded buffalo that had killed Rweendo. And wounded buffalos are terrible and very cunning. They will wait for you until you stumble across them and that's when they charge, keeping their head up high, their eyes trained on you until they dip those horns and pick you up and the horn goes right through and they toss you away.

The people of Sehuba sympathised with me. They said at least Rweendo Muyendi had died a hunter. And I bowed my head and I cried and in between the crying little bits of air came out of my mouth and it was a sound like gasping.

We returned home to eat the funeral food and the meat was cooked without salt so that we should not enjoy it too much. And then they shaved my hair.

Isaac inherited my husband's rifle, of course. He was only a small boy, but he inherited his father's rifle, the one Rweendo's brother Nkapa had given him. Nkapa had passed away a year earlier and I knew his wife and his son Leapile were suffering, but now I was not in a position to help.

What am I looking at? These walls aren't mine. These walls are white when mine are brown. There is something hanging on the wall and I need my glasses. I pat around the bed and then I realise I don't know this bed, it's not mine. The cloth has little tears in it where it has been overwashed. It smells like illness. Then I know I'm at the clinic. There is a sink in the corner just there and half a bar of yellow Sunlight soap which can leave a stain if you don't scrub your clothing hard enough. I can see it's a calendar hanging on the wall and it has a picture of four buffalo. And now I see the other beds, and the other people sleeping here in the clinic.

On the floor by my bed there is a very shiny, hard-edged bag and it's open and inside I can see all manner of things that look new and freshly bought. Isaac must have bought them for me. They look expensive. He is clever, my son. Like his father Rweendo, Isaac could see the changes that were coming and even though he was still a small boy he knew how to make the most of those changes. He knew how to take advantage when Lenny Krause moved next door with his wife and his Land Rover and his parties and his odd little girl as brittle as a winter twig.

Chapter Eight

'*Hey monna, o dira eng?*'

I looked up from where I was hanging out washing. It was a Sunday and our general trading store was closed, but I had plenty of other things to do. My husband had passed away more than a year ago and there was no opportunity for laziness.

From where I stood I could see down the pathway that led from our house and across to the plot of land next door. And it was here that the man's voice was coming from. He sounded angry, he sounded as if he had just found a small boy doing something he shouldn't be doing and so I looked around to check where Isaac was.

On a school day I didn't worry, for I knew where he was. Isaac enjoyed school very much and every morning he asked, 'Where is *my* uniform? Have you ironed *my* uniform? Because I am going to *my* school.' That was still the way he talked, as if everything belonged to him. And he was clever, just like his father. It had been Isaac's idea to go to school and he had troubled me for a long time to send him there. At first I could not afford the uniform, in particular the shoes, so I had refused, but now I could easily pay for everything that was needed. So Isaac set off for school very happily each day and he walked there with my friend Wanga's first-born who was in the same class as him. We had plans that Isaac and the girl would marry when they were older, or at least that was Wanga's idea.

It was Wanga who told me about a certain boy who was teasing my son at school, calling him pencil because his body was so thin. But I told Isaac that as long as he kept on eating as much as he did then soon he would grow up nice and fat. And it was Wanga who told me that the same boy had accused my son of stealing his school bag. So I went to the boy's father and warned him about this lie because I knew Isaac was honest and well brought up and would never take what wasn't his.

That Sunday, when I heard the noise from the plot next door, it was towards the end of the dry season and in our plot most of the trees were bare like ghosts. For some reason the wind was fierce that year, all morning it had been picking up the sand and spitting it all over the place and frequently I had had to stop to wipe the dust from my eyes. The air was grey and hot; we were praying for rain although we knew the rains were a long way off. The day before a spark of summer lightning had caused a fire on the riverbank and I had seen the papyrus catch alight and pop and spark until the flames reached the water and were gone. It was not a time of year I liked, it reminded me of the day my husband had died.

And I also didn't like what I suspected was going on in the plot next door. This plot had been uninhabited for many years, ever since we had arrived in Sehuba, and it was a good place to snare a guinea fowl or a francolin. Several times Isaac had trapped a bird himself and brought it to me so I could cook it. He was very pleased

103

he had been able to do this, that he could begin to provide for me and he saw himself already as a little man. Now he said he wanted to go into Moremi and hunt like his father had done, although I warned him against this. I told him people like us could no longer hunt what and where we wanted.

'Why, Mama? Why is that?' he asked. And what could I say to that?

In the past few months there had been much activity going on at the plot next door, with motor vehicles and men going in and out, and although I had difficulty believing it at first, it seemed someone was building a house there.

Again I heard the man's voice and again he sounded angry. '*A o a utlwa?*' He was asking someone whether or not they were listening, but I heard no reply to the question. Again I hoped it wasn't Isaac who was in trouble. He had been running across to that plot to watch the men clear the grass and remove the trees and he would come back to tell me the news: a man had come across a cobra while erecting the fence and that cobra had spat in his face; another man had been drunk and fallen in wet cement; he had seen a very big car and when he grew up he would buy me one just like it. Isaac was always saying this, always telling me what he would buy me when he grew up. And if I scolded him for something then he would say, 'I am *not* going to buy you that car after all!'

But although I knew that there was plenty of activity going on at that plot next door, still no one had come to us and asked permission to build a house next to ours. And as the Headman could not allocate land until we were consulted, as we were the ones already living here, I had been waiting for someone to come and tell me what was going on.

'*Monna!*' came the man's voice again, and it was such a deep voice, deep and gravely. '*Tswala pompo!*'

So they had a pump next door? They had their own water supply? I continued to put up my washing, very carefully, looking over the top of the sheets as I arranged them to dry, as they slapped this way and that in the wind. This man was giving one order after another and he was shouting at the top of his voice.

I walked away to take more washing from the tub and now I could see smoke rising from the plot next door and I could see a host of men, some on the roof of a low stone house laying out big sheets of shiny tin, others by a big cement mixer, one filling a barrel at a tap. I couldn't tell which one it was that was shouting. No one seemed to be speaking; they were all busy with something. And then I saw him and it was not what I was expecting at all. The man shouting the orders was a white. And I marvelled to hear him, for he sounded just like a true black Motswana.

'*Ke eng se?*' he demanded.

I ducked my head to the tub as the man came to the edge of the plot next door, near enough that I could see him shield his face with one hand and stand there looking around for something. Then I told myself I was the one who lived here, so why was I hiding like this?

105

And all the time I finished putting that washing out I could hear that man shouting. '*O bua maaka!*' he yelled, just like a teacher with a troublesome class. And all that time I could hear no one reply.

Lenny Krause, he was something to look at. He wasn't hairy like a lot of white men, and his body was chunky as if God had squeezed him down a bit at both ends. And the way he walked, as if there was something stuck in his trousers, he rolled as he walked and it was a very smooth, purposeful sort of walk. He had energy and he had youth.

That was the way he walked when he first came over to greet me. He parked his car by the edge of our plot and, leaving it running, he came over.

'The white is coming!' I heard Isaac shout as he came rushing from nowhere into our yard, the band of his catapult fluttering in his hand.

I didn't reply, but I was relieved that now I knew where my son was. He came running up and I almost had to put out a hand to stop him. When he was excited then he still ran as fast as when he had been a small child, running straight into things and then calling out, 'I'm alright! I'm alright!' Even if he'd run into a metal pole and there was blood running down his nose he'd shout, 'I'm alright!' Only recently he had broken a finger while playing football with his school friends, yet he had not asked to go to the clinic until several days had passed.

'Slow down,' I told my son. He was too big to be running like this and besides, I didn't want the white man to think we cared about his appearance that much.

'*Ko ko!*' called Lenny Krause as he came swaggering into our yard. He was well dressed for such a hot day, with a smart long jacket of some thick material with many buckles and buttons, and around his neck was the strangest red cloth and at first I thought he was injured and it was a bandage of some sort. I knew he was a hunter, I could see that at once for I was used to serving them at my general trading store. But unlike most of the hunters he did not wear boots, instead he wore an old pair of patter-patters.

'*Ee,*' I replied. My head was down; I was deciding how to arrange my expression and I was trying not to laugh at the way this man walked, the way he thought he was something. He reminded me of the men who had come for my husband that day, offering him the job with their company, wanting him to work for nothing. But that was long ago, I supported myself now.

'*Dumela Mme,*' Lenny Krause said politely, coming up to where I sat. He took off his hat and wiped his fingers across his forehead. It was a very wide forehead and it was a little less red than the rest of his face where it had been shaded with the hat. 'Hey, *letatsti le a fisa!*'

I agreed that it was a hot day, but other than that I didn't speak. I didn't know what this man wanted and I was suspicious. I didn't know if he were building a house for himself next door to me, or if he were building it for someone else, or whether indeed it was a house at all and not an office or some other such thing.

'*E kae pula?*' Lenny Krause said, and he looked up into the sky so that the lump in his neck flattened out.

I shrugged, I didn't know where the rain was and anyone could see it hadn't come yet.

'Yes, sonny,' Lenny Krause said, seeing my son standing next to me. Isaac had his legs set apart and his hands folded on his chest as if he were my guard.

'*Ee*,' my son replied and he hung his head a little the way he knew he should. But then I could see he had a question to ask and that it was about to burst out of him. He was looking at this Lenny Krause and I knew his eyes were hooked on the white man's shiny-topped penknife which we could see peeping out of his trouser pocket. 'Are you a hunter?' Isaac asked.

Lenny Krause nodded, a single long nod of the head. Then he saw where my son was looking and he pulled out the penknife and held it out. Isaac looked at me and I nodded, so he took it and his face was so surprised as Lenny Krause began to unfold the penknife and show Isaac all the tools so cleverly hidden inside.

'Then where is your gun?' said Isaac, after he had finished inspecting the penknife and handed it back.

'Shshs,' I told him.

But Lenny Krause laughed. 'Must I bring my gun when I come to visit? Sis, it's hot hey?' And he wiped himself again, replacing the hat and looking thoughtfully at Isaac for a while. 'Ever been on a croc hunt, sonny?' he asked at last.

'Yes,' said Isaac, and I had to laugh because I knew this was not true.

'Is that so? Then next time you must come with me, I need a new hook boy.'

'Where?' said Isaac. And I knew he was saying 'where' because he did not know what a hook boy was and nor did I.

'At the camp at Matlapaneng. Plenty of work there. But my wife wants us to settle up here now.' And Lenny Krause sighed and looked around our yard, at the black mulberry tree, a tree that was now so big and with such a wide canopy that the chickens jumped into it and hid there all day. Lenny Krause looked at our house as well, I saw him survey the roundness of the walls and the funnel of the chimney on top and the little window in the attic. And I didn't like the way he looked around him, as if he were at a government auction and deciding what items he would like to take with him.

'So,' he said at last, ' we are to be neighbours.'

'Is that so?' I raised my eyebrows and looked up. This man was not going to be my neighbour if I could help it.

'And your husband, is he around?'

'He is not around.'

And we eyed each other then, Lenny Krause and I, and I saw how his nose was shaped at the end like an arrow.

'My father is dead, he was killed by a buffalo,' Isaac said, and I frowned to hear him volunteering information to a stranger. But I knew he liked to tell this story and it was a story that people in Sehuba listened to patiently whenever it was told. The only one who knew what had happened was my husband's silly friend Haldjimbo and he had died the year before after taking offence to some rats that were bothering him in his house at night. One day Haldjimbo was burning some leaves in the yard when he accidentally caught one of the rats scurrying around outside. So this silly man picked up the rat and threw it on the burning leaves. That rat leapt off the fire, still with some burning leaves attached, and ran right back into the house. And as that house was made from reeds, it soon set alight and burnt right down. Haldjimbo lost everything he had and shortly afterwards he succumbed to TB and died.

I had had friends, of course, since my husband had passed away. The men had come sniffing round almost at once. One had even proposed marriage. But still I stayed alone with my children, as everyone in Sehuba knew very well.

Sometimes a male relative would move in and I would assign him jobs, at the store perhaps. But they never lasted long. They found out that I could manage quite well by myself, that I didn't have much use for them. And if they didn't feel needed then they left. Except for the free loaders who wanted food and a blanket.

'Your husband is not around,' repeated Lenny Krause, and he put his hands in his pockets. 'So the Muyendi store is yours?'

'It is mine.' I spoke easily but inside I was troubled, for now I knew that this white man knew me even before he had come into my yard. But then I told myself that everyone in these parts knew the Muyendi General Trading Store.

That was thanks to me, and it was thanks to my aunty that I knew the value of hard work and didn't rely on the spoils of others. If my husband had lived just a few more months then he would have seen the other general trading store close down after the owner was killed in a plane crash. And now there were many more safari trucks coming by and we were the only ones selling what people wanted: bright orange carrots in cans of salted water, sausages without skin, evaporated milk that stuck to the roof of your mouth, packets of powdered soup with granules of vegetables like green pebbles.

I liked working in that store, standing behind that heavy wooden counter, keeping my accounts on scraps of thick brown paper that every now and again I would sit down and add up altogether. That was when I wished my aunty and father had thought to send me to school, for then these accounting things would have been easier for me to learn. We sold plenty in that shop, whether you wanted a box of matches, or a saddle for your donkey, a kerosene lantern or a new tin bath.

Everyone came to my general trading store, the people in Sehuba, the people from other nearby villages, and the men from the safari companies on their big trucks. The people in Sehuba may have thought it was odd that I was alone, but they relied on my store. If they wanted to gossip then they couldn't because who was going to give them credit when there was no food at home?

I wondered now who had seen this Lenny Krause come into my yard and what they would say about it.

'We should have this finished by the time the rains come,' said Lenny Krause, gesturing at the plot next door. 'At least we'll have the roof on.' And he took a cigarette out of his shirt pocket and he set it in his mouth.

He didn't light it, he just kept it hanging there, stuck to his bottom lip.

'Lenny!' came a high woman's voice and that made us both start a little. Then I saw there was a white woman in the car that was still at the gate to our plot and I watched as she came hurrying into our yard. My eyes almost popped out of my head. She had a pair of shorts like a schoolboy and a white shirt that was twisted up and tucked under so that we could see the bare skin of her stomach.

She was talking quickly in Afrikaans. I knew a few words of Afrikaans by then, from serving the white hunters, although Isaac knew far more than me because he was a quick learner. He was like Lenny Krause; he could switch from Setswana to English to Afrikaans just like that.

The woman sounded agitated and as she talked she gestured back at the men in the plot next door. She didn't seem to have noticed my son or me; she was just heading for Lenny Krause. I admired the silver necklace she had around her neck and the little earrings shaped like drops of rain. And as I looked up then I saw a storm was coming; I saw to the west that the sky had darkened and I sensed the tension in the air as the wind dropped.

'My wife, Marianne,' said Lenny Krause, and he scooped the little woman right under his shoulder and his arm went round her like a python.

'Oh!' Marianne exclaimed, and we all turned to see Kazi walking a little unsteadily out of the house where she had been napping. Still she never slept properly during the night; instead she napped in the day. Kazi's clothes were wrinkled; she had gone to sleep in a little blue dress and panties, a set of clothing that we sold in our general trading store. I grabbed her body and sat her down firmly upon my lap to keep her still, drawing her hands into mine. Kazi always wanted to be touched, sometimes too much so, and if someone offered her a hand then she would run to them. She was forever creeping up behind me and wrapping an arm around my neck, clambering on me as if my knees were steps, patting my face, pulling at me wherever she could. And at night she got so close that sometimes I woke to find her on top of me like she was trying to get back inside.

'This dress is dirty,' she complained, wriggling closer. Kazi was very particular about her clothes and she was very sensitive to anything that she said prickled her or bothered her in some way.

I turned her face to mine and wiped at her mouth with my thumb and around her lips where it was dry and white. Kazi always woke with white on her lips, as if she had been suckling from a hyena in her sleep. Her face reminded me of my late husband's, for it was long like his not round like a girl's should be. And although we tried to keep her out of the sun she had a scattering of freckles on the ridge of her nose like flecks of sand.

I could see that Marianne Krause was entranced by my child. 'Oh she's *beautiful*,' she said, and she bent down and put her hand out towards my daughter and as she did Isaac shuffled closer to me. No one had ever said his sister was beautiful before. A few months earlier Wanga had organised the first beauty contest in Sehuba and I had entered Kazi and of course she did not win because people were prejudiced against her.

Isaac was used to Kazi following him everywhere, especially when he set off for school in the morning, and he was used to saying that she should leave him alone. But he wasn't used to other people showing an interest in her and I could see that he didn't know what to do about this. I looked at Marianne Krause a little differently then, because of the way she had spoken of my daughter. I thought perhaps if she wore adult's clothing then she would not be quite as strange looking.

'We have a daughter also,' said Lenny Krause. But then he left the words hanging there without adding anything else and then he took his arm away from where it had been around his wife. Marianne looked around then and as she did the little girl arrived, as if she knew that just at that moment her parents had been talking about her. She came running into our yard, running in a carefree manner as a child does, not at all concerned about what she looked like. And she had a very interesting way of running; it was as if she were sliding. This child didn't pick up her feet, she slid on them.

The girl came to a stop when she saw my son Isaac and she positioned herself as close to her father as possible. Then she lifted her little face and looked up through her long yellow hair and I saw her eyes just fill up with looking at him. Isaac grew bashful and he busied himself checking his catapult, but that girl just kept on staring as if no one had ever told her this was a rude thing to do.

For a second I saw her look across to her mother, as if seeking something, but I saw that Marianne Krause had already looked away.

'*Mpha* ...' said the girl. She spoke quietly but she was holding out her hand, holding it out for Isaac's catapult.

Isaac laughed to hear a little white girl speaking Setswana, but he quickly put the catapult behind his back.

'Let the girl see it,' I said, amused. 'What's your name?' I asked her.

I expected the girl to hang her head and murmur a reply, and I was surprised when instead she put her head high and looked me in the eye. There is something very strange about blue eyes; they shine a bit too much in the sun. And she was such a little creature, although she was only a year or so younger than Kazi.

'My name is Petra,' she said, as clear as anything. 'What's yours?'

And we all laughed, although I was laughing in annoyance more than anything else. Did her parents not know how to bring up a child? How dare she ask me a question like that!

'This is Mma Muyendi,' said Lenny Krause. 'She is our neighbour.'

Petra looked at me, but almost at once her eyes were drawn to my son again. '*Mpha* ...' she said, and I saw Isaac hesitate, I could see his fingers fiddling with the catapult behind his back. Then he drew out that catapult and he swung it, teasingly, in front of him. He was saying, here is the catapult but you can't have it.

'What gun do you have?' he asked the white man as if

115

they were in the middle of a conversation. 'Is it a rifle? How many do you have?' I wondered if he weren't showing off a little to the white girl with all these questions of his.

'You want I should count them for you, sonny?' Lenny Krause smiled. Then he pulled his hand out of his daughter's, for she was dragging on him as if he would help her to get the catapult.

'My father was a hunter,' said Isaac, and he stuck his chest out as if daring the white man to disagree.

'Is it?'

'*Ee.* He shot everything. He shot elephant, buffalo, crocodile, a hundred kudu . . .'

Lenny Krause listened patiently as Isaac listed the animals his late father had hunted and then, with his eyes gleaming, he asked, 'Ever seen a Martini-Henry? Now that's a gun! You ask your mother,' and he turned to me, 'if she'll allow you to come over and see it.'

'He doesn't have a toe!' said Kazi suddenly, squirming on my lap. 'Mama! The white doesn't have a toe!'

And so we all looked at Lenny Krause's foot.

I had noticed the missing toe myself, as soon as Lenny Krause came into the yard, but it was not something I was going to ask about. Just as I had noticed that he had obtained a plot of land and was building a house illegally but I had not yet asked about that.

Lenny Krause laughed. '*Ja.* I have only nine toes. And I don't miss that tenth one a bit. Never had much use for it anyway.'

My children stared at the white man.

'Just woke up one morning and it was gone.'

Then Marianne Krause muttered something under her breath and took the sunglasses that were on top of her head and slid them down until her eyes were covered.

And then Lenny and Marianne Krause walked out of our yard, my son staring after them, and they got into their car, which all this time had not stopped running. And now I saw that the storm had gone, the sky was blue and the rain had passed us by.

'I'm going to buy you a car like that, Mama,' Isaac said, running back to me. 'What colour would you like? Would you like a red one or a white one?'

'Mrs Muyendi?'

The nurse startles me, I didn't realise she was standing at the door.

'Your son is here,' she says, and she says it quite loud so that other people in the room look up. It takes me a while to remember where I am and why. 'Your son is here, Mma Muyendi,' she says again, and I know what she is telling the other people is this: visitors are not allowed in the clinic at this time, but Isaac Muyendi is.

And here is my son Isaac in his blue suit and his combed hair. He laughs and the air in the room lightens. Then he walks to my bed and his shiny black shoes go clack clack on the clinic floor.

I close my eyes; I feel I can sleep again.

The nurse starts fussing around, I can feel her straightening the sheet over my body, I can hear her tutting her teeth and picking up two dirty cups as if she wasn't the one who left them there herself.

Then I open my eyes because I remember what it is I wanted to ask. 'Have they eaten all the meat?'

Isaac laughs. 'The party ended two days ago, *Mme*.' Then he stops laughing and turns to the nurse. 'So, where is the doctor?'

'*Rra*?'

'Where's the doctor? Where are the results from the tests I asked for? Are we transferring her?'

'*Nnyaa*!' I object. I don't want to be transferred; I don't want to be sent somewhere else. I don't like hospitals, they make me sick.

'The doctor isn't around,' says the nurse.

'Then you will get him,' says my son. 'Now.' He doesn't look at the nurse when he says this, instead he takes his cell phone from his belt and he begins to make a phone call. I can see why some people are afraid of my son, why they try and do what he says they should do. But not me, because I'm his mother.

But then I remember the other thing I wanted to ask him. 'She's back, isn't she?'

Isaac puts his head to one side and holds the phone to his ear. But I know there is no one talking to him on that phone of his because there are very few people in these parts who have a phone like my son.

'I saw her at the party, she is back now, isn't she?'

My son shrugs as if he doesn't know and he doesn't care whether Petra Krause is here or not. But he can't fool me.

BOOK THREE
Petra

Chapter Nine

I love Isaac. He's a boy. I'm eight and Isaac is twelve. I've been eight for two days. Mum marked it on my calendar: May 6, 1976. When I'm ten it will be 1978 and Isaac will be fourteen. When I'm thirteen it will be 1981 and Isaac will be seventeen. He will always be older than me. I will never catch up. And his little sister Kazi will always be older than me too. Man, that isn't fair.

When Isaac's eighteen then he will be allowed to drive. But he already knows how to drive and so do I. Dad says *Yissus*, she's only a girl but she may as well learn. But he says he'll give me a *snot klap* if he finds me trying to drive Betty again. When Dad gets the hell in then I run.

That was Isaac's fault, he dared me. He said I couldn't even reach the pedals because I'm only eight. But I could. Betty cost one thousand rands and she has two tanks, a big tank and a spare tank. When you're in the bush you don't want to run out of gas. She's called Betty because she's not dependable, just like a woman.

When I get in Betty then I play the game. I'm the driver. Sometimes Isaac is the driver. Then I go in the back where there are beds for people to sleep. They are really boxes. At the back it smells of metal and mattress stuffing and grease.

I'm going to buy a Land Rover when I grow up. Isaac

is going to buy one for me and I'm going to buy one for him. But I'm going to buy one for myself too.

I'm not supposed to get in Betty again, but Mum and Dad are asleep and they can't hear me. Man, they had a jawl last night. When I got up in the dark this morning there was such a mess. In the tree outside I found a table hanging. There was a chair as well. Someone must have put them there. I bet it was Dad's boykie Bobby Katz. He can do anything. He shot six lions with six shots once. He can easily put a table in a tree, even though he has a broken arm. Last night he said he might have a broken arm but at least he has ten toes.

Bobby Katz is a Great White Hunter and he says Isaac can be his gun bearer when he grows up. But Isaac says Bobby Katz knows fokol. That's my word, I taught it to Isaac eight days before my birthday. I was seven then.

I'm waiting for Isaac. He knows there was a jawl last night so Mum and Dad are asleep. We're going hunting with catapults. Last month we shot three francolins and two guinea fowl, then we roasted them. Isaac has a new catapult; he gave me the old one. The band is saggy but it still shoots. He gave it to me so I can be like him. It's the first present I ever got that I really wanted.

Dad says I'm as good as a boy at shooting. He thought I was going to be a boy. That's why they called me Petra. They thought Mum was going to have a boy and they were going to call him Peter. Then I came along.

Last night Mum was dressed like Elizabeth Taylor. She's a famous film star and she got married at Chobe. Dad wanted to take her on safari, but she went with someone else. Bloody bastards. Dad wants famous people on his safaris too. Mum wanted to go to Chobe to see Elizabeth Taylor. They have hotels up there and she said we could stay at Chobe River Lodge. So I said and Isaac can come too. 'No he can't,' said Dad. 'Africans aren't allowed,' said Mum. But I thought we were Africans so how come we're allowed?

Mum likes having a jawl. She invites everyone from Maun and says it's good to have fun again. She wore dark sunglasses, a shiny scarf wrapped on her head and some big hoopy earrings. She has a dressing table with three hairbrushes and they have silver on their backs. Once she shouted at me because I was using one to kill a scorpion. She said I would totally ruin it. Mum doesn't like animals being killed. But she doesn't like scorps either. I killed a snake too – Isaac and me found it. It was as tall as me when it stood up. It was going to spit in my face but we killed it. Isaac said he should keep the skin but I said I should. He won because he's older than me and he's a boy.

Isaac hasn't come yet and I've been waiting here for two hours and fifteen minutes. I keep looking back at the house in case he's come in another way. I like the yellow of our house; it's like custard. And I like the roof because it's tin and it makes a din when it rains. It's much better than our last house, the one we had at camp.

That's when we were doing some crocodile hunting. But Mum said it wasn't a good thing to do with a child so we moved up here. I don't like crocs and Dad says that's just fine because crocs don't like me. Dad's killed thousands and millions of crocs. Once he bagged seventeen crocs in eight minutes. They were eating a dead elephant and they didn't see Dad coming. He shot them as they were running out of the elephant. They were so stuffed they didn't run very fast. Then the crocs up-chucked as they died. Man, that river stank.

This is the way Dad kills crocs: if there's no moon then he gets in the boat and he tells Mum to shine the light. Then when he finds one he goes down hard on the throttle and gets a gun and shoots it in the soft bit. Then it's dead and he puts it on the boat. But it still lashes with its tail. A croc can twitch even a day after it's shot. You can't even skin a croc after you've shot it, you have to wait. But you can break its backbone with an axe. That's what the hook boy does.

You can find lots of things inside a croc. Once Dad found half a hippo inside. Bobby Katz shot a twenty-foot croc last month. Inside he found three goats, the horns of a cow, the front of a donkey, and a woman.

It's lunchtime, it's one o'clock. Isaac hasn't come and mum and dad are still asleep. So I need to wake them up.

'Mum!' I whisper round the door. I can see her under the mosquito net but she doesn't move. It's very still in here. The fan is turning; it does about twelve turns a minute. I think about pretending there's a spider in the bed. That will wake her. 'Dad!' I say. Then I look a bit closer. The rug on the floor is slippy and my feet move it out of place. So I bend down to straighten it because Mum likes it straight. Now I'm really near the bed and I can see he's not there.

It can be dangerous at their parties. Sometimes they shoot at each other.

'Petra! Leave Marianne alone!'

'Sorry, Dad.' I come onto the stoep because that's where he is. The stoep is full of empty bottles and old cushions and there are two cartridges as well. There is also half a snake which our cat caught last night. She likes to leave us presents on the stoep, like a frog or a mouse or a snake. All night she goes around the house crying because she thinks she has lost her babies. Mum says, 'Ag shame.' But Dad drowned the babies because we couldn't keep them. Then while she's out there she kills things for us. Our cat doesn't have a name yet because we can't decide what to call her.

'Did you wake her?'

I shake my head. My hair is long enough at the front now that if I do this then it totally covers my eyes.

'Good.' Dad is standing on the stoep scratching his chest. He hasn't shaved this morning. There are sparkly yellow prickles on his chin. 'That was a good *potjie* last night,' he nods at the three-legged pot. 'A good lamb *potjie* should never be rushed, never be stirred. The *potjie* talks to you . . .'

'And you must listen.'

Dad laughs and ruffles my hair. I try to shake his hand off. Dad always says the same thing about a *potjie*. And so does Mum. She says, 'Yes, but where on earth can we get fresh coriander around here?'

Dad says she can send me to find it, I can sniff anything out. I've got a nose like a dog. That's because I'm a mongrel. I'm an African, I'm a German and I'm a Brit. I'm an African because I was born here so this is where I come from. I'm a German because Dad's granddad came from Germany a really long time ago in the old days. He went from Germany on a ship to Africa and then he lived on the coast. We don't have the coast or the sea here, but we have the swamps and that's much better. All round our place is the swamp and on my birthday Isaac and me went out in the boat. He says his father was an expert fisherman. He says that's why he's going to leave school; he already knows what he needs. But I know Isaac is failing his lessons. His mother beats him and Isaac shows me where. Dad beats me too. He says, 'This will hurt me more than it hurts you.' But I don't see him crying.

Then I go and find Isaac and he makes me feel good again. We go to the bush and we do things. We don't do much talking. We pretend to be hunters and hunters need to be quiet. I'm glad we moved to Sehuba and that Isaac is my friend. He's my best friend because I don't have any others. He knows all about the bush and when we go together we go really far. But we always find our way back again.

I'm supposed to be at school too, only there isn't a school round here for me. I can't go to Isaac's school because they don't talk English much. And they don't talk Afrikaans at all. But it's OK because Mrs Van Heerden has arrived now and she's starting her own school. It will be an English medium school so I can go. Mum and Dad were talking about this. I was in bed but I still heard them.

Mum said, 'Lenny, she needs to go to school.' Then she waited till Dad lit her cigarette.

Dad said, 'Why?'

'Because she needs to. She needs friends, Lenny, she needs to be with her own kind.'

'What did school ever do for you?'

Mum doesn't answer. She went to a convent school and she hated that.

Dad says, 'If she were a boy then I could see the point. Sis, Marianne, wait till the Van Heerdens are sorted. Or send her down south.'

That was on the Thursday, four days before my birthday.

Maybe they'll send me to England because I'm a Brit too. My grandmother is from Britain; she came to Africa and married my dad's dad. They nearly locked her up during the war but they didn't, maybe she hid so they couldn't find her. Dad's a mongrel too. Sometimes he says he's an African, and sometimes he says he isn't.

'Go clean your room.' Dad squats down and looks in the pot. I wonder why no one stayed the night after the jawl. Usually they stay and they sleep wherever they want, on the stoep or in the storeroom or just on the sand under the trees. I wish I was an adult too.

'Ah, Dad, I'm too tired.'

'Don't talk kak.' He goes off to the storeroom where I'm not allowed.

I go into my room. My bunk bed is covered in stuff. On the top bunk are my animals and I have to put them all there or one of them will feel left out. I don't want to move them because they are in their right places. Except for Nelly, I need to sit her up a bit more.

Mum says I'm too messy and I should clean my room up. But what about the mess after they have a jawl? When I say this, Dad says she shouldn't take kak from me. Then they have a barnie. I don't know why Nonny can't clean it. That's her job. She gets paid and she gets leftovers and everything. Only Mum can't speak to Nonny because Nonny only speaks Setswana. Mum can say '*Mma*'. But she says it so it rhymes with 'car'. So I have to talk to Nonny instead because I know Setswana better than Mum.

I look in the mirror beside my bed. I look at myself smiling and then I look at myself frowning. Sometimes I look in the mirror to see how I look when I'm crying. Isaac never cries. He says if you hold your breath you don't cry.

I look out the door. Someone's coming because I can hear Roadblock yelping. She doesn't bark, she yelps or sometimes she howls. But dad says that's OK because she's a hunting dog. I love Roadblock because her face is all squishy. I want her to sleep with me but Mum says no.

I can see way down the path but I can't see Isaac. Anyway, Roadblock doesn't yelp at Isaac. She yelps at Kazi.

Kazi drives me mad. She always follows us and I wish I could just hit her. But if I hit her then her mother will come and she's scary. If we play in her general trading store she gets really angry. Dad says, 'Don't mess with

Mma Muyendi.' Isaac's mum isn't friendly. She says Isaac is not around when I know he is. Sometimes when she sees me coming she quickly sends him on an errand. I've been waiting for Isaac to come, not Kazi. When I know he's coming then I feel like it's my birthday again. I get so excited because he's my best friend and now we can go to the bush and do things. Isaac and me are going to live together when we're older. He agreed. We're not going to have children or anything like that. We'll just live together and go driving and hunting. If we feel like it then we'll take people on safari. But not Elizabeth Taylor, not even if she begs.

Kazi always follows Isaac over here. She gets to be with Isaac all the time, why does she have to bother him here as well?

Now she's halfway up the path and she's jumping up and down trying to get away from Roadblock. She's got these clippy cloppy shoes on. You would have to pay me a million zillion rands to wear shoes like that. She's wearing really stupid clothes, like she's going to church. Or a beauty contest. That's what she does, go to beauty contests. Sis. Whenever I get a doll or a dress I give it to Kazi. Mum says 'Ag, shame, that girl is so beautiful.' So I give my dolls and stuff to Kazi. But that's just to get rid of her.

'Mum!' I say, going back into her room. 'When are you getting up?'

'Just now.' She turns over in the bed.

'I'm hungry!'

'Shame,' Mum says, but she's mumbling like she doesn't really care.

Bloody bastards, I say under my breath. Anyway, I'm not hungry. I just feel a bit empty.

Chapter Ten

We're going on safari. Everyone is up early today, even Mum. She spent ages getting dressed. Then Dad shouted, 'Yissus, Marianne, the leopards don't care what you're wearing.'

I'm wearing my new belt. It's just like Isaac's and I can hang my penknife there. When Mum saw what I was wearing she said, 'How about a necklace? How about something cheerful?' She thinks I shouldn't only wear blue or green, but that's what Isaac wears. And boots, really good boots that you can stomp through the bush in.

Roadblock tries to get into Betty but Dad kicks her off. She yelps. Yelp yelp yelp.

'*Ag*, shame,' says Mum, and Roadblock looks at her with gooey eyes. But you can't take a dog on safari, even a hunting one.

First we're going to get Bobby Katz; the hunters are riding with him. He's picking them up in Maun because they are coming all the way from America. We're going to Maun too. Just as soon as Mum gets into Betty.

'Marianne!' Dad shouts because Mum is fixing her lipstick in the wing mirror.

She just laughs and rolls her eyes at me and I laugh back. Once she put lipstick on me and I said it felt like kak, like really sticky pink kak. Mum said it's not kak; it's called Come to Me. She says the ladies in Maun wear lipstick. But she's going to have to put it on a lot of times because it takes some eight hours to get to Maun. Sometimes the sand is two feet deep so we might get stuck. I've got the compass in case we get lost.

I wave at Isaac when we pass his house. We come out of our yard and we turn right and we go right past his yard. I can see Kazi sitting on a blanket with her head down. A big girl is standing over her doing Kazi's hair. And I can see Isaac under the mulberry tree. I think he's carving something on the bark and he shouldn't because his mother will klap him. When he hears Betty roaring past he gives me the thumbs up. But he's not smiling because he's jealous. He says he's going hunting with Peter Mponda. I don't care.

I'm sitting on Betty's roof and it's so high up here I can nearly see down onto Isaac's attic.

When we leave the village I wave bye. When you set off on safari you never know when you'll come back again. This is the first time Mum and me have gone with Dad since we got to Sehuba. He wanted to go alone, but Mum said, 'You're not leaving me here!' I see Mma Muyendi's general trading store and then the school where Isaac goes. It's very small, like a toy, and it's closed because today it's Saturday. I'm going to have to be really good. I'm not allowed to say bloody bastards to the Americans, or fokol.

It's so bumpy it's like we're flying. Mum told me to get off the roof so I have to stay in the back now. But the tarpaulin is flapping and I'm hanging right on the bar and

I can see the road as we pass it. It's like we're leaving the road behind. If I dropped something now I would never be able to get it back.

When we get to Maun we drop Mum off at her friend's house. Her house is called a bungalow and it's so square it's like you could just pick it up. Maun isn't like our village, it's really busy and the road is really smooth. I can see two men tying up their donkeys in front of a big safari sign. Next to that is a big store and I can read the writing outside: A Variety of Fresh & Frozen Essentials.

Mum does her hair before she gets out of Betty. Then she tries to do mine. She pulls it back and tries to put in a pink elastic band but I don't want it.

'I want to stay with Dad!'

'No you don't.' She has me by the hair and it hurts.

'Ah, Dad . . .'

'Sis, Marianne, let the child stay.'

Mum looks at me. I rub my hand across my nose and there's a trail of snot on my arm like a snail leaves. Mum throws the elastic band on the floor and she gets out. I don't want to go into the bungalow and see the ladies. They will say, 'Little Petra! Have you got a boyfriend?' Once I said, 'Yes, he's called Isaac.' And the ladies all laughed too much. 'No he's bloody not your boyfriend,' Dad said. But he is. He's a boy and he's my friend. And we're going to live together when we grow up, he promised.

Man, I love Riley's Hotel. I've never been here but I love it because people have a lot of fun here. There are eight trucks parked outside. They have lots of scratches on the sides and the sides are so dusty I could write my name on them. The fenders are really rumpled. I can see oil dripping down from one of the trucks.

'Let's have a brew,' Dad says, and I follow him across the veranda. It's so hot that it moans and creaks when we walk on it. There are two buildings made from concrete and they have green iron roofs. We go into one and it's like a swamp because the walls are green as well and there is plaster peeling off. It's a bit dark at first but I can see five men sitting in armchairs that look really old. I didn't think Riley's Hotel was going to be like this, I thought it would be big and sparkly. Dad tells me to sit at a table, even though I want to sit on the veranda, while he goes to the bar. But if I sit here quietly then he says he'll buy me a meat pie. The table is horrible. It's covered in black circles where people have put out their cigarettes. I can see out onto the veranda and the tables there are made from wire.

Then Bobby Katz comes in and his arm is still in a sling and he's wearing a cowboy shirt. '*Hoe gaan dit?*'

'Hey there,' says Dad.

Bobby Katz's hat is dark on the bottom and light on the top. The darkness is from his sweat. Bobby Katz always smells of sweat. Mum says men sweat and ladies perspire. And she says Bobby Katz has bedroom eyes. He already has a drink; he has a Lion beer in his hand. Everyone starts moving to say hello to him.

I'm bored. There are no children here, just me. The men are talking really loudly and they don't notice me. Just now I even took a sip from Bobby Katz's beer and he didn't notice. That's because he's busy talking.

'... three buffalo rushed out and came straight for us. Big buggers. So Lenny steps out and shoots the first bull. Slammed that bullet into the brain ...'

Dad laughs and takes a drink. I want someone to notice I drank Bobby Katz's beer so I can say beer tastes *lekker*, even though it doesn't.

'Ja. Just like that.' Bobby Katz slams his hand hard on the table. He has really hairy hands. 'Second buffalo comes round the bush. Lenny fires again. Click. No shots left.'

Dad roars with laughter.

'So where you heading?' asks one of the men.

'North,' Dad says.

'Is it? Who you taking?'

'Americans,' says Bobby Katz.

'Is it? Just you two hey? Sis, how many women?'

Dad frowns at the man and gestures at me. Now he's noticed I'm here.

'Remember that Chobe trip, hey Lenny?' says the man. He turns to the others at the table. 'In the mother's tent at sundown. Out and in the daughter's tent by midnight. Sis!'

Dad shrugs but he looks pleased.

'Chobe,' says Bobby Katz. 'Those fellas are lucky up there, not so?'

'Are they doing well?' asks Dad.

'Well it's hard getting the tourists in with all these bloody liberation wars. But once they get them in they can do what they want. They don't have natives breathing down their necks with all this conservation kak.'

'We're in the crossfire,' nods Dad.

'Only the strong survive,' says Bobby Katz.

A woman comes to the table. She has a hard time getting the empty cans because the men are big and crowding her. But I don't know why she looks so unhappy when she has a job and gets paid and everything.

Man, I'm bored. I'm so bored.

When Bobby Katz says it's time to go to the airport and get the Americans I shout, 'Hurrah!'

I've never seen an American before. But I've heard them singing on Dad's gramophone. He likes Johnny Cash and he calls him Johnny just like he's a friend of his. On the cover of the record it's all black and Johnny is sitting with a guitar and he's holding it like it's a floppy gun. My favourite song is 'Rhinestone Cowboy' and I think a rhinestone is like a diamond but only bigger, like a rhino. Mum likes Dolly Parton and on her record she looks like she's in the bush because there is swishy green stuff all around her. She's smiling like she just had a big dinner.

But I've never seen an American in real life. I think they'll be really big. And because they are really rich they will have lots of money and might give some to me. Isaac says all white people have money. He says if you see a white person then ask them for money and they might give it to you. But I'm a white person and I don't have any money.

The plane comes down and it wobbles on the tarmac.

I see the Americans getting out and man, they look just like Dad and Bobby Katz! I thought they'd be so different, speaking American and everything.

'Here they come,' says Bobby Katz, and my mother laughs. We picked her up from her friend's house and she's happy. Her mouth smells sweet when she kisses me hello again.

The Americans are walking across the tarmac now. They have to go into the wooden house to show their passports. Dad says this will take too long and he vaults over a counter to have a word with someone. Dad knows everyone. If you ever get stuck at a roadblock or anything then it's best to be with Dad.

It takes us all day to get to where we want to stop. Bobby Katz drives in front with the Americans and we drive behind. Mum goes to sleep. Dad taps his fingers on the wheel. I wish Roadblock was here then I would have someone to talk to.

'This is the stop,' says Dad and everyone gets busy. Bobby Katz has two men with him and they put up the tents in the clearing. The tents are really heavy and they both have to hold them to put them up. I want to help but Mum says no. They put the tents up under the trees and then they put out the deckchairs. Mum says I'm allowed to put out the cocktail table. Then they set up the mess tent and inside they put a big table and a freezer and a fridge. The gas canisters are so heavy they have to push them.

Dad says I can help with the food so I carry the boxes and put them in a straight line. Bobby Katz is taking the

Americans out and we're making things nice here, even though I want to go out and see the animals too. But Dad says it's dangerous because the Americans know bugger all.

One of Bobby Katz's men makes a hole in the ground outside because he's going to bake some bread. This evening we're going to eat smoked oysters, gemsbok tail soup, eland steaks, sherry trifle and cream. The adults are going to drink some wine. One of the Americans laughs because he sees we have a big jar of mayonnaise and it's from America, just like him. He shows me his watch and says it's a digital watch and it has a calculator too. He's got ears so big you could easily hang something on them. He shows me a camera too but he won't let me touch it because it's very expensive.

When they leave I take a peek into the bed tent and it's like a little house with windows covered in mesh. There is a washstand which is very clever because it's made from canvas just like the tent and you can fold it and unfold it again. There is a table with a mirror just like Mum has at home, a can of spray to kill the mozzies, and a torch. There is also a bar of new soap, a washcloth and a towel. The beds are really tall and they are made of iron and I want to sleep in one too.

When I go back outside I think there is a storm coming because the trees are shining, the grass has gone all white and the sky is black. It's like someone is playing with the colours because they are so shiny.

When the Americans come back they are really excited because they've shot two kudu. Even though it's easy to shoot kudu, they are really excited. They squat down on the ground and Dad takes their photograph. Then they get in a different order and Dad takes more photographs. Then I go to bed while they are still out there round the fire laughing and talking.

I can hear the Americans and Bobby Katz talking about what the Russians are up to. I don't know who Frelimo is, but I think it will be a good name for our cat. I can hear Bobby Katz's men as well and their voices are low. They must be eating meat because every now and again they stop talking. Then they talk again and it is about the rain.

Mum and me are in our little tent. Mum told me to zip it up so the lions won't get us. You're safe in a tent. The lions just walk around you. I've left my boots outside because Mum says they smell too much to be in the tent. They'll be OK outside because lions don't eat boots and Dad says hyenas don't come near anything made by man.

The next day I'm the first one to see the elephants and I shout at Dad that they're coming. He stops Betty and behind us Bobby Katz stops too. We're leading the way today. There are two adult elephants and a baby and they are not doing much, just walking. They come towards us and then they stop and go to cross the path. They walk one foot at a time, front, back, front, back. I can see their skin stretch as they move and their trunks are like an extra foot as well. It's so funny the way they walk. I want to get out and walk with them. I don't like crocs but I love elephants. Dad stops the car and I put my hand on the door. I'm laughing to see the elephants, I want to touch one.

139

And then BANG!

It's not Dad because he's in the car with me. It's not Bobby Katz because I can see him at the wheel when I turn round. I think Betty has backfired. I think it only sounds like a gun. But then I see the American with the digital watch. He's got out and he's standing on the sand with his rifle. I think he's just playing or maybe having a photo taken. Then his head jolts back and the rifle jolts up. BANG! And I'm right there against the door when the elephants begin to tumble. One of them is howling. Its legs buckle and it goes down and it's slapping the sand with its trunk and the trunk is flopping all over the place.

And there's so much dust that I can't count how many elephants there are now. But I know there are more than there were at the beginning. I think there are five more. I think they are running from everywhere. I don't know if they are running away or running here. Their bodies are like plasticine. It's all mixed up, dust and grey bodies and ears and trunks and tusks. And I don't want to be in the car. It smells wet like someone peed themselves. I want to get out but I can't. That's when I start screaming.

'Don't be such a wuss,' Dad says. He has to shout because there is so much noise. Mum has her head in her hands. The elephants are screaming and I'm screaming and the rifles are going and I think there are three people shooting now. I can't get out and run away because it's like a war out there. If I get out then I'll be shot as well. I can't see the bullets, I can't see anything leaving the rifles, I can only see what happens when they hit the baby elephant. I put my arms round myself very, very tight. There is a big gulp coming out of my mouth and I'm trying to hold it in.

'If you're going to up-chuck then open the window,' Dad says.

He doesn't care. He doesn't care about me or about the elephants. He just gets out and slams the door and he heads after that American.

The elephants are howling and falling over and getting up again and I don't know when it's ever going to stop.

The next day we go home. No one is talking much. Mum has her sunglasses on and she doesn't take them off. The Americans are happy because they have some tusks in the back of Bobby Katz's Land Rover. They are going to give us thousands and thousands of rands. I sit in the back of Betty and bump up and down and think what we can buy with this money. But I'm feeling really grumpy. Everything I do I get told off. This was supposed to be special. I really wanted to go on safari and now I don't. Mum tells me to stop humming that irritating song but I don't.

Dad swears because the gear lever is too hot. The water in the radiator is boiling too. I look out of the window and all I can see is miles and miles of grass and the sand is quivering and I think I can see shade but there isn't any.

Bobby Katz takes the Americans back to the airport and he puts some of the tusks in our Land Rover and then he covers them up really carefully and tells me to sit on top. They are hard and bony and I don't like sitting on them, I want to hang off the back or sit on the roof. 'Owie!' I say, but Dad ignores me.

On the way back home we break down and Dad says the chassis is cracked and he's really angry. He kicks Betty and says bloody bastard. Now we have to camp on our own, we're nearly home but it's night time now. There's not much food left, just some bread which is really hard and crumbly and some mackerel in a tin which really smells. Mum and me sleep in our small tent and Dad sleeps under Betty. He just takes his bedroll and slides under Betty and says it's warm and cosy under there just like a lion's belly. He says there's not enough room for him to stretch out properly inside our little tent.

I'm the first one awake in the morning and it's very quiet. I can see for five kilometres all round me. No one is awake except for the birds. I can see the bush and it's flat and it goes on and on. I'm standing in shadow but in front of me the air is silver and the grass is yellow. I watch the sun coming up; it shoots up from behind some trees which are all alone in the bush like an island. But then I hear them. I hear boys and I get my penknife in my hand and I go investigate. Then I see their tracks and I follow them and I'm so busy looking down to see which way they are going that I walk right into their camp. There is a little fire but it's almost burnt out and there is a tin with its top cut off and it's burnt because someone has been cooking water in it. Then a boy jumps round a bush just next to me and he lands right there. And it is Isaac.

'Ahaha!' he shouts, and he holds out a stick. So I hold

out my penknife and we pretend we're warriors. Then another boy appears and it is Peter Mponda.

'What are you doing?' he asks Isaac.

Isaac stops and he drops the stick.

'Isn't this funny?' I say. 'We're camping here and you're camping here. I've been to Maun and after that we went on safari and the Americans killed two kudu and one of them has this watch and . . .'

'Where's your father?' says Peter Mponda.

'There,' I say.

Peter Mponda starts whispering and he pulls at Isaac and they both run off. So I follow and I see the antelope strung up on the tree and it's really glowing because its skin has been taken off. Peter Mponda starts scrabbling with the rope to get it down but it's too late because we all hear the crunch of footsteps in the bush and when we turn then Dad is there.

Isaac and Peter shift themselves in front of the tree so they hide the antelope. Only they don't because it's much bigger than them and it's dropping blood and the flies are coming too.

'What have we here?' Dad says. He pulls on the bandana round his neck then he just stands there with his hands in his pocket. 'Been hunting, boys?'

'*Ee*,' says Isaac.

'*Ee*,' says Peter Mponda.

They are both looking down now; I can't even see their faces. But I know they're scared. They aren't allowed to just shoot anything they want. They are supposed to have a licence like Dad has, but they don't give licences to

143

children. They give them to adults and Americans. I won't tell anyone. But I feel sick because maybe someone else will. And then the police will come and put Isaac in jail. But maybe Dad can stop them if they do this because the police are friends of his.

Dad's just standing there and he's looking the way he does when he says, 'This will hurt me more than it hurts you.'

'Let's go, Dad,' I say, and I tug on his hand. I tug and tug but he just stands there. Then he scratches his chest. 'Off you go, Petra.'

'Ah, Dad.'

But he flips my hand away from his. Then he just stands there like a stone and I know he won't move until I leave.

I want to say something to Isaac but he doesn't look at me either. I stamp back through the bush and I stamp really hard because it isn't my fault.

Isaac won't play with me today. He hasn't come to our yard for five days. Then I went to his and he refused to come over. He says he'd rather play with his sister. That means I've got to do everything on my own. But it's no fun on my own. Mum says Isaac is in big trouble.

I go to the edge of Isaac's yard and he's playing with Kazi. He's made her a car and they are eating something. Kazi doesn't know how to play properly; she only knows dressing up and girl things like that. I'm so furious with Kazi and I want to get him away from her right now. I put my head right against the fence and I shout, 'Is . . . aac!'

BOOK FOUR
Kazi

Chapter Eleven

The first time my mother put me in a beauty contest it was just a small one and I'm sure I didn't really know what it was all about. I was probably about five. But I do remember a later one, when I was around eight. I remember being woken up early that morning, my mother whispering in the darkness, telling me not to wake Isaac. He was asleep on the mattress we sometimes shared, laying on his back as usual, not moving. Whenever I woke in the night I could hear the gentle rumble of air being pulled in and out of my brother's nostrils. Sometimes listening to Isaac was the only way I could get back to sleep again.

That morning my mother still had sleep in her eyes and there was a crease on her cheek where she had been sleeping with her hand against her face. And then she took me outside to wash and it was as if we were the only ones in Sehuba to be awake that day. I could feel the sky lightening and hear the airy, wooden sounds of doves down in the trees by the river.

I think I was a little young for my age because I can't imagine Maya acting the way I did then. On the outside, I was just so *agreeable* as a child. I went where I was supposed to go, I put on what I was told to put on and in general I obeyed all my mother's commandments.

I understood that how I behaved, and particularly how I behaved in a beauty contest, was important to her. And then there was always the presence of my father hovering in the background, on the lookout for disobedience, according to my mother, even from the grave. 'What would your father think?' she'd ask if I ever came even close to contradicting her. 'What would your father say?' But I had no idea what he would think or say.

I can't remember my father for two reasons: he died when I was so young, and as far as I know no pictures of him exist. In those days and in those parts virtually no one had a camera. I've tried to reconstruct scenes, putting my father in our house, or out in the garden. I've tried to imagine what he would be doing, how he would look, but all I can capture is a general feeling of being ignored. Even when I'm creating these scenes, he just seems so far away from me, but maybe that's because I only had him for such a short time. Isaac always said he remembered our father and I felt he used to hold this over me, the fact he could remember him and I couldn't. Our father was Isaac's hero and even though I couldn't remember him, I wanted him to be my hero too.

'Don't sit on Papa's chair!' Isaac would scold me. 'This is how Papa used to hunt,' he would say, or 'I'm drinking coffee because Papa liked coffee', or 'I'm a fisherman, just like Papa.'

That was what Isaac was doing the day of the beauty contest, the one when I was eight. He was being a fisherman, balancing on a piece of wood and pretending it was a mokoro. As usual he had woken later than we had, and he was always allowed to sleep later than my mother or me. And whenever he got up then my mother would swing into action, making sure there was hot water for him, that he had his tea and bread, that his clothes were ironed. We couldn't live our lives until my mother was sure he had everything he wanted. When Isaac wanted to go to school, he went; it took years before I was allowed to go. And she always talked about his future, how he would one day run the general trading store. But that day of the beauty contest, it was me who took centre stage.

'Stand still!' my mother said, eyeing me as I stood in the bath. She had heated the water especially for me, using a big black-bottomed pan on the fire, and then putting the tin tub in the shade of the mulberry tree. Then she made me stand upright so she could scrub me from top to toe. This was what I remember, my mother totally focusing on me.

'It hurts,' I murmured as she scrubbed me. But it didn't hurt; I just wanted to keep her attention.

'In the old days,' she said, sitting back on her heels for a moment, 'you wouldn't believe how clean the water was then, not like this rubbish water around here. When we lived in Xuku, before masafari threw us out, then the river there . . .'

But I wasn't interested in the old days; I wanted everything to be about now. 'I'm cold,' I said, making myself shiver.

But my mother just took that washing rag and rubbed

even harder. 'Ao!' she objected when I foolishly leant to one side to try and pat the bubbles of soapy froth on my skin.

When I was scrubbed within an inch of my life, when my whole body tingled with the scrubbing, then she told me to get out of the bath and stand on her old red blanket.

'I'm all itchy,' I said.

But my mother just took a towel and dried me with equal vigour. Finally she set about dressing me and getting my hair just right. And all the time Isaac was watching, playing on his imaginary canoe.

'You look silly,' he said as I stood there with just my panties on.

'Hold your tongue,' said my mother, and Isaac opened his mouth in surprise. He wasn't used to my mother defending me.

She did my face last and she creamed it lightly with Vaseline and soon, because it was such a hot day, I could feel that Vaseline steaming on my skin.

Then our neighbour Marianne Krause came by. She didn't use the pathway that we kids used, the one that led from our back door across the yard and into the Krauses' plot; instead she came the long way round. Marianne Krause didn't often come to our house; she seemed to spend most of her time inside her house, but today she had come to see me get ready.

'*Ag*, very nice!' she said in her funny English. She put her hands on her hips and rocked back. 'Don't you look nice?'

I thought it was Marianne Krause who looked nice with her white shirt tied up in a little knot above her belly button. I smiled and smiled, hoping she would give me a present, a doll perhaps with yellow hair, or some jewellery like the chain she had once given me with a little purple flower on the end.

'You will win today, Kazi,' said Marianne.

My mother nodded, a hair clip held between her teeth. She didn't have much time for Marianne Krause; even as a child I sensed that. She always said the Krauses were like squatters, that they'd given themselves the plot next door and no one had asked for her permission. She had a massive grudge against the Krauses.

And then Petra came slipping into our yard, holding out a stick.

'Isaac, see what I've got!' she said, all excited, ignoring everyone except for my brother. On the stick was a monstrous brown chameleon, all humped up, its human-looking fingers grasping the stick, its eyes rolling right the way round in its head.

I yelled in fright and my mother screamed at Petra to get rid of it at once, but Isaac came closer. He loved inspecting animals, even chameleons. He wasn't afraid of animals like I sometimes was. He loved to set off to the bush around our house and pretend to track animals like a hunter, like our father had done.

Isaac watched while Petra showed off her find, and the chameleon with its body like an old man began to slowly put out a leg, jerking it back and forth before finally clasping the stick with its little hands, moving itself

151

forward, not realising if it kept on going then it would soon drop off.

Petra and Isaac watched in fascination and then Petra began to stroke the chameleon and slowly its head began to change colour and its neck puffed up into bright yellow goose bumps. And all the while it kept rolling round its eyes until my mother could take it no more and batted at it with the washing rag.

'How can you bring that into our yard?' she asked Petra. But I knew she was directing the question to Marianne as much as to her daughter. 'Don't you know it's bad luck?'

My mother was always on the lookout for bad luck, and for anyone bringing bad luck into our home. But Marianne appeared not to have heard her.

'Petra!' said my mother. 'If a chameleon bites you, you will laugh until you die. Take it away, now!'

Still Marianne said and did nothing. And I felt uncomfortable because my mother was being rude to Marianne Krause and I didn't want her to be rude to her because Marianne Krause said I was beautiful.

At last Petra took the chameleon away and Isaac followed her out of the yard. Then Marianne left and my mother and me set off to the Sehuba church hall. The hall was built away from the main road, along a narrow pathway that led right and then left from our house. I had been in a beauty contest before but I could feel that this one would be different. I walked so carefully, trying not to get sand in my shiny black shoes that were so hard and stiff that they gave me blisters. God how I loved those shoes, however much pain they inflicted. Each time I wore the shoes the blisters swelled and swelled until my mother pierced them with a needle that she had heated in the fire. That was how she had done my ears as well, she'd pierced them years before with a needle and then she'd stuck a piece of matchstick in the holes so they wouldn't close up. 'Now everyone will know you're a girl,' she'd said.

I only wore those shoes to beauty contests and the rest of the time they spent wrapped in tissue paper in my mother's sideboard. And it was such an ugly thing, that sideboard, so cheaply made. It must have been fashioned out of some sort of fake wood for it was really pale, like the colour of sawdust. And it had a glass front that you were supposed to slide open and shut, only it was stuck and always wedged halfway. Still, the sideboard was the result of the profits she made at our general trading store and she was intensely pleased about it. It showed she was doing well.

She kept my beauty contest shoes right in there along with a plate someone had once given her with gilt edges, a squat little carriage clock which probably came from South Africa, and a plaque with feathers round the edge that she thought was valuable when it was so obviously not.

I can see us trudging across the sand in Sehuba, the sun beating down, my mother holding me by the hand in fingers that were always cool, whatever the weather. I see my mother and me in that flat land, empty but for the thorn trees as we left our house behind, nestled in the clump of trees by the river. I try not to think about home much, it's something I consciously try to push away, but there are times in dreams when I fly into our house like a poltergeist. I circle the top branches of the mulberry tree and then I fly down into the attic and down the steps and all around the house, in and out of the rooms like I'm searching for something, or checking that everything is still how I left it; the sideboard and my beauty pageant shoes wrapped up in tissue paper.

The morning of that beauty contest was particularly hot and dry and it was such a relief when we reached the new slice of tar road and I could walk properly and not worry about getting my shoes and socks sandy. I'd forgotten about those socks, I haven't seen socks like those for years. They were white, naturally, but they only came halfway up my ankle and the tops curled out and were embroidered with flowers. Sometimes I stroked those socks, I loved them so much. My heart would beat a little faster when I looked at them and then when I pulled them on my ankles looked all white and smooth and pretty.

I felt special, being taken to a beauty contest, but I also remember a sense of pressure. If I did well then it was like my mother did well, and if I didn't then it meant people were out to get us. She was convinced that other mothers used *muti* to make sure their daughters won. My mother always believed that someone was out to get her and when things went wrong it just confirmed the negative view of the world that she already had. Once she has an idea in her head then there is no shaking her out of it. If you cross my mother, understand that you have crossed her for life.

And then there I was standing on the stage, just a little wooden box really in a room at the Sehuba church that was used to store supplies. I may have had to recite a hymn, for my mother had taught me my father's favourite hymns; perhaps I just had to stand there very still in my white pleated skirt and matching top. Of course I remember the clothes because my mother liked to discuss them with me, she would even allow me a certain amount of choice. I could have the white skirt or the pink, I could have a bow in my hair or not. This was important to me, the idea that I had a choice, and the idea that clothes fitted the occasion. If you got the clothes right then you would win. And as I stood there I thought, will I win? I'll win, I know I will! They'll choose me. Will I win?

But it wasn't just the idea of choice; it was that I always loved clothes. And I knew from a really early age that the clothes we had in our village were rubbish, that they were cheap and nasty and that somewhere out there there were far better things to be had. If I saw a dress or a skirt in a magazine then that became the focus of my world. I thought if I just had that plaid skirt, that woollen hat with the pom pom, those pair of blue wedge-heeled shoes, that blouse with puffy little sleeves, then I would be happy, I would be really, really happy. I would be complete.

Isaac and Petra had taken another route to the church which went through the bush rather than along the new tar road, and by the time I got on the stage they were standing outside, pushed up against the window, watching. They deliberately had their faces right up against the glass so their lips were blown out like fish. They were mocking me, as they often did. And Isaac was eating bubble gum, chewing on it, rolling it around in his mouth and then blowing out a big pink bubble against the window. I saw Petra laugh as the bubble gum stuck to the glass.

My brother was obsessed with bubble gum. The first time, he'd been given some by a white hunter at our general trading store. He hadn't known what it was, and we weren't supposed to eat things when we didn't know what they were, but Isaac had gone ahead and unwrapped the pink paper and put the brick of thick ribbed gum into his mouth. Then his face filled up with pleasure and his jaw began to chew. And for hours he practised and practised until he could blow one bubble after another, each one bursting with a sticky slap against his face. From that day on Isaac was always on the lookout for more bubble gum. I had seen him take it from the store when our mother wasn't there; I knew where he kept little hoards around the house.

When Isaac blew the bubble against the window of the Sehuba church hall I looked away in a superior fashion. I was keeping my body very still, waiting for the judges to speak. I knew the women doing the judging: Mma Serema from the primary school, a woman who was extremely pleased with the impressive size of her own buttocks, and a woman we called Mrs Fishpaste because she was always ordering fishpaste from our general trading store. They knew who I was, for there were only a few hundred people in Sehuba. But now they were pretending not to know me at all but to be impartial judges whose job it was to choose the fairest of them all. Only, of course, in those days it was not the fairest, it was the darkest girl who won the prizes. And my mother was furious about that.

She always sat on the right of the stage, on the floor with her legs sticking out, and she watched the proceedings with her lips curled up as if she were about to spit on the floor.

I didn't win that contest, but I did come third, and for a moment it was like I had won because they called me back onto the stage, then they called the girl who came second, and then they called the winner. So for a moment I was up there alone with everyone looking and smiling at me. But after the winning girl was given a sash to wear then I became nervous about getting down off the stage. My mother was still sitting down and I ran to her, then I stopped, then I ran to her again. She put out one arm and pulled me in. She didn't say anything; she was actually not even looking at me. She had a way of holding me as if I was a parcel. I wanted to snuggle up next to her; she wanted to hold me at arm's length. Of course she never said so, what she said was, 'Kazi, you are dirtying your dress.'

I waited until she decided which of the judges or the other mothers were to blame for the fact I had come third. Then all the way home I questioned myself. Why

157

had I lost? Why didn't they like me? Why hadn't I won?

And trudging back home along the sand I had a sudden, electrifying thought about running away. I had an idea that I would run to the main road and from there I would hitch a lift and that would be it, I would be gone. I'd go to Maun, which was big; I'd go to Gaborone and live in the city and wear what I liked. It was the first time I had ever had an idea like this and it terrified me and excited me at the same time. It meant I was imagining a world without my mother.

'Mum!'

I'm in the kitchen because it's the only warm place to be on a bleak cold January day like this, an English day with a sky the colour of steel and a chill that I can feel in my bones. Maya is upstairs. She knows I can't hear her properly from down here but that doesn't stop her.

I sit by the window in the kitchen and look out over the backs of the houses behind. I always forget that if I can see what people are doing in their houses then they can see what I'm doing in mine. Only I don't seem to do anything in mine. There is a woman who has her curtains closed all day and then open all night and whenever I get up in the early hours I can see the blue glow of a TV screen. What does she watch all night long and why?

I look down, down at the trees in the gardens behind. They are all so bare, so short. But there is a bird, perhaps a type of pigeon, that likes to rest here and to sing, and its call in the morning is the strangest thing because it sounds just like the African Mourning Dove.

'Mum!' Maya cries, and it's like a goat bleating. 'Maaaaaaa-m!'

'I can't hear you!' I shout. Which is silly because she can presumably work out that if I'm answering her then I must be able to hear her.

'I don't like these blue trousers. Mum!'

'I can't hear you!' I yell again.

'Where's my red ones?' She comes down into the kitchen and stands defiantly at the doorway. She cares deeply about which clothes she wears, just like me. On the day Maya turned six the first thing she did was to put on a Barbie tiara, to crown herself Barbie for the day. Then she put on Phil's old glasses and for a shocking second, standing there in the living room, the glasses made her look just like my mother. I wonder if it's as simple as that, that we just reproduce ourselves, providing another link in the long line of family. Or do we change as we do this, are there subtle differences until the links between one generation and another become looser and looser until they dissolve completely and are gone?

I don't speak much to Maya about my mother because there isn't really any point.

'Mum!' she says. 'Anna says we've got to wear all red because today is a red day and we're doing Africa.'

What red has to do with Africa I have no idea. And I don't like the way her teacher Anna thinks they can 'do' Africa. Which part are you doing? I want to ask. Are you doing the part your mother comes from or are you doing another part? At the end of last term her school was instructed to raise money to buy a goat for families in

Africa. Maya even sold some of her favourite toys. And I wanted to say, are they *sending* a goat to Africa? How, in a padded envelope? Where exactly will they be sending this goat, do we have the names of the people this goat is going to? But Phil says take it easy; at least they're doing something for someone else.

'Maaaaaa-m!' Maya is upstairs again. 'Joe's taken my school bag!'

Maya always blames her brother when she can't find something. I don't answer her; I'll wait until she finds the bag and comes down. I got Joe ready an hour ago; he's still sitting in front of the TV.

When Maya has finally decided on what clothes are acceptable and found her school bag then we are ready to go. And now it's my turn to fuss. There are times I wish I could just go out wearing any old thing but obviously I can't. People expect me to look nice; I expect myself to look nice.

We leave the house and it's freezing outside and oddly misty.

'It's like a monster is smoking,' says Maya as she stands on the steps.

It's been days since we saw blue sky.

We hurry down the road, joining the other parents who are pulling and cajoling their children to school. I shouldn't have worn this jacket; I'd forgotten how short it is. And these heels are perhaps a little too high and they make such a noise on the pavement, it's beginning to give me a headache and fuck, is it cold.

I like to take my time taking Maya to school because

once she's there then I have to go home and hang around with Joe. Diane hasn't called for weeks. I can't even remember the last time she took me out for lunch and it's been months since anyone sent a car to pick me up. These days she offers to meet for coffee and that's all. She won't say there's no work, that's not how she operates. It's one thing I have never got used to about people in England; they just never say what they mean.

Maya joins the line in the playground and puts up her lips for a kiss. It is only a brief kiss; she doesn't like big displays of affection. Two of the boys in her class have begun to refuse to let their mothers kiss them at all. Maya will still let me kiss her, but only just. The more I go to hug her, the more I try to kiss her, the more she pulls away.

I leave Maya at school and push Joe home in the buggy, passing all the other mothers walking jauntily now they've dropped their kids off at school, and suddenly I'm thinking of my old primary school in Sehuba. I wish I could picture it better, but all I can see is a largely empty, sandy yard, a huddle of trees, one long low building painted a salmon pink divided into three classrooms. We had no real playground, nothing to play on like climbing frames, there were no computers like Maya has, half the time there was not even any electricity. Often we were taught under the trees outside, as there were not enough classrooms for everyone.

For several years Isaac and me were at school together, until he started failing his lessons. He hid the reports that said he should pull his socks up and try harder, but our mother found them and she beat him. Isaac couldn't bear to fail, so instead he decided to leave school altogether.

I can remember when he first went to school because I would run after him in the morning as he left our yard. I seemed to spend my childhood running after Isaac, never quite catching up. He wore these little grey shorts and a white shirt and he thought he was so smart. And I would run after him begging to go to school as well and he would turn with an expression of great pleasure on his face and say I couldn't. Then he would run to my mother's friend Wanga's yard and call for her daughter and the two of them would set off together.

'I'm going to *my* school,' he would tell me. 'And I am going with *my* friend.' Our mother thought it was hilarious when he spoke like this.

But it wasn't long before Isaac began to get teased. I heard a boy at our general trading store, a boy from Isaac's class, call him a pencil. And I was shocked because my brother had made out that within his class he was a leader that the others looked up to. Yet I knew he couldn't be if he were being teased.

And then one day I found Isaac in the bush, alone. He had made a fire on which to roast a bird, but it wasn't just a bird that was roasting it was the remains of a new-looking blue and red school bag.

'Yes, sis!' he greeted me when I found him.

I pretended I didn't see the remains of the school bag because I guessed who it belonged to and I felt an overwhelming sense of shame, that my brother was being teased and that he'd stolen the bag. But if Isaac was teased at school, it was me he teased at home. He teased me that I was too young to go to school, he teased me over my complexion and my freckles, he teased me over the beauty contests all the time. He said I'd never win a beauty contest, which was what, more than anything, made me want to win.

Isaac never understood why I had to do beauty contests, but then he was allowed to say no to our mother and I was not. Isaac did what he wanted. If he wanted to watch the catfish run, for example, then he just went. One time I followed him, trailing after Petra and him as I always seemed to do. It was the height of summer, Petra and Isaac wore t-shirts and shorts, but I had a new white dress which my mother said I had to wear although she must have known what would happen. It was actually a little big for me, the dropped waist was nearly at my knees, but it was a fashionable style at the time. It had cost a lot, my mother said, and I was to take good care of it.

We spent the morning hunkered down by the river, at a spot further upstream from where Isaac usually went when he wanted to fish. There we watched the greedy catfish thrashing themselves along the banks of papyrus, chasing out the smaller fish that were hiding and gobbling them up. There was such a commotion it was as if the river were being boiled, as if it were a big pot of bubbling water into which we could fall and be eaten up too.

'Man!' said Petra as she and Isaac leant over the river enjoying the carnage.

'I'm going to catch some big ones,' said Isaac.

'Me also,' said Petra, and at once they began to fish in competition. But I didn't like what was going on in the river; I didn't even want to be there anymore. When I turned to go I stumbled on a root and fell, wet sand splattering over the bodice of my white dress.

Isaac caught two catfish, big ones with sharp teeth, which he took home for our mother. 'See!' he said. 'I'm a fisherman just like Papa!' I trailed behind him in my soiled dress, terrified of what my mother would say. I thought about taking it off and washing it, but I didn't want to be naked by the riverbank with Isaac and Petra. So I dusted off the sand as best as I could.

'How will you win looking like that?' my mother asked when I got home.

'I can get a new dress?' I mumbled hopefully.

'No,' said my mother. 'You will be keeping that one.' And she sent me to break a switch from the mulberry tree.

Chapter Twelve

I was still wearing that white dress the day I first had my picture taken. It was a year or so after the catfish run and we were sitting outside our general trading store, Isaac, Petra and me. The dress was too small for me by now, the dropped waist hung just below my chest and the cloth was no longer white, it was nearly grey. But if I wasn't wearing my school uniform or dressed up for a beauty contest, then my mother insisted I still wear it.

Isaac was on the porch sharpening an axe when a lorry came into view, driving slowly down Sehuba's tar road, and it was close enough that we could see three white men standing up in the back. In recent months we had begun to see more white people arriving in the village, not just the occasional hunters but missionaries and school teachers, and other stranger ones as well. Some of the newcomers were tourists, others were not.

And so we sat outside our store and watched. I was in awe of the new arrivals who had strange accents and often wore wonderful clothes. Sometimes, if I were really lucky, they bought with them, or left behind, magazines or catalogues or wads of glossy adverts which had been inserted into newspapers and which I read as if they were magazines too. I was always the first to get my hands on a magazine anyone had left behind or dropped or thrown away. I took it home and ran up to the attic and sat on the floor with my scissors, a small child's pair of scissors with plastic blades, and spent hours cutting out the pictures, choosing my favourite girls, my favourite ladies, my favourite clothes.

'*Makgoa*,' muttered Isaac, standing on the porch as the lorry drove nearer. He thought of himself as nearly a man now, and he seemed like one to me. His voice had changed, and he was getting secretive, wanting more than ever for me to leave him alone. Everything about him seemed to be exaggerated now, the way he moved, the way he spoke, the way he started giving my mother and me mock bows. Since he'd left school he didn't do much. Sometimes he played football behind the church with old school friends, but mostly he just wandered around being angry. The only person who didn't make him angry was Petra. She was supposed to be at school, along with a handful of foreign children in Sehuba, but I never saw her go there much and no one seemed to tell her off about it.

Isaac and Petra had their arguments; there had been a time when they had stopped talking to each other altogether, or at least Isaac stopped talking to Petra. But it hadn't lasted long and they were soon as close as anything again. And now Isaac had begun running errands for Petra's father and sometimes Lenny Krause gave him some kind of payment, a few coins, a tool of some kind. I was afraid of Lenny Krause and wouldn't have wanted to run errands for him myself, but still I felt left out and envious that he had begun to ask Isaac for help. And it meant Isaac spent even more time at the Krauses' yard with Petra.

As for me, my mother was still persevering with the beauty contests which had become more organised, thanks to her and Wanga's efforts. They were no longer just village affairs; now when there was a contest in Sehuba then girls from other villages came as well.

That morning Isaac was supposed to be watching the store, but he preferred being outside to being inside behind the counter because he thought serving was beneath him. When the lorry stopped with the three white men on board he put the axe to one side and picked up a catapult that he always had close at hand.

'Give me your money!' he demanded in English.

'No money,' said one of the white men, and he pulled out his trouser pockets to show they were empty. Of course we knew this wasn't true.

We watched while the three men got down onto the sand. They had lots of hair; their beards were so thick that the hair on their chin joined the hair on their head. And amidst all the hair their teeth looked very bright.

'Where are you going?' asked Isaac, and he crossed his arms as if he was going to stop them.

'To Sepupa,' said one of the men.

Isaac laughed. Sepupa was to the west, the men were going in the wrong direction. 'Are you hunters?' he asked.

The man smiled. 'No, Peace Corps.'

'What's that?' Isaac asked, and next to him Petra giggled. She was wearing a pair of old khaki shorts that should have been replaced a long time ago. Her hair was so long it went straight down her back but it was tangled and matted at the ends. She looked so small, not like a nine-year-old at all.

'You know,' said the man, 'the Peace Corps, from America. We're helping you guys with roads and dams.'

'Ask them,' said the man's friend. 'Go on.'

The man sighed. 'Any turkeys around here?'

'What?' said Isaac rudely. We knew we could be rude to passing white people, we had learnt that you could behave with them in a different way.

'You know, turkeys?' And the man pulled on his neck and made a gobbling noise. 'For Thanksgiving? John's mom sent him over some dollars to buy a turkey.'

We just stared at them until finally one of the men gave Isaac a few coins. He waited for Isaac to smile in gratitude, which he didn't. Then the men hitched up their stained trousers and two of them went into our general trading store. But the third stayed outside and he took something small and black out of a bag on his back and he uncovered it and held it up. He held it up right close to his eye and squinted at it.

'What's he doing?' I whispered to my brother.

'He's going to take photographs,' said Isaac, and I could see he liked the idea of having his picture taken, for he posed at once with his catapult. I understood then what the man was doing, because I had seen so many photographs in magazines, I had just never seen how they were made. And now I was upset because my brother was wearing his old grey school shorts and the right leg was ripped to shreds and I wanted him to have nice clean new clothes on if he was going to have his picture taken.

'Take another with my sister,' Isaac told the man. Petra had scurried down off the porch the moment the man had taken his camera out and now she watched us from where she stood on the sand.

I shifted myself closer to my brother, happy that he wanted me close, and when the man nodded approvingly I was pleased. But I wished I wasn't wearing my old white dress, I wished I was wearing something beautiful.

When we went home and told our mother what had happened that morning she was furious. She said the men might be American spies and we should not give them any information. But when we told her how many things they had bought at our store then she said perhaps they just wanted to see our animals.

'Why do they want to see our animals?' said Isaac. 'Don't they have any in America?'

My mother shrugged. 'They like travelling, these people. *Ku yendinda ngu wu yani.*'

'To travel is to see,' Isaac said in a bored manner because we had heard the proverb so many times. And although my mother loved this proverb she was not a traveller herself. She never ventured far from Sehuba unless there were reeds or thatching grass to be gathered, and these days she could afford to send other people to do this. My mother didn't want to get away; she wanted to go backwards, back to Xuku and where she'd come from, a place that was supposedly as wonderful as paradise. But I wanted to move forward and I had a growing feeling that I ought to be someplace else. Each time we saw foreigners in the village my feeling of not belonging and my desire to escape only increased.

One day, a late afternoon in the rainy season, we were on the riverbank not far from Sehuba when Isaac spotted three boats coming by. It was the sort of day when the river seemed to steam.

'Outboard motor,' Isaac said knowledgeably as the first boat came into view. It was long and low and made from aluminium. But we couldn't see all of it for this part of the shore was overhung with vines and creepers, leaning over the water, making jagged reflections.

'Hey, it's big,' said Isaac.

'How long?' asked Petra. 'I think sixteen feet. What do you think, Isaac?'

'Fourteen.'

'Kazi?'

I ignored her; I couldn't care less how long a boat was.

The first boat passed by and we saw it had a little canopy at the front, underneath which two white men were sitting on deckchairs. The men both had big thick black-rimmed glasses as if their sight wasn't very good. As we watched, one of the men stood up and I saw the strangest socks, fashioned in a diamond pattern and rolled down once, very precisely, at the top. I stared at the socks, wondering where they were from, wanting them for myself. Then the boats stopped, some weeds had caught in the propellers and they couldn't move.

'Wait!' I said as Isaac stalked off purposefully towards the boats, but he was already halfway there. I looked down at my feet; my mother would kill me if I got my shoes covered in mud. We had been at a beauty contest that morning and my mother had not allowed me to take the shoes off, perhaps as punishment for not having won.

'Your boat is stuck,' said Isaac helpfully in English.

A man with a straw hat on laughed. 'That's the least of our troubles. You kids from here?'

'Yes,' said Isaac. 'Are you hunters?'

The man laughed some more. 'No, we're scientists. You see, kids, we're on a voyage of discovery,' and he looked at the other man as if they were sharing something special.

Petra began to shift from foot to foot in excitement. 'What are you discovering?'

'Well,' said the man and he lowered his voice, 'we're looking for . . . a lost tribe.'

'Why are they lost?' said Petra.

'Not *lost* exactly,' said the man. 'They just haven't been discovered yet. The Swamp Bushmen. Do you know them? Hey, Pieter!' he called to another man. 'I'm asking the kids.'

By now we were right up close to the first boat which was pulled along the shore and inside we could see it was loaded with boxes. We watched while the man peeled one open to take out a cool drink and inside the box we saw cans of Vienna sausages, packets of digestive biscuits, rows of plastic bottles with a yellow bitty sauce inside. Behind these boxes we could see a metal trunk and I was waiting for Isaac to find out what was inside it.

'What's in there?' he asked.

'Here?' the man asked, and he opened the trunk and

at once his fingers were alive with jewels, with chains of beads in reds and yellows, sparkly silver necklaces, rings with coloured stones. They seemed to drip from his fingers. I jerked forward; I so wanted the man to give me the jewels. If I had them and if I could wear them then surely I would win the next beauty contest.

'Treasure!' whispered Petra.

The man laughed. 'Just a few baubles for the Bushmen.' And then he looked at the three of us and then he looked again at me. He squinted his eyes, looking at my face, first sideways and then full on. I knew he was wondering about me, as people sometimes did. For I was a pale skinned girl, I didn't look like my brother, I looked like I belonged to another family, that I came from another place. And the only explanation I was ever given for this was that I took after my maternal grandmother, who died long before I was born, who had a light complexion like mine, and whom nobody seemed to know anything about. I had heard once that she was a Bushman but I didn't know anyone who wanted to say they were a Bushman for everyone else looked down on them.

The man was about to say something when Isaac began with his questions again. 'What's in that other trunk?'

'Here?' said the man, taking his eyes off me at last. 'These are our instruments.' And the man opened up the lid of the trunk very carefully and we all peeked inside. On a soft white cloth there was a row of implements, all metal; some were long and pointed like knives, others were rounded at the end like pincers, one had an attachment that bent out like an open penknife. I was worried that they were weapons of some sort. When Isaac put his hand out to touch them, the man snapped the trunk lid shut.

We returned home that day to tell our mother about the men on the boat and she told us never to talk to such people again. They did experiments, she said, they captured people and measured them. And I felt scared because of the implements we had seen that looked like something a doctor would use, and because of the way the man had squinted his eyes and looked at me and not at Petra or Isaac.

Chapter Thirteen

It took a lot of begging for me to be allowed to go to school, but when I did it turned out I was good at it. School meant memorising, it meant listening to the teacher and then repeating it back. I couldn't see why Isaac had struggled. All I had to do was pay attention and do as I was told.

After I passed my exams, I left for secondary school in Maun and my mother was glad at first; *Ku yendinda ngu wu yani*, she told me. But she had no idea what it was I would discover; I would discover a world which my mother did not control. The night before I left Sehuba I slept even less than usual. I listened to my brother's breathing and I stared at my new bag in the corner of the room, the bag I would be taking with me to Maun.

Maun was a metropolis compared with Sehuba. There was still no street lighting, the chain stores from South Africa were yet to come, but it was a place where people walked faster than they did in our village. From the moment I arrived I was excited by the air of busyness in Maun; people had jobs to go to, they were not just farmers, they had banks and shops to work at, they had uniforms to wear, some even had cars to drive.

Immediately I began to lie to my new classmates and

pretend I didn't come from Sehuba because I was so embarrassed about it.

In Maun there were night time picnics held in the bush along the Thamalakane River where I first drank cider and danced to Brenda Fassie. When the DJ played 'Weekend Special' then everyone danced, the girls in a line, the boys individually with hunched up shoulders and fancy little steps. On Saturdays I would go with my new girlfriends to the shops just opening up in the Old Mall and we would do our best to steal what we could; it didn't matter what, it could be a copper necklace as shiny as gold, a bottle of hair straightener, bleach to make your face pale, a tube of lipstick in its own little case. It was the excitement of taking something glamorous, something that promised to make us look good, and the thrill that we might be caught.

The only thing I didn't like about Maun was the new meat abattoir where all the cattle were killed. When you walked near the abattoir, even half a kilometre away, the air was heavy with the smell of burning flesh which seemed sweet at first until you realised where it came from.

I was a boarding student at Maun Senior Secondary and I liked sleeping in the room with all the other girls. I felt impressive in my uniform with the white socks, the straight blue skirt and tie, the white shirt with sleeves that stopped halfway. I felt excited just going in and out of the school, which was still quite new and built like a city on the river, all contained within itself, the classrooms and the boarding students' building, the playing pitch and the dining hall, the teachers' houses and the staffroom. If I couldn't win a beauty contest then at least I had done what Isaac had failed to do; I had got myself to senior secondary school.

In the rooms at night we whispered and giggled and we renamed ourselves with English names like Star and City Girl. Some of us were bursting out of our dresses by then, we were young women stuffed in child's clothes. And during the day we sat in our lessons and we mapped out the different organs of the body, the progression of the World Wars, the crops they grew in the United States, and all the time we sent each other little secret signals about what we would do in the village that weekend.

But the fact I was hundreds of kilometres away from Sehuba didn't put my mother off when it came to beauty contests. If there was any contest, and she always knew when there was, then she would get the bus down to Maun and make sure I was entered. It could be a village competition, or it could be a pageant at one of the safari lodges near Maun, places we didn't know much about but were longing to go to. It was as if my mother sensed my independence and wanted to put a stop to it as soon as she could. And it was then, in Maun, that I started doing well.

Perhaps it was because there were more white people in the village than there were in Sehuba, many of them very rich white people. There were missionaries and school teachers, as there were in Sehuba, but in Maun there were more hunters, more business people, more safari owners, and most of all more tourists. Now my complexion was

176

not held against me; instead it helped me to win. The more white you looked, the more beautiful you were. To be white was to be successful.

I came third, then second, and then, finally, I won. It was the day my mother and me had been waiting for, the day when the judges conferred and decided I was the one. And it was an important contest, a district affair held in the Maun community hall which had pale blue walls and smelt of dust. The audience were packed in the hall that day, standing elbow to elbow before the stage. The contest was sponsored by a safari company and soft drinks were given out for free. There was music too, traditional music that sounded loud and jerky coming out of the modern sound system.

The sash I received was purple, with Miss Ngamiland written in beautiful cursive silver letters. A man with a shaking hand slipped it over my head and arranged it across my chest.

'Your father would be proud,' said my mother.

It was shortly after the district beauty contest that I finished school and was forced to return to Sehuba. Now that I had had a taste of Maun I didn't want to go back north to the delta, to a village where everyone knew each other and nothing ever happened.

Sehuba had grown in size since I'd first left, it had more bars now, sometimes live music, and there were lots of people passing through, bringing with them ways of doing things differently, but still to me it was the sticks. I had learnt to be more daring while in Maun, to be disobedient in class, to steal things from the shops, to go to places where I wasn't allowed. Now I was home again.

Then one night I learnt a new trick. A friend whose father owned the biggest of the Sehuba bars had asked me to come and spend the evening with her and I knew my mother would never allow it. So I was standing in the attic looking out of the window feeling sorry for myself. And although I had looked out of the window at the mulberry tree for years it was only now that I saw that the way the topmost branches rested just by the window meant that if I went out feet first I would be able to lower myself down. I didn't know if the tree could hold me, if I could scramble down to the thicker branches quickly enough, but I tried and they did.

I landed on the sand which was cool in the evening air and I stood there, thrilled by what I had done. Our garden was silent but for the frogs; the stars were particularly bright. And I ran to my friend's house and spent all night at her place before sneaking back home and climbing up the mulberry tree before the sun was up.

Since then I'd escaped twice more down the tree, but on the third evening Isaac was lying in wait for me. I found him standing at the bottom ready with a torch like a night watchman.

'Where are you going, Kazi?' he asked mockingly, holding the torch up towards my face so that for a second I had to shield my eyes. 'Are they holding beauty contests at night now?'

I landed on the sand with a thud and pretended I had hurt my ankle so that I had to bend and massage it rather than answering him. He knew that I had won the district

178

finals and he knew that this meant tomorrow I would be off to Gaborone to compete in the nationals. And he was annoyed about this and at the attention it brought me. I thought at first he would be proud, as my mother said my father would have been, but he wasn't. In the past few weeks he had been trying to catch me out more than ever, to find something he could report me to our mother for. If I didn't wash a pot to his satisfaction or iron his trousers the way he wanted then he told her so at once.

Isaac flicked the torch around the garden and then he shone it wider so that briefly, on the river outside our plot, we both saw the reflected red glint of crocodile eyes.

'I'm going for a walk,' I said as Isaac turned the torch back to my face. For a moment I wanted to laugh, the idea of going for a walk was ridiculous, and I wanted my brother to laugh too. No one had appointed him the family watchman; he had given himself that job all by himself.

'Have a nice time, *Miss Ngamiland*,' he said, smirking and finally turning off the torch. 'Shall I come with you?'

For years and years I had wanted to be where Isaac was, to go where he went and do what he did, and now he wanted to come with me. I was unsure what to do, whether to give up and climb back into the tree, or whether to continue my pretence and go off walking into the night and eventually end up at the picnic I had been aiming for. If I did walk off then Isaac would tell our mother. But if I went back into the tree and then back into the attic then Isaac would have won as well and I didn't want him to win over anything.

'*Go siame!*' I said as cheerily as possible, leaving my brother with a wave of the hand as if it was daylight and I was simply heading off to the store to get sugar. I walked as normally as I could but I was waiting to see if my brother would follow. I almost wanted him to. Perhaps he would run up beside me and we would go to the picnic together and dance to Brenda. When there was no sound of movement from behind I walked on alone, quickening my pace in fear as the dogs in the Krauses' yard next door began to yelp. The only thing that kept me walking was the fact that the next morning I would be gone.

Chapter Fourteen

The first thing I noticed about Craig MacKinnon was the softness of his face. He was sitting at the end of the judges' table in the hall in Gaborone, the last in a row of chairs, and I noticed that someone had thought to put a small fan on the floor by his feet. I could see at once he was a foreigner; the fan suggested preferential treatment, and then, of course, he was white. And this meant, to me, that he was different, he was exotic. Not exotic like the whites I had seen passing through my village when I was a child, the Peace Corps and the scientists who had looked and behaved so oddly, but still different enough to have an aura of strangeness about him. And he wasn't a white like Lenny Krause was; Craig MacKinnon was handsome.

His elbows rested on the tabletop and below the table I could see that his knees were jiggling up and down. His skin was incredibly smooth for a man and the way his hair was slicked back from his head in a side parting made his face all the more noticeable. I could see even from a distance that his blue eyes had long dark lashes that seemed to sparkle as if they were wet. When he smiled his bottom lip stayed straight and his top lip curled to one side, which on some people could have looked like a sneer but on him looked flirtatious and debonair. And when he did this thing with his lips then a crease formed in his cheek like a dimple.

I saw him as he saw me and he sat upright all at once.

I smiled as I came onto the stage with the other girls, only not too much for it wasn't done for the contestants to look too happy or too pleased with themselves. Beauty contests were a serious business. And I thought, *is* he looking at me? Is that why he's suddenly sitting up? Or is it someone else he's looking at?

The stage was large and made from thick planks of dark wood that were shiny and varnished. This was a proper hall; it was new and clean with strip lighting and a row of clear glass windows along one wall. It was late afternoon and I could see streetlights outside, I could see the traffic and the cars that were so numerous in the city that they resembled cattle being herded, nose to tail, to slaughter. I didn't tell anyone that the cars made me think of cattle; I didn't want them to know I was just a village girl. I had thought Maun was a metropolis; now I could see that compared with Gaborone it was just a backwater.

And then the pageant began. The director of ceremonies was a solid-looking woman who wore a long green dress the colour of emeralds and embroidered cloth tied high on her head like a turban. She held up a large microphone and the sound system crackled and, standing to one side of the stage, I felt my body shiver a little.

'Invited guests, distinguished ladies and gentlemen, I greet you all this beautiful evening,' she said in a voice that was too loud. I could see the sweat on her forehead; the organisation of the pageant had only started that morning and everything was running late. 'It is my distinct honour to be here with you all and to introduce to you the girls of our beloved country . . .'

The people at the front, the invited guests in the two rows of chairs, leant this way and that to see us. And then we walked forward individually and at that point my vision blurred a little for there were strong spotlights on the stage. I only began to see clearly again after the judges conferred and I was the winner. It was 1984; I had just turned eighteen. The hall was so crowded with people standing and jostling for a view by then that my mother wouldn't have been able to sit on the floor, but she wasn't there anyway. I was alone and I had won. I received a certificate and a small amount of money. There were no promises of designer gowns or trips abroad back then, no press interviews, barely any photographers waiting to capture the winner.

The other girls were pissed off, except one or two village girls like me who were too overwhelmed to bear much of a grudge against the winner. But the others were pissed off because they thought I shouldn't have won; there is no solidarity at beauty contests. I knew what they thought, that I was too tall, too thin, and most of all too pale skinned. But there were only two things I was concerned with when it came to my body: the fact that my shoulders sloped and the fact that my lips were so big, like my mother's, that whatever I did I looked sulky. It had annoyed some of the teachers at Maun Secondary

School, I know, for they thought my sloping shoulders meant I wasn't concentrating, that my sulky expression was a challenge to them.

But that didn't bother me now because my school days were over. I could have gone to the university if I'd tried, but I wasn't interested. And I didn't want to stay in Sehuba and work in my mother's general trading store. She said I thought it wasn't good enough for me and she was right. Isaac was proud of the shop, but he didn't want to work behind the counter, he wanted to run it, and in the meantime, while my mother was still in charge, he had been coming up with a series of crazy plans. Just a month ago he'd decided to invest in fish and he had travelled up to Shakawe on the panhandle and bought all the fish he could find. Then he transported them down to Sehuba but the freezer broke down on the way and by the time he arrived the fish were rotten and couldn't be sold. But my brother wasn't put off; like my mother he blamed things going wrong on other people. This time, for example, it was the friend who had lent him the freezer.

Shortly before I'd set off for the pageant in Gaborone, my brother had announced his intention to marry. He still had little to do but mind the shop and, when I was there, report my misdemeanours to our mother. He had no real income, no firm plans for the future, he just dreamt of making money. Perhaps he thought Grace would help him in this, although I don't know how. She was a Sehuba girl, she had been to school for a year and then withdrawn, she was obedient to the point of lunacy. She believed, she had told our mother, that there was only room for one bull in a kraal. I suppose that Isaac impressed her. I didn't know Grace well, and nor, I guessed, did my brother. But he had decided she would make a perfect mate.

'I just wanted to say, well done!'

I was behind the stage, at the back behind the curtain, changing out of my pageant clothes – a white dress with ivory coloured sequins around the neck and fluttery sleeves as thin as paper – when Craig MacKinnon came looking for me. He seemed startled at the sight of the girls taking off their clothes, as if he wasn't prepared for this.

'Thank you,' I said, and I lowered my eyes menacingly at a girl from Francistown who had stopped to stare.

'I voted for you, you know,' Craig said.

I nodded and he laughed. I liked his laugh; he looked loose when he laughed and I liked to see that crease in his cheek again when his lips went up. Then I dipped my eyes the way my mother had taught me when addressed by an elder. And Craig was, I thought, an elder. He was an adult while I still thought of myself as a girl.

'I wondered,' he said, and the other girls were listening closely now, 'if you'd like to join us. Some of us are going to the President's for a wee drink.'

The eyes of the girl from Francistown nearly popped out of her head. She thought Craig was talking about our new President, Ketumile Masire. It was election year; Masire was on the lips of everyone. Yet he was not known in the way our first President Sir Seretse Khama had been, our late President whom we had all been a little in love with. There wasn't a child or adult who didn't know Sir Seretse, his speeches were ingrained in the national consciousness. A nation without a history is a nation without a past. How many times had we heard this? And who hadn't seen the photograph of Sir Seretse and his Englishwoman wife, the day he was inaugurated when he strode triumphantly before the cameras, his arms wide open, a hat in one hand, a slice of white handkerchief just peeping from the pocket of his dapper grey suit. Sir Seretse was a man of charisma, a man of schoolgirl crushes.

But I knew what Craig was talking about; it wasn't President Masire he meant but the President's Hotel.

I shrugged as if I wasn't bothered. But I was astounded. I had been to bars in Maun and in Sehuba, I had been to night time picnics, and I had drunk cider and beer and one time even wine. But I had never, ever been invited by an adult to go to a bar, I had always smuggled myself in with my girlfriends. And the President's Hotel, that seemed a vast building then, full of people from the nearby government buildings and embassies, full of people in power.

'What time?' I asked, which was all I could think of to say. I wanted to show that girl from Francistown just how sophisticated I was.

'Oh, I don't know, about eight?' Craig was still standing a little away from me, and now he put his hands into his pockets. I liked his voice, it was not flat like a lot of white people's; instead it had a quality that was soft and drew me in.

'That's fine,' I said, and I took off my pageant shoes for they were hurting me.

Craig left the backstage area and I had a chance to watch him carefully. He wore long khaki trousers, which were quite fashionably made with a close fit and pockets at the side. I had not seen any shops in Gaborone that sold trousers like that. His back, from behind, was taut and he wore a belt that was obviously expensive. His shoes I admired as well, they were brown boots with a thick clean sole.

I don't know what time I arrived at the President's Hotel but when I got there Craig had obviously been there for some time. I went the back way, walking up the white outside steps that led from the paving stones of the Main Mall. I preferred this to going through the front door where I thought the doorman would ask what I thought I was doing, a young girl entering a hotel on her own at night. This way I could walk up the steps slowly, and because they did not go straight up but went from side to side, it gave me time to look around the tables on the terrace, to see where everyone was.

I saw Craig's table at once, it was to the left of the steps and next to the open glass doors that led to the restaurant inside. There were six people on the table, an elderly very upright man whom I didn't know, and then two of the judges from the pageant and two of the other girls as well. The girls eyed me as I reached the top of the steps and I eyed them back.

Sometimes, after a pageant, men would try to ask a girl out and most would say no. If they said yes, then they quickly gained a reputation. I had never been asked before, but then I had never been at a pageant without my mother before. I was staying with a relative in Gaborone, a woman who taught at a secondary school. But she had gone out for the evening and so, feeling sure she would never know, I had left the house as well.

'Ah, Kazi!' Craig looked up and he rose slightly in his chair. I could see he had been enjoying a large meal; there were the remains of a giant T-bone steak on the plate before him and a couple of thin oiled chips, and from the streaks on his plate it looked as if the juices had been wiped with a cloth.

I stood by the table and suddenly wished I hadn't come. What was I thinking of? Gaborone was still small enough that someone would be certain to see me here and report it back to my relative, and within a day or so that news would work its way back to my mother in Sehuba. She was ill, she said her blood was high, that it was too hot, and that was why she hadn't been able to come.

'Congratulations, my dear,' said the woman next to Craig as I sat down opposite him. Her voice dripped with affection but I knew a niece of hers had been in the contest and I knew she would be furious that it was I who had won.

'A wee drink?' Craig asked.

I asked for a Fanta and Craig laughed as if this were childish. But I didn't care; I was saving up the night to tell my girlfriends about later. And Fanta was such a treat for me, I loved it the way my mother loved her Coke. And then I realised that I wouldn't see many of my girl-friends anymore, for they had left school now as well.

'It must be nerve wracking, being up there on stage,' said Craig as I sipped my Fanta through a straw.

'I quite like it.'

'Not so nice being stared at, though. I'd be far too self-conscious.'

'It is not a case of being stared at,' interrupted the woman judge. 'That is not the aim. The aim is to instil a sense of confidence in our girls, so that they can represent themselves and our country. As the director of ceremonies said ...'

But Craig had stopped listening and had begun a conversation with someone else. 'Oh, you're from Maun?' he said to his neighbour and then he turned back to me as I sat opposite him across the table. 'And where are you from Kazi?'

'The north ...' I said vaguely, for these were city people at the table, people from the south, and when Craig had said 'Maun' it brought a patronising smile to their faces.

'Really? I have a cousin,' said Craig, 'from a wee place called Sooba or something. I don't suppose you know it?'

I leant back and felt the edge of the chair dig into me. I hadn't been expecting this. '*Ee*, Sehuba. I know it.'

Craig was looking at me, waiting for more. And as he sat there his hands began to brush breadcrumbs busily off the tablecloth and into his palms. Then he took the crumbs and tipped them into his plate. Then he took his two neighbours' empty plates and piled them on top of his own. His neighbour, the woman judge, watched him in amazement; I could see that she thought it was the waiter's job to do this.

'Tiny wee place, very wild. My cousin's been there for a while, he used to be a crocodile hunter!' Craig said.

I felt really uncomfortable now. If he had a cousin in Sehuba and if it was someone who had lived there for a while and if he was a hunter, then there was only one person that could be and that was Lenny Krause.

'There are a number of white hunters in Ngamiland,' said the elderly man at the end of the table who had not, until now, spoken. 'There is somewhat of a tradition of English hunters in the north.'

'Really, Professor?' asked the beauty pageant judge, and she turned to him as if this was the most interesting thing she had ever heard.

'*Ee.* You English,' said the Professor, and he looked at Craig, 'have been trying to find our hunting routes for over a hundred years.'

'Scottish.'

'Pardon?'

'I'm a Scot. Not English.'

The Professor laughed and picked up a bread roll which he neatly tore in half. 'Scottish, English ...'

'Aye,' said Craig. 'Quite a difference.'

I busied myself with my Fanta. Although we had done plenty of European geography and history at school, I wasn't quite sure what the difference was. But I thought it explained Craig's voice, it explained the way he talked.

'You do not associate yourself with the English?' asked the Professor, and his eyes were bright. 'So perhaps you identify yourself more with your compatriot Livingstone?' He said 'Livingstone' as if it were something nasty.

Craig didn't reply. He turned in his chair; he seemed to be looking for a waiter.

But the Professor was not to be distracted. 'I believe 1849 was the year he arrived in Ngamiland. Naturally he found people rather preoccupied with other matters. He did not reach Maun, of course, took to his heels when he heard about the tsetse fly. Livingstone! A man who neither discovered anything nor converted anyone.' The Professor smiled and looked around. 'Yes, we have always had the whites, whether the elephant hunters in Ngamiland or the gold diggers in Tati. Gamblers and drinkers, the lot of them. When they weren't running off with our women . . .' The Professor spoke in a soft way, as if he didn't much care, but there was a bitterness in his eyes, and in the way he surveyed the people at the table, and I saw that while he had been speaking he had utterly mashed the bread roll in his hand and now the crumbs were sprinkling everywhere. And I sat a little stiffly at the table, annoyed at his remark, because I thought I didn't belong to anyone, that no one could come and run off with me.

Then we all looked at Craig, to see how he would respond.

'I'm sure you're absolutely right,' he said mildly to the Professor. Then he pushed gently at the pile of plates he had made and got up and went into the restaurant and because my chair was facing the door of the restaurant I could see that at once people began to wave to him across the tables, two men even got up in order to slap him on the shoulder. And to each well-wisher Craig waved back, or shouted out something which I couldn't hear that made them laugh. I could see that Craig MacKinnon was well known around here, that his presence caused a ripple of interest.

'He's an Earl, isn't he?' said the Professor.

'What's that?' asked the woman judge.

'An Earl. A member of what they call the aristocracy. An Earl who has quite a reputation as a ladies' man.'

'Does he?' said the woman judge, and she pushed up one of her breasts as if it were itching her.

I thought this couldn't be true. I thought that the Professor for some reason had taken a dislike to Craig MacKinnon. Or perhaps it was true, but in my case I would change him. I was already thinking along those lines; I had caught Craig MacKinnon's attention and now I wanted to keep it. If he were a ladies' man then that must mean he liked ladies and at once I desperately wanted him to like me.

'I believe our beautiful Botswana has become the adventurers' playground,' said the Professor. When no one replied he picked up another bread roll and picked at it. 'It is such an interesting language, English. Isn't it? Consider this,' and he looked at me and at the others round the table as if we were his students in a lecture hall. 'There is only one letter that separates the words laughter and slaughter. Take the word slaughter, remove the letter "s" and you have the word laughter. I have always thought it very indicative of something.'

We could hear Craig coming back to the table outside now, we could hear people calling out after him, sounding dismayed that he was leaving them.

'And how do you two know each other,' said the woman judge. 'My dear?'

I mumbled something and played with my straw.

'The Scots,' said the Professor just as Craig sat back down opposite me. 'Let us not forget they gave us tarmac. And, of course, the vacuum flask.'

Craig was smiling but he began drumming his thumbs on the tabletop. 'So, Kazi, are you flying back to Maun tomorrow?'

'No,' I said carefully, for I had never been in a plane in my life. I glanced at the Professor at the end of the table and he looked deflated. But then his eyes darted towards me, and I knew that he was the one who would begin the rumour, that he was the one who would make sure my mother knew about this well before I ever returned home to Sehuba. It was scandalous, a young girl like me drinking at a hotel at night with a white man.

'Well how will you get back home then?'

I looked at Craig. I would get back home like everyone else got back home, I would hitch. There was something at once worldly and utterly ignorant about Craig MacKinnon.

'Well you could always use Sara's ticket, couldn't she, Sara?' He turned and shouted to a white woman on another table. 'Sara! You're not using that ticket back to Maun are you?'

So it was all arranged.

Chapter Fifteen

Did he fancy me? That was all I wanted to know. I couldn't let the question alone, I picked at it like a scab on the elbow, like the sort of scab my mother would warn me to leave alone or I would be forever scarred. Did he or did he not? He had voted for me at the pageant, he had invited me to the hotel, so he must like me. But maybe he was like this with other girls; maybe he voted for them and invited them out too.

I left the President's Hotel around twelve that night and walked back to the house near the African Mall where my relative the school teacher stayed. I took a sand pathway that she had shown me earlier, and the sand was cold underfoot, I could feel it sprinkle in my open-toed sandals. There was no one around, no sounds, as if everyone in the world was asleep.

The door to the house was unlocked, as I knew it would be, and I hurried in and went straight to bed. But I hadn't been able to sleep at all. Instead I went over the evening, trying to remember everything that had been said. I thought about the way Craig had resisted being irritated by the Professor, the way the woman judge had pretended to be pleased that I had won the beauty contest, the way the Fanta tasted, the orange fizz on my tongue. I tried to picture Craig MacKinnon's face when he smiled and I thought about him smiling at me. And while I was still thinking the birds began to sing outside and then I could hear the sounds of sweeping from our neighbour's house, the call of people setting off to work as they greeted each other. And it seemed to me, lying in bed listening, that this morning everything was new about the world. I had been waiting for something to happen and finally it had. I was a winner, and I had met Craig MacKinnon.

I left early for the Gaborone airport, spinning a complicated story to my relative about needing to be somewhere to catch a lift home. The airport was so far from the city centre that it had taken me hours to get there. And then I couldn't see Craig MacKinnon anywhere. Two women were pushing big mops across the floor; a man was noisily rolling up the metal front of a car hire shop. A group of white people stood at a desk waiting; they looked weary and as if they had dressed in the dark so that now, in the false light of the airport, their clothes looked unironed and mismatched. It annoyed me that wealthy people didn't take more care of themselves.

I had no idea what to do. So I sat down in a chair that was plastic and shaped like a curled hand, and when I tried to move it I saw it was bolted together with other chairs. Suddenly a large glass door opened at the other end of the airport and people began pouring out. I read a sign; a plane had arrived from Heathrow, London. This was a place where journeys began and journeys ended, where you could start the day in one place in the world and end in another.

'You're here bright and early!' Craig was pushing his way past the people just arriving. He was pulling a leather suitcase on little wheels. 'I thought you might not come. I don't suppose they've opened the check-in yet?' He was speaking quickly as if he was excited and there was a sense of eagerness in the way he pulled that leather suitcase. And I thought how it might be to be someone like Craig MacKinnon, to set off for adventures any time he liked.

I wondered if his comment meant he had been thinking about me too. If he thought that I might not come, then why was that? How intensely had he hoped that I would? He had given me a plane ticket, that must mean something; it must mean he wanted to be with me. But perhaps he was just being polite, perhaps that was just the way he was. Did he like me? That was all I could think about. I never asked myself whether I liked him.

But now he was here and all I had to do was to follow him. I was ashamed of my luggage, my black bag, the type we sold at our general trading store, a bag that never lasted long, a bag whose zip would soon stick and then fall off.

'Is it on time, the flight to Maun?' Craig leant his arms on the counter and waited, drumming his fingers, while a woman checked our tickets.

The woman looked at Craig and then she looked at me and I felt myself shrink a little because I could see what she was thinking: what's this young girl doing travelling in an aeroplane with a white man?

'Can you change that?' Craig asked, handing back the card he'd just been given.

'*Rra*?' The ticket woman stared at him.

'This seat number, it's thirteen. Can you change it?' He spoke with the ease of someone who thinks people will always do something for them, and I stood up straight again, returning the look in the ticket woman's eyes.

As I walked up the steps to that plane my heart was thumping. There were people in front of me, people behind. I had no choice but to continue walking up the steps and when I got inside the plane was shockingly small. Craig was too tall for the plane, he had to duck his head, and he pointed at the seat I was to take. A stewardess watched, without helping. I didn't know what to do with my bag. I held it on my lap but it didn't fit.

'Give it here,' said Craig, and then he opened a little door above the seat and put it in.

'*Ee*, we would also like a white man,' muttered the stewardess in Setswana as she watched Craig helping me, and then she squeezed past him down the aisle. I narrowed my eyes at her as she stomped off down the plane. I looked at Craig from the corner of my eye, but he seemed oblivious of the looks we were getting. I could see the stewardess thought there was only one reason for anyone to go out with a white, and that was money. Black girls who went out with white men were prostitutes, that's what people said; we were cheapening ourselves. And while white men were rich, and their richness made them sexy, they would never marry you. I knew of white men in Maun who picked up schoolgirls and took

198

them for car rides, treating them to dinners at Riley's Hotel, buying them clothes, buying their families clothes. They were their sugar daddies. And then they left the girls pregnant and expelled from school and went off to look for someone new.

And I was still thinking about this when we tore across the runway and then we lifted and were off and I had never felt adrenaline like that in my life. If I had been excited about winning a beauty contest, it was nothing compared to this feeling as we left the city behind, as we turned right in the air like a car.

'You're not afraid of flying, are you?' Craig said.

I shook my head. I could have flown all day; I could have sat in that plane next to Craig MacKinnon and flown all the way across the world. And we were sitting so close that if I had turned then our faces would have touched. For a second I felt juddery, as if my teeth were loose in my head. I wondered what his lips would feel like if he kissed me; they were very thin lips, would they be cool or warm? I had kissed boys before, I had fallen in and out of love with two boys in Maun, but this felt different, this felt grown up.

'My mother was terrified of flying,' said Craig. 'She had to take Valium before even getting on a plane. She died last year. Not on a plane, though, in a car.'

'I'm sorry,' I said.

Craig put out his hand and caught the lid of a table which had just fallen down from the back of the seat in front. 'Don't be. It wasn't your fault. I wouldn't have been able to come to Africa otherwise. I always wanted to come back. I did VSO years ago, in Uganda. It was the first thing I did after school, quite a change from being ruled by sadists with slippers. It changed the way I looked at the world. Then she died and I got the money, so here I am. Everyone thought Botswana was a good idea thanks to Lenny, my aunt's son I told you about. They thought if he was around I wouldn't get up to too much . . . ah, you know . . .'

I laughed because he seemed to want me to.

'It was Lenny's sister who put me up to judging that beauty contest. She's in Gabs and she *made* me . . .'

I laughed again, because it didn't look as if anyone could make Craig MacKinnon do something he didn't want to. He would just, I thought, brush them off.

'It's not the real Botswana, Gabs, is it?' he continued. 'I'm hoping Lenny's place will be better. And I've only got a few months left.'

Craig flipped the tray lid back into the seat in front. I felt the plane level out and the force that had pulled me back in my seat began to lessen. I wanted Craig to say something nice to me; I wanted him to tell me something nice about myself. I couldn't ask him, do you like me?

'So,' said Craig thoughtfully, and I thought he was about to say something important and I listened very hard, waiting. 'So, looking forward to going back to Maun?'

'A little,' I said. 'Only I'm not from Maun. I'm from Sehuba.'

'You're kidding!' Craig turned towards me and I could see a little tickle of hair on his chin and I could see again just how long and dark his eyelashes were. 'You're from Sehuba? Well, you didn't say so. Then do you know Lenny, my cousin?'

'I know him.' I looked the other way now, out of the window at the clouds which were like a range of white mountains between which we were flying.

'You're such a beautiful colour,' said Craig, and his voice was low, almost reverential. 'And you have such beautiful skin.'

I crossed my legs, embarrassed. I waited for more, but now it was Craig's turn to look out of the window.

'That is incredible, isn't it?' he asked after a while, returning to his normal voice and beginning to bounce his legs up and down. 'I mean considering what a huge country Botswana is, that we should both be at the beauty contest, both be heading to Sehuba, both . . .'

'Tea?' demanded the stewardess. 'Or coffee?'

Chapter Sixteen

I lost Craig MacKinnon when we arrived at Maun. One moment we were standing next to each other in line at the airport, and the next a white man in a pilot's uniform was shouting out Craig's name and I saw him look behind as he left the line, as he looked behind to me. I thought when I got through the doors and outside then he would be there waiting for me, but he had gone.

It took me all day to get home to Sehuba. And I sang to myself all the way, my face pressed up against the bus window. The plane trip had saved me money, I had travelled in less than two hours what would have taken me two days, and now I could afford a bus ride.

I couldn't wait to tell my mother that I had won the contest. But as we neared Sehuba I felt a sense of dread, for I feared my mother would already know all about my trip to Gaborone. And I had forgotten, until now, about sneaking down the mulberry tree the night before I'd left.

'Sehuba!' shouted the bus driver, and I struggled to get down the aisle of the bus and then waited while the driver climbed onto the roof and retrieved my pathetic black bag. Then the bus roared off in a cloud of sand. It had stopped on the main road, at the turn off to Sehuba. It was late afternoon and it was hot, the air was as still as it had been inside the aeroplane. I pulled down my dress and pulled up my socks. Then I put my bag on my head, balanced it for a moment with my right hand, and set off.

As I walked I tried to imagine that I was a newcomer to the village, that I had never seen it before, and as I walked the sky began to darken and my feet began to drag on the sand. The sun became obscured behind a big black cloud but the gold of its rays escaped from all round the cloud like an explosion and radiated across the sky. I could see to my right the clump of palm trees with their skinny trunks and their shaggy tops. At the palm trees I would turn right and then I would be in Sehuba itself. I looked up at the sky, at its beauty. But what I wanted to do was to be *in* that sky, in an aeroplane again going somewhere new.

I began to walk quicker now. I turned right onto the main road, passing my primary school and then the Light to the Nation bar where I waved at my girlfriend who was hosing down the outside of the bar with buckets of water, slapping the water down on the sand.

'*O tswa kae?*' she called out, swinging an empty bucket in her hand.

'Gaborone,' I said.

My friend whistled between her teeth. 'How was that?'

'Just OK.' I shrugged nonchalantly and my friend beamed and took her bucket back to the tap.

And then I got to our store and I hoped my mother might be there so that when I got home I would be alone and would be able to think about everything that had happened in the past few days. Our store looked so small compared to the shops I had seen in Gaborone, and although for Sehuba it was modern, to me it now looked very out of date. My mother had had the store painted a creamy coffee colour the year before and the paint was as yet uncracked or stained. At the same time she had hired a man to paint a sign in black letters that ran right along the top of the front wall: Muyendi General Trading Store & Restaurant. But because my mother had paid the man in beer the letters started to get shaky halfway across. I laughed now, at the idea that our shop was a restaurant, for the only food we sold was fat cakes and, on occasion, sausages.

As well as the words, my mother had hired the man to copy a Coke sign in red and white which had taken two days to complete to her satisfaction. But while the paint was fresh, the structure was old. The walls were not quite straight and in places they curved. The sand around the porch was littered with beer cans, with chewed up meat bones, empty cans of pilchards and stubbed out cigarettes. Everything looked used up and thrown away. But on the other side of the road I saw a new house was being built and it stood squat in a raked yard, the blackness of the two front windows still without glass like big square eyes watching me.

I passed close by the store; I thought if I passed on the other side of the road then someone inside might have a better view of me. I passed the two arched open windows on the porch, and then the doorway, and then the final three windows. In the last one a man was sitting; I knew him and he was a drunk.

· The gate onto the pathway to our house opened with

a grating sound. At once I could hear Lenny Krause's dogs barking in the plot next door. His dog Roadblock, a smelly creature that sprayed spit when it ate, had died years ago and now he had a pack of three mangy Setswana dogs. I hated the dogs, they scared me, and now I almost broke into a run. They never bothered my brother, they seemed only to dislike me, and several times I had been bitten and my clothes torn, just as Roadblock had done to me when I was a kid. A day before I had been crowned a beauty queen in a city hall, this morning I had been in an aeroplane with Craig MacKinnon, now here I was running up the pathway, my bag bouncing on my head, afraid of Lenny Krause's dogs.

I thought I heard voices from the garden and I headed round the back to the part of our plot that led down to the river. My mother was sitting there under the mulberry tree, her legs stretched out, a pot of tea beside her, her scarf at an angle where she must have brushed it impatiently away from her head. She looked up and I wanted to run to her, but then I didn't know what I would do once I got there.

'*Ee*,' she said. 'You've arrived.' She smiled and put out one hand and I bent to take it when what I really wanted to do was to jump on her lap. I tried not to look in her eyes, I didn't know what she knew, and anyway, she wouldn't say what that was, not straight away. 'Get your brother a chair!'

Isaac was coming round the side of the house and he looked very pleased with himself. Once he might have been called Pencil he was so thin, but in the past couple of years he'd gained weight and today his cheeks looked as plump as if they were carrying some remains of food inside. I stayed where I was, I had just had a long journey and I wasn't going to rush to get my brother a chair.

As he came closer I could see he was wearing a safari shirt, a green shirt with two pockets on the front and the logo of a flying bird embroidered on the chest. I wondered where he had got the shirt from; perhaps he knew someone who worked at one of the new camps in the delta. I didn't know much about the camps, but I knew we were supposed to be happy about their existence for they bought their supplies from our general trading store, and I knew Isaac had several times tried to get a job at a camp.

'We were talking about the marriage,' said my mother, and she picked up her cup and swallowed her tea in satisfaction.

Inside I groaned. I hadn't come back to talk about my brother's marriage to Grace.

'We're arranging the date,' said my mother.

'And arguing about the bridesmaids,' said Isaac, and he squatted down by my mother and picked up a biscuit from a plate on the sand. He seemed relaxed and I wondered, hopefully, if he hadn't told our mother about my escape down the tree. 'She doesn't want Grace's aunty's girls.'

'*Ee*. They don't fit,' said my mother.

'They don't *fit?*' I said, and Isaac and me smiled at each other.

'*Ee.* They don't go with the dresses, because the dresses are white and they are . . .'

'Very dark?' I offered.

I smiled at Isaac, expecting him to share the joke, expecting him to laugh at our mother's idea of the best-coloured bridesmaids, at the way she had become so entranced with whiteness since I'd started winning beauty contests, but his expression was unhappy now. And I thought, if he hasn't told our mother about my escape down the tree then he will do now.

'So you won,' he said, without looking at me.

My mother laughed and she began to tap her hand on my knee. 'I heard! I heard the news this morning!'

'I'm surprised you bothered coming back here,' said Isaac.

Yes, I wanted to say, so am I. And in my head I thought, what is Craig MacKinnon doing now? Is he thinking about me? Did he mean to leave me just like that? Is that what ladies' men do?

'Tell me about the judges,' said my mother. 'Tell me about the other girls. Were they beautiful? Were they jealous?'

The next morning I slept late. It was dark in the attic room; I had covered the small window with an old t-shirt and when the sun rose I didn't even notice it. I felt lazy. I could hear people downstairs, I heard the young girl who worked for my mother arriving and I could hear my mother saying she was late and that if a person wanted to do well in life then they had to ensure they weren't late and that if she herself were ever late then would her business have been so successful? I felt sorry for the young girl, to be working for my mother who loved being in the position of having someone to boss around.

I heard the soft voice of Grace outside, taking instructions from my brother. '*Ee, Rra*,' she said, '*Ee, Rra*,' and she rolled her tongue around 'Rra' and drew it out to make it sound as agreeable as possible.

I heard the jangle of goats setting off to graze. The room turned light and still I didn't get up. And then I heard him. I heard a male voice and although I couldn't make out the words I knew he was speaking English not Setswana.

'Kazi!' my mother shouted.

I got up guiltily from the mattress and looked around in a panic for what to wear. My clothes were everywhere, thrown all round the floor and none were clean enough. Would I look acceptable as I was? I couldn't decide. I took a mirror, long ago cracked and now half of it missing from its plastic frame. It was too small; I could see either my eyes or my mouth but not my whole face. What should I put on, what should I wear? If it really was Craig MacKinnon downstairs, then why had he come and what did it mean?

Chapter Seventeen

I walked slowly, self-consciously, down the steps from the attic. I had taken an old print of my mother's that she had bought from a Zambian trader and wrapped it around me in the traditional fashion, so that my shoulders and arms were bare. My mother looked up as I came into the living room and she frowned; I could see she thought it was too obvious that I had just got out of bed. She was sitting on our one sofa, a two-seater which sagged in the middle. She had bought it from one of the new furniture chain stores in Maun and she had paid for it in cash; she didn't want to buy it on lay-by like everyone else because if you missed a payment then they came and took the furniture and you lost the money too. In Maun three people had committed suicide when this had happened; one was the father of a girlfriend at school.

'Bring the tea!' said my mother to the maid. 'And bring it nicely!' She meant, of course, bring it in the fancy cups that she kept in her glass-fronted sideboard. '*Ee*,' she said to me, nodding furiously and holding out her palms as if this was far too much for her to deal with.

I came into the living room and found Craig MacKinnon sitting opposite my mother, and I saw with surprise that he was sitting on my late father's Kgotla chair. No one ever sat in that chair and I wondered whether he had innocently sat in it without realising its significance, or even more surprisingly if my mother had offered it to him.

'Your friend has come to see you,' said my mother, and she rolled up her lips.

At once Craig bounced out of the chair. 'Kazi! I hope you don't mind! I just arrived an hour ago, spent the night in Maun, and Lenny and them have gone out so I thought I had to come round and say hello 'cos the girl there said you were neighbours. Sorry about what happened at the airport.'

I frowned at him. I didn't want him to go on, I hadn't told my mother about the plane.

'I met a friend there and then when I looked for you ... Anyway, you got back here OK?'

'Bring the tea!' yelled my mother. 'And the biscuits!'

My mother had obviously decided that Craig MacKinnon was to be treated as an important visitor. She was making it seem that he was welcome here, when in fact he was not. He was not welcome because he was a man, an apparently single man who was apparently interested in her daughter, and he was a white and he was foreign.

'So,' said Craig, and he smiled at my mother. She smiled back, only it wasn't her real smile, it was the smile she used with troublesome customers at the store. Then she made a big fuss about directing the girl to give Craig his tea, and then an equally big fuss about giving him some biscuits on her nicest plate.

Craig seemed quite comfortable with being fussed

over. He dunked three biscuits into his tea one by one, looking round as he did so. 'Nice house,' he said.

My mother nodded.

'I didn't think it would be so ... I thought you'd live in a mud hut or something!' And he smiled but he also looked a little disappointed. 'Who did the buffalo picture?'

My mother looked at the picture on the wall, a print she had taken from somewhere and framed.

'It's a print,' I told him.

'Oh. Have you seen a buffalo, in real life?'

My mother started laughing. Had we seen a buffalo? That was like saying, is it ever sunny around here?

Craig joined in the laughter. 'Was that a stupid question?'

'What did he say?' asked my mother.

I frowned at her. She knew exactly what he had said; she was pretending not to understand English.

'He said, was it a stupid question?' I answered reluctantly.

'He wants to know if he's stupid?'

'No, *Mma*, he didn't say that.'

Then Craig jumped up as Lenny Krause appeared in the doorway to the living room. We all started a little; no one had heard him arrive. His dogs were not with him; there had been no warning barks.

'Mma Muyendi,' said Lenny Krause, bowing a little stiffly in the direction of my mother who all at once got busy stirring sugar into her tea.

Craig strode over to the doorway and he put out his hand, but Lenny grabbed him in a fierce hug. 'How long has it been, sonny?' he asked, and he looked at Craig with fondness which was odd because Lenny Krause was always such a gruff man. I could see my mother was fascinated by this, we had never seen Lenny Krause show affection to anyone other than his wife. 'Our girl told us we had a visitor,' said Lenny Krause. 'Didn't know it was you!'

And then Petra came swaggering into the house behind her father. She wore brown trousers which were mud-splattered at the bottom and her feet were bare. She looked like a boy; she was sixteen and she looked like a boy. A part of me felt sorry for her, I wouldn't have wanted Lenny Krause as my father. But I didn't know why she had to dress like a boy and I didn't know why she always had to appear just when she was least wanted.

Craig bounded back over to the Kgotla chair and I sat down on the arm of the sofa, swinging my legs so they brushed next to Craig's. My mother looked at the way I was sitting and she frowned. I half expected her to tell me to close my legs. And we were quiet then and I looked sideways at Craig to see if he sensed the tension in the room. There was the suppressed aggression emanating from my mother, a solid show of determination from Lenny Krause as he remained in the doorway rather than coming in, my feeling of nervous fear about what my mother would say when Craig MacKinnon left and what I would say in reply. And as I looked sideways at him I saw that Craig seemed so out of place in our house: his legs were too long for my father's chair, his hands were too big for the delicate teacup. And then while we were all sitting there not speaking, Isaac came in.

'He he he,' he laughed. 'House meeting?' he said in English. 'Why wasn't I invited?'

'Get your brother a chair,' my mother said.

And all of a sudden I felt really, really tired. I was tired of wondering what my mother would say, I was tired of all the things we didn't say. And my brother made me tired too, for Isaac was always more enthusiastic when Lenny Krause was around and I didn't know why he had to suck up to him. I realised then that it must have been Lenny Krause who had given Isaac the safari shirt, for that was the world he moved in, he had links with all the safari companies and all the camps.

'We were talking about the wedding,' my mother announced to the room in general, looking round at Craig and then at me and then finally at Petra. 'Have you heard about the wedding, Petra, *my dear*?'

Petra was standing by the wall near the buffalo print, and as my mother spoke I saw her face tighten.

'Of course you haven't!' said my mother, and she smiled at her apparent foolishness. But she knew, as we all knew, that Petra Krause was in love with Isaac and always had been. 'We've only agreed on it ourselves. We've been discussing bridesmaids ...' And my mother looked Petra up and down, from her bare feet to the bandana in her hair, with a look that could not have been more pointed.

Petra put her hands in her pockets and began to whistle, a dry tuneless whistle.

And suddenly I wanted to get away again. I wanted to get away from Sehuba and from my brother and his marriage and from my mother and her general trading store.

That evening Craig came again to our house and I went with him for a walk because he wanted to look round the village. People watched us as we went, turning to stare from where they stood chatting by the flickering light of a paraffin lamp on the counter of a roadside semausu, turning to watch Kazi Muyendi with a white man. But Craig didn't seem to mind; he seemed to enjoy the stir we were creating.

We stopped by the river and he asked me about wild animals and as I told him about them I could feel he was looking very directly at my face, even though I had my eyes held away from him. I continued to talk, only my words got lost because I could feel the pull of his stare. And at last I allowed myself to turn to him and as I did he leant closer and kissed me. I could feel the edge of his tongue, his lips were open a little and they were cool against mine.

'Mmmmmm,' said Craig, pulling away a little. 'God you turn me on.'

I was the only one who wasn't surprised when Craig MacKinnon came round with a little blue box that clicked open like a fridge door. He showed it to me closed and then he opened it and showed me what was inside.

'I've never felt like this about anyone before,' he said.

I looked at the ring, at the gold band and at the shining stone with its clear sharp sides. This meant he was serious; he wasn't playing with me. And the ring would look good on my finger; it would look so good when I showed it around. I would tell our children in years to come, this was the day your father proposed.

'Will you, Kazi?' he asked. 'Marry me?'

And I said, 'Yes.'

'Good! I can't wait to get you home and show you off!'

The first time we slept together was the night we left Botswana. Craig had said we would marry in England. He would give me another ring then; the one he had already given me belonged to Lenny Krause. My mother was furious, at the idea that I would marry a foreign man, and at the idea that I would leave with him for England. But I just looked at her as if I couldn't understand what the fuss was about and told her what she had always told me, that to travel is to see. Isaac was furious too; he was the one who was supposed to be getting married, I had taken away his glory.

We sat at the terrace restaurant at the President's Hotel the night before our flight to England and we drank wine and ate T-bone steaks. I didn't care how people saw us, I was bouncing along in a bubble of happiness. Our hotel room had a green carpet and green blinds at the window that could be either totally closed or totally opened but not left halfway. The phone next to the bed was glued to the table.

'Where have you been all my life?' Craig said, his face next to mine as we lay on the bed.

Still I bubbled with happiness, I had never heard anyone say this before.

I had come out of the bathroom to find him like this, naked in the hotel bed. 'Look!' he said, throwing off the sheet. 'I've got a present for you!'

And without thinking I looked; I really did expect that there might be a present for me wrapped up under that bed sheet.

'It can turn corners,' said Craig and he gave his cock a little flick. And I saw that it was bent out at a right angle like a fat crooked finger. 'Let me show you,' Craig said, and he pulled me close so that I could feel the heat of his body and my skin prickled. I moved around him, my body covering his, but he stopped me. 'Get underneath,' he said. 'It's better that way.' His hands moved over me as if I were made of water and I thought, I'll tell my girlfriends about this.

And then Craig grunted and lay back. I thought he had rolled onto something that had hurt him. 'Sorry,' he said, and I had no idea what he was apologising about. 'It will get better, I promise you,' he said, and he fell asleep straight away.

I wandered alone round the room. And I thought, was that it? Was that all he wanted? And did he still like me? I ate a packet of biscuits from the little fridge and I watched TV and at one point I went to the window and looked down. Our room was at the back of the hotel and I could see the sand pathway that led to the African Mall and to the house where I had stayed with my relative the school teacher the night I had won the beauty pageant. And now I was here again and I was going to England.

216

Chapter Eighteen

It's hard to remember exactly how I found England then; I'm so used to it all now. But I do remember the moving walkway when we arrived at Heathrow because I stumbled on it and was pushed to one side by people who wanted to go so quickly they were even running on a moving runway.

We seemed to be travelling through a tunnel, the walls were white and smooth and bare and there were vents on the ceiling. The people passing me were barely speaking, they were just intent on arriving from somewhere and then getting someplace else as quick as possible.

Then we got to a roped-off area which made me think of the entrance to the Maun meat abattoir where the cattle were herded into narrow spaces and from there to the slaughter. Craig pointed to the queue I was to join, a long one that did not appear to be moving, while he joined another and was soon let through. By the time we came to get our baggage my throat was as dry as the Kalahari.

As we travelled through London I wondered, how long have all these buildings been here? And then I wondered, why doesn't anyone clean them? I had thought London might be like Gaborone, only brighter, cleaner, altogether more modern. The buildings would be taller,

I thought, and there would be more of them, the people would be rich and their clothes would be wonderful. But it wasn't like that at all. The houses were built in one long chain, along every road. When you turned into another road, they just continued, and they were all built of brick. Everywhere I looked there were bricks, brown bricks, grey bricks, dirty bricks. The sun came up slowly and there were buildings where I thought trees should be, and the sky above looked like rubbed-out gold.

But although people back home had warned me about the weather and the cold, it was warm. I had a padded jacket in my luggage which I could see I wouldn't need. But then it was the summer. The summer of 1985. And as we continued driving I saw parks of green grass as vivid as the bush around Sehuba after the rains.

We made our way across London barely speaking. Craig was hunched down in the back of the mini cab. I wanted him to touch me in some way, to hold my hand or to settle me against his arm but he didn't. Someone had been supposed to meet us at the airport and we had waited hours and they hadn't so he'd had to find transport himself and he was annoyed about this.

'How much cash have you on you, Kazi?' he said after we had been travelling for half an hour or more.

'*Rra*?' I couldn't hear properly; my ears were still stinging from the plane.

'How much cash have you got? Only I don't know if I've got enough for the cab. It's going to cost a fucking fortune.'

I flinched at his words and opened my handbag, a new

one which I had bought in Gaborone and which I had thought was very nice-looking until, seeing it now, it looked shabby.

I took out my purse and felt the unfamiliar paper notes, so large and fresh. I began to inspect them, holding them up to see the denomination and to count them. A couple of relatives had given me money, to buy supplies for the journey, and I had changed it excitedly at a bank in Gaborone. Craig put out his hand to take the notes and, joking, I made to snatch them away from him. But he didn't laugh, he scowled.

We arrived at a house in Wembley and Craig paid the cab driver, using every note of money I had with me.

'Here we are then,' Craig said, and he sounded livelier now. We walked up a short stone path to a front door that was mirrored on either side with other, almost identical, front doors, in a street that seemed to go on forever. In the front of the house was a small patch of concrete on which, of course, nothing was growing. I thought what a dismal place this would be for children to play. Then Craig took my arm and steered me around a ladder that was leaning up against the front of the house.

I looked up at the two floors of the house and saw that if someone were to lean out of the window above the front door they would be able to shake hands with someone leaning out of the window in the house next door. I thought that people must be very close neigh-bours in these parts. I liked the colour of the house, the reddish hue of its walls, and the way there was a peaked bit like a hat jutting out over a bigger window on the second floor. But otherwise I didn't like it at all. It looked like the kind of place you could walk in, close the door, and quite disappear. I didn't know then how the English value their homes and how they value their privacy. You couldn't see in, the front door had frosted glass and the windows had curtains. There was no clue as to what life was like inside and that made me feel uncertain as I stood there on the step beside Craig. And I thought it very odd that he didn't have a key with which to let us in.

A woman opened the door and she looked sleepy. 'Jesus Christ, do you know what time it is? Couldn't you have rung or something?' She wore a t-shirt, a very long white one that looked as if it were made for someone far bigger than her. She bent to scratch her legs and as she straightened up again my eyes rested on her face. I could see at once there was something wrong about it but it took me a moment to realise that there was blood encrusted around her nostrils. I thought perhaps she had recently had a nose bleed.

Craig put down his suitcase on the step. 'Well, where was the fucking lift then?'

I stood there, embarrassed, waiting to be told who the woman was; perhaps she was Craig's sister, or an aunt, or some other relative. I had assumed we would be staying with his family. It was not that I looked forward to it; it was just that was the way I knew.

'Aren't you letting us in?' Craig asked. 'It's bad enough you left us stranded in the airport.'

'Well, it's more your house than mine,' said the woman.

'And this is my fiancée, Kazi.' Craig put out his right thumb and gestured to me and I saw the woman smile as if it were a joke.

'Cheers!' she said.

Craig led me upstairs and to a large bedroom, the one I had seen outside with the little turret above.

'I'm shattered,' he said, and he laid down fully clothed and went to sleep.

But I couldn't sleep. It was too bright in the room; the curtains kept on blowing in and out. I could hear the shrieks of children outside and I couldn't tell if the shrieks were in fun or fear. I heard cars passing, the piercing call of a siren, planes overhead in the sky. My legs kept jerking on the bed; my knees had been bent up for so long in the plane that now they didn't seem to be able to rest out straight.

So eventually I went downstairs and found the day had got even hotter. The woman was standing in the front room which had high ceilings and was decorated in the corners with swirls of white plaster flowers. All the windows were open and I felt a little lighter because I could see out, I could feel the air. I didn't want to be indoors; I had been inside the plane, inside the airport, inside the cab, and now I wanted to be outside.

'So, you're from Africa?' asked the woman as I came into the room. She was smoking, and flicking the ash from the cigarette into her left hand which she held out like a cup.

'Yes. I'm from Botswana,' I said, watching to see if she would burn herself.

'Great!' she said, and continued smoking.

I looked round the room and in particular at a thin little fireplace towards the bottom of one wall. I wondered how people used such a fire, for you couldn't sit around it, you would have to sit in front of it. And then you wouldn't be looking at anyone else, you would just be looking at the fire.

Above the fireplace was a shelf and that was full of things: a pale wooden woman with melon-sized breasts entwined with a wooden girl; a dark wooden mask with a grimace of a smile; an ivory sculpture of an elephant running. They looked like the kind of things the Zimbabwean traders sold in Maun, but they were all so ugly, as ugly as the things my mother had in her sideboard at home.

The woman seemed nervous, she began to pace up and down and she sniffed constantly. 'Sleep well?' she asked.

'I didn't sleep.'

'Fuck!' she said suddenly as the doorbell rang.

I moved away from the doorway, thinking she would go and open the front door. But instead she darted to the window and stood to one side, peeking out. 'Fuck!' she said again and the word electrified me, I'd never heard a woman say such a thing. There was something violent about the word, I felt as if something bad were to happen. Then she quickly pulled the curtain shut.

I looked away. I couldn't believe she had a visitor and that she was deliberately not letting them in. The woman stood by the window for a while and then she started sniffing again. She went and put the television on and

I sat there, my handbag on my lap, watching. I clung onto that bag as if it would save me from something.

'There you are,' said Craig, coming into the room much later. He looked sleepy and he was rubbing at the corners of his eyes like a small boy. 'I wondered where you'd got to. Yeah! John, how's things?' He greeted a man who had arrived an hour ago and who was sitting on a beanbag in the corner of the room drinking beer. But although the man replied, he didn't get up and they did not touch.

'Look at that!' John said, nodding at the TV screen.

'What's going on?' asked Craig. I was glad he had asked because I had been watching the TV for a long time and didn't know what was going on. I had seen videos before, American movies at a rich friend's house in Maun and at my relative's home in Gaborone, but I'd never seen TV.

'Live Aid,' said John.

'Live what?'

'Live Aid, it's a big gig, they're raising money for Africa.'

'Is that what all the noise is about?' asked Craig.

'You mean outside? Yeah, it's at Wembley.'

We watched the TV as one band and then another took to the stage, on either side of which were giant outlines of Africa, shaped as if they were guitars. Above the stage was a sign: Feed the World.

'It's Ethiopia,' said John. 'The famine, yeah?'

'It must be hard for you to see your people like this,' offered the woman, lighting another cigarette.

223

'I'm from Botswana,' I said, and Craig patted me on the knee as if to say, don't make a fuss.

And then I saw Princess Diana with her golden hair that was heavily brushed over her head, and her hands clasped in front of her as she stood waiting for something. It was the first time I'd seen a real princess.

I was dying for the toilet, but too shy to ask where it was. Eventually, when I couldn't hold it any longer, I asked Craig and he led me through the kitchen and pointed to a white wooden door. I held back; I couldn't believe anyone would put a toilet right next to a kitchen, that people were to do their business next to where food was prepared. I closed the door of the toilet and sat down. I was here in England now; I was supposed to feel happy. But I felt sad because I had been in the house most of the day and no one had offered me any food.

That night I sat on the bed in the room on the second floor and wrote to my mother to say I had arrived safely. Then I put the end of the pen in my mouth and rattled it up and down against my teeth. I couldn't think what else to write. I looked around the room and I felt as if I were slipping. The walls were covered with patterned paper and it confused me to look at them. I touched the wall near the bed and it was soft and bumpy as if there was something living underneath.

The next day the weather changed, the sky was grey and it rained. And because it rained we all stayed in. I didn't like the way we sat around a small wooden table in the kitchen to eat because I felt forced to sit when I would rather have taken my food and gone outside.

And I didn't like the way we sat around the TV in the living room either, as if we were cold and it was a fire that could warm us.

We stayed at that house for months and every day I wondered, where is his family? I learnt that the woman with the bloody nose and her boyfriend John were house-sitting; they were looking after the house which belonged to Craig's uncle. Then one day Craig said he had had enough, a cheque had come in the post, we were leaving. He didn't tell me why or where we were going and I didn't feel I could ask.

We went to the train station by tube. 'Where is every-one going?' I asked Craig as we took a lift down into the underground and it rattled and the people in it all looked over each other's eyes.

'To work.'

For a second I thought they were all miners.

'Thank God for that,' Craig said, settling himself onto the train seat. I sat opposite him and we had a table between us which was bolted onto the floor.

'Where are we going?' I said at last.

'To my uncle's in Scotland, my uncle the Earl!' And Craig drummed his fingers on the table.

'I thought you were an Earl.' I spoke quietly; I didn't want the people on the train to overhear.

'Where d'you hear that from!' Craig laughed.

I was too embarrassed to answer.

'It's his place in London,' said Craig, 'but he lives in the castle on Mull. And he has no idea we're coming.'

A woman walked down the train then and I could see

her look at Craig, and I could see she liked the look of him and this made him look good to me as well. So I settled back in my train seat and in my mind I pictured Sleeping Beauty's castle and the princess I had seen on TV.

Then Craig went to the buffet car and the longer he was gone the more I began to panic. I looked out of the window to see the city buildings had been replaced by fields and when the train stopped I thought, what if he's got off without me?

Chapter Nineteen

When the ferry came chugging its way across the sea towards us at Oban, its metal bulk slicing through the water, I didn't think it would stop in time. And then it opened itself up and cars drove out of its belly.

At first I was nervous about standing on the ferry deck, but then I went out and it was exhilarating to stand with the spray of the sea on my face. I had learnt at school that seawater was salty, but it was only now that I tasted it that it was true. I felt as if I could fly, as if I could soar off the ferry and join the birds that were circling above us, crying.

And then we passed an island and I could see a tall white lighthouse attached to smaller white buildings that looked like a splattered piece of chewing gum on the deep green land. I couldn't see any people, it looked empty, new but empty. And although it didn't feel as if we were travelling that fast, within minutes we had passed the island and the lighthouse was gone. Then I saw Craignure from across the water and a sprinkling of buildings buried in thick dark trees.

Craig's uncle Stewart met us off the ferry, for Craig had called him before we boarded. It was late evening and Stewart was sitting waiting in a Land Rover, every bit as battered as the one belonging to our neighbour in

Sehuba, Lenny Krause. He wore corduroy trousers and a woollen knitted cardigan and he was reading a newspaper. Craig told me to sshs, before he crept up to the car and knocked violently on the window.

His uncle jumped and dropped the paper. He turned an angry face towards us and I could see his eyebrows as thick and prickly as two fat mophane worms. But then he smiled.

'Should have known it was you!' he said, getting out and making a little grunting noise. 'You could have given us more warning, Celia's been faffing all morning about sheets and things. And who do we have here?' he turned to me.

'This is Kazi,' said Craig. 'My fiancée.'

'You must be awfully cold,' said Stewart.

And suddenly I was cold; the ferry ride had left me shivery as if I had a fever. It wasn't summer anymore.

'All the way from Africa?' Stewart said with some concern. 'You must be terribly cold.'

I sat in the front of the car, which I was pleased about because it meant I was being treated well; back home you could tell someone's status by where they were put in a car and I had never been put in the front of a car before. It also meant I didn't have to sit next to Stewart's dog, a little black and white creature which I hadn't noticed until I'd got in. It sat now on the back seat next to Craig, very upright, panting.

As we drove across Mull I was amazed that Craig had not told me about this place he came from. There were hills of purple as if they'd been sprinkled with bougainvillea petals; there were dense green fir trees, low mountains with deep shadows that crept along the crevices like elderly hands. And when the sun started to go down we turned at a spot on the road, a road that was so narrow that two cars could barely pass each other, where we could see the sea and the water was as orange as the sky.

'It's beautiful,' I said.

'Aye,' said Stewart, and he sounded pleased. 'Aye, it is.'

Behind me Craig didn't speak, but I could feel him jiggling his knees up and down. I had seen a difference in him since we'd arrived in the UK; now he didn't jiggle in excitement, he did it as if he were trapped.

I looked out of the car window and saw a scattering of bricks on a grassy mound of land. It seemed someone had built a house here, and that it had fallen down.

'The clearances,' said Stewart, and he slowed the car. 'You can still see some of the village remains. Have you heard of the clearances? No? Well that was when the Highlanders were evicted to make way for the sheep.' Stewart looked in the rear view mirror as if checking he had Craig's attention. 'The Highlanders, you see, thought they had a right to live on the land of their ancestors, and it turned out that they didn't. So their houses were burnt to the ground.'

In the back of the car I could hear Craig yawn.

'This island has its fair share of tragedies,' Stewart continued cheerily. 'You remember the boulder, Craig?'

When Craig still didn't reply, Stewart looked at me instead. 'He liked to play there as a child. I'll tell you the story. It was the end of the 1700s and a young courting couple had built a wee house under a ledge. On their honeymoon night, off they went to a local dance. That night they came home, went to bed and a boulder came down the hill and crushed them to death. Did you bring your wellies with you?'

I knew we had arrived when we turned abruptly off the road and onto a wide path and then past a low stone building with a sign outside saying 'Gifts and Afternoon Teas'. Then we turned through some big black gates and I saw the castle. It rose up from a wide lawn with grass so short it was almost smooth. Someone had made a pattern with the bushes; they had been trimmed in rows like a furrowed field.

The sky above was almost purple now, yet the house itself was illuminated in some strange light. There were so many windows in the house that it dazed me to look at them, some were arched at the top, others were tiny little rectangles of glass barely big enough to fit a person's face.

I noticed that this house was all over the place. My eyes couldn't decide which part to focus on, for there were strange decorations everywhere, the sort of designs you get from dripping wet sand on a rock. And there were long triangular turrets with golden balls on top and thin spikes and it was as if different bits had been added to the house and no one had cared whether they fitted together nicely or not.

'I'll get that,' said Stewart, giving a grunt as he took our luggage out of the back of the car. Then he opened the back door and let the dog out and it sprang from the car and immediately went to stand by its master's legs. I thanked Stewart, thinking he was a very polite person, politer than anyone I had met yet. When he brushed against me by accident, he immediately apologised and I realised then that people in these parts didn't touch, that in the house we had lived in for the past few months, not once had I seen anyone touch.

'You *have* got a lot just for the weekend!' said Stewart, setting off with the bags. The dog stayed behind for a moment, sniffing suspiciously around my feet.

I looked at Craig, confused. Were we only staying for the weekend? But Craig had gone ahead as well and I could hear his footsteps crunching on the gravel that led to the castle. I followed him through a vast open door where Stewart had stopped and was shouting, 'Celia!'

In front of us was a massive set of stairs, wide enough for half a dozen people to climb at once, and then I looked up and saw the ceiling was hung with antlers. To my right I could see framed photographs going up the length of one wall, and in the photo nearest me was a very blurry looking white woman wearing a long black shirt and in her hand she held a long gun. I looked in vain for pictures of princesses and queens who had once lived in the castle and perhaps still did, but all I could see was this photo of the late Lady MacKinnon with the lion she had shot in 1922.

'Well hello there!' said Celia. She came hurrying lightly down the steps and at once the dog began to bark and zip up and down on the polished floor. She was a small woman, very thin, and she wore a nicely ironed white

231

shirt and a skirt made of thick material that looked more suited to a heavy overcoat. 'That's an awful lot of luggage just for the weekend!' she said, kissing Craig on the cheek. Then she stood at the bottom of the steps with her legs set very wide apart.

'That's what I said,' Stewart agreed. He put our bags down and gave a little gasp.

'Craig?' said Celia, but he had run ahead.

'I'm starving,' he called out over his shoulder. And I saw Celia raise her eyebrows at Stewart and shake her head.

'And you must be Kazi,' she said. She held out her hand and I made to touch it, but she grasped my fingers in hers so hard that I could feel her bones. 'I wish you'd told us earlier that you were coming!' she shouted after Craig.

'That's what I said,' said Stewart.

'Tea is in the library.'

'Sorry?' I said, for I wasn't sure if she were talking to me.

'Tea,' said Celia, smiling. She drew an imaginary cup in the air with her hands and lifted it to her mouth. 'It's a drink, made from . . .'

'Yes, tea,' I said. 'We drink it at home.'

Chapter Twenty

I followed Celia up the stairs to where I could see a corridor going off to the right which then led down to a narrow staircase. There was a little rope strung across the corridor on two brass stands. And hanging from the rope was a homemade sign saying, 'Private'.

'Those are our quarters,' said Celia, leading me in the other direction. 'But for today I thought it would be nice to have tea in the library. You've timed it well, we don't have any more visitors until tomorrow.'

She marched into the library and I followed. I had to squeeze my eyes because the room was so dark, except for a blast of light coming from two tall windows on the left. Everything in the room seemed brown, the squishy leather sofa, the glass-fronted cabinets which ran along one wall, the long beige curtains held together with golden rope, the shiny wooden tables which were of so many different shapes and sizes it was as if someone had kept on changing their mind about what shape they favoured. Even the frames of the mirrors were brown, and the mirrors were so high up that it would be impossible for anyone to see themselves in them. Only the walls were not brown, for they were painted a green that resembled dried peas bleached in the sun.

The room was very still; I could hear the tick tick of a

brown clock on the mantelpiece, and yet it was as if someone had been busy in here. On the desk by the window was an open book. There was a pen and some paper and a glass half full of water. On the floor were two large globes showing the world in blue and green. I walked to the window, drawn by the light.

'That of course is where the ships used to come in,' said Celia. 'You could see them right across the sea.'

I felt giddy at the window, for I could see that the sea was in front of me and on both sides and I felt as if I could fall. Without realising it I began to trace my finger on the desktop and when I lifted it up it was thick with dust.

'Aye, we're the MacKinnons, not the Ma*Cleans*,' laughed Celia. 'But then,' she said, and her voice rose for she was directing her words to her husband who was just coming into the library, 'we do have rather a lot to do.'

Stewart eased himself onto the sofa with a sigh and I wondered if this was a man who could do anything without an accompanying sound effect. The little dog reappeared and it sprang up on the sofa and sat there like a strange-looking person. I waited for someone to tell it off, to slap it back to the floor, but no one did.

'It's a big job running a castle, you know,' said Celia, and she sounded argumentative as if someone had suggested that it wasn't. 'Good Lord, isn't it just! That's been the case since the day I married a MacKinnon.' For a brief second she put her hand on my arm and I felt the pressure from her fingers. 'It's not that old, not as old as Duart's or Torosay, of course. I suppose in some ways you might not even call it a castle at all. But there's enough to keep the likes of us busy.'

'Celia is our tour guide,' offered Stewart. 'Ask her anything.'

When I didn't speak, he said it again, 'Ask her anything.'

'When was your house built?'

'1858,' said Stewart immediately.

'As I was saying,' continued Celia, only then she stopped speaking and busied herself ordering the paper on the desk which I had inadvertently disturbed. When everything was straight again she looked up. 'We can't afford to live in the whole place ourselves any longer and especially not with the children gone. So we've turned the downstairs into a flat and put up private signs.'

'Not that anyone pays any attention to them,' said Stewart. 'Last month we found a couple frolicking in our bedroom. I'll tell you the story; I was just locking up when I heard this noise from our flat. So off I went, and the noise got louder and I thought it was a couple of bairns having a bit of a play. Then I opened the door and would you believe it, there was this gorgeous woman there and she looked up and saw me and . . .'

'An' then yer arse fell off,' snapped Celia. Then she turned to me with a very bright smile and said, 'We've turned the old kitchen into a very nice tearoom.'

'Light snacks and refreshments,' offered Stewart. 'Free parking for coaches outside.'

'Tourism does help,' said Celia, and she sounded

defensive again. 'The farming and fishing isn't what it used to be. Of course we still have the cattle.'

I felt my body relax; if she was going to talk about cattle then at least I could join in.

'And the flocks of blackface sheep,' Celia said, and then she blushed furiously.

'Will you pour?' asked Stewart from the sofa.

'That's my role in life,' said Celia, marching to the table in the centre of the room. 'It's, Celia will you just pour the tea, Celia will you just meet the visitors off the boat, Celia will you just . . .' She began to unstack some thick china cups which she placed carefully on individual saucers. 'Bank holidays are the worst, rounding up the lost children.' She took a little jumper off a teapot and poured the tea. 'And the kids writing "bugger" in the guest book.' She picked up the milk jug. 'Say when!'

She stayed there with the jug, looking at me. But I just stared. I'd watched her unstack the cups, but even so I'd been waiting for her to call someone to serve the tea. Where were the children, who was it that helped her with all of this?

'When,' I said at last, still amazed to be waited on by an elder.

'I haven't poured any in yet!' Celia laughed. She finished adding the milk and then she handed the cup to me and I tried to balance it at the same time as sitting down on an armchair.

'Thanks,' I said, for I had already learnt that people were expected to say thanks. If you didn't say thanks then you were rude, and the only way not to be rude was to say 'thanks'. But I was also beginning to see that there was a way of saying 'thanks' that could be rudeness in itself. Sometimes people said 'thanks' when they meant just the opposite.

'You're more than welcome,' said Celia.

The chair was so soft it seemed to sigh as I sat down, and now that I was sitting I saw a handwritten sign taped on the wall, 'Please sit down if you wish.'

Celia gave Craig his tea and she stood there in front of him watching him drink it, as if the tea were medicine that it was important for him to finish. 'Will you not have some cake?' she asked Craig. 'He's looking a bit peely wally,' she said to her husband, and I looked at Craig because I didn't know what she was talking about.

We had supper in the library too, while the wind howled outside. Only once was I asked to do something and that was when Stewart asked me to take a bottle of wine out of a pan of hot water and bring it to him.

We began with soup and I thought perhaps they were very poor to be drinking water with spoons, but then we had meat – roast beef which Stewart was very pleased about – and little spongy Yorkshire puddings. I didn't like the food; the meat was without fat or marrow and it sat rather sadly on the plate in thin little slices. But the trifle I enjoyed, and so did the dog for it was given some too, in a china bowl with paw prints around the edge.

Again I wrote a letter home that night. We were in the bedroom next to Celia and Stewart's and I was anxious about making a noise. But Craig was not. He wanted to kiss and to play around. I had noticed that Craig always wanted to have sex when I was doing something else. If I was watching TV, or if I wanted to talk about something, and especially if I was writing a letter home.

I would not take my clothes off until I had written my letter, and once it was in the envelope then I wrote 'Africa' and I underlined it, hard, several times.

We didn't stay a weekend at the castle, we stayed a year. It was an odd sort of life they lived, Stewart and Celia, like guests in their own home. At any moment a visitor might appear, despite it being before opening or after closing time. I always found myself hurrying away from groups of people coming up or down stairways, and I always seemed to find myself outside doorways hearing snatches of conversation, visitors talking about a painting they were looking at, a room they had seen, what time the coach was leaving, if they would have fish that night.

'Let's talk about your intentions,' said Stewart one evening in the library after the castle had been locked up for the night.

'My intentions for what?' asked Craig, helping himself to whisky from a big glass decanter on a table next to the fireplace.

'Well,' said Stewart with a grunt as he moved over to let the dog jump up next to him. 'About the future?'

And I thought, he wants us to leave; he's trying to find out when we're going.

'I might go back to Africa,' said Craig.

I sat up straight on the sofa, surprised.

'Or I might go to Asia, never been to Asia.'

'Craig has always been the adventurer in the family,' said Celia.

'You mean the loser,' said Craig, and he finished his whisky and straight away poured another one.

In the winter it snowed and I woke one morning to see the deep green rock of hillside layered with white. I felt disorientated; the land was white and the clouds were white and there seemed to be nothing in between. When I went outside the trees were like iron and the light from inside the castle behind me was almost pink as if something strange were being burnt upon a fire.

Then spring came and the flowers appeared, wild yellow ones by the shore of the ocean, scattered on sandy rocks like tiny lemons, and bluebells, their soft heads bent in clusters. But although I saw these things around me, although I saw their strangeness and their beauty, it was also the beginning of the loneliness. I had never known such loneliness in my life. And there was nothing I could do about it; it came down on me like a sea fog.

I continued to write letters home, and when I put a letter out on the tray in the hall to be posted I willed it home in my head. I saw it being put in a bag, in a car, in a ferry and a train. I saw it being flown in a plane across Europe, across Africa, until finally, finally, my letter arrived in Sehuba where I pictured my mother sitting under the mulberry tree, drinking tea and Isaac standing beside her reading the letter out loud. 'Is it a letter from Kazi?' she would say, and she would be smiling, eager to hear how I was doing in the UK.

I didn't know how long a letter would take to get to

Sehuba or how long it would take to get one back. I thought perhaps some got lost on the way. I thought up all sorts of reasons why I wasn't getting a reply. But eventually I had to face what was going on: my mother was deliberately not replying, she was not going to forgive me for leaving with Craig MacKinnon, for disobeying her, for marrying a white. And now I was in a place where no one knew me, they didn't know my family, they didn't know where I came from. And I became less than known, I became no one.

BOOK FIVE
Nanthewa

Chapter Twenty-One

The day my son married was a wonderful day; we had known when the rain came the night before that the ancestors were pleased. The marriage had been delayed, of course, after Kazi left, but eventually it took place. I woke early that day, as was my custom, and I sat there on my mattress listening to the rain outside and it made me think of the old days, when it would rain at Xuku and how pleased we were then. Of course the rain sounded gentler in a reed house, and that was when it rained a lot, not like these days. These days we don't have any rain, and the white people have even put chemicals in the Okavango so that the water dries up. That's why we have all this drought.

There was much to do that day, a wedding doesn't organise itself; we were expecting guests from all over the place and it was important that nothing went wrong. Isaac had made invitations and they had been printed in Maun, and they looked very nice with a photograph of him and Grace on the cover and little red hearts around the edge. We had two celebrations, in the traditional manner, one at Grace's home and one at ours. Of course the one at ours was bigger, for Isaac wanted everything just right, as did I.

Wanga helped me organise the supplies and her

daughters worked hard that day, except for her third-born, Abu, who was unable to come. Wanga boasted a lot about Abu; she had won a scholarship to Maruapula where the clever rich children went and she intended to go to the university and after that to the UK to study even more. But I ignored Wanga's boasting that day, for I had a wedding to run and everything went well, everyone behaved themselves, there was food so plentiful that people were even throwing it away.

We showed Grace's family how a wedding should be and I could see they were impressed. The preacher was a white man, a Dutch man, and although I hadn't wanted him there, because he had been referred to us by Lenny Krause, he did his job well. And the way he looked in that white suit, he went very well with the bridesmaids that day.

And when the ceremony and the party was over, then the women led Grace into our house and I welcomed my new daughter just as many years ago Rweendo's mother had welcomed me. The only thing that was missing, the only thing that made me feel things were not quite right, was that Isaac's father was not there to see him become an adult. Because I wanted to show him: see how our children have grown? See how things are now, how well I have worked for our family?

Right from the day of the wedding I was waiting for Grace to tell me she was pregnant because I knew about these things and I would be able to help. But even when a full year had passed, still I had no grandchildren.

And as for Kazi, for all I knew she had fallen out of

that plane with the Englishman who walked as if he had a rash and who was always jiggling his limbs up and down. She was far away now and she had turned her back on us. She knew I couldn't read, just enough to run my store and do my accounts, but Isaac could have read a letter to me. He could read letters to me as if they were stories so that I was always disappointed when he came to the end of the page, even if it were just a letter from the bank in Maun. But Kazi had forgotten about us.

Isaac had wanted to change the way we did things. He was a married man now, an adult, and he wanted more control of the business. At first I had been reluctant, but eventually I had agreed. We kept our money in a bank account now, we hired foreigner workers from Zimbabwe and Angola because they were cheaper, and we sold in bulk to the safari camps. All these things were Isaac's idea.

But as for Kazi, she had left her home and abandoned her family. She wouldn't listen to me because she couldn't see what I could see. Children are not supposed to forsake their mother; they are supposed to remember where they come from. So I was angry that I had to rely on Lenny Krause for news.

'Mma Muyendi,' he said one morning, speaking as nice as anything. He always stood in the doorway when he came to see me, and he never let anyone know he was on his way. I didn't invite him to my house, I didn't make him welcome in my home, but still he came, just like he had come that first time many years before. And now Lenny Krause was a big man, there was no one in the village with as much power as him. People weren't really listening to the Headman anymore, but they listened to Lenny Krause because it was Lenny Krause who brought the tourists into Sehuba in their big noisy trucks.

We had our tar road now, just as my late husband had said we would, the tar road that went all the way down to Maun and then to Francistown and then to Gaborone and then to Johannesburg, and there wasn't a person in Sehuba who hadn't seen those tourists come in. Lenny Krause had his own mobile safari company and he was very busy bringing people in from South Africa and showing them around, camping in Moremi and making plenty of money.

The government was in charge of the reserve now. But still, there weren't many ways that we Batswana could make money from Moremi, from the land that had been our land. We did not own the companies, we did not own the camps, we did not own the land. I knew what Isaac had been doing, I knew he was buying hunting licences at citizen prices and then selling them to Lenny Krause. For that was the only way that people like us could make money from masafari. Isaac had ambition, he tried the honest way to get a job in the camps, but like his father before him, he found that masafari didn't offer much to people like us.

'Are you well?' Lenny Krause asked, and he was mumbling a bit so that I knew, even without looking up, that he was poking a matchstick in and out of his mouth. Now that he didn't smoke that was what he did, chew on a matchstick all the time like a cow with a sharp blade of grass.

'*Ee*,' I said. I was sewing an old dress of mine and I needed to concentrate for my eyes were giving me trouble. When Lenny Krause didn't say any more I looked up and what I saw made me prick that needle right into the skin under my fingernail. Because now I saw that Lenny Krause wasn't just standing in the doorway, he was using the doorway for support. And I could see terrible scars on his right leg, below his shorts and above his socks. I knew about the attack, everyone in Sehuba had heard about the lion that had attacked some foreigners on a safari in the Linyanti, but I didn't realise, until then, just how serious it had been. It looked as if Lenny Krause had borrowed a leg from someone else, for the one with the scars was very thin, and it was so very pale and hairless as if it had been wrapped in a bandage for many years.

And so, seeing him like that, I couldn't help but ask him in. I shook my head slowly from side to side as I watched him cross the room and sit down uncomfortably on the sofa. Then he rested that leg out as if it were made from wood and was no longer able to bend.

'Doesn't hurt a bit!' he said, rubbing it up and down. 'Here, Mma Muyendi, is where the bugger got me first.' He tapped the outside of his knee. 'And then I was under that beast's belly and it was lovely and warm under there.'

'Hey,' I kept on shaking my head.

'My own fault,' said Lenny.

I didn't contradict him because I thought this was probably true.

Then Lenny laughed and he shifted as best he could on the sofa. 'So, Kazi doing well?'

'Yes, very well,' I put my head back to my sewing, but inside I was furious. I wanted to say, is she? Is she well? Because I myself have no idea.

'Of course they're in Scotland now, at Stewart's castle.'

'Of course,' I echoed, and all at once I could feel the end of my finger pumping from where I had pricked it earlier on.

'From mud hut to castle, hey?'

I put my sewing down for a second and looked round the room, looking so that Lenny Krause would look too and see that we did not live in a mud hut. This was a brick room in a brick house, here was my sofa which I had bought with cash, here was my cabinet and here were my plates and clock behind the glass.

Lenny threw his hands in the air. 'Come on, Mma Muyendi, we're relatives now, isn't it?'

So I gave him a very nice smile. Yes, we were relatives now because my foolish daughter had agreed to marry his ugly foot-jiggling cousin, but I hadn't chosen these relatives, there had been no discussions, no consensus, so as far as I was concerned these people were nothing to me. I could see through that Craig whatever his name was, I could see just what he was after, and like a fool Kazi had fallen for him. Marriage! I knew he would never marry her.

'I wonder if they will come back at Christmas,' I said

in a soft voice, like it was something Kazi had told me and I was musing on whether it would happen or not.

And Lenny Krause took to the bait immediately. '*Sis*, they've said they are, but who knows, man. Who knows where Craig might get it in his head to go next?'

So it was true, Kazi was coming home for Christmas.

'And how is your wife?' I asked, because I wasn't as angry with Lenny Krause anymore.

'Not good,' he said, and he was not smiling now.

I could not remember the last time I'd seen Marianne Krause, but in the village when people talked about her now they called her the ghost. For she was very, very thin and people said it was as if she were fading away.

'It's malaria?' I asked.

'*Ag*, who knows.'

'If it is malaria then you need a doctor.'

'I'm not going to those buggers at the hospital.'

'I mean the traditional doctor.' I bit the thread and it caught uncomfortably between my teeth.

Lenny Krause shrugged. 'Whatever it is she won't listen to me.'

We sat quietly for a while and it was so quiet that I could hear splashes from the river and the sounds of children playing.

'About these diamonds,' I said at last, because what Lenny Krause did or did not do about his wife was not my business. I was not one of those women overly concerned with the details of other people's lives. 'Do you think it was true, that they tried to sell them to a policeman?'

Lenny Krause chuckled and he looked relieved not to be talking about Marianne anymore. 'That's what I've heard.'

Everyone in Sehuba was talking about the two men who had been arrested the week before and taken to Maun. People were asking who the men were and where they were from and who they worked for, and they were discussing everything from the length of their hair to the size of their boots. And they laughed at the idea that the two men had come to the delta and tried to sell illegal diamonds to a policeman.

'And were the diamonds really glass?' I finished my sewing and laid the dress on my lap. 'They must be very stupid people.'

And Lenny Krause leant forward then so that one elbow rested on his good knee, so that it was almost as if he could have toppled out of that chair and right on top of me. And when he spoke his voice was not friendly at all. 'I wouldn't use words like that, Mma Muyendi.'

And then I just knew it was true, what people were saying, that Lenny Krause wasn't just taking ivory and selling it like we knew he had been doing for years, even when this was not allowed anymore, that he wasn't rich just because of his safari company, that he was involved in other things too.

'And where is Petra?' I asked, as if diamond smuggling were nothing to me.

'Ag, you know Petra.' Lenny eased himself back on the sofa. 'She's in the bush.'

In the bush at her age! She should have been thinking

of marrying herself by now, although I didn't know of anyone in the village who would take her.

'She's getting too big for Sehuba, Marianne says. Says we should have sent her away years ago.'

I thought that he spoke of his daughter as if she were an animal who had outgrown its cage. But then Petra was a strange girl, she always had been, and so was her mother with her way of dressing in children's clothes and her wild parties that went on all night and disturbed the sleep of people who worked hard. I thanked the ancestors that, with the marriage, Isaac was out of her way for I had never liked their friendship; I had never liked the way Petra clung to Isaac and followed him like a shadow. Grace was not a clever girl, she would never be any help with the business, but she was obedient and she made a good daughter.

'And Isaac?' Lenny Krause asked. 'How's he?'

'Oh, he is just OK,' I replied modestly. 'Business is as good as can be expected with all this drought and illness we have these days. He works hard, my son, he knows how to make an honest living, he is running the store well.' And I paused when I said the word 'honest' and I eyed Lenny Krause where he sat with his leg stretched out like wood.

'That's why I wanted to see him,' said Lenny, and I didn't like the way he looked at his watch, for then I realised that a meeting had been arranged, that all along he had come not to see me but my son.

And now Isaac walked into the room and he looked very fresh. Grace had not given me any grandchildren,

251

but at least she could wash and iron his clothes properly. I watched my son as he bent to greet Lenny Krause, stooping to take his hand. Lenny Krause had done a lot for Isaac, he had contributed to the wedding expenses, he had brought business to the store, and I could not remember exactly when this had started, this father and son relationship they had nowadays. But there had come a time when, if I didn't remember to say that Lenny Krause had been around our yard looking for him at a certain time, then Isaac got very upset with me.

Lenny tried to get off the sofa as if he were leaving. 'Got the licences, hey?' he asked my son.

Isaac nodded. 'How is the leg?'

'*Ag*, man.' Lenny began rubbing at his scars again.

Isaac did not seem surprised by the sight of the leg; he seemed to have already seen it.

'Best we talk,' said Lenny Krause, and he looked at me as if wishing me away.

'My mother should listen to whatever is said,' replied Isaac. And I smiled a big fat smile to hear him talk like this, for a child should never keep anything from his mother.

'Right then.' Lenny sat back again. 'This is the deal: you know my company, you know how it's going, and I want to expand. These camps in the delta, they're doing well, and with hunting not as good as it was, and with my leg ...' Again Lenny stroked the scars on his leg and it was as if he didn't even realise he was doing this. And as I watched him do this I puzzled over that lion that had attacked him, for now I could see that the scar that was

252

most prominent was one that was shaped like a single hole.

'So I'm selling the mobile operation,' said Lenny Krause. 'I want a camp. Only we're talking a permanent, luxury lodge. Not something that you put up and take down, something that's there all year round. The tourists want luxury now; they don't want sleeping bags and some kak brandy. This photography tourism, that's the new thing, that's our market.'

Isaac nodded. But I could sense that he was holding back, that he was anticipating what was to come, and in that way Isaac reminded me of his father.

'I've had some discussions . . .' said Lenny Krause, 'with the people concerned. And I have a site, near Khwai.'

The word Khwai hung alive and sharp in the air. That was where we had once lived, those people had been our neighbours at Xuku, that was where some of the people had been relocated.

'What will my son do?' I asked, because I was thinking of the whites who had come for my late husband that one time and wanted him to work for their company.

Both men looked at me as if I shouldn't interrupt.

'I need a co-owner,' said Lenny at last and he laced his fingers together. 'So he'll be co-owner.'

'You need a citizen on board,' agreed Isaac. 'If you have a citizen then you can move forward, that's what the government wants. And it's time we Batswana made a profit from our own resources.'

Lenny Krause laughed. 'You're the citizen, I'm the financier.'

'I would be in charge of the camp?'

'*Ja*. You know the area.'

'I know the area.' And Isaac looked at me as if to say, see, *Mme*, see how this person needs me? And I knew he was thinking of the proverb I had always told him, that those at the back will one day be in front.

'Of course, you'll need to buy some shares,' said Lenny Krause. 'Once you can.'

'Of course,' said Isaac as if he already knew this, as if this wasn't a problem to him.

'What will you call the camp?' I asked.

'Nare Lodge,' said Isaac at once. 'That would be a good name, there are plenty of buffalo around Khwai. Or Tshukudu, all the tourists want to see rhinoceros.'

'No ways!' laughed Lenny Krause. 'Not some foreign word. Wilderness is good, Wilderness Camp.'

Chapter Twenty-Two

I barely saw my son after that day; he was so determined to make the camp of his successful that he set off at once with Lenny Krause. They had a site, as he had said, not far from where we used to live at Xuku and they brought the men in to build the camp. News travelled back to us in Sehuba that the building was going well and after some few months I sent word that I would visit. But the reply I received was that it wasn't yet time and that I should wait. Christmas and New Year passed, Kazi did not come home and I had no news from Lenny Krause about this.

By the time the water was high, I thought they must be ready to open that camp, yet still I was not invited to visit. Grace went, Isaac called for her, but not for me. So one day I decided to go there for myself on a truck taking supplies from our general trading store. I packed my red blanket and some few pots, and arranged for the store to be looked after, because with Isaac now at his camp it had fallen to me once more to manage it.

The driver picked me up at my home early in the morning and I was waiting for him with my things all ready on the sand. Grace had prepared some food for me, as well as some biltong to take for Isaac. Although it was early in the morning there were still a few people to see me leaving in that truck, and they waved as I went by for they could guess where I was going. Everyone knew Isaac had a camp, he was the first Motswana to part own a camp and everyone wanted a job there.

When we passed near Xuku it nearly made my heart cry for I could remember the day we had watched our village being burnt down by that game warden. I could remember how Isaac had been on my hip, his mouth wide open, and the question in his eyes: Why are they burning down our homes, Mama? I felt there was a bad spirit in that place now. Where our houses had been it was overgrown with bush, there was no sign of our lives, no sign of our past.

The trees in the nearby bush were the same, only they had been stripped by the elephants which were troubling a lot of people who lived on the periphery of Moremi. We had not had that much trouble with elephants in the old days, unless a white hunter had injured one and left it to roam, but now there were more people and more elephants and they trampled crops and there was nothing the farmers could do. If you couldn't shoot an elephant because it was destroying your livelihood, then how could you provide for your family? It was only the whites who had the money to buy a licence to shoot an elephant, and it was said that soon there would not be any shooting allowed at all. It seemed like these days animals were eating us instead of us eating animals.

We drove away from Xuku and then, when we reached the water, my heart lifted again. I could see the Okavango and it was beautiful to me, even the birds walking across the lily pads were beautiful. It was not like our river in

Sehuba; that was a stream, a trail of urine, compared with this. And I sat there and filled my heart with the sight of the Okavango and the country of rivers that I had known as a child.

Eventually the truck driver stopped by a sign that was made from wood and I knew that sign said Wilderness Camp, the name Lenny Krause had chosen for the camp. I got off the truck and I rearranged my clothes, undoing my scarf and then tying it tight around my head again, dusting the sand from my body. It had been a very uncomfortable journey to make by truck.

I followed the driver down a path and we passed a reed house built in the traditional manner, only without much skill for I could see that the walls were not tight enough and that it would not last that long. A lot of bushes must have been cut in order to clear the path we walked along, but when I looked up I was happy to see so many familiar trees: a sycamore fig far older than any we had in Sehuba, and the first mowana I had seen for a very long time. The mowana is the elephant of trees and I knew that this one would have been here for many years. I thought of the mowana at Kasane that my late husband had told me about, the one which the British had used as a jail, locking people up inside who refused to pay their hut tax. I wondered if that tree had also survived, just like this one, and if it had then it must have had many stories to tell.

Then we reached a clearing and I found my son standing on a big deck made from wood and the deck was raised and from here we could see right to the water, to a jetty also made from wood, and I could see three mekoro tied up there on the banks of the river. And my heart lifted again for I could not remember the last time I had been in a mokoro; I thought it was when Rweendo had still been alive.

Isaac was busy telling the men what to do, for they were building a frame over the deck and hammering in those nails as quickly as anything. I recognised two of the men as Isaac's age mates from Sehuba, including his old friend Peter Mponda who had always been a bad influence on my son.

'*Dumelang Borra*,' I said.

'*Mme*!' said Isaac, turning in surprise.

I smiled shyly; I knew he would be happy to see me.

'What are you doing here?' He frowned and folded his arms.

'I have brought the supplies that were ordered,' I said calmly, only I wasn't feeling calm because I didn't like the way Isaac had replied. He was looking around that camp as if deciding where he could hide me. 'And so that I can see this camp of yours.'

'But it's not ready,' he said.

I shrugged; that didn't matter to me.

'And we have some tourists coming.'

So they were not ready but they had some tourists coming? That didn't make sense to me. Did my son not want me around? I told the truck driver, quite sharply, to get my things, and then I sat down on the sand next to the deck.

I sat there for some time, watching the men building.

I sent one of them for water and then, as the sun moved overhead, I made myself comfortable under a tree.

When I woke the air was very still and quiet. The men had gone, leaving only Isaac.

'Hey I'm tired, *Mma*,' he sighed, coming up to the tree where I sat. 'I've been working flat out. I haven't slept for three days. Lenny's not around, this is all down to me, I'm totally in charge of this. I've got to get this structure up and the bar built in the next forty-eight hours, I'm still waiting for half the supplies, I've got two guides now but I've still got job interviews all afternoon.'

I curled my lip. I was no stranger to hard work and I didn't like to hear people complaining just because they had a job to do.

'OK, OK.' Isaac put down the measuring tool he had in his hand. 'You want to see the place? We'll go by mokoro, I want to check one of the channels.'

As I settled myself down onto the mokoro, as I felt it wobble beneath me, I felt like a small child setting off for a day's fishing. I admired the way my son took the pole and without a word began to steer us away from the camp. His father had been a good poler, as had his grandfather, my father, and it seemed right to see him like this. He had the manner just right, he was neither too stiff nor too loose, he did not dip that pole too quickly like some polers I had known, he just pulled us on as if that mokoro were part of him.

We were alone on the water and we glided without speaking, past the papyrus on the shore, their heads bowed as if they were trying to drink. There is something

259

about travelling by mokoro that makes you want to dream; you have time to think while you're sitting there, low down, on the water. And you see things from a different perspective, because from down there in that mokoro the land around you seems so large, the papyrus are like giant trees, the fish eagle coming down to hunt is so big it's almost as if you could be its prey. It makes you very small, being down on the river. And this makes some people afraid, when they realise what a tiny little thing they are in life, but then that is what we are, tiny things in a big land.

Then out of nowhere we heard a terrible noise, a churning noise something like a tractor, and I could feel everything round us grow tense and frightened, the birds began crying, there were rustles in the grass, the water beneath us started to tremble.

And then we saw a speedboat come tearing down the river channel towards us. It was lifted high up in the air at the front and it was roaring through that water, slapping up and down, churning the river up so much so that as the speedboat passed I bent my head and still I was covered in spray. I had only a moment to glimpse a white man in sunglasses standing at the front of the speedboat and he waved a can at us and was gone. It took a while before the air was quiet again, before the birds stopped crying and the land seemed to settle back to how it had been.

'What was that?' I asked.

'It's a boat from Chief's Island,' Isaac said, sounding envious. 'They've started taking people out on river rides, mornings and evenings. They've got a big boat too, for sundowner cruises. Lenny's looking into getting one for us.'

'Well, they're making too much noise, this isn't a tar road.'

Isaac laughed. 'The hippos hate them.'

'Then they will attack them.'

'They can't catch them, *Mma*,' Isaac said as if I were a stupid somebody. 'The speedboats go too fast, you've just seen that one fly past.'

And then we saw another mokoro coming silently down the river towards us.

'Hey, Electricity!' Isaac shouted out to a very tall boy who was poling two white people.

The boy laughed, and so did I to hear his name. And he did look as if he had some electricity in him because he had been poling that mokoro very fast and even now, standing still, his face was very busy looking around. '*Dumela Rra, Dumela Mme*,' he said, and he bowed his head a little so that I knew that he knew who my son was and that made me proud.

'Don't you know him?' Isaac said to me in a teasing voice, gesturing at the boy with the pole. 'He is a Muyendi.'

I studied the boy. He was tall, I had already noticed that, with long lean arms and legs. His face was bright and his eyelids a little heavy in an attractive way. On his top lip I could see the fine shadow of a new moustache.

'*Mme*,' said my son, 'this is Leapile Muyendi's boy, Leapile, the son of . . .'

261

'I know who Leapile Muyendi is,' I said. He didn't need to tell me my own relatives! 'So you are Leapile's son?' I asked.

'*Ee, Mma*,' said the boy, again very respectfully. He smiled and his eyelids folded slightly and I thought that this is a boy who is going to break some hearts.

'And how is your father?'

Electricity looked confused for a moment and he glanced at Isaac.

'Leapile is fine,' Isaac laughed. 'I just hired him yesterday, he came across from Khwai asking for a job.'

'Good,' I nodded, because it was only right that my son should help the family out. And then I looked again at Electricity and I saw that indeed he had a look about him, mainly in the eyes and in the forehead, that resembled his grandfather Nkapa, my late husband's brother who had worked in the Rand mines. I asked further about his parents and his village and established that all was well with his family, but I could see the white man in the mokoro wasn't pleased about all the chit chat. He put out an arm on which he wore a big shiny watch and he began to tap on it and show it to Electricity.

'Do excuse us,' said Isaac in English to the people in the boat, and they looked so startled I couldn't help but laugh. 'Who are you working for?' Isaac turned back to Electricity.

'Hey,' sighed Electricity, sounding weary just like an old man. 'I'm working for the whites at Chief's Island. Right now I'm taking my tourists to move camp.'

I thought then that he was very young to do this job

and wondered why he wasn't at school. But then I thought where would he go to school around here?

'We stayed near Chief's Island last night,' continued Electricity, 'now we're heading downstream.'

'And after that?'

'And after that,' said Electricity, and he looked at my son in a cheeky fashion, 'after that I'm coming to your camp so you can give me a better job. Those people at Chief's Island,' and Electricity cleared his throat and emptied it into the river, 'are paying me peanuts.'

The two white people in the mokoro looked a little nervous when Electricity spat like that. They were looking at our faces and their expressions looked stupid, the way people do when they are listening to something that they can't understand.

'Check me later, I need some new guides,' said Isaac. 'I'm looking for a manager as well, someone with experience, let me know if you know of anyone. Even if they're not that experienced, as long as they are a Motswana they can get trained up.' He was about to pole off when he noticed something in Electricity's boat. 'That's a nice knife you've got there.'

I peered forward as well to see what Isaac was talking about and I saw a very big knife on the bottom of the boat of a type I hadn't seen before.

'I wouldn't mind one myself,' said Isaac, and Electricity looked happy at the compliment and, smiling broadly, he pulled off.

We returned to camp shortly afterwards for I said I was tired and needed to rest and Isaac replied that in that case I should not have come all this way. We had just reached a fireplace which was being built on the grass near the deck structure when I saw a man sitting on an oil drum, his head bent in concentration, whittling away on a stick. I saw at once it was Leapile Muyendi. Although I had not seen him since he was a small boy, some years after he was born and after we'd moved to Sehuba, I would have recognised him anywhere, even if I had not just met his son and been reminded of him. The shape of his head was like his father's, like my late brother-in-law Nkapa's. It was very square and very firm and set on his shoulders like a rock. For a moment, looking at him like that, I was back in Xuku, back in the time when Rweendo was alive and full of plans, the time when he sent money to Nkapa to buy me the red blanket.

Leapile looked up as we approached. Then he stood and wiped his hands down his trouser legs, ready to receive a greeting.

'Where are the builders?' Isaac asked rudely before I had a chance to speak, and he pointed at the fireplace where a circle of cement had been half completed. 'This was supposed to have been finished this morning. When the tourists get here, we have to have this done. *Sis!*'

I frowned at my son. He hadn't even greeted his own cousin properly!

'Perhaps something has happened?' I said in a voice that was gentle, so gentle it was to serve as a warning to him that he should change his manner.

'*Ee*,' said Isaac. 'Something has happened. They've buggered off.'

'There was a disagreement,' said Leapile, and he spoke quietly and kept his face turned away. Now I saw that he was very different in fact from his father Nkapa, for his voice had a mild quality to it, like he was a man used to soothing disagreements rather than provoking them.

'Between whom?' Isaac demanded.

'They will tell you,' said Leapile, and he bent down and began tightening the laces on his boots and I could see this was unnecessary because the boots were very new and the laces were already tied nice and tight.

'Well, you tell me and then they can tell me,' said Isaac impatiently.

I tutted, to show Isaac that he shouldn't speak to Leapile like this.

'While you were on the river,' Leapile spoke at last, his eyes on the ground, 'the white man came and said they were lazy, so he sent them to chop down some trees.'

'Lenny Krause was here?' Isaac asked, and he looked tense.

'No, not him,' said Leapile, 'the other one.'

'What other one?'

'They will tell you.'

And then we saw a thin little man in the distance and I could see he had shorts on and a very bright yellow shirt. I wondered no one had told him not to wear bright clothes like that in the bush. Then he came closer and I had to laugh for this man had hitched his shorts up so high that his private parts were pushed to one side like a bag of fruit.

'Isaac?' said the man, and as he came towards us he

held out his hand even though we were too far away to touch it. 'Tim!' said the man, and he sounded very happy about this. 'Tim Loveless, I'm your new manager.'

Chapter Twenty-Three

I left my son at his camp and returned home with a heavy heart. I could see that Isaac believed that life was finally giving him what he wanted, but I feared he was not as clever as he thought he was. I didn't like Tim Loveless; I didn't like it that a stranger was to manage that camp when it was supposed to belong to my son, and I could see at once that he was a stranger. It was not just his ridiculous yellow shirt, or the way he had failed to acknowledge me, it was that Tim Loveless was a foreigner and so he knew nothing about our land. And if you don't know the name of our plants then how can you teach them to someone else? If you don't know how to pole a mokoro then how can you take people into our Okavango?

I could see that Isaac was angry that Lenny Krause had appointed a manager without consulting him. But this hurt his sense of pride so much so that he would pretend he was not upset. I wondered why my son didn't stand up to Lenny Krause and say he didn't want Tim Loveless as the manager.

And then I forgot all about the camp because when I returned to Sehuba I could see that at last Grace was pregnant.

'Don't lie like that,' I told her the morning after

I arrived. We had been washing clothes and when the heat grew too intense we had both lain down to rest. Only she was lying on her side like a big dozy dog.

'*Mme*?' Grace opened her eyes, those big round eyes of hers that would be very useful to have if you were a criminal because they look so very innocent.

'Don't lie like that, it's bad for the baby, you must lie on your back.'

'What baby?'

I laughed. 'My daughter, don't take me for some stupid somebody. I have eyes. Look at you!' And then I lowered my voice, 'You haven't told anyone, have you?'

'No.' Grace moved over onto her back obediently. Then she absent-mindedly dipped her fingers into the bowl of sugar I was using for my tea and began to suck them.

'Well don't, because this is the time when they can bewitch you, this is the time when bad things can happen.'

I got up then, I no longer needed a rest. Inside I was singing to myself, for at last I would have a grandchild. I had lost my daughter, Kazi no longer belonged to me, but now our family would begin to expand as it should. I couldn't wait to tell Wanga when the time came, for I was tired of hearing her news about her child Abu who was in the UK and who wrote to her mother regularly as a daughter should. And then I felt afraid because I remembered my pregnancy which had ended in the bush after we moved to Sehuba. A family should have as many children as possible; I had only managed two and this was because someone had cursed me.

From the plot next door I could hear a generator just starting up and I was surprised because things had been quiet for a very long time at our neighbour's house. Ever since they had buried Marianne Krause, it had been quiet. She had died in the winter on a day when I was sitting outside under the mulberry tree. I had heard a sound that morning, the whirring sound that the quelea birds make when they gather together to invade the crops. I looked up to see the birds on the other side of the river and they were swarming, making sudden changes of direction for no reason at all. And then suddenly they crossed the river and converged on the trees in Lenny Krause's yard, and at once the trees darkened like a cloud covering the sun. That was the morning Marianne Krause died.

I went over at once and others came as well to offer their condolences, but Lenny Krause was like a dead man himself, he had no idea what to do. We had to help him with all the arrangements, and provide the food, and notify the people who needed to be notified. Then they took her body somewhere, perhaps back to Namibia, and since then I had barely seen Lenny Krause. But I knew that his daughter Petra had been sent away from Sehuba, that she had finally been sent south.

The day Candy was born was a very dry day, the sky was black with smoke from fires in the delta and it was not a nice air to breathe. I was irritated and anxious that morning. Grace had returned to her mother's to have the baby but I had explained my experience in the business of childbirth, for I had delivered so many babies in Sehuba, and I sent word that she should call on me when the time came. But when I woke that morning I knew, in my blood, that something had already happened.

I put on my best headscarf and wrapped a light shawl around my shoulders and set off for Grace's mother's house. But I could not walk as fast as I used to and the sand was so dry, so deep, that I slipped a little. In my mind I was walking fast but my feet didn't seem to have got this message.

When I arrived I went into the house where Grace was and there she sat on the mattress, her hair all a mess and this big silly smile on her face.

'He has arrived,' I said, breathing hard and easing myself down onto the floor. 'He is a fat little baby, he looks just like his father and we will call him Ketumile.'

Grace laughed, and I was surprised at this for it was almost as if she were laughing at me. 'He's a girl, *Mme*! See,' and she unwrapped the blanket from around the baby so that I could see it was true. And although I wanted a boy, for if you have a girl she will just be taken away from you, it still took my breath away to see that fat little newborn and to be able to greet my first grandchild.

'See your grandmother, Candy,' Grace said, and she was crooning those words into the baby's ears. 'Ah, Mama's baby,' she said, and she kissed that newborn all over its face.

'Candy?' I asked, trying to keep my voice low. 'What sort of name is Candy?'

Grace smiled at me; she smiled even though she could see I was upset. 'It means sweet, a candy is a sweet, *Mme*. This baby is like sugar to me!'

And Candy was a sweet baby; perhaps it was all the sugar Grace had eaten during her pregnancy. She even smelt a little like sugar as well. She was a sweet, happy, placid little baby. There were never any problems with her sleeping or eating or crying. Instead she seemed very happy to be in this world, as if she had already been promised that life would be sweet for her.

One morning, shortly after the umbilical cord had healed, I had a fright. I had been napping inside the house, and when I woke I thought I heard Candy crying. So I got myself off the mattress and I went to find her, and I went in and out of every room, and in and out of the kitchen outside, and in and out of the garden and I couldn't find Candy and I couldn't find her mother. Then just as I was really growing afraid, I heard Grace at the gate outside.

I was standing waiting for her. 'Where have you been?'

Grace smiled and held her hand in greeting.

'Where have you been?' I said, only louder. 'That baby's too small, what are you thinking, taking her out like that?'

'We were at the clinic, *Mme*. It is the day for her injection. Tuesday the fourth, that is injection day.'

'Tuesday the fourth?' I said, very angry now. 'What is this, "Tuesday the fourth"? What does that mean to me? You will give an old woman a heart attack sneaking out of the house with a baby like that.'

Grace hung her head and shifted Candy on her back.

'And what injection is this? You can't give a small baby an injection, do you want to kill her?' Then I saw that tears had filled Grace's eyes, I saw I had got my point across.

'The nurse at the clinic said you have to have an injection . . .'

'The nurse? What does she know?'

'She knows,' said Grace, only she spoke so quietly that if my ears hadn't been so sharp I wouldn't have heard her.

I eyed my daughter-in-law until she dropped her head. And then Candy gave a little cry and I rushed around Grace to take my grandchild down. But as I went to do this, Grace also turned and I found myself chasing her backside like a dog wanting to catch its own tail.

'Let me take her, she's crying,' I said.

'No, no, she is fine.'

'Let me take her.'

And at last Grace took Candy off her back and she handed her over. And I swung that baby around a bit to see how she was, and I pulled on those legs of hers because someone had to do it, someone had to make sure she grew up strong. She was always doing this, Grace. She seemed to want that baby all to herself. She didn't even like me carrying her; she behaved as if she was the only person in the world to have ever had a baby. 'Mama's baby!' she crooned morning, noon and night. 'Mama's baby!'

The months went by and still Candy was a sweet, happy, placid little baby. Isaac returned from his camp for a while and he was happy. He said the white manager Tim Loveless had been sent packing because he had no experience managing a safari camp, and Lenny Krause had someone else in mind.

And still Grace kept Candy close. She would not listen to my advice, not even when I told her that I could look after Candy, that she and my son should be working on getting another baby now. Why didn't she go to camp with him, I asked. But she always had an excuse.

One afternoon, when Grace was asleep, again I woke to hear Candy cry out. This time I found her at once, snuggled up close to her mother on the bed. So in order that she wouldn't wake her mother, I picked her up and I took her into my bedroom.

I could smell at once that she was dirty. That was the problem with the nappies Grace wanted to use, they were made of some plastic material and they soaked up all the mess a baby made and it smelt terrible. I had just ironed a set of cloth nappies and I had them right in my bedroom, so I decided now was the time to use one. I laid Candy on the bed, right in the middle of my old red blanket, and I busied myself looking for cream and a nice big pin.

And then, from the corner of my eye, I saw her. She just flew past me, that little baby. She just flew off that bed and landed on the floor with the sort of thud you hear when a watermelon has been dropped, just before the hard green skin splits open. I didn't know how it had happened. She had been in the middle of the bed, she hadn't even learnt how to stand up on her own yet, but somehow she had raised herself up and toppled to the edge of the mattress and then fallen, head over heels onto that hard stone floor. It was as if something had done that to her, picked her up like that and thrown her off the bed.

And I thought all these things in that second that I saw her fly and at once I was down on the floor and holding her in my arms. 'Cry,' I said to her, 'cry.' I knew if she cried she would be OK. And I hugged her too hard, willing her to cry.

Then at last she did and then Grace came rushing into my room. 'What's wrong?' she asked, looking round wildly.

'It is nothing,' I said calmly, cradling Candy, quietening her down. 'She's hungry.'

Grace fumbled at her dress and took out her breast and held out her hands for Candy. But now Candy began to scream.

'What is it?' Grace said.

'It is nothing,' I repeated, patting Candy firmly on the back as her mother flapped her arms.

'See?' I said, 'she is quiet now. You go and do the tea.' And I began to sing very softly to Candy. But the moment her mother was out of the room I began feverishly to check her. I checked her head, her neck, all over her body, and I couldn't find a wound, there was no cut, only some soft skin on the side of the head that would soon bruise and I knew which plant could be used for that. Thank God, I said to myself, thank God. And I put my face very close up to Candy's and smelt that sweetness and I promised I wouldn't let anything bad happen to her again.

I did not take Candy to the doctor. I had examined her and I had found she was fine. There was no need to tell Grace what had happened, that would only worry her. And Grace was showing signs of stubbornness; I did not want ill feelings in our household. But as Candy grew I could see something was not quite right. She became a fussy child. She was either fussy or, at other times, I would catch her just sitting there staring into space. And as she stared she licked her lips, as if they were dry, as if they were bothering her somehow.

'Stop it with the lips!' I said the first few times. And Candy would start, as if coming out of her world and into mine. And when she looked at me I knew she had no idea what her lips had been doing.

Yet the rest of the time that child had no fear, she ran around just as her father had done when he was a child. She would run too close to the fire; she would approach a snake when she saw one instead of going in the opposite direction. It made me nervous to leave her alone. Either she was running towards danger, or she was in a world of her own. One time I found her with one of my reed knives and she had it in her hand and she was just sitting there, the long sharp blade resting on her naked leg.

So I knew I had no choice but to keep that child close.

And I did keep her close; we were as close as anything, Candy and I. And because Candy was close to me, she saw the things that I saw, the things that no one else did. One evening, just before the sky grew dark, we were sitting together under the mulberry tree when she saw the smoke.

'Mama!' she whispered, and I could tell from her voice that something wonderful had happened.

'What is it, my child?'

'Look, the tree is breathing!'

And I looked and I saw the curl of smoke from the swollen berries on the tree and I took my fingers and I squeezed little Candy's cheeks. 'We will keep this between ourselves,' I told her. 'Tell other people and they will laugh at you like they laughed at me.'

'Is it a witch?' Candy asked, and her little hand came creeping over for mine.

'It could be,' I smiled. 'It could be a witch.'

BOOK SIX
Kazi

Chapter Twenty-Four

I wanted to leave the castle and I didn't know how.

'Kazi?' Celia asked, her head around the bedroom door. 'You're looking awful peely wally. Do you not think some fresh air would do you good?'

'That's what I said,' Stewart agreed, joining his wife at the door. He wore his tartan hat, the one that looked like a tea cosy. If he was wearing this hat then he was going out, and if he was going out then that meant we had visitors coming. I pulled up the top of the duvet, feeling cold. After my chores were done in the morning then I often went back to bed and huddled for a while, and every time Celia found me in bed she asked if I had woman's trouble. If I shook my head then she asked, rather excitedly, if I was *late*. But I wasn't going to be late because Craig didn't want children. I had never known a man who didn't want children; it hadn't occurred to me that there could be such a man, so I'd never even asked him. Now I felt he'd taken away my future.

Two days ago we'd been returning from Tobermory when we'd stopped by the sea. I looked at the wet, moss-coloured rocks that jumbled over each other into the slate-coloured water and thought how far I was from home. And then I'd seen two children playing on the rocks and I'd said, 'What do you think our children will look like?'

And Craig had said, '*Our* children? You must be kidding.'

I looked at the sea and I kept my voice very quiet. 'You don't want children?'

'Of course not.'

'But why?'

Craig looked at me and his face was annoyed. 'I don't want to be tied down, Kazi. I don't like being tied down.'

And all of a sudden I felt like an ornament that a traveller had brought home with him, an ornament that the traveller just didn't want anymore.

'Is Craig at the gift shop?' asked Celia, still with her head round the door.

'I think so,' I said as I saw Stewart padding off down the hallway.

'Craig's helping quite a bit with the tours these days, isn't he?' said Celia. 'You want to watch him.'

That made me sit up. What did she mean, I wanted to watch him? Watch him doing what? But I already knew; she meant the way Craig was with other women. The way he flattered the women who worked in the gift shop and the women who came on the tours. He would stand next to them, very close, and sometimes he would brush a hand against their shoulders or their hair and then, if I walked in, he would look at me as if I were the maid. And the times I'd seen him do this, the women liked it, they liked him flirting with them. A few days earlier I had come into the gift shop to hear him say to one of the women behind the till, 'Where have you been all my life?'

I got up quickly and stood in front of our wardrobe wondering what to wear. I wanted something bright, something colourful and determined, but there wasn't anything. I felt I was turning into a winter tree; everything I owned was brown and black. I was only twenty-one; I didn't want to look like Celia, I wanted to dress up and go somewhere nice.

I left the bedroom and found Craig in the tearoom in the basement of the castle, a room with uneven walls something like the colour of milk. He was setting out the cups, putting them face down on a row of saucers. A big group must be coming; there were plenty of cups on the table.

'Were you here earlier?' Craig asked as I came in.

'What?'

'Were you here earlier?' Craig repeated, and his voice was steely. 'There are two dirty cups here, Kazi.'

'Oh,' I said, about to move nearer.

'So,' Craig snapped, and I stopped where I was. 'Who were you drinking with?'

This was the way he'd begun to speak, as if I were guilty of living a secret life.

'All ready then?' asked Celia, coming into the tearoom. 'Sorry! Didn't mean to interrupt the newly weds!'

I looked at Craig and he avoided my eyes. The wedding had been a dismal affair; I didn't even like the ring he'd given me. No one had sung, no one had cried. There had been no one there to give me any advice. We had just signed our names in what looked like a visitor's book and then hurried through the rain to the pub.

'The ferry's due,' said Celia, on her way out of the room. 'They should be about half an hour.'

'Fine,' said Craig, and he began rattling around in the box that held the teaspoons. 'So,' he turned to me, 'what will you be doing today? Reading your magazines?' He began to take out some forks that had been put in the box where the spoons were supposed to be, noisily putting them in their rightful place.

I drew out one of the tearoom chairs and sat down. I knew it would annoy him that I had brought a magazine down to the basement with me but I set it on the table and opened it. Sometimes I read Celia's favourite magazine, *My Weekly*. She liked the recipes for beef and ham gumbo and baked stuffed peppers, and she liked the knitting patterns, complex lists of instructions that allowed her to fashion a cardigan with smock-stitch cuffs decorated with pearl beads. But I liked the complete stories. *Once upon a time, there were three girls who were good friends. And they each married the man of their choice. But who lived happily ever after?* I loved the stories about marital problems with their pencil drawings of white men with windswept hair and women with cascading locks. *She needed help and understanding. Could she expect to find them in a village where she'd always been an outsider?* That was me, I thought. I was the outsider. For more than a year I had not met another African. I had not spoken Setswana to anyone, not even to myself; I had even begun dreaming in English. One night I dreamt I was looking at myself in a mirror and thinking I must cut my hair, and I woke in fear because in the dream my hair was yellow which meant that in my dream I was white.

Apart from *My Weekly*, sometimes Celia bought *Vogue* as well and I waited with suppressed excitement while she went through it in the evening after the visitors had gone, always with one eye on the TV watching *EastEnders*. We both liked watching *EastEnders*; we enjoyed watching other people suffer.

Today it was my own magazine that I had brought down to the tearoom with me and it was *Elle* I read with the most satisfaction. First I read the fashion pages, salivating over Jasper Conran raw silk skirts, Red Tab Levi 501s, red and white polka dot canvas platform sandals available by mail order from a shop on London's King's Road. I loved the broad-shouldered jackets teamed with tight short skirts, the earrings that were as big as saucers, the Ferragamo shoes the colour of a green apple with golden buckles. The models looked full of life, they leapt through the air, they put a pink-gloved finger between their lips, they ran up a set of brown stone steps. And I thought, I could do that, I could leap through the air on the desert sand, I could sit on a horse on a white chalky cliff. I could stand on a boat with a Chanel bag and my ankles crossed, I could sit on a rock in a toga, I could hold onto my hat in a busy city street. I'd look good in that dress, those shoes would fit me just right.

And then I read the beauty pages, the instructions for mixing contrasting shades of eyeshadow, how to sweep raspberry over the lid, then cornflower blue from the inner corner. But I didn't have these powders, and even if I did I knew they would look wrong on me. The make-up was for white women.

But still I fantasised. Perhaps I would be walking in the castle grounds one day and someone would approach me and say, 'You could be a model, here's lots and lots of money!' Or someone would come into the castle, they would see me in the hallway and they would say, 'That's her! That's the one we've been looking for!'

I must have sighed while reading about Yasmin Le Bon, how she had signed up with Elite, and why now she had decided to give up the catwalk.

'You're dreaming, Kazi,' said Craig. He was standing over me, a tea cloth in his hand. 'Those things aren't real in there, those houses, those people ... Who do you think you are, the next Grace Jones!'

'How do you become a model?' I asked. I said the question quickly so that then, I thought, I might get a real reply.

'Oh come, Kazi!' Craig laughed, and the crease appeared in his cheek, the crease I didn't find so attractive anymore. 'Look at you, no tits to speak of and legs like brown spaghetti.'

I looked down at my legs and I thought, I was a beauty queen when you met me, people thought me beautiful then.

'Oh, OK,' said Craig, drawing back a little, pretending to be serious now. 'Well first I think you need to have a portfolio. Do you have a portfolio? No? So you'll need someone to take some photos. Know any professional photographers? No? So you'll need to hire one to take your photos then. Oh, I'm *sorry*, you don't actually *have* any money? Oh, I see, your husband supports you? And that would be because you don't actually *have a job yourself*?'

I wanted to scream. I wanted to scream so badly that I cut myself turning the pages of that magazine, a paper cut, a very long thin fine paper cut that made me want to weep.

Two days later I had the strangest phone call. It was strange from the moment I answered, standing in the hallway near the great entrance to the castle. The phone here had its own little table, set beneath a giant oil painting of a man holding a gun, two dogs by his side. The man looked satisfied with himself, just like Craig.

I answered the phone quickly; Craig didn't like me answering the phone. 'Hello?' I said and waited, expecting someone to ask me about opening times or parking for coaches or play areas for children. When the dog came up and started to sniff I kicked it away and it looked at me and curled its lips.

'*Dumela Mma*,' said the voice on the phone. '*Ke* Kazi?'

My stomach lurched. I thought it was a joke, that someone was playing a trick on me. I had had no contact with my family back home, they did not write, they did not ring. I knew my mother didn't have a phone, but Isaac must have access to one by now, I thought, he could have arranged a call. And I thought, she's calling me! My mother's calling me! After all this time she wasn't ignoring me at all, she still loved me.

'*Ee*,' I said, and my voice was all shaky. '*Ee*, *ke* Kazi.'

The woman at the other end of the line began laughing. 'Oh Kazi, I'm so glad. I've been trying this number over and over. Oh I'm so miserable here.'

I had no idea who I was talking to.

'It's me! Abu!'

'Abu?'

'*Ee*! Abu from Sehuba. Wanga's daughter!'

I began to fiddle with the cord of the phone, untangling its loops. Wanga was my mother's old friend, a woman with whom she had her usual love-hate relationship, but I couldn't picture Abu. Wanga had four children, I thought, all girls. But which one was Abu? She must be the clever one Wanga was always boasting about.

'Where are you?' I asked a little nervously.

'I'm here.'

'*Here*?'

'In the UK. In London.'

'Oh.' I felt such relief that she wasn't on Mull. I didn't want her coming here, what would I have to show for myself? What would I have to show for my two years in Britain? I didn't want anyone to know how unhappy I was, that I had nothing here. People were supposed to go to the UK and make a name for themselves, they were supposed to make a lot of money and bring lots of nice things back with them. And all I had was a borrowed pair of Wellington boots.

'I've been here for a term and I can't call my mother anymore because I just start crying. No one talks to me here. Oh Kazi, I didn't think it would be like this.'

'Are you studying?'

'*Ee*, I'm at LSE,' and for a second her voice lifted and she sounded proud. 'They're OK, the professors are nice. But that's all we do, go into classes and go out again. I don't even know anyone's names. And hey it's sooo cold.'

She laughed then and I laughed too.

'I'm coming,' said Abu. 'I'm coming there to see you, I need to see a home girl.'

'No,' I said quickly. 'I'll come to you.'

Chapter Twenty-Five

It took me the next few days to organise my trip to London and I was worried that when I asked Craig for money he would say no.

'I have to meet a friend, a friend from Botswana.'

'Really? Which friend is this?' Craig was opening the post, sitting at the table in the library, the letters and packets in neat piles. Until recently this had been Stewart's job, now Craig did it instead. It was a clear day outside, a sunny day, but the curtains were partially closed. I had been told that sunlight damaged the old books, but I had only recently discovered that the books on the bottom shelves were fake. Their spines were thick and brown and had titles embossed in gold, but if you looked on the top you saw they were all joined together with cardboard.

'A friend, someone you don't know.'

'You're being very mysterious. How do I know you're not running off to see a boyfriend?'

I laughed out loud.

'So it's funny?' Craig asked as he sliced through a letter with a thin gold-coloured knife.

'I'm going to meet Abu,' I sighed. 'She's the daughter of a family friend. She's studying at LSE and she's sad and lonely down there.' I tried to think how else I would get money. I did a lot of work around the castle, I cleaned and swept the kitchen every day, I tided the tearoom after the visitors had gone, I hoovered the rooms upstairs, I changed the bed sheets, I even cleaned the toilet bowls. But no one had ever mentioned any payment for this, it was just something they expected me to do and I expected to do. I wondered what Celia would say if I asked her for money.

'Here,' said Craig at last, taking his wallet from his pocket, and I had a sudden memory of the way he had taken the money from me in the cab from Heathrow, all the money I'd had.

It was Stewart who gave me a lift to the ferry.

'That's an awful lot of luggage just for the weekend,' said Celia, watching me leave.

'That's what I said,' agreed Stewart.

I picked up my bags a little guiltily. I had packed a lot and I didn't really know why.

It was a long time before I got to my train, before I could finally sit down and breathe easily. And then I found that my seat faced the wrong way, I was seeing what I already knew, passing the landscape that had been my temporary home, instead of facing the way I was now going.

Two stops later and the train filled up and all the seats were taken so that I had to hold my elbows in as I read my magazine, otherwise they would knock against my neighbour and I knew people didn't like that. I saw the man at once; he had a way of drawing attention to himself. He stopped very deliberately in the train aisle to put his briefcase on the rack, even though there were several people trying to get down the aisle behind him. And as he did this he waved his head around, as if showing everyone that he had a ponytail because when he waved his head the ponytail swung back and forth. When he sat down diagonally to me, a black bag around his neck, I felt his eyes on my face. The more I felt this, the more I was unable to look up. When he got up later to go to the bar he still had the bag round his neck. Only once did I look up as he was looking at me and immediately the man smiled. So I put my head back into my magazine.

An hour before London my neighbour left and to my alarm the man with the bag moved next to me.

'I'm sorry,' he said, although he didn't look sorry at all. 'But have you ever done any professional modelling?'

A woman opposite me raised her eyebrows in distaste.

'No,' I said. I thought it was cruel, that this man should pick exactly on something that I wanted to do.

'You should think about it,' said the man. 'And I don't mean glamour, I mean editorial.'

The woman opposite looked pointedly out of the window.

'You've got the features, the figure ...' the man said, and he leant away as if to see me better.

I licked my finger and turned a page in my magazine, as if he were interrupting something I really wanted to read.

'That's one of mine,' said the man, tapping the page. 'Sean Taylor. You've probably seen my name. Here's my card, go on, take it, you know you want to.'

I got off the train and now the people who had been sitting still for so long burst into life and rushed along the King's Cross platform. I felt myself jostled along, suitcases bumping my ankles, men's elbows poking my arms. Above me pigeons gathered in the metal rafters of the vast curved roof, the voice on the tannoy system echoed unintelligibly around the station, broken shards of sunlight lit the faces of the people around me. And then I saw Abu waiting; she was right near the ticket barrier, standing with her arms folded. And she came running up to me, her arms held out wide now, laughing.

'Kazi!' she said, grasping me by the shoulders. Then she put her head back. 'You're so thin!'

'Hi Abu,' I said, looking her over, seeing the sort of face I had not seen for a long time. Everything about her said Botswana to me, the light in her eyes, the way she at once took my hand and held it and her fingers felt soft in mine, the heavy cardigan she wore around her shoulders when, for England, it was a warm spring day.

As we stood there I looked at her face, at its roundness and the sheen on her forehead from which her straightened hair was slicked back. She had not done a very good job with her hair, I thought. I would offer to do it for her. I remembered her clearly now, I could see her as a child, I could remember that at school she was a year or two below me. I remembered how I had admired her traditional dancing, how she had always led the other girls at village events.

There was something at once stubborn about Abu, the way she strode off through the station not making way for anyone, and at the same time haphazard. I saw that although she had her ears pierced, one of her earrings was missing. And her clothes did not fit at all, her trousers were too big for her and were held in awkwardly with a leather belt, her jumper was blue and her cardigan was orange and the colours did not complement each other at all.

I followed Abu past a row of plastic flowers hung by hooks on the station's stone wall. 'Where are we going?' I asked.

'I have a room in Camden. My mother's cousin is a nurse and she found me a room. You'll like it. How was your trip? Hey Kazi *we*! I can't believe you came all the way to see me.'

I squeezed her hand but I felt a little guilty. I didn't know if I had come all this way to see her or if it was to get away from Craig.

'My mother says you live in a castle!'

'That's right,' I said. I didn't have the words, then, to say how things really were. 'How does she know?'

'Your mother told her,' Abu laughed.

And I had an odd feeling then, almost like fear, to think that people spoke about me back home. To think that my mother did talk about me, to think that she took the time to tell her friends that I lived in a castle. So what about my letters then? Why couldn't she reply to them? She must be getting them if she knew about the castle.

'Don't forget my card. Call me!' said the man from the train with the bag. He was a step ahead of us and I watched as he went into one of the station's shops, heading for a display of flowers.

'Who was that?' asked Abu.

'A man from the train.'

Abu laughed as if I had done something naughty. 'Let's see the card he's talking about.'

'I threw it away.'

We went to Abu's house, an old house the outside of which seemed to be crumbling. It was built above a newsagent's and the house opposite had broken windows that were boarded up. Inside the hall smelt of bacon that had been fried long ago.

'You OK?' Abu asked as I sat down on the bed in her room.

I smiled to show her I was.

'I'll make some tea.'

I looked around the room; it was very sparse. The bed had a creased white cover. There was a small desk in the corner and above this on the wall a notice board covered with papers, timetables and letters. In the middle of the notice board was a photograph of Abu's mother and sisters. I knew where it had been taken, at the photographic studio in Maun, for I could see the women standing stiffly before a backdrop, a painted scene of yellow sand and green palm trees like an image of a Caribbean beach in a magazine. Then I saw that on the window Abu had stuck a large Botswana flag and I felt unnerved because for a second, as I stared at it, I didn't know what it was.

'Here,' said Abu, handing me a cracked mug of tea. She

did not ask me how much milk or how much sugar I wanted, she had just gone ahead and put a lot in.

'So what are you studying?' I asked.

'International Relations.' Abu sat down on the bed and the mattress sagged.

'Oh.' I sipped my tea. 'And is it very difficult?'

'Difficult!' Abu laughed. 'Not at all. I'm way beyond the UK students. Look at the background I've had, I know more about the colonisers than I do about my own country.'

'So you'll stay in the UK?' I curled my hands around my mug for they were cold.

'What's here for me?' Abu laughed again, and we both looked around the room, which seemed to be shrinking the longer we sat in it. 'I'm taking what they have to offer, Kazi. And then I'll go home.'

Two days later I called Sean Taylor, using the payphone at Abu's house. I'd lied to her; I hadn't thrown away his card at all. All the way to the studio near Tottenham Court Road I was so excited I couldn't speak. But I was also worried, was this photographer called Sean Taylor for real or was he playing with me? I had checked my magazines, I had seen his name, but part of me thought it was a joke, that he was simply laughing at me.

As I stood outside the studio I saw a young blonde woman come down the road and she was pulling a trolley behind her and the wheels made a rattling noise. She stood at the same doorway as me and rang the bell.

'Hi!' she said in a friendly way. 'I'm late, I'm always

late. I couldn't get the back closed, and one of the wheels fell off.'

I looked down at the woman's trolley.

'Are you booked in for today?' she asked. 'I'm make-up. I'm supposed to be doing a new girl at ten. Sue?' she said, holding out her hand. She said her name with a question mark as if she was querying whether it was hers or not.

And I smiled really hard at Sue because I thought the new girl might be me. And I couldn't believe that she had a whole trolley full of make-up, I couldn't wait for her to open it so I could look inside.

'Fuck,' said Sue, 'this bum bag is killing me. Just hold this for me, hon.' And I watched as she pulled a pouch from around her waist, adjusted it on one side, and rang the bell again.

We went up in a lift and I saw myself in the mirror inside and felt nervous. My dress was too short and my legs looked like brown spaghetti.

'You're gorgeous,' said Sue, also looking in the mirror. 'Just don't let Sean give you any shit, you know what photographers are like.'

And I narrowed my eyes in the mirror so I looked like someone who wouldn't take any shit.

'And get some pads. You'll be wearing a body suit, right? Think how many other girls will have worn it. You don't want someone else's thrush, do you?'

The lift stopped and Sue bundled out her trolley with the broken wheel and I followed her along a thin white corridor, my heart thumping so hard that when I looked down I could see the cloth of my dress fluttering over my chest.

'I'm this way!' she said, and she opened a door and inside I could see a room with three women sitting in a row in front of mirrors which each had light bulbs around the edge. The women were having make-up applied and they were looking seriously at themselves in the mirrors, trying out expressions, pouting lips, raising eyebrows, tilting necks.

'You go to reception, hon,' said Sue, 'they'll tell you what to do. All the best! And remember, don't sign anything unless you read the small print, don't sign anything that will make you legally theirs for ever and ever!' And she went into the room with the mirrors and the women and closed the door behind her.

I continued walking and I thought, I must remember everything that happens today because it's going to change my life.

The receptionist took me to the studio and when she opened the door I was amazed at the size of the room. It was something like a gym with a wooden floor and a raw, empty feel. I kept my eyes in front of me rather than looking all over the place, so that when Sean Taylor came in he wouldn't think I wasn't used to this. But from the corners of my eyes I could see giant lights like metal flowers with bulbs and shades on top, wires all over the floor and up the walls, massive rolled sheets of paper that were too bright to look at.

Sean Taylor didn't arrive for another hour and when he did begin to photograph me my face felt very bare.

I was not the ten o'clock girl Sue was expecting; no one had come to put make-up on me.

'Where are the heels?' Sean demanded of a woman standing nervously to one side. 'Fucking stylists,' he muttered to himself.

The woman hurried out and came back with a pair of black shoes with heels pointed like an umbrella. Cautiously I put them on and then, as I walked towards Sean, I felt a rush to the head. I had seen shoes like these in magazines, I had wanted shoes like these for years, but I hadn't thought they would make me feel as if I were tipping over a precipice.

'Don't smile!' snapped Sean. So I didn't; instead I thought of Craig and how I had nothing to show for myself and I let my face go into a sulk.

'That's it!' said Sean. 'Good. Good. Close your mouth. Keep your mouth closed.' And he started moving back and forth in front of me, sometimes crouching, sometimes on his tiptoes. He told me he would do some test pictures, that I could have them for free and then I could put them in my portfolio, a portfolio I didn't tell him that I didn't have.

'Some girls,' said Sean, resting his camera on his knee, 'don't have a personality. You have.'

And I thought, but shouldn't I be smiling if I get to wear all the nice clothes they have in the magazines?

And then Sean gave me a Polaroid and I looked at it and although it was my face, it didn't look like me. The way the light shone on my cheeks was so clever it made my cheeks seem as if they were made from wood.

Chapter Twenty-Six

I stayed with Abu for the next few weeks and I think she was happy to have a home girl around. She liked having someone she could tell about her day, about how her classes were going, about which professor looked like a warthog, about the Zimbabwean man with lovely eyes who worked in the canteen. But as the days went on I felt edgy. I thought the Polaroid meant I was going to be a model and I didn't know what to do next. Would I have to go back to Craig? If I couldn't earn any money then I would have to return. Why hadn't Sean Taylor called me, was I not good enough?

And then the agency called.

'Kazi?' a woman's voice demanded. 'Ah ... I can't get the last name ...'

'Muyendi,' I said. I had given Sean Taylor my own name; I wasn't going to use Craig's.

'Yes darling. Is this you?' The woman took a sudden breath and I got the feeling she was so busy that she would just be able to deliver some information before putting the phone down. 'This is Diane Kinksly, darling. From Top Girls.' She said it with a pause, she said it like I should know who she was and what Top Girls was, and of course I did.

'Hello,' I said, sounding stupid; the call had taken me by surprise.

'We loved the pictures Sean showed us. I'm not even going to pass you to a booker, I want you for myself! Let's arrange an interview. I have a window on Friday at . . .' I heard the noise of paper flicking. 'Ten.'

And that was how it happened, that was how it all began. My first thought was, what would I wear? I was paralysed by indecision. How would I get something that would be the sort of thing a model would wear to meet an agent as big as Diane Kinksly? I went to Oxford Street and I spent hours going in and out of the shops and touching the clothes and trying them on. Then I went to Covent Garden and did the same. The new clothes for spring were in; I wanted cream, I wanted linen, I wanted a pair of shoes with golden straps. But I knew I couldn't buy anything because I still didn't have any money. Abu said I could borrow her clothes, so I wore some of my own blue jeans and one of Abu's tops; it was red with a square neck and padded shoulders and I thought it suited me. I thought I looked so smart setting off for my interview with Diane Kinksly. If my mother could see me now, I thought. If Isaac and Craig could just see me now. And then as I got nearer to the agency in Kensington other thoughts took over: what if they didn't like me? Perhaps red was the wrong colour. And I should have worn a warmer jacket; the sky was blue but the air freezing. What if they didn't like me? Only Abu believed in me; she said the fashion world was shallow but if

I wanted to be a model then that's what I should do. She was becoming like a sister to me.

There was something about the agency building that made me think of a hospital. The walls were white, the floor was wood only painted white and there were lights all over the place. There were five other women in the waiting room and the way they sat made me nervous. They were all arranged, they were not just sitting on a sofa or a chair, they had their legs folded in a certain way, an arm extended in a certain way, a profile offered in a certain way, like statues that someone had dotted around a hospital.

'I've come to see Diane Kinksly,' I said.

'Where are you from?' the woman at the desk asked, a woman with a short bob and sweat on her upper lip.

I hesitated. Did she mean where I had come from just now, or where I had come from before that, or did she mean where I really came from? I spoke English fluently now; I didn't think she could tell that I wasn't from here.

'Who sent you?' said the woman a little sharply.

'Diane rang, she asked me to come.'

'Oh,' said the woman, looking surprised, and she pressed a button that was hidden under her desk.

Diane's room had a lot of glass in it and from the window behind where she sat I could see a view of London, thin grey buildings reaching up into a sky that was criss crossed with the plumes of passing planes.

'Kazi,' said Diane, holding out her hand but not getting up. She had spiky hair as red as a tomato. I went towards her with my hand out, ready to give hers a firm shake because she looked like someone who wanted a firm shake. But as I got to her desk her phone rang and she turned her hand up flat towards me as if to ward me off.

'Give me ten minutes, darling,' she said into the phone. As she spoke she began to pat a doll she had propped on her table in front of a very new typewriter. The doll had chunky fabric arms and blue eyes with a band of white around the edges which made them look as if they were being forcibly held open.

'Sit!' Diane said to me. 'As I said, we loved the pics. Normally we do our own test pics, but Sean is good. And it's a good time for girls like you. Ethnic is quite *in*.' Then she grabbed her ringing phone again and spat into the receiver, 'No, she doesn't do snow. It's bad for her skin. Talk to the booker, darling, I don't even know how you got through to me.'

I waited for her to finish and I looked around the walls in her office and at all the pictures of models who were where I wanted to be.

'Far more black girls now,' said Diane, putting down the phone. 'Well, far more than there were ten years ago! It's quite a trend, Iman, Naomi Campbell's very sweet . . .'

And I thought, a trend? Does she think at some point we will all just go away again? But I kept my smile because I wanted to be a model.

'Of course, you're not going to be the next Timotei girl!' And Diane laughed so much she began to cough. 'So, darling, a little bit of background. Age? Oh, I've got that here. Yes, well that's OK, a little older than average, but black girls age so well, don't they?' The phone rang yet again and she picked it up. 'Give me another two minutes, darling.' Then she put her elbows on the desk and stared at me. 'You *are* a lovely colour.'

I smiled back, but I thought, a lovely colour for what? A lovely colour to be a model?

'Not too dark,' said Diane thoughtfully. 'The camera doesn't like dark faces. Any experience?'

'I've done a lot of beauty contests . . .'

Diane trilled with laughter.

'Back home.'

'And where would home be?'

'Botswana.'

'Uhuh. Just explain to me where that is.'

'Africa.'

'Love it! Did you see *Out of Africa*? Wonderful film. Robert Redford, wouldn't kick him out of my bed. And your name, Kazi. What does that mean? I do love these African names, they always mean something, don't they?'

I stared at her, how could a name not mean something? 'Kazi,' I said. 'It's a Shiyeyi name, the language of my father's people. It comes from the word for woman.'

'OK! Got you. Love it! But the surname, darling, that's a mouthful. Can we shorten it? No, I don't see how we could shorten it. How about a new surname? No, how about no surname at all? One-word names, that's going to be very *in*. Right, Kazi darling, we are going to build you a career. I'm talking prestige. This isn't usual but I've got a casting for you.'

Diane gave me a yellow Post-it note with an address written in blue scrawl. I held it in my hand and stepped back out onto the street. The sky was blue now, so blue that the buildings around me gleamed as if they had just been washed, and in a park nearby I could see the sparkling yellow of dozens of daffodils, their complicated heads heavy on the thin green stalks. I hadn't remembered London as beautiful; I only remembered the summer I had arrived and how muggy it had been.

I stood and read the address on the Post-it note a few times, as if that would help me to know where to go. But in the end I went back into the agency and asked the woman with the bob how I was to get there. And I wanted to ask what exactly a casting was, but it was too quiet in the agency's waiting room and I didn't want the others to overhear me and think me stupid.

I arrived on time and when I entered the office, one of many in a squat grey building, a building that had nothing at all glamorous about it, I found I wasn't the only one to be photographed. The place was full of young women; there were two women in the hall, a dozen standing and leaning against the walls in a long corridor, another dozen in the waiting area. And they all looked so much the same, all were tall, some even taller than me, nearly all were white, most had hair in shades of yellow, although some had hair that was brown. There was a feeling of rigidity as if all the women were holding themselves in, ready for something, ready to be told suddenly to move. And then suddenly a name was called and a woman did move; she disappeared behind a door and a few minutes later, as I was still standing there, she came out again in tears.

I couldn't get to the desk I could see across the waiting

area without forcing my way through, so I asked a woman by the door, 'Is this the casting?'

'Which one?'

I shrugged and showed her the Post-it note in case that gave a clue.

'Oh,' said the woman and she looked impressed. 'Benetton.'

Now I knew what it was I was doing, I pushed my way as carefully as I could to the desk. I knew about Benetton, I had seen the ads in *Elle* and other magazines because they were the ones with black people in them. Only they were odd ads; people wearing flags sticking out of hats, people wearing green and blue jumpers, green and blue hair. The people in the ads didn't really look like models at all; they didn't look like the sort of model I wanted to look like. I wanted to be photographed dancing on a beach for *Elle*.

'Kazi? Twelve-thirty, wait there,' said the woman at the desk.

When at last it was my turn I was more prepared than I had been with Sean Taylor. When I entered the studio I had an idea of what the room would look like; I had an idea of what my approach should be. I would not smile, I would sulk and stick my chest out and arrange my body in the sort of poses I had seen the women at the agency do. But then I realised they were photographing us in groups and that I was to join three other women already standing in front of a white screen.

'Good colour combination,' muttered one of three men standing at the back of the room. 'Can you get them to play?'

'Play!' yelled the photographer, a very thin man dressed all in camouflage.

I looked at the other women and they looked at me. One was white, so white it was as if she did not have any blood in her at all. On my other side was a woman with a deep pink colour, her cheeks livid.

'Tell them it's a story,' said one of the men at the back, and as he spoke he looked only at the photographer, as if he didn't think we could hear even though we were there in front of him.

I didn't know what we were to play with. But the snow white woman seemed to have an idea and she batted me on the arm and then threw her head back and shrieked very loudly like a little girl in a school playground.

'OK,' said the photographer. 'Work it, girls! Now all of you ... PLAY!'

A few hours after I had arrived back at Abu's house, the agency rang to say I had the job. And the payment for the job was one thousand pounds. One thousand pounds! I had to think about this for a long time, I had to think really hard about it to make sure it was true. One thousand pounds. That was ten thousand pula. Ten thousand pula could build a house back home. Then I hugged Abu and she said, 'Your mother will be sooo pleased!'

I didn't answer; I thought this was a careless thing to say because Abu knew by now that I wasn't in touch with my family. And I knew, from the things she had told me here and there, that my mother was letting it be known that I had run off with some strange white man to the UK and forsaken her. And this was so unfair it made me furious; I wasn't there to put the story straight. I hadn't forsaken her, that was what she'd done to me.

And then Abu went to a lecture and I sat in her living room and watched TV and I wanted so much to have someone else to tell. I decided I would send my mother money, I would send off some money casually as if earning money like this was something I had been doing for years. They would think I was rich but who cared, maybe I could be rich. And then maybe she would write to me. I had been trying not to regret coming to the UK, but now I was beginning to feel happy again.

And I wanted to tell Craig about the job, it gave me a reason not to return to the castle.

'Hi,' I said when I phoned him, my voice crazy with excitement; I had almost convinced myself that Craig would be pleased with what I had to tell him.

'Oh it's you,' he said flatly. 'Having fun with your *friend*?' he asked.

'Yes, Abu's fine.'

'So, busy having fun. And how's the great modelling career?'

'Actually,' I said, 'you can see me in the Benetton campaign next month and my *agency* says . . .'

'Well, if you want my news,' Craig interrupted, 'not that you've asked or anything, but I'm going to Zimbabwe.'

After Craig had hung up I went out shoe shopping and I bought a pair of blue polka dot canvas espadrilles. That night I put the shoes on the floor by my mattress in Abu's room so that when I woke the shoes would be the first thing I saw and that way I would wake happy.

Chapter Twenty-Seven

The work followed fast after the Benetton ad and in the next few months Diane sent me for one magazine editorial after another. *Elle* chose me for a spread on black and white, the autumn colours of that year. I wore white, the white girl wore black. I did an editorial on holiday dressing and a prestigious two-page perfume campaign. The days were long and we were expected to work hard, but most of all we were expected to wait; we spent our days endlessly waiting. But still it was easy for me. I had waited all those years in beauty contests, waited while my mother got me ready, waited to go on stage, waited for the judgement to begin. And I was loved, I was finally beginning to be loved, and I was being paid to be loved. I didn't have to go back to Craig after all.

The first time I made a cover of a magazine I could barely sleep the night before. In the morning I didn't need my wake-up call from the agency, I rushed straight out and bought five copies of *iD* magazine. I wanted to tell everyone that that was me on that magazine, that I had known I could do it and now I had. Then I sent one home to my mother.

A few days later, Diane called me in. I was familiar with the agency now and no longer intimidated by the place or the people. And walking to the agency, even in the cold, London seemed beautiful to me. I loved the way the pavements were strewn with brown and golden leaves, still soft, only recently fallen from the trees. As the day went on the leaves would turn into crispy piles, curled and shattered along dark dry veins, so that it looked as if entire London squares were covered with cornflakes.

'Things going well?' Diane asked. She had dyed her hair again, now it was not so much red but purple like an over-ripe avocado.

'Yes,' I said, 'they're going very well.'

'Good.' Diane held out her fingernails and rattled them on the front of her desk. 'Darling. We need to talk. A word of advice. Never, ever forget how important the photographers are.'

I nodded. I already knew this.

'Kazi,' she sighed. 'You need to make them love you. You need to make them *want to fuck you*. On Monday you had Dave Truman, yes? He found you a little ... frigid. Modelling is like sex, darling. You have to make that man want you. And if you do, you'll be a star.'

I thought of Dave Truman, who was just getting started then, and of the other photographers I had worked with in the past few months. Some I liked; I liked the ones who told me to *feel* the clothes, who enjoyed their work like I enjoyed mine. But some of the photographers moved too fast, pumping out their shots, and some like Dave Truman wanted to touch me, wanted to move around me, so close they could have sniffed my private parts. When I modelled a gold rubber dress so

308

tight I could barely move, Dave Truman had wanted me to squat down in it as if I were in a pit latrine.

'OK?' asked Diane, and she picked up her ringing phone and that was the sign for me to leave.

One of the people in Abu's house moved out so I moved in. The agency sent me to Paris and to Milan for runway shows, and I thought, look at me now, I'm in *Paris*! This is me walking down a street in *Paris*; this is me on my way to work. I loved the build up before the show, the way the air became tight with cigarettes and perfume, Perrier and champagne, the way everyone rushed around me and then suddenly I was on and then everyone loved me and called my name and then in a moment I was off and the next girl came on. It was so fleeting, this burst of attention, and the build up was so long. And then once it was over I wanted to have it again.

But I knew I was lucky. I hadn't started at the bottom like some girls had, I had started somewhere near the top. And I thought I knew what I was doing; I wasn't disturbed like some of the other girls, so disturbed that I didn't know how they got up in the morning. I met girls who weighed themselves every hour, day and night, who only ever ate a quarter of the food on any given plate. I met a girl whose breasts were lifted so high up for a shoot that they only fell back into place four days later. I met girls who had been abused by their agents and photographers, who had been forced to do unmentionable things at the hotel they called the Fuck Palace in Milan. I saw how cocaine kept you going and how it killed you. I met a girl who liked to have sex right before a runway show and then strut out with semen running down her leg.

But I was OK, I thought. I was in charge of myself. And the way I was treated by some people just made me even more determined to succeed.

One day I was waiting, as ever, outside an office door. I had just returned from Paris and Diane was on her way; there was some contract work to be sorted out. And the door opened and a woman in a tight little secretary's outfit came out and she closed the door behind her, but not well enough because it swung a little open again. And from where I sat on a white leather sofa I could see the backs of two white men in blue striped suits.

'Who's next?' asked one of the men.

'The black one, I think,' said his colleague.

'I don't like black girls.'

'I'm not keen on them either. Is it the African one?'

And then I knew they were talking about me.

The first man sighed. 'Africa would be great, wouldn't it, it would be a great country if they were all white?'

And I thought, fuck you. That was the way I was beginning to speak then. I said fuck if I dropped a pen, if a cab was late, if it was raining and I didn't have an umbrella. Fuck fuck fuck, that was the way people talked all around me. Fuck you, I thought, just watch me.

Then one day Sue told me about the Africa job, that a new glossy women's magazine was casting for a fashion shoot and they were going to do something new and shoot it abroad. I rang Diane at once. And when I rang her, I was always put straight through.

'Am I up for the Africa job?'

'Of course, darling.'

'And where is it, where are they going?'

'Africa, darling.'

'Yes, but where?'

'Somewhere exotic. Begins with a "B". Lots of elephants.'

'You mean Botswana?' and I held my breath.

'Yes, that sounds right, darling.'

And I wanted that job like nothing else; it was my home, they had to choose me. And I was arrogant now, people were telling me every day that I was beautiful, that I was wonderful, and I believed it. I believed it when they said it, but then later, in the cab home, or alone in bed, I would think, but how long will it last? What if they don't like me tomorrow, what if I am no one again next month?

But then I got the Africa job.

We set off for Heathrow in the dark; some of the others had caught a couple of hours' sleep first but not me. I had spent the night packing, folding everything so carefully, folding all the things I would be taking home. I had a camisole for my mother made of a material so fine, so expensive, that I wanted to close my eyes when I felt it. I had some warm boots for her as well, for winter, and a brooch in the shape of a feather. For Isaac I had a belt, a thick leather belt with a golden buckle. And I had baby things too, for I had heard that my brother and Grace had a daughter now. Abu had told me; she said the baby was called Candy. I almost cried when she told me this. I was an aunty, there was someone in this world who would call me aunty, but my brother had not even thought to tell me.

We didn't have to check in at the airport, it was all done for us. It was only when we got onto the plane, when people eyed us enviously as we headed for the soft chairs of business class, that I heard the pilot say that the travelling time to Johannesburg would be approximately eleven hours.

'When's our plane to Botswana?' I asked Bibi, another model who was sitting behind me. She was very young, not even eighteen. She was wearing a short black dress and just above her left nipple was a round white badge saying, 'Milk's gotta lotta bottle'.

'Uh?'

'How long is the wait at Jo'burg? Do you know?'

'No,' Bibi said, and she began rummaging around in a bag.

'I hope we don't have to wait hours for a connecting flight.'

Bibi gave me a blank look. 'What do you mean?'

'I'm asking when we get to Botswana,' I said.

'Uh?'

'Botswana,' I said, and now I could feel that something was not right.

'No, I don't think it's Botswana. It's Bopswana or something.'

'Bophuthatswana?'

'Yeah.' Bibi found what she was looking for in her bag, a small plastic bottle with a nozzle on top.

'It can't be!'

'Well, wherever Sun City is,' and Bibi began spraying her face with water.

'Bophuthatswana?' I wailed. 'Bophuthatswana! That's not even a country, that's a fucking homeland!' I had turned completely round in my seat now; other people were looking as if the sound of my voice was disturbing them. I thought about how I had been watching TV with Abu two days earlier. 'They just had a coup! Didn't you see it? I'm not fucking going there!'

'A coup?' Bibi looked a little worried now.

And there I was, trapped in a plane going to South Africa, land of apartheid; a place where people like me could be shot.

It was a three-day trip and there was another job beginning the day after we got back to London, and then another after that. I began to think how I could get home from Bophuthatswana. Even if I flew it would take at least a day and I hadn't been paid yet. And then we set off down the runway and I just knew that it wasn't going to happen, that I was going to pass over my country and yet not stop in it. I put my head back and I closed my eyes and I tried not to care. I'm doing OK, I thought, is anyone missing me down there anyway? They don't write, they don't call, they are happily living their lives without me, and however much I longed to tell them I'd made a mistake, that marrying Craig had been a big mistake, I wouldn't get the opportunity now.

Then I must have dozed for I woke with a stiff neck and a feeling that I was looking down upon myself, looking down upon someone crying. I could feel behind my eyelids how the tears were building up and how they just seeped out without me wanting them to and ran in a thick continuous stream like warm sap down my face.

Chapter Twenty-Eight

I first met Phil at the BBC, in a room known as the green room even though it wasn't green at all. It was beige and hot and it felt like being inside someone's handbag. When I arrived I was assigned a minder; it was only the second time I'd been on radio and I still didn't have a clue. The idea of talking on air made me feel on edge and I had been feeling on edge ever since I'd returned from South Africa, where I'd been photographed at Sun City in a bikini, holding a spear, next to an elephant which appeared to be drugged, but not as drugged as the other model Bibi. It was the worst shoot ever.

And I knew that my mother knew that I had been in Africa, because Abu had told her mother I was going. And I knew she wouldn't understand, that it would be one more thing she would hold against me.

Diane called when I got back and left a message about a calendar job. It was a high-profile calendar, she said, the theme was the seasons and I would be summer. But I didn't want to do it.

And then out of the blue a journalist rang and asked what I thought of Nelson Mandela; perhaps I was the only African the journalist could think of to ask, perhaps he didn't know any other Africans. I said Mandela was my hero, what else was there to say? And then the press printed that old halterneck swimwear picture of mine with the headline, 'Why I think Mandela is sexy'. And then I got the invitation to come on the radio.

The first time I was put in a room alone, except for a smiling woman who was there to show me what to do. On the table was a very large, soft-looking microphone that I thought was a child's toy.

'Four minutes to go,' said the woman, and I followed her gaze to a big clock on the wall. Then I put the headphones on and I heard a man's voice: 'So, Kazi, as an African yourself, how do you think Mandela's release will affect people at home?'

I had got so used to people thinking that because I was a model I was stupid. Now I was actually being asked something other than my skin care routine. But I couldn't see the man asking me the questions; I needed to see whom I was speaking to, and so every time I started a sentence my voice trailed off into space. And I thought, fuck, I should have asked Abu what to say.

But I couldn't have been that bad for Diane rang at once and said I had another interview booked. And that was how I ended up at the BBC.

I spent half an hour before the show in the green room with three other people. I didn't know who they were but they were not Africans and they all seemed nervous as we were led into a studio and placed around a large shiny-topped table. I realised they were supposed to be experts; they were supposed to analyse the meaning of Mandela's imminent release. I was there to add some human interest; the fact that I wasn't actually from South

Africa didn't seem to bother anyone at all. The only downside about radio, Diane said, was that they couldn't see how gorgeous I was.

I looked behind me and saw three men behind a glass wall, but I wasn't sure if they could see properly or not because they appeared to be looking straight through us. I couldn't get comfortable; I kept trying to sit up in the squishy chair and leaning too close into the microphone. But then I looked at the man opposite me and saw his hands were trembling violently as he picked up a glass of water. In front of him on the table he had three big thick books in a pile, full of paper bookmarks sticking out, and he started to fiddle with the bookmarks as the presenter began speaking.

'And today we have four very exciting and very different guests, author Greg Youngster who has written a wonderful book on the ANC ...'

I didn't hear the other people's names; I only heard when the presenter came to me.

'... and last but by no means least, top fashion model Kazi who's recently returned from South Africa herself.'

I saw the man opposite me smirk.

'Kazi, let's start with you!' said the presenter and her eyes were eager as if she had drunk too much coffee. 'You've just come back from South Africa. How was it being back home? Are people there *terribly* excited about Mandela's release?'

'I'm not actually from South Africa ...'

'Of course you're not,' the presenter said brightly, looking down at her notes. 'You're from Botswana.'

'But yes,' I said, trying to be agreeable, 'people are excited. His release is long overdue because he shouldn't have been imprisoned in the first place ...'

'And is it hot over there at the moment?'

'Hot?' I looked at her, confused. I thought she would want to know what it had been like living in a front-line state, and for hours the previous evening I had grilled Abu for her views so I could decide what to say.

Twenty minutes later the show was over.

'I didn't get to tell any of my anecdotes,' complained the man who had written the book on the ANC.

Afterwards I felt exhausted and I slumped down in a chair in the overheated green room and began to eat from a tray of croissants that none of the other guests had touched. I was waiting for my minder to show me out again.

'Nice to see a model eating,' said a man in the corner of the room. I had seen him tying up a cable; I thought he was some sort of technician.

'Do you have a problem with that?' I asked. Could he not let me eat in peace, wasn't it bad enough that I felt like a performing animal? Suddenly the croissant didn't taste so good anymore, but I very deliberately started on another one.

'Sorry,' said the man, and he took the band of his Walkman off from around his ears. He smiled then, a wide smile that showed his teeth, bright and white in a strong square face. I saw he had a camera in his hand and without thinking I straightened up on the chair.

'I heard you talking just now. It was an OK show;

usually they just talk a lot of crap. But she shouldn't have kept on cutting you off like that.'

The man was smiling and he had a cheeky face. His hair was thick and springy and he had a beard that almost looked as if it had been glued on. And his glasses, thin rectangular with black frames, looked like play glasses. When he smiled his ears went up.

'I'd like to go to Botswana myself one day,' he said, and he crossed his arms against his chest and I thought he seemed to be waiting to see if this was OK. He hadn't turned his Walkman off; I could hear a muffled background beat.

'Why?' I asked, still feeling rude.

I felt bad the moment he'd left the room, and there seemed to be a gap, a space where he'd been standing as if he'd left something, something playful, in the room.

The next day Diane rang again about the calendar job and this time I said yes because I needed the money. The shoot was in an old office block near King's Cross and twice I got propositioned on the way. By the time I arrived I was feeling nervy.

'Kazi? You're late,' said the booker. 'Surprise surprise.'

I scowled at her, I was never late. I made a point of not being late; I knew what they said about black girls like me.

'Patrick is waiting for you,' she said, and she pointed up a set of spiral stairs in the middle of the office.

I went up, walking carefully for the steps were metal strips and I thought I would get a heel caught, and I didn't like the way when I looked down I saw two men looking up at me, watching my progression up the perilous stairs.

'Hi, sorry I'm late,' I said as I got into the studio. I still didn't think I was late, but I would be apologetic anyway.

A man in the corner of the studio, leaning up against a kitchen counter, opened a bottle of water and began to drink. Then he sighed and walked off, he just walked straight past me and through another door. I stayed where I was because there was nowhere to sit, until eventually he came back, walked past me again, and finally nodded, 'On the floor, baby.'

I couldn't believe he was talking to me.

'If you could shift your ass that would help. Get the clothes on, then get on the floor. Or I suppose you want a line first?' He moved to a marble-topped counter and took out a gold credit card.

'No,' I said.

'There you go,' he offered.

Hadn't he heard me say no?

And then I posed with my gorgeous clothes on, my soft orange dress the colour of summer, and I thought, what am I doing? Why am I selling this calendar, these clothes? Why does it matter whether anyone buys this calendar, these clothes, or not? And I knew that what I was selling was myself; I was allowing myself to be sold. I hadn't made anything in my life; I hadn't produced anything of my own.

'Arrogance doesn't suit you, Kazi,' said Diane the next day. We were in her office and she was sitting very erect at her table, for on her head was a bowler hat with a big silver clock balanced on the front and she didn't want it to fall off.

'Patrick was a dickhead,' I said.

'Yes, well. He's very well regarded. And he wants you again.'

'No.'

'Kazi, darling. You're not big enough to pick and choose. You did well last year, darling. But this is this year, OK?'

I didn't reply, I just stared at her; I had still not forgiven her for sending me to South Africa.

'I've got something here that *pays*, darling.' She held up a catalogue, a thin one with a curling front page, and waved it in the air. And I thought, I was on the cover of *iD* magazine, I've been in *Elle*, I've worked Paris and Milan, and this is all you can give me?

Diane might not like it, but I was feeling arrogant. I didn't want to do as I was told. I had wanted to become a model to prove something, and this was when I saw that this was exactly why my mother had put me in beauty contests, to prove something. That was what we models all seemed to be doing, proving to somebody or other that we were worthy, that our worthiness was in our beauty. We competed with each other for love.

'So you'll think about it?' Diane asked, making it sound like a statement.

The door opened suddenly and a man put his head in. 'Oh, sorry!'

'Darling,' Diane crooned. 'Come in, come in! This is Kazi,' she pointed at me on the chair.

'We've met,' said the man.

And then I saw who it was; it was the man from the BBC green room. It was Phil. He wasn't a technician at all, he was a photographer.

'Have you indeed?' asked Diane.

Phil beamed, took off his Walkman and let it hang around his neck and then he shook my hand and his fingers were warm and dry, his nails were as beautifully formed as short square shells. And for a second it was as if he was saying, it's just you and me, shake my hand and it will be just you and me. And I liked his shirt because it was a tight red and white print and I liked the way it was unbuttoned at the neck and rolled up at the sleeves. I could see his muscles; see their existence beneath the cotton on his arms.

Chapter Twenty-Nine

'Why don't you call him?' Abu asked. We were sitting in the living room watching the *Krypton Factor*, waiting for the intelligence test which was Abu's favourite part.

'If he wanted to he'd call me,' I said.

'But how does he know you like him? If you don't call him then how will he know?' Abu was trying to be patient but I could see she was getting annoyed. She didn't agonise over things the way I did, she just did them. 'You give off this thing, you know, Kazi. This, I'm a model, don't touch me.'

'He's probably got a girlfriend.'

'Well, why don't you find out? Shshs! I want to watch this bit.'

So I decided that Abu was right; if I wanted something or someone then I should go after it, not wait to be asked. I got Phil's number from Diane and I called. But the moment I dialled his number I started quivering. What if he just hung up on me? What if he wasn't interested at all? What if he said, you must be kidding?

'Hi,' I said, as businesslike as I could. 'Is this Phil?'

'Yes,' he said cautiously, and I could hear the sound of people laughing in the background.

'This is Kazi. We met . . .'

'Oh, hi Kazi. So, how's things? Just a minute, I'll move somewhere quieter ...'

I smiled to myself, that I hadn't had to remind him who I was.

'Is this something to do with Top Girls?' he asked.

'No.'

'Thank God, because that Diane's a handful, isn't she? So, what can I do you for?'

'I was wondering,' I said, 'I need some new photos for my portfolio, d'you know anyone?' I wanted to ask him to take them but at the last moment I panicked. He must be able to see through me, I thought, he must know if I needed new photos then the agency would get them done. He must be able to see that this was a set up.

'Let me see,' he said thoughtfully. 'It depends on what you want. Sorry, what? I can't hear that well, there's lots of ...'

'Are you at a party?'

'No,' he laughed. 'This is my mum's.'

'I've called you at your mum's? This was the number Diane gave me.'

'That's OK, it's the one I give out. But it's always noisy here, and my sister's just turned up and she's got three kids.'

'Oh,' I said, and I felt tight with envy. He had a family, he had a mother and a sister and he could just pop in on them like that. And they must *like* each other; they must actually get pleasure from being with each other for I could still hear the sound of laughter.

'Have you got any nieces or nephews?'

'Yes,' I said, and then wished I hadn't. When people in the profession asked me personal questions I avoided answering them. I couldn't understand how other models met up once for a shoot and unburdened themselves of everything about their lives.

'Yes?' prompted Phil.

'My brother has a daughter called Candy,' I sighed. 'But I've never met her.'

'That's sad,' Phil said, and I could tell that he was holding the phone right near his mouth now for his voice was close and a little muffled.

'Well, I haven't been back, you see. I haven't been back to Botswana for years.'

'How long?'

I had to think, I had to go back in my mind over arriving at Heathrow, staying in Wembley, going to Mull and my time in the castle, and then coming down to London and starting over again. 'I left in 1985. And I just haven't been able to get back.' It sounded weak, it sounded like an excuse, but I couldn't say my family didn't want to speak to me anymore. I was too ashamed, too saddened to tell anyone. 'And my brother's had another child now, a boy.' I tried to keep my voice light but Abu had just told me the news and once again I felt left out. I had written to my mother and to Isaac at once; the moment I had heard about Bulldog I wrote that I was planning a trip, that I was coming within a few months and would that be good? But as yet I had had no reply. And I told myself, if they don't reply then that's it, because they don't want me, they don't even want me as an aunty for those children. I held the phone so hard against my head that my ear began to pound.

'So,' Phil said, as if reminding me what we were supposed to be talking about, 'I have a friend in south London. He's good, you'll like him.'

But I want *you*, I wanted to say.

'I'll get you his number.'

'Or we could meet,' I said very hurriedly. 'We could meet and you can give it to me then.'

'Is this a date?' Phil asked, and I could hear he was smiling.

Phil suggested we meet on Primrose Hill and for once I didn't think so much about what I was going to wear; I changed my mind only twice. But as I walked up the hill I began to worry that I had made a mistake. I had arranged this date; I was the one who had forced it out of him. And yet maybe the person I thought he was, or could be, wasn't right at all.

It had been three years since I'd last seen Craig. Celia had sent some of my things down from the castle and enclosed a short note saying Craig had left for Zimbabwe and I'd thought, what about our marriage, what am I going to do about that?

There hadn't been anyone in my life since Craig and I'd been determined not to make such a mistake again. I was too busy for relationships, I often insisted, echoing what the other girls said, but I was lying.

It was hot that day; at the bottom of the hill lay a white haze of heat and on the top of the hill the air seemed to shimmy before me. I walked up the pathway, passing people just setting out picnics on the grass, marking out football goals with hurriedly removed t-shirts. I got to the top and looked down on London and on the aviary of London Zoo. At least the birds had a little space to fly in; at least they could feel the sun even if they were still trapped inside.

I looked around for Phil and saw him at once, sitting with his back to me on a wooden bench. And my heart sank; he was shorter than I remembered, he looked slumped.

Quickly I looked around, trying to work out whether I could get back down the hill before he turned and saw me. Or could I cut off further to the right, would that be a better way to disappear? But it was too late, he had turned. And then I saw it was a man in his fifties and he had a dog with him and it was not Phil at all. The man didn't even look like Phil; there was no resemblance at all. Phil was sitting on the slope of the hill, on the grass in a patch of shade, his Walkman on his ears, his head back and his eyes closed.

'Hi!' I said, coming up, ridiculously happy about the mistake over the other man.

And Phil must have caught my enthusiasm because he opened his eyes and smiled and then he shifted as if to make space for me, although it was a big patch of shade and there was plenty of room. And I thought, he is one of these English people who doesn't like to touch, he's not even going to touch to say hello. So I bent down and I kissed him on the cheek the way models did with each other.

327

Phil looked surprised. 'How's your day been?' he asked, as if we always met like this, on a hill, to see how we were.

I sat down and put my legs out in front of me on the grass that was cool and prickly under the tree. 'Good,' I said. 'Good and getting better.'

Phil smiled and I wondered what he was reading into my words and what I wanted him to read into them.

'I love this park,' he said, taking his eyes from mine. 'It's posh, but I love some of the trees. I've been taking photos every month for a year, this is my last month. See that tree over there? The oak?'

'Which one is the oak?' I asked, but really I was looking at Phil and at a triangle of flesh that was his stomach, just visible where a button had come undone.

Phil looked surprised again. 'Very thick trunk, quite spread out leaves. It's the tallest of those three trees there. I've been taking a picture of that one on the last day of every month for a year. At the same time of day,' and he shrugged. 'Does that sound a bit stupid? I thought it was a really good idea at the time.' And he burst out laughing. 'But it's clouds that really get me.'

'Clouds?' I asked.

'Yeah, it's real daydreamers' stuff, isn't it? I like their drama.'

I looked up at the sky now, searching for clouds.

'Wouldn't it be dull without them?' asked Phil.

'I suppose so.' I thought perhaps he was a little mad, but then my eyes fixed on a small puff of cloud far over near the horizon and I began to watch it move.

328

'That's cumulus,' said Phil. 'A really bubbly, fair weather cloud . . . Not to be confused with . . .' He shifted on the grass and smiled. 'You must think I'm a right nutter. But don't you love the way we're in the middle of one of the busiest cities in the world and here we are in a patch of green? You can't even hear a car.'

And I listened and it was true.

'Where I come from,' I said at last, 'it's like this all the time. I mean, you don't have to leave home to be surrounded by silence.'

And Phil didn't say anything and I didn't say anything, but I had heard my voice and I had heard the sound of my own sadness. I was glad he didn't ask me about this, that he wasn't going to start firing off questions, that he would leave me to talk if I wanted.

We sat there for an hour or more, and then we walked down the hill and across into Regent's Park. As we walked along a wide path, bordered on either side with white urns bursting with red and yellow flowers and new trees planted exact distances apart, I felt an air of contentment, the contentment of a summer's day in England. People had enough space to sit and play, they had ice creams and cool boxes, they had balls and newspapers. No one was shouting at each other, no one was fighting. It was as if time had been turned down, as if it had been slowed down so that people could just be people and enjoy the sun.

We appeared to leave the park then, but by just crossing a road we came to another part and we walked over a bridge and by a pond where the trees hung down like green mops that someone had forgotten to rinse out. In the middle of the pond was a massive eagle about to pierce itself, beak first, into the water. It was only when we got nearer that I saw it was a sculpture. But my senses were heightened; I seemed to see possibilities all around me.

'Shall we go and get a drink?' I asked at last, and all the way I was thinking, can I touch you? Can I put my hand on your chin and hold your face?

Then we went to a café where two young girls asked for an autograph and their mothers whispered about me as they sat drinking cappuccino. And I felt as if I'd walked into a previous life, that my identity as a model had happened years ago.

Chapter Thirty

There are times in a life when you meet the right person and I knew this person was right because of his smell. I smelt him first on the grass on the hill that day; it sort of came at me as I was redoing the laces on my pink Converse. It was not a smell of perfume, or of clothes, or of shampoo. It was more like he had washed himself with soap that had nothing in it, that was just soap without anything added. So that behind the clean smell there was smell that was just his, that was just Phil. I thought perhaps it was soil, warm soil after rain, or perhaps the soil you find on a potato after you pull it from the earth.

A smell can be addictive; even though you can't pinpoint it and even though you can't quite describe it, you can believe you need that smell just to get through a day, just to survive.

The day after we met on Primrose Hill I spent lazing around. I couldn't concentrate on anything. I didn't return a call from Diane, I lost track during a conversation with Abu, I rang the doctor's to make an appointment, forgetting it was Thursday afternoon and they were closed, I made food because it was lunchtime but then I just stared at it.

'You look nice today, what are you using on your cheeks?' asked Sue. She was in our living room, her trolley open, going through her supplies on the way to a shoot.

I touched my cheeks as if to find out what might be on them.

'Hello? Kazi? Anyone there?'

And I started smiling over nothing at all.

'Has she met someone?' Sue asked as Abu came in.

Abu looked puzzled. She was on her way to class with a rucksack full of books in one hand and I could see her mind was on the assignment she had been doing until late the night before.

'Well look at her with that silly grin on her face!' said Sue. 'She's met a bloke, hasn't she?'

So Abu looked at me and there was something hurt in her face and I knew it was because I should have told her I'd met Phil.

'So you rang him?' Abu asked, and she put her rucksack down.

'Who is *him*?' asked Sue.

'He's a photographer.' Abu went to the TV and put it on as though she couldn't care less.

Sue groaned. 'You're not going out with a photographer?'

'He's a nice one,' I said.

'You're mad, Kazi. Photographers are the worst. I should know, I've slept with enough of them. Beware men with big lenses. Talk about fucking egos.'

Abu looked disapproving.

'So,' said Sue, stuffing her make-up back into the trolley. 'When did you see him?'

'Yesterday.'

'What did you do?'

'Oh, we went to the park, to Primrose Hill.'

'Not an expensive date then?' Sue laughed. She squatted down by her bag and zipped it shut.

'He takes pictures of trees,' I said. 'And clouds.'

'*Clouds*?' Sue stared at me.

I shrugged, embarrassed.

'So what's he like? Is he tall? Nice body? Nice bum?'

'I didn't really notice.'

'Don't get coy on me! How could you not notice a bum? So when are you seeing him again?'

Now I felt nervous, because I didn't know. And now I felt stupid too, that Sue was teasing me over someone I might not even meet again.

'He hasn't called you?' asked Sue.

I shrugged. 'I'll call him.'

'You can't!'

'Why not?'

'You don't want him to think you're too keen.'

I got up, Sue was making me confused.

'Can't stop thinking about him?' she asked sympathetically.

'Yeah.'

'Yeah,' said Sue. 'It can make you really self-obsessed, fancying someone.'

'She's already self-obsessed,' said Abu.

I looked at her as she stood there by the TV, unable to believe what she'd just said. Abu was never mean, she didn't bitch about people the way Sue did. Then I laughed because maybe she was joking. But Abu wasn't even looking at me; she was staring now at something out of the window so I could only see her profile, and it looked hard and made me think of my mother.

'Of course she's self-obsessed, she's a model!' said Sue.

But Abu didn't smile; she just kept on staring out of the window and her body as she stood there was rigid like she was holding herself in.

'What do you mean, *tsala ya me*, I'm self-obsessed?' I worded it carefully; I worded it so that Abu knew I was talking to her as a friend.

'Well,' she said at last, 'you think about yourself all the time. You're the centre of your own universe, all you think about is how other people see you. Do you look good? Have you got the right clothes on? How should you do your hair? What about the rest of us?'

'Don't be so jealous,' said Sue mildly.

'I'm not jealous,' spat Abu and she turned to me now and put her hands on her hips. 'You need to think about other people once in a while, *mosadi*. You've turned into an English woman.'

'Thanks very much,' said Sue.

'What do you mean?' I asked.

'I mean,' said Abu, 'that you think about yourself first, you think about money, you think about fame. It's me, me, me. Look at you! You never even *think* about where you come from.'

'Fuck off,' I muttered.

'You see?' Abu said, and she picked up her rucksack and went to the door.

'That's not fair,' I called after her. 'You know about everything at home, you *know* I'm the one who's been writing; they're the ones who have never replied, they're the ones who have cut me from their lives. It's not like I don't want to go back.'

'Isn't it?' Abu said. And she left.

When both Sue and Abu had gone I called Phil. If he didn't like me then he didn't like me, but I wasn't going to wait to find out. We met again at Regent's Park and again it was a sunny day, full of people slowed down by the heat, stopping to point out flowers on the grass or ducks on the boating lake as if they had never seen flowers or ducks before. And as we walked I could feel an electricity between us, like something was at once joining us together and keeping us apart. And I thought, to hell with Abu. She can go back home, but why should I when no one wanted me there?

When Phil had to leave to go to work I kissed him once on the lips and then suddenly his body was right there against mine, and I could feel his hardness and I pulled him in so roughly that his glasses fell off onto the grass.

'I don't want to be a model anymore,' I said the next day. We were at the same café we had been at before.

'No?' Phil asked. He rested comfortably back in his seat, as if he were in no rush, as if he were happy to just sit.

'No. I don't think I ever wanted to be a model.'

'Well, you did well at it. There was a time when your face was all over the place.'

I looked at him. So he already knew about me? 'I think I've had enough now, I'm nearly twenty-seven.'

Phil laughed. 'Twenty-seven! You make it sound old.'

'Well, how old are you?'

'Thirty-two. Definitely old enough to settle down. Mum keeps on asking me when she can wear her hat.'

'What hat?'

'You know, a hat for a wedding. Anyway,' he sat up a little on the chair then, as if regretting what he'd said, 'what about the modelling?'

'I was sort of pushed into it,' I said. 'Ever since I was little. It was all about proving something. Oh, I don't know how to explain it ...' I stopped and looked out of the window and when I turned back to Phil he was sitting in exactly the same pose, waiting, listening.

But I didn't want to say anything else, because then I saw I was looking at Phil as a way out, as if meeting him was an excuse to do something new. That's what I'd done with Craig. Why did I see men in this way, why couldn't I be the one who changed my life?

Then we both watched as a woman and a small boy came into the café and the boy had chocolate ice cream all round his mouth and he was licking intently on a naked wooden lolly stick as if not realising the ice cream had gone.

'Ahh,' said Phil, looking at the boy and beaming.

When we went to see Phil's parents his father opened the door, a thick glass door which had a chiming bell attached, and gave me a kiss.

'Come in, love,' he said. And then he said something

else, but I didn't catch it because we were ushered through the house and into the garden and it was full of people. I could see the woman with the yellow velour tracksuit was Phil's mum, that the young woman with straight black hair had to be his sister, that the children were all his nieces and nephews. And I realised that I hadn't been in a family for years; I almost didn't know what to do.

'What would you like to drink, love?' asked Phil's dad, yelling in my ear. 'Doing well, son?' He put out an arm and held it on Phil's.

'Yeah, doing good, Dad.'

Then Phil's mum came and steered me inside saying she needed a hand, and I stood in the kitchen, taking peeks into the room next door because I could see a glass cabinet so similar to the one my mother had in Sehuba. And then for a second I could feel the scorching heat of a summer's day in Botswana, I could see the glint of the sun on the glass-fronted cabinet which held my beauty pageant shoes, and I could see my mother sitting in the shade of the mulberry tree in our yard drinking tea.

Then I saw a pile of books and a hairbrush next to a table in the other room. The hairbrush had a heavy silver back and it took me a moment to think where I'd seen one before. Then I knew it was a hairbrush like our neighbour Marianne Krause used to have. I had never written to her, never thought about her much over the years, but when I had thought about her, I had seen her as she was when I left. Now I tried to add up the years, to think about how old she was now. I wondered if she was still wearing a white shirt tied up over her belly button.

'Just take this for me, love,' said Phil's mum, and she handed me a tray piled high with choc ices and I walked out into the garden with it and the children saw me and came running.

When I told Phil I was pregnant I was worried what he would say. I thought perhaps he would reject me like Craig had done, that maybe it would turn out he didn't want children at all. But when I came out of the bathroom one morning and showed him the kit I'd bought from the chemist he had tears in his eyes. 'That's all I've ever wanted in life,' he said.

Chapter Thirty-One

'You're not going to get much bigger, are you?' Sue asked, looking sideways at my tummy. We were sitting in the flat that Phil and I had rented six months ago; it was still quite empty inside. I didn't want to fill it up; I wanted everything to be just right. I was happy now; I had no need to worry about getting back to Botswana. Let them get on with their lives, I thought. I had Phil and soon I would have a baby.

'Big is good,' said Abu. She loved my pregnancy, it seemed to make her love me again, and she came over every day, sometimes bringing baby things she said she couldn't resist.

And Phil couldn't resist baby things either. While our living room and bedroom had very little in, the baby's room was getting crowded. He had made a cot of white painted wood, he had hung a mobile of suns and moons and clouds from the ceiling, he had two little jumpsuits that looked small enough for a doll. But I was fearful of the things he bought, I tried to tuck them away, putting the jumpsuits high up on a shelf so they couldn't be seen because I worried that it was bad luck to prepare for things this way.

'Of course big is good!' laughed Sue. 'Of course it is!'

But I could see she didn't believe this, that my fatness made her uncomfortable.

Diane had said that pregnancy would be the end of my career, but she was wrong. Instead it was as if no one had ever thought of photographing a pregnant model before until I suggested it. And now when I was photographed I had something to show, something that I had made. Look at my belly! I wanted to say, I made this myself! And those shots caused some controversy; you weren't supposed to be glamorous when you were pregnant, you weren't supposed to show bare breasts and bare stomachs in this way. I was criticised for sexualising pregnancy, for having no morals, for having no shame, but it was a decision I made myself.

'I think she looks great,' Abu said, looking at Sue, making her point.

I gave birth to Maya on a June day, one of the hottest days of the year. When the pains started Phil and I rushed to hospital to find the place was being knocked down. Normally the hospital looked like an office block, today it looked like a demolition site. I got out of the car to see three men in hard hats and yellow jackets standing dwarfed next to a digger; the air was full of dust, the land was trembling.

Once inside, the midwife gave me two paracetamol and told me to try and relax. 'We're flat out at the minute,' she said. 'Can you hold on for a while?'

I stared at the pink cap she wore on her head; it looked as if she was expecting rain.

The room was white, it was so white that it didn't

seem real, and everything was metal and sharp, from the corners of the trolley on wheels to the gleaming poles with machines on top. Then I felt a dull breeze and I saw a window was open and all around the window were daddy long legs flitting around on their spindly limbs.

It was several hours later that the midwife came back and offered me gas and air, and when Phil helped to put the mouthpiece between my lips I felt I was going underwater diving.

'You can have it when you want,' said the midwife.

And so I sucked away until I grew light headed and until my hand just flopped from my face and the mouthpiece fell down. Then the midwife started fiddling and the next thing I knew my waters had gushed out; they exploded over Phil and I started laughing, even with the contractions, I started laughing at the look on his face.

'Make sure you masturbate between your contractions,' said the midwife encouragingly.

'What?' I said, pulling on the gas and air. I hissed at Phil, 'She wants me to masturbate between the contractions.'

Phil began giggling.

'Rest,' said the midwife looking alarmed. 'I said *rest* between your contractions.'

And then in between the laughing I was shouting and I was still shouting when a consultant came in, and he came forward crouching a little like a photographer might and I could see he was heading for my ugly green gown.

And I didn't want him anywhere near me, he hadn't even introduced himself.

'Keep your fucking hands to yourself!'

The consultant stopped, his hands twitching.

And another contraction came and I shut my eyes and reached out for the nearest thing to grab and I grabbed and it was soft and when I opened my eyes I saw I had grabbed hold of the midwife's breast. And then I looked at Phil and I saw this line of blood that spurted over his face, across the walls, on the floor. It flew around the room like water from a hosepipe, only it was red and it came from me. And then Maya was born and her hair was sticking up in fright.

My room was full of flowers and I couldn't decide which were the most beautiful, it was as if a garden had come inside.

'What will you call your baby?' asked a new midwife the next morning.

I looked at Phil; he was asleep on the chair next to the bed, his glasses down upon the end of his nose, his Walkman on his lap.

'Maya,' I said softly.

'That's nice,' the midwife nodded.

'It means, she has come.' I was about to add that it was a Shiyeyi name, but I stopped myself because what did an English midwife know about Shiyeyi? I had thought about names a lot, I wanted our child to have a name from home, but then I had thought about the old names and I had realised how sad they were. Why did my people have such sad names? Why were the girls and women of my people called Kushanda, to suffer, or Mishwezi, tears, or Ncapa, the rejected one? Why were they called Saywa, the one who is hated, or Narefo, the mother of death? Those were the names I had grown up with and now, in England, it had taken me a long time to remember them and even longer to remember what they meant. So I called her Maya, she has come. Because I had been waiting for her for years.

Then Phil's family came to the hospital and I pretended they were mine, that this jolly woman with the pink track-suit on was my mother, that this man with a big bag of grapes and an instamatic camera round his neck was my father. And Phil got onto the bed with me and his father took a picture and I smiled like I had never smiled before.

'Maaaam!' Maya shouts from upstairs. 'I'm ready!' She is waiting to go to school, wearing a ra ra skirt as pink as the tulips I can see growing in the pots on the windowsill of the house that backs onto ours. I can see the second-storey window is wide open and I can hear the muffled sound of a theme tune on the TV, but the pigeons are louder, the pigeons that sound like the African Mourning Dove, are far louder than the TV. I look down into the garden at the back and I can see someone has taken half of their furniture and put it outside under a tree that is so heavy with white blossom it looks like snow. The English really do spring clean at springtime.

'What does *cling* mean?' Maya asks. She comes into the kitchen, holding one of her reading books. She has brushed her hair too hard; she is desperate to turn it into straight hair like Barbie's, but instead it looks wild around her face.

'Is it in one of your books?'

'Mum! What does cling *mean*?'

'Well, it means when you sort of hang on to something. Like, if you say, stop clinging on to me then ...' But I can see I've lost Maya's interest, she wants short answers, quick explanations, unlike Joe who likes stories and it doesn't matter to him whether they make sense or not. But however dissimilar they are in character, they are both so competitive. Yesterday Maya said, 'I was born the natural way, wasn't I, Mum?' And although Joe didn't understand what this meant, he understood the challenge in his sister's voice so he said, 'I was too, wasn't I, Mum?' And I told him he was born by Caesarean and I showed him the scar again thinking that would impress him, but Maya said, 'That's not natural. I was born the natural way. And I was born first.'

Maya busily puts her reading books into her school bag. 'And,' she says as if we are continuing a discussion, 'why don't people have whiskers?'

When I say I don't know she scowls; she thinks I'm laughing at her. Sometimes I don't know how to handle her questions; some of them are just unanswerable. Why does sunshine shine on us? How do clouds know it's daytime? Why do lamp posts stand there? What is water made from? I wish Abu were here, she's good at Maya's questions. But Abu is doing her PhD now and she's too busy to come round.

'What are you doing at school today?' I ask, and as I

344

ask I'm doing ten other things, I'm getting Joe's shoes ready and I'm turning off the lights in the kitchen and I'm picking up my bag and I'm seeing how much credit I have on my mobile. I'm doing so many things at once I could be running a multi-national company not just getting two kids ready to go out.

Suddenly I think of yesterday. I was at Tescos on my own and I was in the queue feeling I had forgotten something because normally I'm looking to see where Maya and Joe are, that they're not taking sweets down from the shelf that the shop puts right at child level. The queue was long but I wasn't in a hurry because I was alone and I was enjoying listening to the two girls in front of me, they were schoolgirls on their lunch break and they had taken so much time with their hair and clothes, copying styles you see in the new women's magazines and adapting them to their own. Now they were chatting about what to do on Saturday and they were eyeing up another group of girls just coming into the shop. And I thought of my schoolgirl days and how we would hang around in the sandy mall of Maun thinking we were so special, checking each other out. And then a man in a Tescos apron touched me by the elbow.

'Madam,' he said, steering me lightly forward, around the girls and towards another till that was just opening.

The girls looked at me, furious. They had been in front of me.

'There you go, madam,' said the man as he delivered me to the till.

And I thought, who is he calling madam? All the time

345

I'd been seeing myself as one of the chattering girls, I'd been thinking about how a belly button ring would look and whether it would hurt to get it done and if I should go for silver or gold. Now this man, this boy, had made me see I was heading for middle age. I was thirty-three and I wasn't a chattering girl anymore.

'Where's Dad?' asks Maya.

'He's at work.'

'Why?'

'You know why.' I'm getting annoyed now. Ever since Phil set up his own studio he's there day and night; he may as well live there. And he always seems to be waiting on the results of a big contract; he's up for a job now but I can't remember which one because I'm just a useless middle-aged madam who is too weak to stand in line at Tescos. Phil was going to take Joe with him because Joe will behave himself in the studio while Maya will not. Sometimes I think Maya and me are the problem ones in this family.

I go to the wall and look at my calendar and see it's a whole week before the *Parenting* magazine shoot. Diane wants Maya to be photographed too, she wants us to do a celebrity mother and daughter feature and I've refused. They aren't paying much anyway, but however many times I say I've given up modelling I can't think what else to do.

'Here's your coat,' I tell Maya, handing her a blue rain jacket.

'I'm not wearing that!' and she holds her hands stubbornly across her chest.

'Why on earth not?'

'It's blue!' she wails.

'And so?'

'It's for boys!'

'There's no such thing as for boys,' I say, but there is, there are boy things and girl things, and we live in the UK so we all know that. I don't want her to worry so much about what she looks like, but she does. Last week I saw her standing in the bathroom and she had her back to the mirror and was twisting her body round so she could see how her bum looked from behind, just like me.

'Vanity thy name is woman,' Phil said, coming into the bathroom looking for something. As he came in Maya went out.

'It's not vanity,' I said.

'Well what is it then?'

I could hear Maya's footsteps stop, feel her hesitating on the landing and then finally setting off downstairs.

'It's fear,' I said. 'It's fear about how we look because people are always looking at us! How many times do people tell Maya she's beautiful? Almost every day! You know that. And I've got that fear too, that fear about how I look, and why do you think that is?'

Phil took the nail clippers from next to the sink. He didn't like conflict; he didn't like it when I got angry.

But I was furious; I could feel anger filling me like adrenaline. 'If you're always taught to think about how you look, then is that vanity? It's not, it's fear. If you're put in beauty contests from the age of five, how does that work? What do you think that does to you? And if I didn't care how I looked and if I didn't work hard and

347

get paid good money, and manage to get a mortgage on a flat ... then it pays to be vain, doesn't it?'

I could see Phil stiffening and I could hear I wasn't making any sense.

'If you say so,' he mumbled. 'You're the model.'

'Men work, don't they, Mum?' asks Maya. She thinks she's going to be able to distract me from the raincoat, that she'll get away with not wearing it.

'And women work,' I say.

'And men like football, don't they, Mum?'

'Goal!' shouts Joe from the living room.

Then the phone rings and Maya runs for it. I stay in the kitchen but sharpen my ears to hear who it is. Maya comes back looking puzzled. 'It's someone funny on the phone.'

So I get up with a sigh and go into the other room. 'Hello?'

'*Ee, Mosadi.*'

My heart flips and my chest feels like it's stinging. It's not Abu, she is the only one who speaks Setswana to me. And it's a man.

'*Oa re eng?*' the man laughs and his voice buzzes down the line.

I know that voice; somewhere inside me I know that voice.

'*Ga o nkitse?*'

Don't I know him? But how can I know him, he hasn't said who he is. Maya comes in; she's sensed something odd is happening.

'*Ke mang?*' I ask sharply.

'It's me, sis. It's your brother.'

BOOK SEVEN
Candy

Chapter Thirty-Two

I'm sitting on the floor next to my grandmother's mattress and we are all in a row with our backs against the wall, my grandmother and Wanga and me. My grandmother's black cycling shorts are hanging over the edge of the chair in the corner of the room, but I don't think she will be wearing them again because she says they gave her a rash. My grandmother came home from the clinic last night and she says it was a horrible place and she will not be going back even if someone was to try and carry her there. She's drinking water now like she's really thirsty and I'm watching her eyelids carefully in case they do that droopy thing again. I didn't sleep while my grandmother was away.

'Hey it is hot,' says my grandmother. '*Batho ba modimo!*' and she waves her cup of water.

'Winter is coming,' says Wanga.

'Oh, winter is far away, we have a long time to put up with this suffering,' says my grandmother.

Wanga laughs. 'Winter is coming.' She smooths her hand down across one of her legs which she usually says is sore and is troubling her. But she doesn't say it's sore today, because if she does then my grandmother will tell us all about the clinic again. They put needles in her in the clinic, they just jabbed them right into her buttocks,

351

and she says her heart was beating so fast she thought she would die. My grandmother doesn't trust modern doctors.

Under the chair, beneath my grandmother's black cycling shorts, are a pile of party plates, very soft paper plates that bend in the middle when you put food on them. But these plates are still covered in wrapping because we never even got the chance to use them at the party. After they took my grandmother off in the ambulance then no one really felt like having a party anymore. Everyone left very quickly after that, and Petra Krause with her hair like fire gave a lot of people a lift. We still have some food left from the party, even though the doctor and the headmaster and MaNeo tried to eat as much as they could. I have some of it in my room; I have covered the birthday cake with a towel. I wanted to keep it nice for my grandmother but the icing on the top has slid off the sponge now and I've been eating it in little bits, enjoying the chocolate as it sinks down my throat.

I haven't done anything since my grandmother went to the clinic; our general trading store was closed so I didn't have to go there and my father forgot all about my going to school. I don't want to go to school anyway because Mary and her friends have been spreading stories about my family and saying my grandmother was bewitched, and if she isn't bewitched then she has Aids and that's why she collapsed and went to the clinic. And I know what else Mary and the others are saying, that these things are the same, that someone is behind this, someone who doesn't like us, because why did the hyena take the child at our camp and why was it my grandmother who collapsed? They are both in our family, my uncle Leapile's child who was taken by the hyena and my grandmother. Now I feel that I will be next.

'Where's the *tea*?' my grandmother shouts, and she pushes herself away from the wall and fumbles around on the mattress for her stick. 'Candy we, go and see what's happened to the tea.'

But I don't get up because I can hear the maid outside and I can hear that she is coming now. I know my grandmother would rather take Coke than tea but my father says he's not going to allow that anymore.

I'm supposed to be doing the floor today, it is too dusty inside my grandmother's room, but if I do the floor then everyone will have to move out of the room and it doesn't look like my grandmother is going anywhere. She is behaving like she has been away for a very long time and not just three days. 'Look at the grass!' she said when she came back from the clinic last night, as if she cannot remember that it rained just before the party and that that grass has been busily growing since then.

The maid comes in with the tea and now the door is open I can hear other things outside. I can hear children setting off for school and I can hear the jangle jangle of cow bells. Then I hear Bulldog shouting that he doesn't want to go to school, he wants to stay in the mulberry tree, and my mother shouts back that she will beat him if this goes on and he knows she is late and has to go to Gumare. But she doesn't bother me because I'm not going to school, my grandmother needs me here. And

I'm really pleased about this because this is what my father told my grandmother last night: Aunty Kazi is coming. Aunty Kazi is coming all the way from the UK, and when she does I want to know everything that goes on.

I am going to take my Aunty Kazi all around Sehuba and show her to everyone because I haven't got any aunties here. I have uncles but my mother's sisters don't live here anymore and I want an aunty like my friend Mary has because you can tell things to your aunty that you can't tell anyone else.

I get up and squat down by the tray the maid has brought and I pour my grandmother's tea from the teapot that is brown like a palm nut. And I say, 'Is she very beautiful, Aunty Kazi?'

I don't turn from the teapot but I know my grandmother has her lips puffed out; I'm only brave enough to ask her this question when I have my back to her.

'Oh she is so beautiful!' says Wanga at once. 'Put in another sugar,' she tells me as I begin on her tea.

'You didn't always think she was,' objects my grandmother.

'Me?' says Wanga, and she taps herself on the chest. 'Are you saying I didn't always think she was beautiful?'

'*Ee*,' my grandmother says, and she's chuckling now. 'I'm talking about you.'

'Well!' Wanga takes her tea and blows on it a few times. 'Who was the one who first told you about the beauty contests?'

My grandmother chuckles some more and Wanga

joins in and then she moves her legs and she knocks over a packet of rice that I forgot about and left on the floor.

'*Hela*, you were always a clumsy one,' says my grandmother, and she tells me to clear up the mess.

'Me, clumsy?' says Wanga. 'Who was it who tripped me over the very first day we met?'

'Tripped?' says my grandmother. 'You're saying I tripped you? It was you who fell and me who helped you up!'

'I only fell,' says Wanga, 'because you put out your great big foot and that tripped me over.'

'And how is Abu?' says my grandmother when she's finished chuckling.

'She called last night like she does every week,' says Wanga, and her face is serious now. 'She has her final exams soon and then she'll come back with her PhD. But whether she'll come back here, to Sehuba ...'

My grandmother nods in sympathy. 'There isn't much for young people here. And she'll be used to the English ways. These children just leave us as soon as they can.'

My grandmother and Wanga drink their tea and they go all quiet. Then my grandmother gets all fidgety with her legs. 'What time is it?' she asks. My grandmother never asks what time it is, but she wants to know the time now because my father said he would be back with Aunty Kazi at five o'clock. He rang Aunty Kazi in the UK when my grandmother was in the clinic and now she's coming back. After all these years I've been thinking about her and now I am going to see her at last.

I can't wait to see what will happen when my Aunty

Kazi arrives, because ever since I was small my grandmother has been telling me that her daughter Kazi has forsaken her, but now she is coming. It makes me feel itchy all over. I wonder what she will bring with her? I've been thinking about this at night when I don't sleep; I think that if I think about something nice then I won't have my bad dreams. And just in case I have my bad dreams and someone bewitches me in my sleep, I have stayed awake to be safe. I think the spirit in the attic is back as well, I heard some funny sounds from there last night and I was too afraid to go and look. I think I should tell my father about this because perhaps Aunty Kazi will sleep in the attic like she used to and so she needs to know there is a spirit in there.

I pour myself a cup of tea and then I take it with me. I want to go to my room and sneak some more cake and look at the pictures of Aunty Kazi that my father threw out, and especially my favourite which is when she is with an elephant and she looks very small but very proud.

'Where's your father?' my grandmother asks as I get to the door.

'*Mma*?'

'Wake up, child! Is there something wrong with your ears, I said where's your father?'

I feel my face get hot because I don't like it when my grandmother scolds me. And she knows where my father has gone; he's gone to Maun to get Aunty Kazi, has she forgotten that?

'How are things at the camp?' asks Wanga.

'*Hela*,' says my grandmother, shaking her head.

And then they both shake their heads back and forth and back and forth. We mustn't talk about what happened in the camp and the hyena that took Leapile's boy, even though everyone else is talking about it and it was on the radio news again yesterday. On the news the man said that Leapile's son left his tent and everyone knows you shouldn't do that and so the hyena took him by the face and ate him all up.

My father says if we don't want to harm his reputation then we should keep our mouths shut about what happened and ignore the gossip as well. But I heard Bulldog talk about it and no one told him off.

I stop in the doorway and I make my voice very loud and clear. 'I'm going to get ready for my Aunty Kazi so that I look really nice.'

My grandmother splutters her tea all over the saucer and Wanga begins stroking her bad leg up and down and I leave to go and drink my tea. We might be waiting a long time, it will take my father a long time to get to Maun and back again.

Bulldog has come back from school and he wants food. He's lucky because I have made some nice soft *motogo* just like our mother makes, but she couldn't do it because she has gone to Gumare to see someone who needs help and I don't know when she will get back.

My mother left before she heard the news about Aunty Kazi and maybe it will make her happy when she hears it. Maybe it will make my father stop shouting at her.

I have been very busy today. I have gone all around our plot and I have inspected all our flowers and I have watered them with rain water. My favourite part of the plot is down where the banana trees are because when you get yourself in there, squeezing in between the trees, then it's cool and green and the leaves are so big they flap like elephant ears. I will show my Aunty Kazi this place; she will look very beautiful in here.

After watering the plants I did some cooking and I helped my grandmother to wash and prepare herself. She took a long time today and she complained about the water, that it wasn't hot enough, and she sent me back to heat some more. She is very grumbly today and she says she aches in the buttocks where the nurse injected her. Now she's sitting on a mat outside under the mulberry tree and she's grumbling to Wanga about the clinic and about Bulldog making noise with his friend down by the river and about winter being too far away. The grumbles are getting more and more until I think she's going to shout at someone, and then finally what we have been waiting for happens: my Aunty Kazi arrives.

We can hear my father's car from a long way away, and when it passes Lenny Krause's house next door then we can see the dust in the air and we can hear the wheels grinding on the sand. My father drives fast; he says you have to drive fast around here if you want to get anything done. When he pulls up at our gate I am ready, I am all ready to fly to him and my Aunty Kazi, and I'm happy because I'm wearing my special party dress again. But Bulldog beats me to it, he gets down to the gate and he opens it and my father roars in.

'This heat is killing me,' grumbles my grandmother.

And I want to jump up and down and shout, They're here! They're here!

Chapter Thirty-Three

I can't believe what I'm seeing; I can't believe that is my Aunty Kazi. I see her get out of the car but I don't think it's her; I think it's someone else. I have seen her pictures in the magazines but still I thought she would look like my father, like him only a woman. But I know it must be her because she's the only woman getting out of the car. And she is wearing trousers! My Aunty Kazi is wearing trousers. If she's wearing trousers then maybe I can wear mine too. I can't wait to see what my grandmother will say.

My Aunty Kazi leaves the car and as she leaves she looks back at my father, who is her brother, but he's leaning on the bonnet of the car speaking on his cell phone and he has one finger in his ear and he's frowning.

'They are here,' I tell my grandmother, and now I'm feeling really, really shy and I make myself like a cat and get down close next to her on the mat under the mulberry tree. But my grandmother's fidgeting, she moves on the mat and her knee knocks me and so I have to shift myself to the edge. And as I watch my Aunty Kazi and the man and the two children coming across the grass I know for certain that nothing will ever be the same around here. They are our family and look at them! What sort of people are they?

'Is there something wrong with her legs?' my grand-mother says to Wanga, and I look at my Aunty Kazi and I see that she is walking like a flamingo. She is very thin so she must have been really, really ill and her jeans are very tight so her legs look like pipes. She has a very beautiful handbag on her shoulder and it is brown and white and I just know there are some good things in there. Even though she is walking quickly she seems to be walking very slowly, because I'm still watching her and she still hasn't reached me where I'm sitting feeling itchy under the mulberry tree.

'Hi!' she says, and she looks at us standing there and her eyes are moving very quickly.

My grandmother looks at Wanga in disbelief.

'*Dumelang Bomme,*' Aunty Kazi says then, and my grandmother nods, that is a better way to speak.

Aunty Kazi stumbles, she has caught her high heel on the edge of the mat and she puts out her hands. I think she is putting them out to stop herself from falling but then I see she wants to hug my grandmother but my grandmother folds her arms across her breasts so that Aunty Kazi's arms are just left hanging there. Then my grandmother unfolds her arms and she pulls me in next to her and I snuggle there and feel much better. I look up at my Aunty Kazi and the skin on her face has gone all tight. I like her lipstick; I like the way it's red like a mulberry that isn't ripe.

I look behind my Aunty and I see the man; he looks funny, he's all smiling and he's looking this way and that and I like him at once. And he has the two children with him, a little girl wearing a pink skirt that is pointy at the end and she has a hat on her head that is striped and makes me think of a sweet and she is talking really loud and really fast. Then the man stops and he goes back to the car and he takes something out with handles and wheels. He bends down and he kicks it with his foot and just like that it shoots out and I see it is some kind of a chair. Then he picks up the little boy who is wearing shorts and a t-shirt like the Sehuba football team only a different colour. The boy doesn't look as if he is really awake and the man puts him in that chair and pats him on the head. There must be something wrong with that boy that they have to put him in a thing like that.

When I look at my grandmother her face is wobbling and I watch her eyelids in case they are going to get droopy again. My Aunty Kazi bends down on the mat so her knees are on it and it looks as if she is begging. My grandmother moves a little and she takes Aunty Kazi's hand but she's not looking at her, she's looking down by the river where the grass is tall with all the rain. Then I'm happy because when I look up I can see a rain cloud and it is travelling quickly over the sky to us. It makes us very quiet, waiting for the rain cloud to come, and that's why no one is speaking.

'Hi!' says the man who is my Uncle Phil as he comes up and shakes my grandmother's hand, although first he tries to kiss her but she doesn't like that. 'I'm Kazi's partner, Phil.'

My grandmother looks at Aunty Kazi and removes her hand. 'Your husband?'

'No,' says Aunty Kazi.

'Great place,' says the man called Phil who is my uncle. 'Unbelievable the drive here,' he says, and he sits down on the sand like a woman. 'We saw ostriches on the way, didn't we, Joe?'

'And I saw them,' says the little girl.

'Bring a chair!' my grandmother tells me.

Aunty Kazi looks like she doesn't know what to do and she's still kneeling on the mat when I come back with the chair. I give it to Uncle Phil because men need chairs.

'How *are* you?' Aunty Kazi asks at last. She's looking at my grandmother like she's worried about her, but she looks annoyed too.

'Not too bad,' says my grandmother like she doesn't really want to talk about it, and she fiddles with her glasses like they are bothering her. She's been getting excited and grumbling all day because her daughter, my Aunty Kazi, is coming, but now she's not talking much at all.

'Kazi we,' says Wanga, and she leans forward and takes hold of my Aunty Kazi by the knee. 'How is my daughter Abu?'

'Oh, she's fine,' says Aunty Kazi, and she stops kneeling and sits down properly on the mat. 'I have a parcel from her, I'll get it in a minute. And she sends her love.'

Wanga smiles and hugs on her legs.

'So, how *are* you?' Aunty Kazi asks my grandmother again. I look from my Aunty Kazi to my grandmother; they are facing each other and although their complexions

363

are not the same, and my grandmother has cracks on her face and Aunty Kazi doesn't, their lips are just the same and they are both hunched in the shoulders. I wonder if I will look like Aunty Kazi when I'm older, if I can change my colour, and after that when I'm an elder I wonder if I will look like my grandmother. The leaves in the mulberry tree start to rustle, the wind is coming and it's bringing the rain.

'*Hela*,' my grandmother fidgets on the mat. 'My elbows are killing me, and I've got high blood, and at night I get so hot.'

'No,' says Aunty Kazi and she sighs, 'I meant with the collapse and everything. When Isaac rang he said you were in hospital?'

'She was in the clinic,' says Wanga, and my grandmother frowns at her.

'So we got here as soon as we could,' says Aunty Kazi. 'I was expecting to see you in bed or something. So are you fine now? What did the doctors say?'

'Doctors!' says my grandmother and she spits on the ground. 'Where's the *tea*?' she shouts.

'She looks fine to me,' says Aunty Kazi. I can hear her because I have followed her inside the house; we have finished our tea and she has come to find some sun cream for the children. The rain has gone, it didn't last long, and by the time we got up to go inside it had already stopped. Now it's hotter than it ever was.

'Hello, Candy!' says Uncle Phil. He says it in a very friendly way, only quite loudly because he wants Aunty

Kazi to know that I am here, that I have followed them up the steps to the attic.

'The way Isaac was talking you'd have thought she was on her death bed,' says Aunty Kazi, and I can tell by her breathing that she is lifting something. 'I can't believe he made it out like that. All these years without news! They didn't even tell me when the kids were born! Then suddenly, out of the blue, after God knows how many years, I get a call, I get summoned just like that. If we've come halfway across the world ...'

'Is this your room?' Uncle Phil says to me, and he steps away from the door in case I want to come in.

I shake my head but he is still looking at me as if expecting more, and I think, did my Aunty Kazi not know about me, does she mean no one told her when I was born? All this time I've been thinking about her and she didn't even know about me!

'It's a very nice room,' says Uncle Phil, and he's speaking very slowly. Perhaps he thinks I don't understand English, but I am not like Bulldog, I don't speak gibberish, I can speak it fine if I want to. I don't know why he thinks this is my room, but then he doesn't know I am not allowed up into the attic anymore.

'It used to be mine,' says Aunty Kazi. She thumps a suitcase on the bed; it's metal like a tin roof with hard sides. 'She hasn't even put clean sheets on,' she says.

'Come on, Kazi!' says Uncle Phil, and he laughs and I think he wants us all to laugh too.

I stand and watch while my Aunty Kazi takes the things out of her case; she doesn't do it very carefully, she just lifts out a big pile of things and I see colours that I haven't seen in clothes before, blues and greens that look as if something has been added to them, or perhaps taken away. I don't know what colour her t-shirt is, I don't know the name for that colour, but it looks like berries mixed with sour milk, and I can see the strap of her bra and it matches the t-shirt exactly. I can't stop looking at my Aunty Kazi's face because even though I look and look I can't find anything wrong with it. It is perfect; it is so perfect that I can't concentrate on what she's saying. She is more pale skinned than I thought she would be, even though I have seen her pictures in the magazines, and that is why she wants sun cream; she doesn't want to be black like me, and I wonder if she will give me some too.

I watch her unpack and it's like she doesn't know what is what or what is where. It's so hot up here and I can see some big spider webs on the ceiling. She opens another suitcase, it's a smaller one and it has pictures of three little girls on the side and the material is pink and so are the girls. This must be the girl's suitcase because as Aunty Kazi opens it all manner of clothes and books and toys come out. I wonder which of those clothes she will give me; my dream is to enter the competition we are having next month. The name of the contest is Miss HIV Stigma Free Beauty Contest. I don't have HIV and my grandmother and my mother and my father say I can't enter it, but I want to, if I just had something nice to wear, if I just had something from the UK.

'I'm going to check on Joe,' says Uncle Phil.

'I'll do it.'

'No, it's fine, you get yourself sorted and I'll go get him. He's probably still asleep, he could do with a sleep.'

My Uncle Phil seems like a very kind man, he seems like the kind of person that will volunteer to help you just like that. And then he puts his hand in his pocket and he takes out a small tube wrapped in green. 'Polo?'

I hang my head.

'Would you like a Polo? A sweet?'

And then I am sure he's the nicest man I've ever seen.

'Maybe she's not allowed them, Phil ... Where's the fucking sun cream?'

'Where's Maya?' he asks. 'Anyone seen Maya?'

I think he's embarrassed because of what Aunty Kazi just said, a bad word like that can get you thrashed at the Kgotla. I'm so shocked I'm going to pretend that I didn't hear her say that word; people in my family don't even know that I know that word.

'She is on the swing,' I say, and I point to the little window in the attic. We go to the window together, my Uncle Phil and me, and we look down over the branches of the mulberry tree and we can see Maya on the swing and her hat has fallen off and is on the ground and now it's wet.

'It's very beautiful here,' says my Uncle Phil. 'Those rain clouds were unbelievable! And that tree down there is just like a Van Gogh painting, isn't it, Kazi?'

'Huh?'

'You know, one of those swirly ones where the tree looks like some mad hairstyle.'

'Found it!' says Aunty Kazi.

When I get outside my grandmother asks me where I have been, she says the maid has disappeared and she needs some fresh tea. The mat is too damp to sit on so I have brought the tarpaulin.

'I was in the attic,' I say.

'She was with me,' adds Aunty Kazi because she has come outside now as well. 'God I'm exhausted, we didn't sleep at all on the plane, it's impossible with two kids running up and down the aisle the whole time.' The way she speaks Setswana is really strange, the words don't go together well and it is as if she is reading from a book, not talking to someone.

'She is not allowed in there,' says my grandmother.

'Where?'

'The attic.'

'Why not?' asks Aunty Kazi.

I sit down and I hunch myself up because you are not allowed to talk to my grandmother like that.

'Because she's not,' says my grandmother, but she doesn't seem angry with me and she pats the tarpaulin so that I will move closer to her. I don't know if she wants me to get the tea now or not and I look at Aunty Kazi still standing there and her skin is all tight again. In the mulberry tree the birds start squabbling. 'It is not a place for a child,' says my grandmother.

'Why not?' asks Aunty Kazi again. 'I was in that attic on my own for years.'

'Get your brother a chair,' says my grandmother, and I think she's speaking to me and I'm confused because

I don't even know where Bulldog is and anyway, he never sits in a chair. But then I see she's talking to Aunty Kazi and Aunty Kazi just looks at my grandmother as if she has never met her before. My father has come up from the car, but then he just walks straight past us and goes round the back of the house talking on his cell phone.

'Are those trousers of yours comfortable?' asks my grandmother. She stretches out her legs and she picks at one of her toes because it has a lump growing on it.

'Yes thank you,' says Aunty Kazi in English.

'It's a wonderful house,' says Uncle Phil as he comes out into the garden as well. 'Has this place changed much?'

'Fifteen years,' says Aunty Kazi. 'It's been fifteen years, of course it's changed!'

My grandmother tells me to go get the tea and to get it now. Then she asks Aunty Kazi another question: 'Is there no food in England?'

Aunty Kazi is about to say something, but then she sees what my grandmother means and I think she changes her mind. 'People like you thin in England.'

'What did she say?' asks Phil.

'England!' says my grandmother. 'I don't know why you ever had to go there.'

'*Ku yendinda ngu wu yani,*' says Aunty Kazi, and she snaps it out like that. 'That was what you always said.'

'What's going on?' asks Uncle Phil. He's looking from my grandmother to Aunty Kazi very quickly, like a chicken.

369

'*Ku yendinda ngu wu yani*,' repeats Aunty Kazi. 'To travel is to discover.'

'Is that a proverb?' asks Uncle Phil.

'I guess so, it's like a family motto.'

'It's true, isn't it, though, to travel is to see. What do we say in English, travel broadens your horizons?'

'It's just stating the obvious,' says Aunty Kazi, and Uncle Phil looks hurt.

'Tell your mum it's very beautiful here,' he says. 'Tell her we've been looking forward to seeing her and we're really glad she's better. And say how great it is, that I've always heard about Botswana and all the wildlife and everything.'

Aunty Kazi tells this to my grandmother and my grandmother gets very interested and leans forward so her breasts are almost on her knees. '*Ee*, it's beautiful. And this was our land, a long time ago before we were kicked off the place where the tourists now come . . .'

'OK, Mum,' says Aunty Kazi. 'He didn't take it off you.'

My grandmother puffs up her lips. She likes to speak about the old days when she lived in Xuku and the living was good and they had everything they needed and the food was plentiful. But then when she speaks about the old days she soon gets angry because when the reserve was made then my grandmother was kicked off that land like a piece of rubbish.

Later I bring the tea and the adults go quiet and they drink it slowly. I go to the little boy Joe who is in that funny chair and he's awake now so I pick him up.

370

'Careful!' says Uncle Phil as I swing the boy onto my hip. I want to show Joe the banana trees. I think he likes me; I want to make him like me. I don't know why Uncle Phil and Aunty Kazi are looking at me like that; I'm only carrying him to the banana trees.

When I come back everyone seems very annoyed. Aunty Kazi has her hands on her hips and she's saying, 'I was only asking how I can recharge my phone.'

'There is no power,' says my grandmother.

'You mean there's been a power cut? What, because of the rain?'

'No, I mean there is no power.'

'You still don't have any electricity?'

'No.'

Uncle Phil asks what's going on and then he gets out his cell phone too and looks at it. 'I'm supposed to be hearing about that job.'

'Well we can do that,' says Aunty Kazi, 'we can get electricity installed, it can't be that hard. I saw power lines on the way in, other people must have it.'

'She doesn't want electricity,' says my father coming out through the house.

My Aunty Kazi turns to look at him and she looks sort of helpless standing there. 'You don't think my mother needs electricity?'

'Our mother,' says my father. Then he sees that Aunty Kazi and Uncle Phil have their cell phones out so he gets his out as well.

'Don't you think *our* mother needs electricity?' asks Aunty Kazi.

371

'Not particularly.'

'Has she got a phone at home?'

'She has not.' My father isn't laughing today and he's speaking the way he does when someone wants a job and he says there isn't any.

'So what if she needed to call for help?'

'I'm around,' says my father, and now he smiles a great big smile. 'If she needs help. What, sis, are we too backward for you?'

Aunty Kazi narrows her eyes and she looks quite scary now.

I thought they were going to love each other, I didn't think it was going to be like this. I wish my mother were back from Gumare.

'Daddy!' cries Maya, and she comes running up from the swing she's been playing on and she's shouting in a really loud voice, 'That tree is huge! Why is it so big? Why can't I push my legs on it? Why don't we have a swing like that at our home? When are we going to give the presents?'

'What is she saying?' asks my grandmother.

'Presents,' sighs Aunty Kazi. 'She wants to give you the presents.'

My grandmother smiles and she waves with her fingers that Maya should come to her. I move closer, I don't want Maya too near my grandmother, but Maya doesn't want to go to her either so that's good.

'I wasn't sure what to bring,' says Aunty Kazi. 'I asked if there was anything you wanted, in my last letter.' And she says the word *letter* like it is something really, really bad.

'She's tired,' says my father suddenly, and he helps my grandmother up even though she hasn't asked to be helped up and she doesn't like people lifting her like that. 'She needs to rest,' he says. 'She's been ill, you know. You're going to tire her out.' And he leads my grandmother into the house and she goes with him even though she looks confused.

'Lenny Krause has been looking for you,' my grandmother says over her shoulder.

Aunty Kazi stiffens.

'He wants a word with you about what you did with that husband of yours.'

I see Aunty Kazi clench her hands as she follows my father and grandmother into the house.

'What did she say?' asks my Uncle Phil who is standing outside next to me.

So I tell him the words in English and he says, 'Husband? What husband?'

Chapter Thirty-Four

During the night I heard so many things. I heard whispering coming from my grandmother's room, but when I went and peeped in she was asleep so I don't know who was doing the whispering. Then I heard someone shouting, 'Goal!' and I lay there very still listening and I think it was the little boy Joe because the sound was coming from the attic. Then I heard people going up and down the steps to the attic and the steps were creaking like my grandmother's knees. Then the wind started outside and I could hear something dropping, ping ping ping, on the roof, only it wasn't rain.

I wonder how long a person can last without sleeping?

Maybe that's why everything looks strange today. It is very, very still outside like something is going to happen, and when I look at the sky the clouds seem heavy. I am sitting on the step at the back of our house and I'm not doing anything, just watching the chickens fighting over some corn. I was going to wear my trousers this morning because Aunty Kazi wears trousers, but when I took them out of the cupboard I saw the moths have made sticky soft patches all over the legs. The cockerel comes and all the chickens run away because he's the strongest fighter, he's the one that woke me this morning. My father says the cockerel says this: I peed on a log! I peed on a log! That's what he's saying when he wakes us in the morning.

In the kitchen opposite me the maid is cleaning and she's cleaning really hard because it's payday today. I can't see her through the window but I can hear her sweeping and then I can hear a pot falling on the kitchen floor.

Then our gate squeaks open. It can't be my Aunty Kazi or any of her family because they are all asleep, my grandmother is round the other side of the house washing, and my father went out a long time ago. If it was Lenny Krause then I would know because he has a way of walking, one foot goes much slower than the other and you can hear this just by listening to his feet on the gravel and then on the sand. I can hear a very faint sound of panting and I know it's the Krauses' dog because it's so old that it pants wherever it goes.

'*Yissus*! You gave me a fright!' Petra Krause has only just seen me. I've been watching her walking up towards the house and her lips have been moving because she is talking to herself so she might be a little crazy like my grandmother says her mother was.

I put my knees together and pull down on my nightie.

'*Howzit?*' asks Petra when she gets to the steps. She puts her hands in her shorts' pockets and then she takes one hand out and she pushes down at something in her back pocket. '*Oa re eng?*' she asks when I don't reply, because I don't know what to say to 'Howzit?' But I know Petra Krause can speak Setswana, she can speak it just like her father who my grandmother says sounds like

375

a true black Motswana. Petra Krause can speak Setswana better than my Aunty Kazi can.

'Is your father around?' she asks me.

I shake my head. I knew it, I knew she wanted my father.

'Where's he gone? I haven't seen him at all since the party.'

I shrug, because of course my father doesn't tell me where he's going.

'Will he be back soon?'

'*Ee*,' I say, because sometimes it is easier to lie.

Petra pushes her hair away from her forehead. 'And how's your grandmother?'

'She is fine. My Aunty Kazi is here.'

'Is that so?' Petra looks really surprised and I like it when I make people look surprised. 'No one told me.'

'*Ee*. She arrived yesterday. From the UK.' This is the first time I have been able to tell someone my Aunty Kazi is here and I'm really proud about it.

Petra sits down next to me on the steps as if she is a child too, and now she's sitting here I want to stand up but I'm feeling all dizzy.

'Well ...' she says, and she takes a stick and starts scraping it back and forth on the sand. 'It's a nice spot, this. I used to sit here. Did you know your father and me were friends?'

'*Ee*,' I say. She's making me feel shy.

'When I was the age you are now, we were best mates.' Then Petra Krause turns because there is the sound of people talking coming from inside the house and she looks like she wants to run away. But now I want to stay because I know Petra Krause and my Aunty Kazi were never friends and it is Aunty Kazi I can hear.

'Maya, I've told you, I don't have any idea where your Barbie is.'

'But Mum!'

'Do you want something to eat? Let's go and see if . . .' and now Aunty Kazi has seen that we are out here sitting on the step. 'Morning, hon,' she says to me and she pats me on the head. I look up and I see she is wearing a red dress that is very, very short; it is the sort of dress that my grandmother says you shouldn't wear. 'I hope we didn't keep you awake last night. We had a dreadful night; it's always like that when you sleep somewhere new, isn't it? Oh, hi, I'm Kazi,' she says to Petra who is still on the step next to me. And I think, this place isn't new, this is where she comes from and she used to live here just like I do.

I wait while the two women look at each other.

'Oh my God!' says Aunty Kazi. 'It's you!'

Petra looks a little nervous and she stands up and starts pushing down on her back pocket again. 'I heard you were back just now.'

Aunty Kazi nods and smiles and nods again.

'Mum!' says Maya.

'This is . . .' Aunty Kazi says. She is going to introduce her daughter to Petra Krause but it is as if she has forgotten her name. 'This is an old friend,' she says, then she looks as if this is not the right word.

'And who are you?' Petra says to Maya, and she says it like she doesn't normally meet children.

'Goal!' shouts little Joe, and he bursts through the doorway and Bulldog is with him and they both run off and the cockerel dodges back and forth in front of them like crazy.

'So you're back,' says Petra, because Maya hasn't answered her.

'So I'm back,' says Aunty Kazi. 'It's really nice of you to come round and see us.'

I get up then; I know why Petra Krause has come round, she hasn't come to see Aunty Kazi or me. I saw how she looked at my father at my grandmother's party.

Then I'm surprised because Aunty Kazi and Petra Krause go and sit together under the mulberry tree. I want to go and sit with them but I also want to play with the new toys. These children have so many toys. Maya has dollies and she has a plastic slate that you can write on and then you can wipe away what you have written and start again. And she has so many things for her hair, clips with butterflies and flowers, puffs that are all sparkly, a band that is soft and made from velvet. And Joe has even more toys; he has a truck that lifts up at the back like the ones the road builders use and lots of little men dressed like army men. Yesterday they were following me, Maya and Joe. They are my cousins and they were following me. But these children don't know anything; they don't even know bananas grow on trees. I told them about the snakes and one day I might tell them about the spirit in the attic who was blowing the sheet at the window in and out when Mary was still my friend.

Uncle Phil comes out of the house and he says Joe

needs a nap and he puts him in the little chair and pushes him down to the riverbank because he says that will send him off. Bulldog goes to play at his friend's house and Maya gets on the swing again. So now I can borrow her magic drawing slate and go and sit with my Aunty Kazi and Petra Krause.

'I had no idea you didn't live here anymore,' says Aunty Kazi. She is sitting on the tarpaulin and Petra Krause is sitting opposite her with her back against the mulberry tree. 'Whenever I thought of this place, I just sort of pictured you here, as a thirteen-year-old and everything. Actually, you look just the same as you always did! When did you leave Sehuba?'

Petra laughs and she puts her notebook and a pen on the grass. '*Ag*, they sent me to South Africa after Mum died. Dad couldn't cope.'

'She *died*?' Aunty Kazi has her mouth open like she needs water. 'Your mother died,' she whispers. 'I didn't know, I had no idea, no one told ...' Her voice stumbles and I think she's going to cry. She puts her hand out but Petra Krause moves even further back against the mulberry tree.

'She was ill for a long time.' Petra says it like it doesn't matter. Then I see her body all sink down like a punctured tyre.

The women are quiet and we can hear the wind in the mulberry tree. I try to draw a picture of the tree on Maya's slate and then I wipe it clean again.

'So you've been in South Africa all these years?' says Aunty Kazi.

379

'*Ja*. It's my first time back.'

'Just like me,' says Aunty Kazi. 'How does that feel? Does it feel strange?'

'It's a work trip,' says Petra, and she picks up the pen and puts it on top of her notebook.

'Oh. What kind of work do you do?'

'I'm a journalist.' Petra is frowning. 'I used to write for the *Argus*. That's how I got back here. I got a commission.' Now Petra is looking at my Aunty Kazi and I know she is admiring how beautiful she is. '*Yissus*,' she sighs, 'it's weird to be back in Sehuba.'

'Isn't it?' Aunty Kazi looks relieved, like she's suddenly got comfortable, and she moves her leg so it rests right next to Petra Krause. 'I keep on meaning to have a walk around, to see what's new, but it's like I don't even have the energy.'

'Well it hasn't changed at all,' says Petra, 'Sehuba is just the same. At least on the outside. There's the tar road, the police station, they're new. But your school is still there. And the bar. And everything else. It's like time stands still up here.'

Aunty Kazi takes off her shoes and she stretches her toes and she looks at them and I wonder whether she likes the colour she has painted her nails or not. 'Tell me about it,' she says. 'So what are you writing about?'

'Oh, it's supposed to be a travel feature. You know, a piece on the camps. The success of high cost, low volume tourism, impact on the environment, community conservation, that sort of thing.'

Aunty Kazi nods but I don't think she's really listening.

'But then the day I arrived ...'

'How's your dad?' asks Aunty Kazi.

Petra looks startled and then she laughs. 'He's just the same.' She pulls her head away from the mulberry tree and she looks at our house like she's waiting for something. '*Ja*,' she nods. 'A travel feature. That was the idea. But then ...' She leans forward towards my Aunty Kazi. 'I'm more interested in all these attacks.'

I draw very hard on the magic slate, I don't want the women to think about me being here, I want them to go on talking.

'Attacks?' asks Aunty Kazi, and she folds up her legs. 'What sort of attacks?'

'Isaac hasn't told you?'

'I just got here yesterday.' Aunty Kazi waves away a fly that wants to sit on her toenail.

'*Ja*, of course. Well, there's been a number of elephant-related deaths. One just before I got here. And then the boy attacked at Wilderness Camp. That was three days ago.'

'A boy was attacked at a camp? By what?'

'Hyenas. A whole pack of them.'

'God,' says Aunty Kazi. She shivers so her head and her shoulders shake. 'Hyenas? Is he ...' She looks around, perhaps she is looking for Maya or for Joe. 'Is he ...?'

'Dead?' says Petra Krause. '*Ja*. According to radio reports he left the tent. He is – or was – the son of one of the camp staff. I thought you knew. It's your relative, Leapile Muyendi.'

381

'My *relative?*' says Aunty Kazi, and she draws up her feet so she's sitting cross-legged.

'The boy wasn't supposed to even be there. The staff aren't allowed to have family with them.'

'Those are the rules at the camp?' Aunty Kazi looks surprised and I wonder at her eyebrows and how straight they are, like someone drew them with a pen. 'So who's in charge?'

Petra Krause laughs again, then she stops and stares. 'Your brother. That's Isaac's camp. You didn't know?'

Aunty Kazi shrugs as if she might know and she might not. 'You're sitting here very quietly,' she says to me.

I keep my head down; I want them to talk more about the boy.

'Wilderness Camp is a joint venture, your brother, my dad.'

Aunty Kazi looks puzzled. 'Where is it?'

'Near Khwai.'

'Khwai?' Aunty Kazi looks amazed.

'It's part of these new community areas. There's been a lot of change in the industry.' Petra stops and she stares across at our house again. 'Remember how it was all hunting? Then there was a shift into photographic safaris. That would have been about the time you left. Then it got complicated. The government broke up the concessions in the Delta and handed out wildlife management areas, some to hunting companies, some to photographic companies, some to communities. The idea was the community is now in charge of the land, they keep the resources and they decide who to go into

382

business with. There's been a lot of talk about helping communities set up their own businesses, but I wouldn't be surprised if that's just talk.'

'How do you know all this?' asks Aunty Kazi.

'I'm a journalist,' says Petra Krause. 'I read.'

'Well,' says Aunty Kazi, looking at her toenails again. 'Community areas sound like a good idea.'

'*Ja*, in theory, a good idea,' nods Petra Krause. 'But is it working? Look at all the Delta camps, there's still no Batswana in charge. Except your brother.'

'Really?' asks Aunty Kazi. 'I guess I don't know much about it.'

Petra Krause sighs and looks around. She looks at the chickens hurrying across the sand and she looks up at the sky which is too hot for rain and then she turns suddenly and pats the mulberry tree with her hand. 'I've often thought of this tree.'

'Me too,' says Aunty Kazi, and she's laughing again. 'I remember coming out of my window,' and she looks up at the attic, 'one night, and I thought I was being really quiet, but Isaac was waiting for me at the bottom.'

'I love this tree,' I say, and I say it before I think about it and then both the women are looking at me like they had forgotten I was here, and I slip Maya's slate under my buttocks so they don't see it and take it away.

'*Ja*,' says Petra, '*morus nigra*. Black mulberry.' Then she sits up a little. 'They're classified as alien invaders down south.'

'Alien invader?' asks Aunty Kazi.

'A species that some idiot brings with them from

abroad. They take over the indigenous plants. That's why the black mulberry is supposed to be removed. They're being pulled up all over the place down south, in people's gardens, everywhere.'

I stop drawing now because I feel very sad. They are going to come and cut down our tree and we have always had this tree. It makes me want to cry thinking about this and I don't know what we can do to stop these people from coming and doing that.

'Cheer up!' says Aunty Kazi, and she puts an arm around me. She gives me a squeeze and then she says, 'Is that your mum, Candy?'

I look at where she is looking, down to the pathway and the gate, and I can see this little woman coming along with a big bag of things on her head and for a moment I have forgotten her, I have forgotten my mother.

'Mama!' I cry, and I hold out my arms. Next to me Petra and Aunty Kazi look at each other and it's like they are saying something to each other with their eyes but I don't know what. I run to my mother and I hug her round the waist only she can't hug me back because she has the bag on her head and she has a scythe in one hand and a plastic bag in the other.

'*Dumela* little one.' She smiles down at me and kisses me and says, 'Mama's baby, Mama's baby.' It's been a long time since she said that and I can see her face is glowing and she's happy today. 'Who are the visitors?' she asks.

'It's Aunty Kazi!' I cry, and I'm so happy to be the one to give her the news. 'It's Daddy's sister! She's my aunty, you know.'

'*Ee*, little one, I know.'

'She's come from the UK!'

'The UK?' My mother looks impressed, but then I see she is just copying me. 'Well, let me go and greet them then.'

Chapter Thirty-Five

I'm feeling left out. My mother has been sitting here for ages and ages gossiping with Aunty Kazi and Petra Krause. She hasn't even unpacked her bags; they are still lying there on the tarpaulin where she put them down, and so is the scythe. I go and check on my grandmother and make sure her eyelids aren't drooping and then I come back again. The women are sitting so close that I can't get near them and their bodies are making a triangle. But they look strange together, Petra Krause has naked legs all the way up to her shorts and yellow hair on them, Aunty Kazi has smooth brown legs and painted toenails, my mother has scars on her leg and big veins.

'So tell us what happened after you went to the UK,' says Petra Krause. She takes a squished packet of cigarettes out of her shorts' pocket and opens it up. 'You married Craig and then ...?' Petra lights a cigarette and she turns her head to the left and blows out a whoosh of smoke.

'And then ...' says Aunty Kazi, and she looks like she doesn't know where to begin.

'I heard he came back a while ago,' says Petra.

'He did?' Aunty Kazi looks surprised.

'*Ja*, he runs one of the camps on Chief's Island. I'd

like to talk to him, he's the one they radioed when the boy was killed.'

'Oh God,' says my Aunty Kazi. 'The last I heard he was off to Zimbabwe, so he ended up back here? And he's in charge of a camp! That's ridiculous. Craig couldn't run a thing, he's the laziest person I've ever met.'

'But you married him?' asks Petra.

'We all do stupid things when we're young.' Aunty Kazi swivels around on the tarpaulin like a dog on a hot day trying to get cool.

'What was his problem then?' asks Petra, and she blows out some more smoke.

'What wasn't his problem?' says Aunty Kazi.

My mother giggles suddenly and that makes me worried because my mother never giggles, and at first I think she is trying to swallow something in her throat.

'You know,' says Aunty Kazi, 'people told me right from the start that your dad's cousin was a ladies' man.'

'So he had affairs?' asks Petra. She puts out her cigarette on the sand and she picks up her pen and I think she's going to write this down.

'I've no idea,' shrugs Aunty Kazi, 'if he actually did, but he certainly wanted to, or he certainly wanted me to think that he wanted to.'

'That's what men are like,' agrees my mother. I look at her in alarm and she looks at me and then she ducks her head.

'Even my brother?' asks Aunty Kazi, and she is looking at my mother very closely.

But my mother is frowning, she is frowning at me and

387

I don't think she wants me to be here. Then she quickly tucks her skirt between her legs and she stands up and she picks up her bags and I see my father is back because we can hear his car roaring in.

'He he he,' my father says as he gets out of his car and comes towards us. '*Dumelang Bomma*,' he says and he bows. 'Candy, Candy, you are looking very sweet today! Go and help your grandmother.'

I stand up and I walk backwards a little, I don't turn round properly because I want to look at everyone and see who is thinking what. Petra is kneeling now, she is picking up her notebook and putting it in her back pocket and her face is all red. And now I know for sure what is going on. My mother says my father is having affairs and that means having girlfriends and this is his girlfriend, Petra Krause. That is why she has come round here, to see her boyfriend that is my father. That is why my mother and father are always fighting nowadays.

'Have you made your grandmother some tea?' asks my father. He has come inside the house to find me and I have come in here because there are too many people at our place now. I want to be alone and sneak some more of the party cake, but when I came in my grandmother called me so I'm in her room now. It's dark in here and very hot.

'*Ee, Rra.*' I come to the doorway to answer him.

'Well go and make some more.' My father waits until I leave my grandmother's bedroom because I know he wants to say something to her and he's rattling his car keys in his pocket. My grandmother is lying on her side on the mattress and she says her legs are paining her and also that her blood is high.

'I don't like it,' I hear my father say. 'I don't want Candy hanging round with them, you know what Kazi's always been like.'

My grandmother mumbles something but I can't hear what she's saying.

'And what's that?' It is my Aunty Kazi speaking; her voice is very loud like Maya's. 'What have I always been like, Isaac?' She is at the doorway to my grandmother's room now and she is banging a bottle of cream up and down against the palm of her hand.

'You shouldn't sneak up on people,' complains my father.

'And you shouldn't bitch about them, especially not in front of your child, Isaac.' She looks around for me, only she can't see me because I'm right up against the wall and there are prickles of dust floating in the air all around me.

'*Batho ba modimo!*' says my grandmother, and I want to tell them they shouldn't fight because then maybe my grandmother's eyelid will get all droopy again and they will have to call for the ambulance and Mary and her friends are going to say bad things about my family.

'Just leave Candy out of this,' says my father, and I can hear his jaw is all clenched.

'What on earth are you talking about?' asks Aunty Kazi. She still can't see me but I can see her.

'My mother is tired, she needs to rest.'

'*Your* mother?' says Aunty Kazi, and I know they are

389

going to have the same falling out that they had yesterday.

'Our mother,' snaps my father. 'Don't start bothering her with all this.'

'All what? Anyway, is Candy at school?'

'What?' My father sounds confused and I am too, I don't know why Aunty Kazi wants to talk about this.

'Is she at school? Only she doesn't seem to go to school.'

'Yes she is at school, she will be back there tomorrow.'

And I think, no! I don't want to go to school, don't send me to school when I have to stay here and see what happens. My legs are itchy now and I really need to get something and scratch them.

'It's amazing to think that she's at the same school we went to, isn't it, Isaac?'

Aunty Kazi is putting cream on her face, stroking it up and down against her skin.

'Not really,' says my father.

Aunty Kazi looks annoyed.

'*Rra?*' calls my grandmother in a wavery voice from inside the room.

'What is it, Mum?' asks Aunty Kazi, and she moves forward because she wants to get into my grandmother's room, but my father is still there at the doorway and he won't move to let her in.

'Where is Candy?' my grandmother calls out. 'I need water.'

I come to the doorway too now because I am being called and my father moves so I can go in. Then I see my mother through the window, she is outside standing on

390

the sand. I can't see what she's doing; she just seems to be standing there and her face looks very sad.

Now it is the evening and I'm outside on the step at the back of the house and my Aunty Kazi and my Uncle Phil and the children are playing. Maya is on the swing and Joe has a ball and Aunty Kazi has her arm around Uncle Phil. She is saying, 'Let's put some music on,' and Uncle Phil is saying, 'OK, babe.' My mother is washing herself and my grandmother is resting and I'm just here watching everyone and they haven't even asked me if I want to dance too. It's like they don't even see me.

Then Lenny Krause and my Aunty Kazi are having a big argument. It's night time and I've come outside because I can't sleep. Lenny Krause and Aunty Kazi are standing on either side of the fence that runs around our plot. I can hear their voices going up and down but I can only hear some of the words. Aunty Kazi says, 'Oh for God's sake' and 'He's not some wonder boy' and Lenny Krause says, 'Bugger' and 'Girls like you.'

Everyone is arguing at our house nowadays and even my grandmother is too busy for me.

I don't like being at school because if I'm here then I don't know what is going on at home. And I don't like it when Rra Klap starts walking up and down the rows of chairs in our classroom because I know what's going to happen. We are in a new classroom and it even has lockers outside, but I don't use a locker because people will steal things from it. If you have something precious you must hide it. We call him Rra Klap because that's what he does to you; he claps you if you don't do your homework or if you don't answer him properly. On Mondays he does this a lot because he has a *babbalas* from the weekend; he must have drunk a lot of beer yesterday because he tried to drive his car through the school gate and missed. He has a small car and the gate is very big but still he missed and he drove the car right into the side of the gate and smashed the window. And the reason we know about this is because Rra Klap had a Form Two girl in the car with him and she had to go to hospital.

Now he's in a really bad mood and he's put a box of reading books on his table and told us to take one and read it and not make noise. Then he will ask for our homework and I haven't done my homework because I haven't been at school ever since my grandmother collapsed and in a moment he is going to get to my desk and he is going to know this.

'Candy *Muyendi*,' he says. 'So nice of you to join us.' I can smell his breath and it smells like a dead something.

I hear Mary and her friends at the back and they are pretending to try not to giggle. All morning they have been giggling at me and making noises like a hyena and pointing at me and hiding their mouths behind their hands.

Rra Klap doesn't like me; once he asked my father for a job and my father said no. I keep my hands really stiff under my desk and I know he is going to ask to see my homework and my book and I have forgotten to bring my English book, I don't even know where it is. I was supposed to cover it; I was going to cover it with pictures of my Aunty Kazi.

Rra Klap holds out his hand. 'Homework,' he says.

I hang my head even further over my desk.

'*Mosadinyana*! Give it to me!' he says.

'I don't see it,' I mumbled.

'You don't *see* it? Because you haven't *done* it?'

And I say, '*Ee*,' really quietly because there is no point lying to Rra Klap.

Then Rra Klap sends me out to get a switch and he tells me to make sure it is a strong one and a long one because he doesn't want to break it, he wants to use it for some time. But I don't want to go outside and get the switch because if I do then I will run all through the school and through the gate and all the way home before they come and cut the tree down and before my mother finds out about my father and Petra Krause.

And that's when the itching gets too bad.

First I start giggling like Mary and her friends and Rra Klap looks at me like I have turned into a snake, and he has to watch me even though he doesn't want to. Then the giggling gets higher and higher and all crazy and then I really start laughing. And then I wave my arms out and I laugh and laugh and I throw myself on the floor and my head hurts when I hit the floor and I'm glad I've hit the floor because it's hard and holds me in place.

I wave my head back and forth and back and forth and this is nice and it makes me feel dizzy and I wonder if this is how my grandmother felt after her eyelid drooped, and I know everyone is looking at me, everyone in this room is looking at me and two of the girls near the front must be itchy because I can see they are scratching themselves too, and now I feel more powerful even than Rra Klap.

BOOK EIGHT

Petra

Chapter Thirty-Six

Yissus, that Candy is strange. I'm not surprised she freaked at school. She's like a pulley wound too tight. Like a cable car sliding up Table Mountain, you wonder how it stays on the wire sometimes. I could see something was not right the other morning when I rocked up at Mma Muyendi's yard. Candy was so excited about Kazi I thought she'd explode. And the way she looked at Kazi and me, head this way, head that way, dying for some drama. She's used to being at the centre of that family. She's troubled, that girl.

The moment she freaked at school the other girls started doing it too, the giggling and the itching and the fainting. They started scratching themselves with anything; stones, walls, scrubbing brushes, rulers, pens. So obviously they started bleeding. On day one the parents tried Calamine lotion. On day two they tried petrol. Then the headmaster sent Candy home. He told her not to come back till she was cured.

But cured of what? No one's said. I've read of it before, though. Last year there was an incident at a Sepopa school. And down south, in the Cape Province. It's always the girls who start it, odd behaviour that spreads like wildfire. It makes me think of nineteenth-century hysteria, the fact it's always girls.

Some people said what happened here is witchcraft. Witchcraft! I'd forgotten about that. Things go wrong, people say it's witchcraft. *Yissus*, they said it when Mum died. At two pm she was pronounced dead. By five pm people outside our house were already talking witchcraft. Best not think about that.

I've been sitting here staring through the window all morning. I got up at five as usual, now it's nearly eight. Normally I'd long be working by now. It's when I open my bedroom window and look right, out at Table Mountain. The slopes are still in shadow; higher up the granite is bright. To the left are the shiny towers of office land and below that the tangerine light of the bay. It's when the silver glow of porch lights left on overnight are too bright in the early morning. That's the best time to work, before I head to the office. Only since I turned freelance there's no office to go to. There are a lot of pros to being freelance. I don't have to offer to make anyone coffee. Or hear about people's weekends. But the cons are you don't always hear about work. If I hadn't gone into the office a month ago, to pick up old mail, I wouldn't have heard about the Botswana supplement. They might even have forgotten to commission me.

For years I've read anything I can about home. I've cut out every feature on the Delta: wetlands, rhinos, dredging, archaeological finds, wild dogs, flood alerts. Mainly it's travel and tourism, or conservation. If it's anywhere near the front of the paper then it's a wildlife attack. If the tourist is a South African then it will be front page. There are more wildlife attacks in Botswana than any other southern African country. That's what I read three weeks ago. Can that be true?

From this window I can see the Muyendi driveway. It's littered with Land Rover parts. There are mulberries squashed on the paving stones. The purple is so dark it's almost as black as octopus blood.

My cell beeps and I snap it open. That's what I like about this cell, the way you can snap it shut when you've finished with someone. It's a message from Kirk. I can't be bothered.

This is my old room and it hasn't changed a bit. I'm still expected to sleep on the bloody bunk bed. The first night I got up there and found Nelly covered in dust. No one's touched her for years and her stitching is coming undone. I try to remember how it was to believe Nelly was real and that I had to look after her. The day they shot the elephants was the day I didn't want her anymore.

I can't see the Muyendis' house as well as I used to, it's too overgrown by trees. I used to be able to see Isaac from here, then I'd run right over. We were going to live together. I really thought we were going to live together! I used to get him to promise me. We were going to buy each other Land Rovers just like Betty. Betty's in parts now, and I've seen some of them in the Muyendis' yard. Isaac must have taken her apart after I left.

Dad always said she was undependable. Like a woman, he said. You hear a lot of kak when you're young. Women were undependable, irrational, weak, and too concerned with their personal appearance. You grow up hearing this and you believe it. It was only when I got away that I began to see things differently.

I can't afford a Land Rover; all I can afford is the bakkie. But the drive here was good, I hung my head out of that window and I felt as free as I did when I used to sit on top of Betty. I only stopped when I rocked up at Riley's Hotel. That's changed, that's a three-star hotel now full of businessmen having conferences. It's all green lawns and larney signposts showing how many ks it is to Gaborone. And the lounge, where I used to go with Dad, that's all table lamps and low lighting. The sofas even looked clean. Only the buffalo heads on the walls were the same.

I've hardly seen Isaac at all since I got here. And that was a week ago. I knew he was successful, if you measure success by money and power, which most people do. He's made it and there's not a lot of Batswana to make it in the tourist industry. So I wanted to see what he was like now, if we still had what we used to. *Yissus*! This is a stupid way to be thinking.

Our fence needs work; the corner posts at the gate aren't even straight. Along the river new telephone poles have been rammed in the sand. I would have enjoyed watching them being put in as a child. That's the sort of thing that would have kept Isaac and me busy for hours.

What happened to the swamp? The river used to be right up to our house, we'd have to drag a boat right up to the steps or it would slide down to the water. Now the river has shrunk, there are trees where there used to be swamp. Is it some sort of cycle, or is it a sign of things to come? I can't decide if the Delta is as fragile as some people make out.

Isaac is married. He's got two children. A little boy they call Bulldog, which can't be his real name. And the girl Candy, who's going crazy. The wife Grace seems OK; OK but under his thumb. When he rocked up yesterday she scrambled to her feet as quick as anything. She should stand up to him; I'd stand up to him. He's got fat now and the funny thing is, it suits him. He has this presence.

When I saw him at the party I could feel him even when I was at the other end of the Muyendis' garden. I knew he'd seen me and I knew he knew this. Then his mother collapsed. I was just gearing up to talk to him when all hell broke loose and they commandeered my bakkie to take people home. If you've got a car in these parts then it belongs to everyone. I've already been asked to help with two funerals.

I look down at my notebooks on my mother's old desk. Why has Dad put it in here, because he can't stand to see it? Her hairbrushes are still here. I pick one up and the silver inlaid back feels cool. I can see my mother sitting at this desk brushing her hair. How old was she when she died? Thirty-six? That's only a few years older than me. Man, that seems strange.

I wonder what happened to our maid Nonny? She might still be in Sehuba. Did she have kids of her own? I can't even remember. I can't remember because she wasn't like a person to me, that's the way I was brought up. I really thought she should be happy getting leftovers.

There are five notebooks in this pile, only the first one

has been written in. And that's mainly the notes I made at the Kgotla last week. I felt forced to make notes because people expect it. When you're interviewing some official they always stare at you and your notebook and then pause for you to write down their words. They think what they've said is just so important. They think because I'm listening to them then what they're saying is interesting. Most of the time they know fokol. That's why I went freelance. I'd had enough of being sent to interview people about drownings and road deaths, court cases and prison fights.

The Kgotla was totally mad; I'm pissed about it even now. That's the thing, you get these men, put them on a stage, and what do they do? Ban a woman wearing trousers. *Yissus*! I saw them, the way they looked at me when I first rocked up. They basically watched while pretending not to watch. And I had to decide where I should park myself: at the front standing with the men, or at the side sitting with the women?

I went as near to the front as I could. It was quite cool, barely twenty degrees, the sort of morning when you just want to put your *takkies* on and run by the river. But I was on a mission; I wanted to know what they would say about the boy. I couldn't see how they could hold a Kgotla meeting and not speak about the boy. And if they spoke about the boy then they'd speak about the camps. That's what I wanted to know about, the camps. I needed something different to write about. It happened the day I first arrived. Dad told me about it. 'Kid's been chomped at Wilderness Camp,' he said. 'You been at my brandy, Petra?' If the dates are right, it happened that evening.

The Kgotla was different. It used to be held under a tree but now there's this larny stage where the dignitaries sit under a shade cloth. It was eleven-twenty when I got there. The men were only on item three of the agenda. They had only just begun to talk about the polio campaign. *Yissus!* Last year people hid their children in the bush when the mobile health patrols came. They said the polio campaign was a government plot of Biblical proportions. They basically said that instead of being immunised, the children would be killed.

I parked myself next to a man with a wiry body, slumped on one leg, wearing blue overalls. Then I knew who it was, Isaac's old friend Peter Mponda. He looked old, his face had that saggy quality men get when they're no longer young.

I got out my notebook but I wasn't writing anything. Then the Headman got to the microphone. I hadn't even seen him take the stand. I hadn't been aware he was about to speak. I was thinking of Peter Mponda and the day I found him and Isaac with the antelope in the bush. I was so terrified Isaac would be taken away. Dad must have sorted it out. Only I didn't see that then. All I knew was that Isaac stopped talking to me for a while.

I remember the Headman's uncle. He had these sharp cheekbones and a gnarled old knobkerrie which he used to stomp on the sand during disputes.

'It is not according to our culture,' said Headman Kariba.

403

People turned to look at me.

What? I thought, what's not according to our culture? Why are you looking at me?

'And therefore,' said the Headman, 'and therefore any woman wearing trousers should not be present at a Kgotla.'

I nodded as if I quite agreed. But my head was spinning. Just what was his problem? He was supposed to be talking about the polio campaign, now he was talking about me. Only he wasn't looking at me, he was looking at the people at the Kgotla, the women on the sand with their legs sticking out, the men splayed on wooden chairs, hats shielding their faces.

'I am therefore giving instruction that those people wearing inappropriate clothing should leave and change into more appropriate clothing,' said the Headman.

Those people! He meant me.

'Trousers are contrary to Tswana culture. There are too many Batswana imitating other nations' cultures these days.'

I stubbornly kept looking in front of me. Since when was I an 'other culture'? Doesn't he know me? His uncle knew me as a child. I knew *him* when he was a child!

I looked one by one at the men on the stage and I saw they wanted to send a message. And they wanted to show their power, not to me, or even to the other women, but to themselves. Because they've lost it, haven't they? They have lost their power. Who listens to the Headmen or Chiefs these days? It's the government that makes the decisions. Then the decisions trickle down to the people.

And what was the Headman wearing anyway? A baseball cap turned the wrong way round.

What good is it sending me out of the Kgotla? They have to pick on someone. They have to say, you're different, get out! Like me wearing trousers is that much of a threat. My face was burning. But I just walked back through the people at the Kgotla, nodding. This is where I come from, so why do I have to make a point of it? Yissus! We're all immigrants here; we've all come from somewhere else.

'The white is leaving,' I heard someone say just as I passed a group of men. Yes, that's right, I was leaving. They think I don't belong here. So what the hell am I then? People in South Africa are always asking: is there a place for white people in Africa? Obviously it's white people that ask this. I'd always laughed at that. But then I didn't think I'd be so unwelcome here. Maybe I wasn't even welcome as a child, only I didn't know it then.

On the way out of the Kgotla I passed a government reporter sitting upright in his van, writing notes. Then I passed by Mma Muyendi, sitting with her legs set apart, her eyes beady behind those thick-rimmed glasses; she's had the same glasses for twenty years. I nodded in her direction; I've known the woman most of my life. Don't mess with Mma Muyendi, Dad used to say. And we never did. If there was one person I was more scared of than Dad, it was Mma Muyendi. She murmured something when I came past and the women around her drew back. They were not sure whether to follow her lead and acknowledge me or not. Village life, it's so fraught with worrying about what everyone else is doing. And right now it's me they're worried about.

Chapter Thirty-Seven

'What's this kak?'

Dad is back. He's in the kitchen. I can hear the sound of an iron lid as he lifts it and slams it back. He's found the vegetable stew.

'Is this your kak?' he shouts out.

I can hear his stick thumping across the kitchen floor. It's as if he's killing beetles on the way, stomping on their brittle backs. Yissus! Then down the corridor he comes. I can hear Stitches pattering as he hurries to keep up. Stitches is old, he's not playful with a squishy face like Roadblock was. But he's still fierce. Dad called him Stitches because when he bites you, you're going to need stitches. That's the sort of joke Dad finds funny.

Dad stops. He's rearranging the frames on the wall. First he adjusts the one of the fish. This is the picture where he is standing on the banks of the Linyanti. He looks a little awkward because he's holding up a pole with a fish that reaches from his toes to his armpits. It's heavy; Dad's shoulders are leaning over to one side. His face is in shadow, under the rim of his trilby, and his nose is as thin as the crease in the hat.

At the end of the corridor are the clients' pictures, the ones they used to send Dad when they got back home. There's Ed Justice from Missouri, an orange-faced man in a khaki cap. He's wearing a heavy leather jacket and black gloves like a golfer. He looks sheepish, as well he might. He's only holding up a couple of birds. Then there are the group ones. Why do men always sit the same when they have their picture taken after shooting something? They crouch with one knee higher than the other, a gun on the right knee, the barrel resting over their left forearm. What sort of pose is that?

'Petra?' Dad says at the doorway.

I turn from the desk, Mum's old desk. My cell beeps and I snap it open. It's Kirk again. So I snap it shut. Stitches pads into the room and collapses with a sigh on the floor under my old bunk bed. I count to five, then Stitches farts.

Dad comes over to the desk. He looks a mess. His hair is brushed to one side of his head and his face is all squinted up. His eyebrows are white and bushy. The skin on his neck is like a tortoise. Yet still he wears his natty kerchief. It is the red one with white spots that he has worn since I was a baby. Once, a long, long time ago, it made him look like a matinee idol. That's what Mum said. What is he now, fifty-four?

I'd only been a week in South Africa when I heard what they call Afrikaners. They call them rock spiders. This is what Dad looks like now. He looks like a spider which has crawled out from under a rock. His checked shirt is wrinkled and unbuttoned halfway down. He looks like someone who needs someone else to look after him. His arms, though, are still strong. His forearms are bronzed and taut.

Dad is a 'whenwe'. He's one of those men who always talk about whenwe. When we ruled Africa, when things were good.

I shouldn't be here. I should have known we couldn't live together again. It's been seven days and I'm going crazy. First the Kgotla meeting, then the Muyendi party, now I'm stuck here. I'm supposed to be working but he keeps on telling me to run errands. I need to get out there and see some camps.

At least I took a run this morning. I ran along the main road, past the Muyendi store, the bottle store and the bar, the school. The sand was cool and white like snow. It was just me and the goats. Then I turned left onto the road out. Then right at the tar road by the new green sign with its thick white letters: Sehuba. And then I left the village behind and ran north towards South Gate and Moremi, until the road met with the buffalo fence. I'd read about the buffalo fence; the government's been putting them up all round the Delta. The idea was to separate wildlife and cattle. There's been a lot of animal deaths along those fences. I've seen the pictures; horns and flesh caught on the wire.

I hung a right at the fence and ran for five ks quite alone. Once you are out there then it's just you and the sand and the shrubs and the sky. It's a highway to nowhere. That's why I wanted to come back. One thing Dad and me like is the bush. I got that from him, that and being a loner. Nothing else.

I remember the day I arrived in South Africa all alone. I got a kombi along the freeway into Johannesburg. I could see the unreachable sky-rise buildings of the city. I kept on expecting the smog to lift, to reveal something sparkly and new, and it didn't. Dad's uncle met me and didn't ask much. I felt like a buffalo in a tearoom at his house, all larny doilies on the table, plastic covers on the settees. Dad's Aunty Antjie burst into tears when she saw me. 'You look just like Marianne!' she wailed. Which was a lie because I didn't look like my mother at all.

I stayed there until uni. Then I made my move and left.

Cape Town was so different; it was buzzing. You had the sea and the mountains, and you always had the wind. It was evening when I arrived, all excited, ready to be a uni student. The sun was setting and Table Mountain looked as if it was guarding the entrance to something magnificent. Then I saw the giant smoke stacks. And then I saw the uni, set right under the mountain on the slopes of Devil's Peak, like no one had ever thought about land-slides. On a dark day Devil's Peak looked like something about to explode.

That was the year the police sent in the riot brigade. Up the thin grey steps they went towards the white columns of Jammie Plaza. Then they *shambokked* students in the library. Botha wouldn't let the Cape papers report what happened. That's when I first thought about being a journalist.

I look at my cell. It's almost noon. What the hell have I been doing all morning? Down in Cape Town they'll be about to fire the gun. When I first arrived I was told some man up there on Signal Hill was loading up a cannon and firing off the noon gun like they'd been doing every day since 1902. Then I found out the shot is triggered from someplace else.

'There's a *tokoloshe* in that house,' Dad says, waving his stick in the direction of the Muyendis' yard.

I roll my eyes and flex my feet. My feet are bare now and my soles are stinging; I ran too hard this morning.

'*Ja*,' he says with a chuckle. 'And that *tokoloshe* has been starting fires.' His chuckle turns into a cough. 'That girl Candy, she's been setting fire to things, I tell you, even before she started all this kak at school. Something not quite right up there.' Dad taps his temple with a knuckle.

'What d'you mean, fires?'

'Set her own mattress on fire. *Ja*, said it burst into flames while she was looking at it!'

'And the school?'

'Silly buggers,' says Dad. 'Closing the school. They've sent most of the *picanins* home now.'

I open a drawer in the desk and take out a calculator. I'm going to work out my mileage. I don't want to get drawn into a discussion about the Muyendi family or the *picanins*.

'What's this?' asks Dad, poking at some papers on my desk. I brought them with me from Cape Town as background reading. There are so many travel pieces on the Okavango and I had to wade through them all, trying to find something different.

'Work,' I say.

'Ag,' he says dismissively. 'Don't talk kak.'

I'm dying to take my papers off him but I keep my hands on the desktop. He thinks work is something you

411

do outside. With a tool. Perhaps a gun. Ideally it's something you oversee other people doing.

'I've told you, Petra, I've told you there's a job at the camp any time you want it.' He pokes at a footstool on the floor made from an elephant's foot. He pokes at it with his stick as if checking it is still dead.

'I have a job. I'm a journalist.'

'Ag,' says Dad, and he picks his nose. 'Journalists. Bloody bastards.'

'We haven't talked about the boy,' I say.

'What boy?'

'You know what boy, the boy at the camp. It's odd, isn't it, that a hyena took him from a tent? From *inside* a tent? If you're inside a tent, you're safe, that's what you always said.'

'The boy left the tent, what do you expect?'

The more dismissive Dad is, the more I can't leave it alone. 'How do you know he left the tent?'

'Petra . . .' Dad says it like a warning. 'It was a one off.'

'I think it's interesting. All these attacks.'

'What do you mean, all these attacks?' Dad sounds exasperated. I know that exasperation, I get it too.

'Look,' I say, and I pick up a notebook. 'I've already got four fatalities. Each happened in or near safari camps. There's the woman taken by a croc up round Linyanti.'

'That was months ago,' says Dad.

'Thirteen weeks. Then there's the hippos, the man who was killed by the hippos at the lodge outside Maun?'

'That was territorial. The man just got in the way.'

'And then,' I continue, 'the one on the radio yesterday,

412

the man trampled by an elephant up near Sankoyo?'

Dad shrugs.

'Did you hear that? Yissus! He was in the back of a bakkie with seven others. They were about twenty ks from Sankoyo and these elephants were blocking the road. One of the elephants left the pack and began to charge. So this man jumped out of the bakkie in fright; the others lay down in the back. Then when the elephant went after the man, the driver saw his chance and drove off. One of the passengers told the driver to stop; the others urged him to drive on.' I look at Dad but he's not saying anything. 'I would have made that driver stop, wouldn't you?' When Dad still doesn't answer, I start again. 'So if tourists are getting attacked, don't you think that's interesting?'

'The Sankoyo man was a local.' Dad turns, ready to leave the room. Stitches twitches his tail in anticipation.

'But isn't it freaking the tourists out, especially with the boy? Doesn't it suggest something is wrong? Won't it impact on the industry?'

'Impact?' says Dad, and he pulls on the kerchief round his neck. He's mocking me now.

'Have an effect,' I say wearily.

'Ag, man, there's always something going on. There's always complaints about something, people always bleeding complaining about racism this, give me more wages that, can I take two years' sick leave ... Anyway, the tourists are a bunch of wussies,' Dad chuckles. 'Africa is not for sissies.'

'Apart from Isaac Muyendi,' I say, and my voice gets a

little strange, 'is there any other Motswana anywhere high up in a camp? Only I haven't heard of any. Any management couples? Anyone black in charge?'

'Petra,' says Dad, and he taps his hand against his good leg. 'These people pay a lot of money, they want an intelligent conversation around the fire at night. They don't want some village idiot who can't speak English.' He taps his hand against his good leg again. I don't look at the bad leg, the one the lion chomped all those years ago after I left for South Africa, after I was sent away. To look at, or to ask about, my dad's leg means trouble. It means hearing about the old days. It basically means being told about those thirty-six hours in 1972 when he and seven others killed seventeen buffalo, five wilde-beest, three impala and a warthog. It means hearing about all the exploits of Dad and Bobby Katz. Bobby Katz, my dad's own *boykie*. Bobby Katz who arrived with his family on an ox wagon from Zambia, who rode a zebra for the hell of it, who trekked cattle across the Kalahari trailed by lions, who knew how to tweak an elephant's tail. That's what I was always told about Bobby Katz, the Great White Hunter. Dad's one of the few left now. Maybe that's worth a feature. But then why would I want to glorify them when they've been glorifying themselves for years?

Most of the old white hunters got chomped sooner or later. But Dad always said you don't get evil animals, only evil people. So you have no one to blame if you're chomped except yourself. So I'm guessing Dad blames Bobby Katz for the fact he died last year. I remember

Bobby Katz well. I remember he smelt of sweat and Mum said he had bedroom eyes. I thought that meant dark, like a bedroom. *Yissus*, the kak you hear as a child.

Perhaps she said it to irritate the hell out of Dad. But what if Mum wasn't joking? What if she and Bobby Katz had a thing? I think of the day they shot the elephants, he was there then. We were following him. Then we put the tusks in the back of the Land Rover. Then what happened to them? Was it even legal then?

'Have you eaten?' I ask. I don't know why I said that.

'Ag, I'm not hungry,' says Dad.

I look up and focus on the picture just to his left. This is his favourite photograph. He's wearing a long khaki jacket, so long it is tied tightly with a belt in the middle. I count seven buttons on the jacket. This picture is twenty years old. Dad has eyes that are just beginning to crinkle, his lips are dry. He's got his foot on the running board of an old Ford. On the side of the car is a metal sign: *Lenny Krause. Professional Hunter*. He looks sexy, like a young Johnny Cash.

I am about to say, 'You should eat.' But I stop myself. That's not my job. I don't need to tell him about the stew I've made. He's already seen that. He will take it as an insult. Vegetables are not proper food. Vegetables are for women. They're probably undependable too. He will prefer instead to drink from his half-jack of Klipdrift brandy on the counter. I know what he wants, a real *potjie*. A lamb *potjie*, not rushed, never stirred. I'm overcome with impatience.

I decide I will talk about myself. I'm testing him. If

I talk about myself will he listen? 'Did I tell you about the Kgotla last week?'

Dad stares out the window.

'Headman Kariba sent me away for wearing trousers!' I laugh out loud. It sounds so ridiculous now, that I should have been angry.

'Is it?' Dad asks. I look at him from the corner of my eye. He always likes the chance to laugh at Headman Kariba. Or anyone else in Sehuba. But he doesn't like the way I dress either. He treated me like a boy till I was seventeen. I learnt to drive, I could shoot as good as anyone. Then Mum died and I was supposed to be girly, which is what Mum wanted, which is what Aunty Antjie wanted. Now Dad thinks I should wear dresses as well. Yesterday he asked if I had a boyfriend.

'So let's go, hey?'

Stitches wakes again and struggles to his feet.

'Where?' I ask. But I get up anyway and put on my takkies. He wants me to drive him somewhere. I want to buy some cigarettes.

Outside Frelimo the cat has left a present on the stoep. It's a thin grass snake neatly bitten in two. That must be the third or fourth cat we've had called Frelimo. They always died, or got killed, or disappeared. I climb into the bakkie, kicking away an empty beer can, an empty Coke can, an empty gun cartridge. But Dad doesn't get in. He's standing on the sand watching a man come up the pathway.

'*Baas*,' the man says as he gets nearer. He keeps his eyes trained on the ground. I grip the gear stick in

416

annoyance. *Yissus*! We're not down the mines now.

Dad might not be able to drive too good anymore, he might look like a rock spider, but he's still respected around here. Yesterday I saw him come out of the cop station and three cops came out after him calling good-bye. He probably paid their school fees.

I look at our house through the rear view mirror. When did it become so shabby? Was it always like this, or is it something that has come just now? It used to be yellow, now the colour has gone. The floor of the stoep is cracked. The vine that runs up the back wall is saggy. The house looks like a mobile home, as if it has wheels sunk into the sand. There used to be a path that led from our porch straight to the Muyendi house. Isaac and me were up and down that path all day long. Sometimes Kazi followed; she was always following us, and we told her, '*Voetsak*!'

Kazi loved attention. She was always entering these beauty contests and she acted like they were so important. Mum always said, 'Ag, that girl is so beautiful,' and she said it like it hurt her. 'What do you do?' That's what she asked me the day before yesterday. Well, Kazi, what do *you* do? Take your clothes off and let someone photograph you? 'I didn't know you were a journalist,' she said, like it wasn't something to write home about. She had no idea Isaac and Dad even have a camp.

I knew she was a model in the UK, which is a pretty useless thing to do with your life, and I knew she went off with Craig. Dad says she just wanted a way into the UK. That he always knew she'd dump Craig for the next man

417

who came along. She never was the brightest crayon in the box, but she seems a bit sharper now.

She's married too now, I guess. She's got this fella from England who smiles a lot and jumps whenever his cell rings. There was only one time I could have got married and that was to Kirk. I met him on Jay Bay, a surfer who rose with the sun, always waking me to say the waves were smoking. I loved to see him run on the beach. He taught me the term forest family, when your pubes get stuck in your wetsuit and you can't get your hands in to untangle them. But he smoked too much doob and in the end it got too much. So when he sends me a message now I don't reply.

I stand in the garden while the man talks. Then Dad pats him on the back and says there is no work. The man beams. He begins to walk away, walking backwards. He edges past our pet cemetery where Roadblock is buried and two of her puppies and scores of kittens. I thought people around here treat Dad with respect, but is it respect or is it fear? It could even be hate.

I put the bakkie in gear and as I reverse out of the plot I think of the Kgotla again, of the village and the people I know. I've been away too long. All that time I'd been looking for an excuse to return. I don't want a travel feature, I want something else. And if Dad knew what I was going to do he'd kill me.

Chapter Thirty-Eight

April Fool's and I'm the fool, sitting here at the window again. The bakkie had a flat and I couldn't find a decent spare. I can't believe I didn't bring one with. So I'm stuck.

The school's still closed. I thought about filing a piece. Muti closes school. Girls go insane.

I've seen Candy, she's still at home, and I've heard Kazi yelling at her kids, but I haven't caught sight of Isaac at all. I've been thinking of excuses to get myself over there.

I put on the radio in time for the news. I'm surprised it's the first report. The announcer sounds serious. 'Sehuba community junior secondary school in Ngamiland will reopen next week following its closure after an outbreak of a psychiatric problem described as anxiety mass hysteria.' The announcer doesn't even draw breath; he reads as if he's speaking one long word.

I lean back on my chair. So they're going to reopen it again? Without having found out what happened or why?

'The school's deputy head said it was not yet known how many students were affected. The disease which was started last week with one student hit the school for three days and the number of affected students rose to ninety-four.'

Yissus, that must have been most of the girls in the school.

'The students were said to be behaving in an abnormal manner. They were itching, laughing, crying and throwing stones and other dangerous objects. At first it was suspected that the disease was malaria but blood samples did not show any signs of the disease. Health officials analysed a number of book lice found at the school but said they did not pose any threat to human health.'

I laugh out loud. My chair creaks.

'The Ministry of Education has consulted with teachers, local authorities and community leaders then acted on the recommendations of health officials to close the school. However it is to reopen on Monday.'

So they didn't mention Candy, they didn't mention her by name. I wonder if that's because she's Isaac's daughter.

It's pre dawn. Dad had a bit of a jawl at the bar last night. He's asleep when I leave. I jog through Sehuba, rucksack bouncing. The sand takes my feet; it's just twenty minutes to the crossroads. The supplies truck won't even be here yet. The compounds look closed up. Soon the land will be fizzling in the sun. I pass the Muyendis' General Trading Store and there's a woman sweeping the stoep. The beer bottles make a clanking noise. There's a woman out sweeping in front of Light to the Nation too, where Dad was last night. It will take him a while to realise I've gone. Like when he wants coffee for instance. I pass the school and it looks empty. What happened to Mrs Van Heerden's primary school?

I pass the house where it used to be but it's clearly not a school anymore.

At the crossroads the driver's waiting for me. He thinks I'm on a mission for Dad. I get in the back and fit myself in and when we pull off, the sand flies from the ground. The journey's going to take most of the day. I've got plenty of water.

We pass small villages which I can't remember existing. But still, they seem familiar. Not everyone has a brick house, there's plenty of old style homes. I smell wild sage. My eyes follow tracks in the sand. But if I get out now people will shout. Children will shout, '*Lekgoa*! Give us money!' Just like Isaac used to do. I get down even further in the back of the truck and cover my face with a scarf.

I see the sign from five metres away. Wilderness Camp. The truck comes to a stop and I stand up in the back and stretch. This is the first time I've been to Dad's camp. The first time at this camp. For a second I don't know what to do.

'You're late.' A white man with khaki shorts hitched up high comes walking down a pathway.

The driver gets out of the front and slams the door. '*Dumela Rra*,' he says, flat like that.

'You were supposed to be here hours ago,' says the white man.

I see the driver's face as he comes round to the back to unload the supplies. I've been sitting for hours wedged between boxes of detergent, bags of flour, planks of wood, two gas canisters. The driver has his face closed

421

the way I close mine when I'm talking to Dad. From the back where I'm standing I can see the camp built between the trees. It's impressive. It cost plenty of money to build this.

'Oh!' says the man. 'I didn't see *you* up there!'

'Petra,' I say, leaping down from the truck. 'Petra Krause.'

'Petra … from?'

'Krause. From Sehuba.'

'What, something to do with Lenny?' The man looks alarmed.

'That's right.' I brush off some sand. 'I'm his daughter.'

The man's all smiles now. 'We didn't know you were coming.'

'Neither did I.' I pull down my rucksack and put it on my back. Then suddenly four women come running along the pathway. They've got headscarves and aprons on; one is still tying the apron around her tummy.

'OK, OK,' says the white man, and he waves at them with one hand so they stop in their tracks. 'Tim,' says the man to me, 'Tim Loveless. Camp manager. I'm sure your father has told you all about me!'

'You're the manager?'

'That's right,' he says, and he smiles and his eyes crinkle up and I just know he thinks he looks good.

'I thought Isaac was the manager.'

'Isaac?'

'Isaac Muyendi.'

'Oh, right.' Tim puts one hand on my back and steers me forward. I can't stand it when people do that.

I shake off his hand. 'And where are you from?'

Tim smiles some more. 'I'm a citizen of the world!'

'How long have you been manager?' I ask. He looks taken aback but I wait for his answer.

'Let me see,' he says, and I know he's pretending to think about this. '. . . started back in the eighties, then I moved on, then I came back.'

'Is that so?' I ask. I don't like this man. Why can't he answer a simple question?

'Is Lenny on his way?' asks Tim as we walk down the pathway, passing a little reed curio shop and an office, a large baobab tree, and a building I take to be the kitchen. Someone is cooking; the air is white with smoke. 'Only we're full at the moment. The tent he usually stays in has guests. How long are you staying?'

'That's OK. I can sleep anywhere.'

Tim looks worried. He doesn't know what to do with me. I hear some drumming start; a light uneven drumming like the person is tired.

'Afternoon tea,' says Tim. And suddenly we come to a clearing and the sky is vast overhead and there's a trestle table set out on the grass and a white tablecloth that's billowing in the breeze. I think I've seen this scene in a movie.

'Julie!' shouts Tim. A white woman at the table turns and waves and Tim marches me forward. 'This is Julie, operations manager. Julie, this is Petra, Lenny's daughter.'

'Whose daughter?' The woman has a very shiny face and a little clip in her hair like a kid.

423

'Lenny's,' says Tim, and he's giving Julie a significant look with his eyes.

'No worries,' says Julie, although I haven't said I am worried. 'Cup of tea?'

'Yes,' I say. 'Sure.' I hadn't realised how thirsty I was.

I can see the person drumming now, it's a man hunched down under a jackleberry tree. He keeps on drumming as people begin to trickle out onto the lawn. They come in twos, they come in threes; they come in khaki and white. They have cameras and binoculars around their necks. The man stops drumming and puts the drum gently to one side. Then he stands and I see he's over six foot tall.

'Cucumber?' asks Julie. 'Or salmon? Ah, Klaus,' she says to a big man with a camouflage hat on, 'we were wondering where you'd got to! Scone? Or brownie? Coffee? Or tea?'

'Coffee with cake,' says Klaus. 'If it is real.'

'Well of course the coffee is real! You should know that by now!' Julie laughs prettily. 'This is Klaus,' she says to me.

The man shakes my hand with clammy fingers.

'Lovely,' I say, without really thinking.

'Yes,' says Klaus. 'It is very lovely. Although we were supposed to leave last week after what happened.'

'Oh!' says Julie. She's trying to distract him with something but she's looking around and she can't think what. 'Isn't it *hot* today? Did you hear about the leopard sighting?'

424

'But they gave us some extra days,' says Klaus. 'For free.'

I take a cup of tea and the cup is very small and thin. I could break it easily. The guests are speaking quietly, politely, like at a cocktail party. I'm dying for Julie to go so I can find out what Klaus knows. He must have been here when the boy was attacked.

'So,' says Tim. He's back and he's standing very close to me. I slouch down on one leg, away from him. 'So, business or pleasure?' He says it as if it's suggestive in some way.

'A bit of both,' I say.

'Do you work for your father? I wasn't sure. I know he's mentioned you . . .'

I smile because I know he's lying. Why would my father mention me? 'I'm a journalist.'

This is the wrong thing to say. Tim stiffens; he actually moves a step away from me. Then he catches himself and tries to smile.

'I'm doing a travel feature,' I say, and this relaxes him.

The tall man who was drumming comes up. He's fit, about my age. He has the best-trimmed moustache I've ever seen and eyelids that seem to fold down over his eyes. 'Mr Loveless,' the man says.

'Yes?' demands Tim without looking at him.

'I'm asking if I can take Lesego's walkie-talkie for the game drive.'

'Later,' says Tim and he brushes him away.

I ask the man if he's a driver. I ask in Setswana and

the man looks surprised. 'I'm an understudy,' he says. 'Electricity Muyendi.' He shakes my hand.

So he's a Muyendi. For a second our eyes touch.

'A what?' I ask.

'I understudy this man,' Electricity gestures at Tim. 'And if I don't understudy him properly, I get fired.'

I want to laugh. He's taking a risk, I think. It's almost like he's daring me. But then I realise Tim has no idea what has just been said.

'You can speak the language?' Tim asks.

I put my tea down. 'I'm from these parts.'

'Of course, of course. Ah, Electricity, could we talk about that walkie-talkie issue just now? Is that OK?' Tim is talking differently now; he's trying to be nice.

Electricity nods but he has a smirk on his face as he stands to one side.

'Ladies and gentlemen,' Tim claps his hands together and the people gathered around the trestle table with the billowing white cloth stop talking. 'I'd like to welcome Mr and Mrs Stringer,' he nods at a short couple who look identical to each other in khaki tops and trousers, 'who just arrived this morning. And, for their benefit, I'd like to go through the day's events. For those who already know, please bear with me. We're traditionalists up here; if it's the old Africa you've come to see then you won't be disappointed.'

The man called Klaus gives a satisfied laugh and sticks his belly out.

'Your wake up call will be about five-thirty . . .'

'Goodness!' says Mrs Stringer, and she fiddles with a

necklace of pearls around a neck which is going pink in the sun.

Tim smiles. 'You'll get used to it. Tea and coffee at six. Then the activity of your choice. A walk, a game drive. Ten-thirty, eleven, it's back to camp for brunch. Followed by siesta. You're free to wander the grounds, we have a pool, there are books on the patio area, there is the curio shop ... Although please don't leave the perimeter of the camp.'

'Why is that?' asks Mr Stringer.

'Wild animals,' says Tim.

Mr Stringer looks embarrassed.

'I'm interested in the birds,' says Mrs Stringer meekly.

'Oh! Two days ago we had a great sighting,' says Tim. 'On one of our morning walks. Python caught a fish eagle by the wing mid air, wrapped himself round it, dislodged its jaw and that was it. Ah,' sighs Tim, 'the perennial drama of the bushveld.'

Mrs Stringer looks upset, but she accepts a brownie from the tray Julie offers.

'Afternoon tea,' Tim continues, and he raises his cup to show he's drinking it, 'is, as you've seen, at three. Then there is a game drive again, or a mokoro trip. You return around six-thirty, relax, take a shower, then sundowners around the fire before dinner. Ladies, gentlemen, please, enjoy!'

I pick up a scone as the people begin to talk to each other again.

'And what would you like to do?' Tim asks.

'Oh,' I shrug. 'Just hang around here, have a chat.'

Tim looks alarmed again. 'What about a game drive? Would you like someone to take you out?'

'Yeah, sure.'

'Electricity!' shouts Tim. 'Can you take Mrs . . .?'

'Ms,' I say.

'Can you take *Ms* Krause out? This afternoon?'

I'm back at the front of the camp again. There are three vehicles all in a row, the guests are getting on board, the drivers are lifting in the cool boxes. The vehicles don't look too good, the fender is hanging off one and on mine there's a hole in the side at the front.

I ask Electricity what happened.

'Mr Tim hit a tree.'

'Yissus. Was he drunk?'

Electricity looks as if he's considering something. Then he sees Tim heading our way and he laughs. '*Ee*, he was drunk.'

I watch Tim approach. 'OK? OK?' he asks as he rounds up the rest of the guests and gets them on board.

And I realise what he's thinking; he's thinking this is his private kingdom.

Chapter Thirty-Nine

I slept good last night. I felt like a kid camping, like when Dad used to take us to the bush. I always slept better in a tent, or inside Betty, much better than I ever did at home.

Tim Loveless put me in the tent the camp's pilots use, just behind the bar near the outside toilet. The bed was saggy and the mosquito net fell down. But still, I slept good. I've seen the guest tents; they're far smarter than the tents Dad used to have, this is high-class luxury now. The beds have new wooden frames carved from mukwa, there's even room for a small bookcase and a writing desk, both made from mukwa too. No wonder it's an endangered wood. There are bathrooms at the back of the tents, and inside there are creams and shampoos and thick white towels. I wonder what the staff tents are like. But every time I went anywhere near the staff quarters yesterday, Tim Loveless popped up and led me away. There are three groups here: the staff, the guests, Tim and the Aussie woman. Operations manager! The woman didn't even know what to do when the generator broke down last night. It took me just thirty-five minutes to fix it. Things like that, they either work or they don't, you either have the solution or you don't.

I'm down at the jetty before anyone else. Some of the guests are still stuffing themselves at afternoon tea. My feet feel bouncy today. I'm keen to go on a mokoro ride.

'Are you poling us?' I ask Electricity as I see him coming down to the river across the lawn.

'*Ee*,' he says, and he begins to untie the boats.

I get the feeling I'm interrupting him. He's not in a talkative mood today. Maybe he doesn't want to talk to me because of Dad, because I'm the boss's daughter. Maybe he regrets what he said about being an understudy and about Tim being drunk. Maybe Tim has warned him off talking to me.

I leap into the mokoro and settle myself down. I hope no one else is getting in here with me; I want to have my legs out. Then I see the knife resting on the bottom of the boat. It's an unusual one, with a wide blade and a handle wrapped in brown leather, just long enough to fit a fist around. At the base of the blade there's a slip of metal that curves up in a decorative way. I wonder where Electricity got something like this.

Now the guests are coming. All the cake must have gone to their heads; they are almost running down to the jetty in one noisy group. I can sense creatures in the grass scattering away; above me a fish eagle cries in warning.

Electricity sets off first and I wonder if he'll let me have a go later. I used to pole with Isaac, although he always said he was better than me. But still, I'd like to try again. It feels good being sunk down on the water so low.

We travel in convoy along the river, passing tributaries that meander off into the distance. The sky is blemish free. If we were in South Africa, the river would be chock-a-block with tourists by now.

One of the other guides overtakes, he's leading the way and Electricity doesn't look too keen about this; I can see he's picking up speed. The first poler is young, his strokes are a little uncertain. But the tourists in his boat are the most glamorous; the man has slicked back hair and an expensive camcorder, the woman has a white scarf wrapped around her neck and big black sunglasses like Mum used to wear. The woman's got heels on too; I saw her tottering in them as she got into the boat.

'Are there many hippos around?' I call to Electricity.

'Plenty!'

I hear a roaring noise and then, around a bend in the river, the white brow of a speedboat. The river is narrow here; there is barely room for the speedboat to pass. But it does and our boats rock in its wake.

'There's one,' says Electricity.

I look where he's looking and I see two tiny triangles, the tips of a hippo's ears. A second later and they are gone. I begin to count; I know how long a hippo can stay under. Electricity steers us to the right but the young poler in front is going straight. I wonder if he hasn't seen the hippo's ears. And then the water breaks and the hippo throws itself out. *Yissus*, it's a big one! A male, around three thousand kilograms. The boat looks miniature now, it's bang slam on top of the hippo and the hippo just opens it mouth so wide that I feel my own jaw tighten. I can see its incisors, sharp as knife tips; I can see the bristles round its mouth. And then it bites. But before it bites the water is already going red. It's not blood; it's what happens when a hippo fights.

431

'Oh my God!' A woman is screaming in the boat behind us. I think it's Mrs Stringer, the one who wants to see the birds. But I'm trying to focus on what's happening in front, I need to concentrate. Everything is very still and very quiet. Electricity has steered us parallel to the empty boat and the hippo has gone. It must be right under us. I'm looking for a weapon; I'm looking for that strange knife I saw at the bottom of the boat. But Electricity already has it and he swings it up over his shoulder, poised just like that, waiting. There's a commotion to my right and I see a man and a woman on the reed beds. It's the people from the first boat; they've managed to get to shore, but where is the poler?

I see Electricity rear back and I rear back too because I know what's going to happen now. Five minutes have passed; the hippo has to come up. It can't keep its ears and nostrils closed much longer. The tension holds me down in the boat; the whole river is waiting, even the birds have stopped. Then Electricity lunges forward as the hippo's head comes out, and he plunges the knife right into its forehead. It's stuck in there, like an arrow in a target. Electricity must have really thrust it in. But still, it looks flimsy, a little shiny piece of metal on the vast hippo head.

A piece of the broken mokoro suddenly bobs up next to me on the water. It shakes me; it reminds me what's happening. The boat is totally destroyed, and we're next. There is nowhere we can get to in time. Then I hear the woman behind screaming again. The hippo is out; the knife is floating near the shore and the hippo is storming out of the water. Now I can see the scars on the hippo's flank. Some are old but there is one that looks fresh, it's only recently been fighting. It roars as it reaches the riverbank, its stubby legs crashing through the papyrus, flattening everything around it.

'Let's go!' I shout, and I try to paddle us away with my arms in the water.

But the hippo snorts and throws itself back into the river and the splashing is deafening. The water's so mixed up I can't follow what's happening, until I see the hippo is out again. And now it's going after the tourists on the reed bed. The woman is trying to run onto firm ground but she's got those high heels on and I can hear her crying. She's slipping and crying, slipping and crying.

'The knife!' I yell at Electricity. But he's already got it back, just as the hippo double backs and throws itself right at us again. Electricity stabs the hippo in the neck and it submerges, fighting with the knife underwater. A woman's handbag pops out of the water, all swollen.

Now there is real blood and Electricity is on the shore, he's picked up a dead log and he's bashing the hippo on the head, pounding it as if it were a small dog. His face has no expression at all. The hippo grabs the log, I'm amazed by its stubbornness, and then Electricity seems to decide something and he lets go. Then the hippo is off, thundering along the riverbank, and I see the missing poler swimming desperately to shore.

'My handbag!' wails the woman on the shore.

'The camera! It's not insured!' shouts the man.

And I want to laugh. This man has just saved their

lives, she's worried about her handbag and he's worried about his camera. I expect Electricity to look triumphant, but he just starts walking round, picking up bits of broken boat, a camera case, a pair of binoculars snapped in two. Carefully, he stores them in a pile, as if it matters that they are neat.

'Help me,' he calls to the other polers. They've been watching from the side of the river where they must have paddled to for safety. Now they jump into action, looking scared and ashamed.

I'm at the bar, mesmerised by the bottles, the way they are reflected in the mirror at the back of the bar. They look so inviting. The way they shine, their fresh square labels, the clear liquid inside. There is a crazy atmosphere at the camp. Down at the fire Tim Loveless has been trying to soothe the tourists' nerves. Mr Stringer is threatening to sue. 'I'm going to sue!' he shouts out every few minutes.

'Have a brandy,' says Tim Loveless.

'Wow,' says Mrs Stringer. 'Wow. I used to think hippos were so adorable.'

'No bones broken,' says Tim. He's way out of his depth; he hasn't a clue what to do. Every few minutes he scurries off to radio someone. Perhaps Dad? Perhaps Isaac? He says he's informed the wildlife department and they will, he tells the Stringers, come and shoot the hippo. But he doesn't say how they will know which one to shoot. The Aussie woman Julie is red in the face and she's flustering round down by the fire offering everyone canapés. The big man called Klaus seems affronted. I think he's jealous he didn't come out with us earlier, that he missed the drama.

Electricity is next to me at the bar. He's sitting very upright on a shiny-topped stool. He looks odd, because he has a great big dirty bandage wrapped too loosely round his head. I think he's still in shock; he seems very calm, like he doesn't want to frighten anyone.

'Are they flying you out?' I ask.

He picks up a bottle of Lion beer and looks at it like he doesn't know what it is. I gulp mine down.

'He says there's no plane.'

At that very moment a Cessna flies overhead and we see the white smoke splatter a trail across the deep blue sky. It's close, it's going to be landing somewhere near.

'Can I interview you?' I say. I have my notebook in my back pocket. I pull it out and see it's still half soggy. My trousers have dried, but I forgot about the notebook.

'For sure,' says Electricity, and then when he looks me in the eye I feel exposed. I pull over a napkin and look around for a pen.

'You saved their lives, our lives.'

Electricity nods, he looks solemn.

This is so weird, we're sitting at a bar and the bottles of booze are gleaming and this man in front of me fought a hippo and won. I grew up with stories of men fighting animals, I've heard of men fighting elephants, crocs and buffalo. But I've never actually seen anyone do it, and do it just to save other people, not to get something for themselves.

'Ah, Electricity, my brother,' says Tim Loveless. He's left the tourists by the fire and come up to the bar area. 'Never had anything like this in all the years,' he says to me. 'Not a single incident.' He looks like he's going to tell me to write this down.

'Except the boy,' I say.

I don't know if Tim hasn't heard me, or if he's pretending not to have. 'You OK?' he says to Electricity. 'Got everything you need? Not too many beers tonight, hey!'

Electricity very purposefully lifts the bottle of Lion beer to his lips and drinks. Yissus, he's thirsty, he just drinks and drinks. 'We guides are not allowed alcohol,' he says to me when he's finished, 'in case we get drunk.' Then he stops and we both listen to the sounds of drunken laughter from down by the fire.

'Where did you get that knife?' I ask Electricity as Tim heads back to the guests.

Electricity's eyes look brighter now. 'Mail order from Hong Kong. It's a Kung Fu knife, a butterfly one.'

'How much?' I asked, dazed.

'One hundred and thirty-two US dollars.'

'So . . .' I pull across another pile of napkins to write on. 'Is that true, that nothing like this has happened before?'

'Not like this exactly, no.' Electricity shakes his head and the bandage slips. 'But the hippos have been getting more dangerous because the speedboats drive them crazy. The animals aren't afraid anymore. I've been working here since the mid eighties, in the past there would be an attack perhaps once a year, now it happens several times a month.'

'So their behaviour is changing?' I lower my voice, I can see Tim heading back here again and I want to get my question out quickly. 'And the hyena? What happened with that?'

Electricity turns and looks over his shoulder, down to the fireplace. 'There are some funny things going on around here, including what happened to my brother.'

'Your brother?' I stop writing. 'It was your *brother* who was attacked by the hyena?' I don't know why I hadn't worked this out until now.

Electricity looks at me and there's a challenge in his eyes. 'He's not doing so good,' he says at last. 'My father says ...'

'How do you mean,' I say cautiously, 'he's not doing too good?'

'He has terrible injuries.'

'The boy is *here*?'

Electricity begins stroking the condensation from the bottle of beer. Then he wipes his wet fingers on the top of the bar. He doesn't say anything, but I know his answer. So the boy is not dead at all.

This is what Tim has being trying to hide; this is what my father knew too. And Isaac.

'What happened?' I ask, leaning forward, keeping my voice low. 'Did he leave the tent?' Down by the fireplace I can hear the tourists laughing, Mrs Stringer sounds totally hysterical.

'No, of course he didn't leave the tent,' says Electricity, and he leans back on his stool, annoyed. 'Why would he leave the tent? And he was ill, that was the thing, he had a fever so he wasn't strong enough to leave the tent even if he'd wanted to. The hyena opened the tent itself.'

I sit back on my bar stool as well and feel the legs wobble.

'They've learnt to do this,' says Electricity. 'They started by coming into the camp and taking things, someone's boots left outside a tent, perhaps, a shirt on the line. One time they even tried to eat a wheel on the plane,' he laughs, only he sounds bitter. 'Then they learnt how to open the tents; first they took food and so on and then . . .' Electricity guesses what my next question is before I ask it. 'We told Tim. He knows about these things. We asked for padlocks, he said there were none.'

'Why isn't your brother at the hospital?' I ask.

Electricity sighs. 'He was taken to the clinic after the attack, they said he should be transferred to Maun. Tim said there were no vehicles and no plane, that they would bring a doctor up here to see him. They haven't. I wanted to take him myself, but he's too weak. My father says he shouldn't be moved, it will make him worse. Yesterday I told Tim if he didn't get a doctor up then I was reporting him to immigration.'

'Immigration?'

'You think he's here legally?' Electricity snaps. 'I know Tim Loveless, he arrived here with a toothbrush and change of shorts when I was still a boy. He worked here for a while, messed the place up, got fired, then he came back again. He's a mechanic, a rubbish mechanic, not a manager. And Julie? She's his girlfriend and she's a hairdresser!'

I can't believe Isaac hasn't dealt with this. Isn't he supposed to be in charge? I can't decide whether he knows what's going on. And what's worse, that he doesn't know or that he does know and hasn't done anything? Either way, it tells me something. What I remembered was Isaac as a boy, that's the memory I've been chasing. A boy who loved the bush. Who loved to hunt. Who was my only friend. And I've been completely wasting my time. Because if this is the way he runs a camp then he's turned into someone who cares for nothing but himself.

'Let's go,' says Electricity, and we leave the bar before Tim can check on us again. I follow Electricity through the camp, taking a path I haven't been along yet. Dusk is coming; I can feel the light fading, the warmth of the day oozing away. The staff tents are right at the back of the camp, some ten metres from the entrance sign. There are four of them, flimsy green tents like I used to have as a child. They are erected in a square around a small burnt-out fire. The day feels musty; I can smell my own sweat. The grass underfoot has been cleared but it's growing back in patches and there's rubbish everywhere: an empty plastic bottle of Fanta, two bashed cartons of Kentucky Fried Chicken that must have come all the way from Maun, a used sanitary towel, burnt matches, pieces of hard green mosquito coil.

'The baboons,' says Electricity, waving at the mess. 'There aren't any proper bins in the staff quarters. There are no toilets either, or showers.'

In the distance I hear the clapping and the sound of

women ululating. Some guests must have arrived at the camp entrance. The Cessna we saw earlier must have brought them. I hear a car door slam and the sound of voices. And I know one voice at once: it's Kazi.

Electricity bends to open the flap of one of the tents; it's badly torn and has been stuck together with gaffer tape and giant safety pins like the ones used on babies' nappies. He gestures that I come closer but I don't really want to look inside. I don't want to see the boy but I have to.

BOOK NINE

Kazi

Chapter Forty

Ever since we'd arrived in Sehuba there was one image that I couldn't get out of my head. It was the moment we'd got to Johannesburg, when we'd got into the airport proper, that I felt both at home and completely out of place. I had a dim memory of the big square tiles on the floor from years ago, from when Diane had sent me to Bophuthatswana, the way they looked freshly cleaned and slippy but weren't. And then as we joined the queue, as Maya raised her voice even louder to be heard above the crowd, I saw an influx of travellers with faces that seemed achingly familiar. A man to my left looked like an old school friend, a boy named Ketsile whom I'd once kissed in Maun. But then I thought, would Ketsile look like this now, would he be this short? Would he be carrying a conference case and have a gold watch round his wrist? And anyway, what would he be doing in Jan Smuts airport, what were the chances of that? Then I saw a woman behind him who looked like Mma Serema from Sehuba, one of the women who'd judged me in the beauty contest when I was eight. However unlikely it seemed, I kept on looking at her, aware that I was staring, but desperate to establish if it was her or not. And then I watched a young man carrying a baby, casually but lovingly over one shoulder and

I thought, I haven't seen a man hold a child like that for years.

And then I watched a group of three men in suits laughing together, purposefully telling their stories loudly so that others could enjoy them and join in.

I had not seen so many people that looked like Batswana for years. Some were South Africans, of course, but some, for sure, were Batswana and getting the connecting flight to Maun just like us.

I stayed in the queue, it wasn't moving, I had plenty of time to look around, and I wondered, where do I fit in? Do I look like I belong with these people joining the queue next to ours, or do I look like I belong with Phil and my children standing just behind me? Recognise me, I wanted to say to the people. Recognise me.

'Kazi Muyendi,' said a man's voice.

It was the man who looked like Ketsile. And suddenly I felt very dizzy standing there on the shiny floor tiles.

'I thought it was you,' he said as if it were perfectly normal that we would meet like this. And then he began to talk to me in Setswana and I thought, this is such a sweet language. And it felt like a private language too for not everyone in the airport queue could understand us. Next to me Phil couldn't understand it. And nor could my children.

And then when Ketsile left I realised we needed to be in two queues. Phil and the kids should be in the queue for foreign nationals to our right, while I could stay in the African queue.

The rest of the journey I didn't remember, the plane to

Maun, the drive to Sehuba. I didn't even remember what I thought when Isaac picked us up at the airport. I was too worried, worried about Mum, about her collapse and how I would find her. From what Isaac had said on the phone, it sounded like a stroke. I never thought I'd arrive to see her sipping tea under the mulberry tree as if nothing had happened at all.

I said it was jet lag, the fact I couldn't get up any energy in the first few days. But it was defeat. I thought the phone call meant I was being welcomed home. I thought Mum and me would sit and chat, we would talk and talk, we would fill in the years. If there were misunderstandings then we would smooth them out. She'd want to know all about my life in the years I'd been away and I would tell her. I had pictured myself at her sick bed, handing her medicine perhaps, making her comfortable, talking.

For so long I'd suppressed my yearning for her and for home. I'd told myself I didn't care that my family had turned their back on me, that I was OK, that I had made a new life for myself in the UK. Yet always I had been waiting for that letter or that call, the one that would bring me home again. But from the second I arrived my mother snubbed me. And Isaac didn't want me on his turf at all. I didn't even know why he'd called me home.

The first day I sat outside and looked at a sky strewn with clouds. It rained a little, but then it was hot. The air got stiller as the day wore on. By late afternoon the sounds were muted. A dove, a woodpecker, a car in the distance like a single passing wave. I watched a

445

yellow-headed bird alight on a tree, the twig swayed, then became still like everything else. I knew it wouldn't rain again. The day wouldn't do anything at all. It would just get dark and then continue with the heat the next morning.

On the second day I went and looked around the kitchen, the same outside kitchen we'd always had. Phil had taken the kids on a walk, Mum was napping. I opened the first cupboard, above the cooker. There was a jar of Ricoffy, a jar exactly as it had always been, a metal tin with a plastic top that would sigh a little when it was opened. There was a picture of two women, one white, one black, laughing on the orangey brown label. I couldn't remember the picture but I squeezed open the lid and smelt the granules and remembered them at once.

And then I really began to hunt around, quickly as if I was doing something I shouldn't be doing. I took down a big packet of A1 super maize meal and held it in my hand, feeling its satisfying soft heaviness. A1 was *the taste of success*; White Star super maize meal was *the clever choice*. My mother's cupboard had packets of both.

I put my hand further into the cupboard and brought down a blue carton of Ultra Mel milk, a can of Koo baked beans, some Ecco corned beef, a very old jar of Black Cat peanut butter, several packets of Knorr curry vegetable soup. I lined everything up in front of me, as if I had found treasure. I had not seen these foods for years. I hadn't even thought about them, but now that I saw them again I felt I was plugging a hole in something that had been missing.

446

I moved to the gas-powered fridge and opened the door. There were red viennas the colour of spam, a big rubbery polony like a giant plastic-wrapped sausage, a jar of Crosse and Blackwell mayonnaise. I didn't have to taste them now to remember how they tasted. I could see myself on the porch of my mother's general trading store eating from a packet of viennas, feel the wet floppiness in my mouth. I could see my mother opening some Ecco corned beef, the way she lifted the little metal key and rolled back the lethal jagged top. I could smell Knorr soup, see how it sank on top of a mound of *bogobe* on days when there was no chicken and no goat to eat.

'Mum!' yelled Maya. 'Maaa-aaam!'

I closed the fridge door, left the food still lined up on the counter, and went to find her.

'If Mum's fine,' I said to Phil on the fourth day, 'as she obviously is, then we may as well have a holiday. We've come all this way on false pretences, let's at least get into the Delta.' We were in the attic, without the kids for once. 'She's not ill, is she? Whatever happened, she's fine now. I don't even know why they wanted me here, I don't think they even did.'

'OK,' he shrugged. He wasn't really concentrating; he was peering at his shoulder, inspecting his tan.

'Shall we then?' I could hear the impatience in my voice, an impatience that had been with me ever since I'd woken up, an impatience that had been growing inside since the moment we'd arrived.

'Shall we what?' Phil sat down on the bed and the mattress sagged, it was the same mattress I'd slept on as a

447

girl and it upset me that Mum, or Isaac, couldn't have given us something better to sleep on.

The attic was a crowded mess, the kids' mattress was on the floor and the sheet was sprinkled with sand and footprints, clothes lay everywhere for Maya hadn't been able to decide what to wear that morning. And then there were the household supplies, a hessian sack of mealie, empty Chibuku cartons that were perhaps going to be used to plant seedlings in, a blanket still in a thick plastic cover. They were things no one wanted right now, so they had been put in the attic, just like me.

'I'm saying, shall we have a holiday?'

'Aren't we on holiday already?' Phil bounced a little on the bed.

'You might be, but it doesn't feel like a holiday to me.' I went to the bed and put my hands up his t-shirt and felt the warmth of his chest. These days we could only snatch touches of each other, we always seemed to be setting off to do something else. I wondered for a second what was wrong between us, if there was anything wrong, or if it was just me.

'Aren't you happy here?' Phil asked, but he sounded distracted, like he didn't really care.

I was touching him but he wasn't touching me back. I put my face tight against him. 'No.'

Chapter Forty-One

'Kazi! Kazi we!' Mum called from downstairs. She sounded annoyed as if she'd been calling for ages.

'Oh God,' I said to Phil, 'there must be another visitor.'

For the past few days every time someone came round I was expected to swing into daughter mode and offer tea and have them look me up and down as if I was at a beauty contest, taking in my body, my clothes, my face. So here she is from the UK, I could feel the visitors thinking, doesn't she think she's something? And, as I waited while they looked me over, or as Mum sent me to make tea, then suddenly I wasn't an adult anymore, an adult with my own family, I was a child again.

I picked up some shoes and looked inside them. I had not looked inside shoes to check for scorpions for years and for a second I didn't know what I was looking for.

'Here she is,' said Mum as I came down the attic steps and into the living room. It was gloomy in the room, as if it needed to be dusted, and at once I wanted to be outside. But Mum was waiting for me, sitting on the two-seater sofa, next to a woman dressed in a green and orange print dress with big puffed out sleeves. The woman looked up as I came in, I could see she was watching me with a mixture of suspicion and envy. So

I greeted her carefully, with great elaboration until Mum looked satisfied.

'This is MaNeo,' she said, patting her friend on the thigh. 'She is a friend of Isaac's.'

'Oh!' laughed MaNeo. 'We are all friends of Isaac's.'

Mum nodded. 'Hey it is hot,' she said, and she fanned her face with a large white envelope that I could see had been opened and resealed again. I looked at the envelope as she laid it on the arm of the sofa and I felt a little tremor of excitement.

'So my child,' said MaNeo, 'how is the UK?'

'Fine,' I said. I looked at my father's old Kgotla chair, wondering if I could sit on it. I could not say the UK was wonderful, that would not go down well, but I could not say it was terrible either.

'And now you are back,' said MaNeo, and she had her eyes on my shoes, she was silently admiring them.

'And now I am back,' I smiled at her, feeling my cheeks harden. MaNeo was like a lot of other visitors to my mother's house, they treated me like I thought I was too good for this place, but if that were the case then why would I have come back? And I knew there had been a campaign of disinformation, orchestrated by Mum, so they all thought she had been short-changed somehow, that I was not the respectful daughter I should be. It was like she was holding me up for inspection, so that others could criticise me rather than her having to do it herself.

'And is this the first time you've been back in fifteen years?' asked MaNeo, and she said it with a sideways glance at Mum. And I couldn't explain, I didn't have the energy to say you know what, for fifteen years I've been writing to my mum, for ten years I've been sending her money, and do you know what? She never once replied.

It wasn't supposed to be like this, this wasn't the way I wanted it to be. I'd thought I would come back and spend my time walking round the village, people would wave and I would wave back. I would catch up with old friends, catch up with the gossip. But even though I hadn't yet gone into the village, Sehuba was already stifling me. I wasn't used to heat so strong, at night the mosquitoes whined in my ears, during the day the visitors came and stared at me. I felt trapped in the house and I felt out of control, I was no longer in charge of when and what we ate, of when the kids should wash, of when they should go to sleep. I could hear Maya and Joe outside, Maya was on the swing again, Joe was playing with Bulldog. I didn't know whether they had eaten, I could not remember if I had washed Joe's face.

'He he he!' Isaac came to the doorway of the living room and poked his head in.

'My son, my son!' said Mum.

Next to her MaNeo straightened up and beamed.

'Get your brother a chair,' Mum nodded at me.

I ignored her.

Then Phil came down from the attic and into the room. 'Morning,' he said to everyone. He was wearing my favourite t-shirt; he must have just changed into it, a soft black t-shirt with a silver cloud on the front.

'*Dumela Rra,*' my brother replied. I looked at the two men, Phil and my brother, and the way they mirrored each other, both standing with their hands in their pockets, like they were squaring up for a fight. I had never seen Phil do this before and for a moment I was pleased, I felt I had someone on my side.

'Sleep well?' asked Isaac.

'Yeah, we're feeling a bit more settled now,' I lied. 'How's your camp?' I asked. Petra had told me about the camp, but Isaac was yet to mention it.

'Still there the last time I checked,' Isaac laughed.

'I'd like to see it,' I said.

'Oh we'd love to see it,' agreed Phil. 'I'd love to take some landscape shots.'

'I thought you came here to see our mother?' said Isaac, and as I looked at him in the open doorway I wondered why he had never got round to putting in a door.

'Yes, I did come to see Mum, of course I did,' I spoke carefully. 'But as she's not actually in *hospital*, as she's apparently fine now, I'd like to see your camp.'

'Oh his camp is wonderful,' gushed MaNeo. 'So successful. So many famous people stay there, don't they, *Rra*? Why, even the President has been there!'

Isaac let his shoulders relax.

'We'd love a holiday there, Isaac.'

'A holiday?' my brother said, and he raised his eyebrows and looked at me as if to say, you should be so lucky. 'I'm afraid it's booked way in advance.'

'Is it *totally* full? Couldn't you get us in, if only for the night? Phil's dying to see the Delta, and the kids would love it.'

'Children need to be eight or above,' said Isaac.

'Why?'

Isaac rattled his car keys in his pocket. 'Although we did have an American kid a week or so back.'

I stared at him, waiting. I wondered if I continued being nice to him, if I continued behaving as if I wanted a favour from him, some thing only he had the power to grant, then we could be on good terms. He hadn't changed a bit, I thought, he was still in his gatekeeper role; the one he'd first assumed in adolescence. He was still the brother who had caught me climbing out of the mulberry tree, only now he really thought he was the boss and that Mum belonged to him. 'Mum could come too?' I asked.

'*Ao!*' she objected from the sofa.

'Why not?' I said, and my voice sounded sulky like a child's because my brother and my mother were united against me. 'Why can't we all go?'

'Because she is not well,' said Isaac, and he moved into the room and took up position next to Mum. He motioned that she move forward and then he placed a cushion behind her back. For the past few days he hadn't let me anywhere near her, every time I found her alone, every time I tried to have a talk with her, he appeared and insisted she needed to rest.

'How's Candy?' I asked, feeling nasty. 'I haven't seen her this morning.' I saw Phil frown as he left the room, hurrying to answer Joe's urgent shouting from outside.

'Candy is fine,' snapped my brother, heading back to the doorway.

'Has their school opened again?'

'The school has opened again.'

'And she's OK, is she?'

'Yes.'

'So, you'll see if you can get us in to your camp?'

'I will see,' said Isaac.

And then I sat down on my father's Kgotla chair, daring anyone to tell me to move, and as I sat down MaNeo got up to leave.

'Is that one of my letters?' I asked as Isaac showed MaNeo out.

Mum didn't reply. I couldn't see her eyes properly beneath her glasses; I couldn't gauge what her expression was.

'That one there, is that one of mine?' I leant forward from the chair and pointed to the letter she had been fanning herself with earlier.

She looked confused. 'This one?' She picked it up from the arm of the sofa. 'This is from the bank.'

'Oh. So it's not one of mine?'

'Yours?' my mother laughed. 'What letters did you ever write? No, my child, I gave up waiting for news of you years ago.'

'What do you mean?' I could hear my voice, it sounded like a wail, it sounded like Maya when I told her to turn off the TV when she was watching her favourite programme. 'What do you mean, *what letters*? The letters I sent, every month, ever since I got to the UK I wrote to you. Right from the very first day I arrived.'

My mother waved her hand dismissively in front of her face.

'She's tired,' said Isaac. I looked up to see my brother

454

had come back into the room. I wondered how long he'd been standing there. 'You're tiring her out,' he said, and he took hold of her arm, about to help her up from her chair.

'Wait!' she said. 'I want to hear some more of this rubbish she's speaking.'

'It's not rubbish!' I felt my skin prickle. 'I sent you letters; it was you who never replied. Tell her, Isaac, you must have seen them, you tell her.'

'Your brother is a very hard worker,' said my mother.

'What?'

'While you have been away, my child, enjoying yourself in the UK, your brother has been working hard to make a name for himself, to make a camp. He worked hard for many years and he put all his money into that camp and now it's a huge success.'

And me, Mum, I wanted to say, haven't I been a success as well? 'So you're saying you never got any of my letters?' I stood up and pulled down on my dress. 'How is that possible?'

My mother shrugged as if that wasn't her concern.

'So are you saying you never got any of the money either? Because it was sent, it certainly left my account!'

'What money?' my mother asked impatiently, and when again Isaac bent as if to help her up, this time she brushed him away. 'What is your sister talking about?'

'The letters, Mum. I'm talking about the letters.' Then I looked at Isaac, saw the desperation on his face, saw the way he was once again trying to get Mum up from the sofa, and all at once I knew. 'You took them, didn't you?'

455

Isaac rammed his hands into his pockets and I could hear the muffled jangle of keys.

'Tell her,' I said, furious. 'Go on, tell her.'

'It was Kazi's,' he said at last.

'What was Kazi's?' asked my mother.

'The money.'

'*Rra*?' My mother was frowning now.

'She wrote a few letters . . .'

'A few!' I shouted.

'She wrote some letters,' said Isaac casually, but his hands were still rammed in his pockets. 'But I knew it would upset you to see them.'

Mum's face quivered for a second.

'I was protecting you from that, *Mma*. I didn't want you getting upset.'

'And the money?' I demanded.

'Money too,' he nodded at Mum. 'I was keeping it for you.'

'So where is it?' I asked.

'Over time it built up,' said Isaac, and he was speaking softly now, as if talking to himself. 'I thought I could use it.'

'What are you saying?' my mother asked, and she looked scared.

But I understood, I understood completely what was going on; Isaac had kept my letters and he had kept the money and he had taken it for himself. 'That was my modelling money, Mum. I worked hard for that. The minute I got my first job, after I left Craig.' I looked at her, willing her to understand how serious this was.

'I sent you money. And you never replied, but I still kept on sending it.'

'You sent cash?' Mum asked.

'What does it matter what I sent! No, of course it wasn't cash, I sent bank drafts.'

'But I don't go to banks. Isaac does the banking for me.'

I held my breath, waiting until she realised what she'd just said. 'So what did you do, use the money I sent for your own business?' I turned to Isaac and I could feel my voice was trembling now because I had just realised something as well. 'So this camp of yours is mine!'

'Well it's more Lenny's really,' said Isaac.

But he was not going to put me off. 'Lenny Krause put money in too? How much?'

'I can't work it all out now,' Isaac objected.

'Why not?'

'Well he put up the initial sum ... and I matched it with some more.'

'The *initial sum*,' I mimicked my brother. 'And what would that have been?'

'This was years ago, sis. I can't remember now. Some few thousand. But it's as much his camp as it is mine.'

'It's not yours at all!'

'He paid the building costs,' Isaac continued. 'He got the land, he hired people at the beginning. He did the marketing, he got the clients in from South Africa and America.'

'Ah,' I said, putting my hand up to stop him. 'But where did Lenny Krause get his money from? He's a crook, Isaac, we all know that. Mum always said he was a crook, didn't you?'

Mum nodded, but her lips had started trembling.

'So if you used my money then it's my camp. All this time it's been mine. And you've been acting like it's yours! Just now you let me *beg* you to go there! You actually stood here and said I couldn't come. The camp is full, you said! *My* camp is full. So that's easy then, we'll go tomorrow.'

'Hey, you children are making noise. I'm tired,' said Mum, and when Isaac went forward to help her up she batted away his hand. 'I will do it myself.'

I watched her fumbling to find her stick and then I watched as she walked unevenly across the floor to her bedroom. Aren't you going to apologise, I thought, aren't you going to say sorry? But perhaps she had nothing to say sorry for, because during all the years I'd been away she really thought I'd never contacted her, in all those years she really thought she hadn't heard a word from me.

While Mum slept that afternoon I went to visit Dad's grave. It was the first time I'd had the chance to walk through Sehuba and I took the pathway from our house, heading away from the river, past the Krauses' house and onto the tar road. On either side of the road the land was pitted with marks like a sand pit children had just left after playing there all day long. I saw a group of round houses amid a clump of acacia trees and the houses were the colour of earth, of dry parched soil. I took in a pile of firewood, the jumble of dusty logs, a structure made from

458

v-shape poles holding golden bunches of thatching grass.

I began to feel the heat bearing down on me and I longed to cross the road and stand in the shadows the trees made on the sand. I used to know this land, I thought. Why don't I feel like I know it? And as I walked on, I felt as if I was looking down upon myself, the way I did when I was in the UK and dreaming of Sehuba.

The first shop I passed was my mother's general trading store and it looked old and weather beaten, as if it were hundreds of years old rather than just a few decades. I remembered coming the other way past the store the day I returned from Gaborone after winning the national beauty contest, I could feel those pageant shoes on my feet, feel the way they pinched me. And then I started to remember things I hadn't thought about for ages, that I wasn't even aware were memories, like the shape of the anthill near the store and how I would play for ages looking for termites and poking them with sticks. I thought of the day Isaac planted the banana trees at home. I remembered a terrifying thunderstorm when several houses in Sehuba had been flooded and the people had had to ask the government for help. I remembered the day I found Isaac in the bush with the stolen school bag he was burning, trying to get rid of the evidence.

I passed a standpipe and a group of kids in torn t-shirts waiting for their turn at the tap, one small girl with a baby tied upon her back. I passed two boys standing on the roof of a new house, balanced on a round skeleton of twigs. And then I saw another house that had half collapsed, as if pushing down the reed wall next door, and the only thing that was alive and growing was a tall grand paw paw tree.

I passed the bottle store and bar, and then I saw my old school. I could just see it between two trees; the long low school rooms were painted white now and at the end of the first building was a tree leaning over at such an angle that it looked as if it had been blown by a strong wind and then frozen there, never to grow straight again. I walked on, still feeling angry. That was my camp. All these years it had been my camp, that was where my money had gone.

I remembered the cemetery as a lonely, empty place, on the outskirts of the village past the butcher's and the Kgotla, on an unmade track. Sometimes Mum would take us there on a Sunday, to leave flowers, or to tell us about our father and what a skilled hunter he had been. But now it was like a car park, one grave next to another, barely any room between. I couldn't remember people using metal frames over graves; I could only remember humps of soil. But now there were dozens of metal frames with green roofs on top as if to give the deceased some shade. Notices were hung on one end of the frames, giving the person's date of birth and death, burnt with coal into a slab of wood or written with white paint on a piece of tin. The frames stretched off into the distance like a shanty town seen from the air, and as I passed two freshly dug graves showing the earth dark and moist inside, I shivered despite the sun.

Dad's grave, the grave we were always told was a

mausoleum, as if that were something impressive, looked pitiful. I looked at it, trying to feel something, trying to feel I had a father. I thought of speaking to him, of telling him about my life now, of everything that had happened to me since I'd left Sehuba. Of how I'd made it in the UK, of how I owned a safari camp, right on the land he used to come from, right on his old hunting grounds.

Chapter Forty-Two

It was a long, hot drive back to Maun and we saw nothing on the way, no other cars, no other people, nothing. Isaac had lent us a car and organised our flights; he couldn't stop me from going to the camp now. At first Phil drove and I read a paper I had found on the back seat. It was a Maun paper, it seemed to all be court reports. A man had killed a kudu without a licence last year; he had just been sentenced to six months in jail. Another had killed a springbok and when he was fined P100 he had pleaded for a lighter sentence; he was sixty-eight and had a big family to support. I couldn't believe they were still sending people to prison just for killing an animal for the pot.

'Mum!' said Maya from the back. 'I'm bored. When are we going to get there? When are we going to see some tigers? I want to see the animals!'

'There are no tigers in Africa,' I said without turning my head.

'Why not!' Maya wailed.

When Phil got tired I drove, and the emptiness of the road, the horizon shimmering on the tar as if the tar was wet, began to make me feel a little crazy. But then I began to enjoy it, to enjoy just driving rather than being stuck in a London traffic jam. And then I just wanted to keep on driving, faster and faster, to eat up the road, to travel to the horizon and never stop.

'What do you make of my brother?' I asked as we passed a sign for Maun.

'He's OK,' said Phil, and he turned round to see what Maya and Joe were doing.

'He's OK,' I echoed. 'But what do you make of him, what about the whole deal with the camp?'

'He's your brother, Kazi, what can I say?' When I didn't answer Phil turned back round and sighed. 'I think he's jealous of you.'

'*Jealous* of me? That's ridiculous!'

'Why is it ridiculous?'

'Because Isaac was always the favourite one in our family.'

'Where are we going, Mum?' Maya asked when I pulled up at the Maun airport. 'Are we going back to England now?'

'No, we're going to the Delta,' I said. 'Come on, get your stuff out of the car.'

Maya got out clutching her Barbie doll. 'Can we buy something?' she asked. 'Please?'

'Like what?' I said. But I could see two shops opposite the airport and I had an urge, just like Maya, to consume. I hadn't been in a shop for days. 'OK, some postcards maybe. Phil! We're just going in here.'

Phil put Joe in the buggy and started unloading our bags.

The shop was cool and crowded inside, a sparkly den of trinkets and baubles, baskets like Mum used to make, a display of rings and earrings and necklaces, mobiles and posters and CDs, wooden ornaments and fly whisks and other curios. I didn't remember any of these as a child; I couldn't remember the Maun shops ever selling tourist things like this.

I picked up a piece of grey stone sculpted into a turtle and turned it over to see it said *Made in Zimbabwe*. I picked up another ornament, a wooden candleholder, and on the bottom I read a handwritten Shona name.

I was just going to ask if anything was locally made when I saw Maya was on her tiptoes, reaching up to the postcard rack and beginning to take them down. 'I want this one and this one and this one,' she said, taking down a photo of a fish eagle in mid flight, a baobab tree on a salt pan, two children standing on a porch, a girl with a white dress, a boy with a catapult in his hand, three women naked from the waist up gathering *tswii* in the river, a Kgotla scene of old men on wooden chairs. I looked at the back of the postcards, to see who the people were, but they weren't named and nor were the places where they had been taken.

'Just get some animal ones,' I told Maya.

'But Mum! I want these ones.'

I turned them over again and that's when I saw, when I really looked at the two children standing on the porch, the girl in the white dress and the boy with the catapult in his hand, and I realised it was Isaac and me. It couldn't be, I thought. But it was. Isaac was at the front, his body thin beneath an open shirt. He had his hand on one hip and his belly, small as it was, was protruding slightly over a pair of ragged grey shorts that were torn down one leg. There was an openness in the way he stood, as if he were utterly relaxed, as if he had nothing in the world to hide.

And there I was in the white dress that I had been forced to wear even after I had ruined it a year before at the catfish run. I was standing on Isaac's left with both arms against his shoulder, my nose level with his armpit, my face squashed against him. Both of us were smiling, although Isaac had a slight squint in his eyes.

In the background, just at the side of the picture, was a door, and I knew that was the door of our general trading store. I couldn't decide who had taken the picture and when. Then I looked at Isaac's shorts again and I remembered the day the Peace Corps came by on the back of the truck and how one of them had taken our picture and how ashamed I had been because Isaac's shorts were so badly torn. That was the very first time I'd had my picture taken. They were the same shorts, this was Isaac and this was me and we looked so happy. That was what I couldn't get over; we looked so close and so happy.

'I don't believe it,' I said. I held the postcard nearer as if I were short sighted, squeezing my eyes a little, trying to squeeze myself back to how things had been then, when Isaac was still a boy and I was still his little sister following after him.

'What, Mum?' Maya sounded worried, as if I were about to make a scene.

'Look at this!' I showed her the card. 'Who do they look like?'

'Dunno,' she said, moving to the counter and trailing

her fingers along it, attracted by a basket of Perspex key rings with dried flowers inside.

'Bastard,' I said, under my breath. The bastard American man had taken a picture of my brother and me and made it into a postcard. There was no date on the card, no photographer's name. I didn't know if this was a new thing, something that had only recently been printed, or if it had been around for years. I didn't know how it had ended up being sold in a shop in Maun. How many tourists had bought a postcard of my brother and me and sent it home saying here they were in Botswana having a lovely time? Wish you were here! Maybe Isaac and his catapult, me and my white dress, were pinned up on notice boards in offices in America, held on kitchen fridges with magnets – who knew where our images could be now?

To the man who had taken the photo, we were just kids. Just two little African kids that he thought were cute. He had never even asked our names.

'Kazi!' Phil had his head in the doorway. 'We're supposed to be checking in.'

And I put the postcard of Isaac and me in my bag and walked out.

Chapter Forty-Three

'Hey, guys!' A young white man with a nametag on his dark green khaki shirt saying 'Chris' came sauntering up to us on the airport tarmac. 'I'm your pilot, Wilderness Camp, right?' He put his hand in the air and made to give Phil a high five.

'Right,' I said. I looked at Chris and at the wraparound silver glasses over his eyes that made him look like an alien. We were standing outside the terminal building and all round us people were striding either out of or into planes, ducking their heads under a wing or a propeller, lugging rucksacks and pulling trolleys, striding in sensible boots.

'Here we are, guys!' said Chris, stopping in front of a plane that had a bright red stripe along its flank and which stood, balanced, on a single tyre at the front. Chris opened the back door and Phil bent to get on board.

'It's really small, isn't it, Mum?' asked Maya.

We watched while Chris got into the pilot's seat and strapped himself in. Then he took a crash helmet from the passenger seat next to him and popped it on his head.

'Mum,' said Maya, wriggling on her seat. 'He's wearing a crash helmet.'

'Mmm.'

'Can't I have one?'

But Chris had started the engine and, with a deafening roar, the plane began to taxi along the runway.

'Look, Joe!' Phil said. 'See those animals down there?'

But Joe's eyes were all over the place. He couldn't focus on anything; he was just so excited to be in the plane. And I thought perhaps it was all too much for him, and I wondered when memories first form and whether Joe would even remember anything of this trip to Botswana at all. How could Botswana mean anything to him, or to Maya, if they only saw it fleetingly like this?

As soon as we flew away from Maun the world became greener, and as I looked down at a river of blue I thought of an earthquake, as if the land had been cracked, as if the river were a split of water along a fault line. And then the patches of blue became bigger as if the water were pushing the land away, pushing it away until it formed into little islands floating in the blue.

I felt a rush of beauty seeing the Okavango below as if it was something I had had inside me that I hadn't been able to think about for a very long time. This is mine, I thought, this is where I come from, so it's mine. And I wanted to dive out of the plane and embrace it. I couldn't believe that somewhere down there was a camp that was mine.

'Look, Joe!' Phil said again. He was trying to make Joe see the big herd of buffalo like tiny brown sperm with legs, thundering towards a watering hole. But Joe just wanted to look at the fly that was trapped inside the plane, buzzing against the glass. It was like he could only focus on something that was right up in front of him.

'Kazi, this place is amazing!' Phil said, draping his arm across my seat. 'And the clouds!'

And I smiled, as if I'd made it myself. But I wondered why, when I was at Maun secondary school, they had never taken us into the Delta. We may have known about the camps being built, and the teachers telling us that tourism was good for the economy, but schoolchildren were never actually taken into the Delta. Why was that? But unlike some of my classmates, I knew the Delta because it was part of my family, because I always knew that was where I came from, until we were moved out. And now I wanted to know, in detail, who was moved and by whom and why, and I wanted my mother here so I could ask her. As a child it had bored me, her reliving of the past, now I wanted to know.

'Can buffalo eat you, Mum?' asked Maya.

I turned to her and saw her face looked worried. 'No of course not, they wouldn't want to eat you.'

'What about a lion? That could eat me. And Joe.'

'Nothing's going to eat you, hon,' I said. I put her hand in mine but she pulled it out.

'Where did you get that from?' I asked as Phil pulled a brochure from his camera bag and opened it up.

'The airport.'

I looked over his shoulder at a picture of a swimming pool and an elephant and beside that a map. 'Is that the camp?'

'Yup,' said Phil, and he began to read it out, his finger travelling along the words as the plane juddered in the air. 'At Wilderness Camp you can feel Africa's heartbeat; a heartbeat that connects you to a place that has not changed since life began.'

I snorted. 'Who wrote that?'

'Your brother?'

'It doesn't sound like him.'

'It says here something about Moremi Game Reserve, that's what we're flying over, right? Hunted by the Bushman thousands of years ago, initiated by the Botswana tribe.'

'The *Botswana* tribe?' I shifted irritably on my seat. 'What the hell is that? You can't say the Botswana tribe. It's like saying, the England tribe. Who writes this crap?'

'What's wrong, Mum?' said Maya.

Phil sighed and folded up the brochure and put it away and I fiddled with my trousers, wishing I hadn't worn linen because now they were as creased as a concertina.

'Mum!' said Maya. 'Are we inside or are we out?'

'What?'

'Are we inside the sky or are we outside, in the plane?'

'Look,' I said, 'see the Delta down there? Now see the clouds? We're in the sky, hon, we're flying.' And I leant back in the cramped little plane, thinking back to the very first time I'd been on a plane, when I'd gone with Craig MacKinnon, and how excited I'd been then. I thought my life was just beginning then and that I could do anything I wanted. I thought that if I could just get away then everything would be good.

'I'm African, aren't I, Mum?' asked Maya, and she prodded me in the side with her elbow.

470

'Yes.' I put out my hand to stroke her hair but she ducked.

'I'm half African, aren't I, Mum?'

'Yes.'

'And me!' said Joe, and he thumped a podgy finger against the window, trying and failing to touch the fly.

'And you.'

'Am I half or am I quarter African, Mum?'

'You're half.'

'See?' said Maya to her brother as if she had won an argument.

'OK, guys,' said the pilot, yelling above the noise. 'We're going down.' And we swooped down and for a moment I couldn't see where on earth we could land. Closer and closer we flew; I could see the blur of animals, the smooth golden shanks of impala as they scattered through the trees. And then I saw the landing strip and down we bounced, coming to a stop in a burst of dust.

'Mum!' Maya said, her voice hot in my ear. 'You stole that postcard, didn't you?'

Chapter Forty-Four

'I want to go home now,' said Maya, sitting very straight on her plane seat, holding her Barbie doll tightly on her lap.

'Don't be silly,' said Phil. 'Stay there, I want to film you all getting out.'

So we waited until Phil got out and exchanged his digital for his camcorder, and then we got out and my legs felt a little shaky as I bundled Joe onto my hip, as if I'd had to run somewhere and now I was weak. The moment we were out of the plane and upright on the sand the pilot revved up the engine, adjusted his crash helmet, and he was off, just managing to lift into the air before the runway ended and disappeared into the bush.

I stood and watched the plane go and when I turned to Phil he was already heading for the safari car parked to one side of the landing strip, a large open-topped vehicle with three raised rows of seats.

'Welcome,' said the driver, an elderly man in a rumpled khaki shirt and a baseball cap on his head. 'Welcome to Wilderness Camp.' I thought he spoke with forced gaiety, like these were the lines he'd been rehearsing and someone had advised him to put more heart into it.

'Say "*Dumela Rra*",' I told Maya.

She scowled.

472

'Come on, be polite.'

'It doesn't matter,' said Phil.

'Yes it does,' I said, but I didn't know why it mattered, I didn't know why I was feeling so irritated. Perhaps I wanted to be on my own, perhaps I didn't want to have to wait while Phil took pictures, to worry whether Maya had enough sun cream on, to look for a wet wipe for Joe. I just wanted to be here by myself, to be in a place that I had not been for years.

'*Dumela Rra*,' said Maya.

The driver laughed and pushed up the tip of his cap.

The drive to camp was short, the sun above bore down on us, and as the vehicle tore through the shrub land acacia thorns scraped along its green shiny sides. The land seemed so barren, so parched, after all the water we had seen from the air, and I reminded myself that it was the dry season, that the hunting season had just begun.

'Why are they dancing, Mum?' asked Maya when we reached the camp and a group of women came running up and formed a line by the car, at once beginning to clap and ululate. 'Is it because they are happy?'

'I guess so,' I said doubtfully as the women continued to sing and dance. I could see them staring from me to Phil and back again and I wondered if they'd never had a black guest before. I hoped this wasn't Isaac's idea; welcome to Africa and the all singing, all dancing natives.

'Ah! You've arrived!' said a white man coming jauntily up to the car. 'Perfect timing! Tim, Tim Loveless.' He held out his hand to Phil, identifying him as the leader of our group. 'How was the flight? All ready to see some game?' Tim wore a green paisley scarf around his head something like a pirate, and I wondered if he had looked at himself in a mirror recently and seen that he looked a prat. A white woman came up then, wearing a slightly more glamorous khaki outfit which jarred with her flushed red face.

And I thought, Tim thinks I'm a guest from England, he has no idea I'm Isaac's sister. And he has no idea this is my camp.

'Don't I know you from somewhere?' asked the woman, and she had a very cheery voice like a presenter on a children's TV show, completely delighted with herself.

Tim stopped and looked me up and down, from my crumpled linen trousers to my white vest top.

'Only if you read fashion magazines,' said Phil. He moved to take our cases from the car, but the driver had beaten him to it and now he stood there as if he no longer had a role in life. I didn't like the way he'd said that, the way he was dismissing my career in a single sentence. What do you mean, I wanted to say.

'Why, are you a model?' asked Tim.

The woman started laughing delightedly. 'You're Kazi, aren't you? Oh my God! You're *Kazi*! I've read all about you! I *love* your trousers.' She looked me up and down as well. 'And your top.'

'My mum's famous,' said Maya.

'You must be very proud of her,' said the woman with a pat on Maya's head, and to my surprise Maya didn't move away, she stayed there with the woman's hand resting on her head as if she enjoyed it.

Tim led us through the camp, along one pathway and then another, and I could hear the airy, wooden sound of doves and then the sound of a crested crane, honking as if it were affronted. We walked in single file behind Tim until we came to two fever berry trees and then, sheltered beneath them, a row of tents built on wooden platforms like individual tree houses. They looked right; they looked exactly where tents should be. Isaac had done a good job, I thought. I'd almost been hoping to be disappointed, but the camp was far nicer than I'd imagined and there was a feeling of peace, an air of tranquillity about the place.

'There's your parents' tent,' Tim told Maya, 'and there's yours.'

Maya's eyes widened; she couldn't decide whether she liked this idea or not. 'I get to sleep in my own tent? Because I'm a big girl?'

'With your brother too,' said Tim. 'If you want.'

'Look at this!' said Phil, stepping onto the porch and going into the first tent. 'Lovely bathroom,' he shouted out. 'Come and look, kids!'

And we went and looked inside, at the large bed with its white sheet, at the two covered windows on the side, at the wardrobe whose door was open showing spotless shelves. And then we looked in the bathroom, at the wooden shelf with two porcelain bowls fitted snugly inside and the old-fashioned knobbly taps gleaming and freshly cleaned. It was more tasteful than I'd expected, as if everything had been crafted carefully by hand using only the best materials. Everything here had cost money, and I thought most of the things must have been imported from someplace else.

I left Phil and the kids admiring the bathroom and went back outside onto the deck, which was set out with two canvas chairs and a fold-out table. From here I could see the river, and as I looked a group of elephants appeared on the opposite shore, a baby in the centre of the group. They began walking lazily into the water and as they did so the air around me began to grow golden.

Then the sound came. 'Wuwu we! Wuwu we!'

'What was that, Mum?' asked Maya, running out onto the deck, a towel she had taken from the bathroom wrapped around her as if she had just had a shower.

'Just baboons,' said Tim. 'Dinner will be ready shortly. If you'd like to freshen up first?'

I stared at him, those weren't baboons!

'I'm tired,' said Maya. 'I'm really, really tired and I want to go into my *own* tent.' She looked at Joe, hoping he would complain about this.

'Let's go and eat first,' said Phil. 'What the hell is that?' and he pointed over the deck at a moporoto tree and at the long, rope-like stalks of fruit.

'Sausage tree,' said Tim.

'What's its local name?' asked Phil.

Tim looked stumped. Then he put his finger to his lips. 'Shshs! Look over there.'

The moment he said this I saw the cheetah, saw its slinky shoulders as it moved through the long grass beyond the riverbank, grass as long as hair and the colour of burnt butter. The cheetah stopped by a mound so its head was just visible. Then suddenly it flicked its tail, gathered itself up and trotted away.

'Wow,' said Phil. 'A leopard! Did you see the leopard, kids?'

'It's a cheetah, Phil,' I said, as kindly as possible.

'How can you tell?'

'It's the size of the head, and the way it walks.'

'How do you know that?' Phil looked impressed.

I shrugged; it was just something I knew.

We went back across the lawn and the grass looked black now in the darkening evening. There was a quietness, a silence broken only by the bats, by the rustles in the grass and by a slight gentle wind in the trees.

We passed a toilet made from reeds and then took a stone path down to an expanse of lawn, and even in the dark it was so green compared to the barren land we had driven through that it seemed like a carpet that had just been rolled out. To my left I could see a thatched bar and, further in the distance, a raised area that I took to be a swimming pool. I was amazed at the size of the place; from the entrance it had seemed deceptively small, but once you got into the camp itself, it was huge. I wondered how many people worked here, what they did and where they came from. How much did it cost on a daily basis to run a place like this?

The other guests were already settled around the fireplace. I could see two men wearing flak jackets like they were off-duty war correspondents or about to have a skirmish with armed guerrillas.

Phil sat down with a sleepy Joe in his lap, but Maya took her own chair and set it next to mine.

'What's that?' she said, her voice all quiet.

'Frogs,' I said.

'What are they doing?'

'They are being frogs.'

'I don't like it.'

'Don't be silly,' said Phil. 'Mmm, this beer tastes great.'

And it was then that I looked up and saw Petra Krause. It took me a second to place her, to realise that the thin white woman hurrying across the grass was actually Petra. I couldn't think how she had got here and I felt furious for a moment, as I did in the old days when she would follow Isaac and me. We had come for a peaceful family holiday, we had come to get away from Sehuba, and now here was our neighbour Petra Krause.

She was moving quickly and I wasn't sure at first if she had seen us or was heading for someone else. I didn't know whether to stand up and draw attention to where we sat, or just see where she was going. And as I watched I had an old, aching feeling of jealousy. When I'd first seen her a few days ago I'd felt sorry for her. I hadn't known about Marianne, I hadn't known her mother had died. I hadn't known she'd been sent south and I thought it must have been a shock, to go from Sehuba to South Africa. But she still had an assurance about her, an assurance she'd always had as a child, and I envied the independence in the way she walked.

I'd always thought she was a cold fish who could talk about how big something was, how long, how fast, but

478

not about how she felt about it. She was a child who liked numbers, facts and figures, but she'd rarely showed any emotions. And now I thought perhaps she didn't hide what she felt, perhaps that was just how she was. Why couldn't I be more like that?

Petra got to the fireplace and immediately stuck her hands in her pockets like she was trying to weigh herself down. I could see that her face, now that she was near the fire, looked very bright.

'So,' she said, as if it was perfectly normal that we should all be here. 'So,' she said again, looking around.

'Ladies, a glass of wine?' asked Tim Loveless, and he called for a uniformed woman to bring a tray of drinks.

Petra bent down then, right by my chair, and for a crazy second I thought she was going to kiss me. 'I've got to tell you something,' she hissed. When I opened my mouth to ask what, she put a finger against her lips in warning.

I accepted a glass of wine from the waitress but Petra declined. She seemed flushed and impatient.

'How did you get here?' Maya asked Petra.

'By truck,' Petra said. 'Kazi, I need to ...'

'Ladies, some salmon?' Tim held out a tray with strips of smoked salmon arranged beautifully amid slices of lemon and soft, just toasted bread.

I took one and began to eat.

'Are the kids in your tent tonight?' Petra asked, and she spoke urgently, as if it were vitally important that they should be.

As Tim turned with the tray, ready to offer it to the

other guests, Petra motioned me to one side with her hand. When I still didn't get up, she took my arm and quite determinedly pulled me away from the fireplace.

'What is it?' I asked, half annoyed, half intrigued.

'This way,' she said, hurrying me off along a pathway that was now lit up with flickering candles. 'Right,' she said, stopping under a jackleberry tree. 'The boy who was attacked a couple of weeks ago. He's here.'

'What?' I felt disorientated standing there in the darkness.

'Kazi,' Petra said. 'The boy wasn't killed at all, he's still here. This way, mind that log.'

She pulled me on, along another path, and we passed the reed toilet, then a large green tent and then what looked like a curio shop. 'Tim wouldn't fly him out,' Petra said, speaking over her shoulder, striding ahead. 'They took him to a clinic and then they just sent him back here.'

She stopped at last in a small clearing where I could just make out a handful of tents. My foot crunched on something and I kicked at it, seeing a Fanta can go bouncing off into the darkness.

'He's in here.' Petra stopped in front of one of the tents and put her hand out towards a badly patched up flap.

'What's that?' I asked.

'What?'

'On your hand.' I took Petra's arm, which was much frailer than I thought it would be; I had seen a strange mark as she was about to open the tent and now I could see it was a large purple bruise.

Petra looked down and was about to reply when we both heard the sound of footsteps in the bush behind us. 'Look,' she hissed. 'Just look.'

Reluctantly I put my head inside the tent. I waited until my eyes adjusted to the dim light inside and then I saw the frail body of a boy lying curled up on his side. He lay completely and utterly still, like children do when they are fast asleep from illness or exhaustion. I saw he was wearing a pair of khaki shorts and that he had his hand resting on his cheek. I saw a small metal bowl on the floor next to his head and beside that a napkin that someone had folded carefully in half and then half again. Then I looked at his legs wrapped in wads of bandages and at the vivid stains, perhaps of iodine, on the cloth.

Quickly I put my head back outside.

'We need to get him to hospital,' Petra hissed.

'How are you going to do that?'

'Where's the plane you just came in on?'

'It left the moment we got off.'

'Oh. Oh, OK.'

'What's that?' I heard footsteps again, only now they were nearer.

'What?'

'Ladies! Here you are!' Tim was walking towards us shining a torch this way and that as if he thought we were hiding in the undergrowth. 'What on earth are you doing here?' he laughed.

'Well,' said Petra, about to answer.

But Tim continued speaking, 'Just to say, dinner is

served. Your husband is already at the dining tent,' he said to me. 'Did Maya find you?'

And then we heard the sound again. Wuwu we! Wuwu we! The whoops started low, like a bubble of noise, like excited children hollering at a football game, and then they got louder and became whiny and mad and then there was total pandemonium.

Chapter Forty-Five

I just didn't know what happened; one minute I was standing outside the boy's tent and the next I was running through the bush screaming for my child. It took only a second to connect the two things: the sound of the hyena and the fact Maya was missing. And so I ran, I just cut straight through the trees, not even bothering to try and retrace my steps. I didn't care about paths or about what route I should take; it was like I was being pulled on a piece of rope because I knew, somehow, where she was even though at first I couldn't hear her. I could feel where Maya was and I crashed on, pushing my way through the bush, slapping at branches. I didn't care about plants underfoot or about snakes in the undergrowth, I was oblivious to everything but getting to where I needed to be. Yet I didn't seem to be going fast enough, I didn't seem to be making any progress at all. Then I heard her, heard a scream that could only be hers, a noise that tugged inside of me, that fired me on so that nothing could stand in my way. And when I saw her, huddled down on the sand beside the reed toilet that I had passed only a few minutes before, I pounced.

And suddenly there were people all over the place, two of the tourist men in their flak jackets, a guide in uniform with a cigarette in his hand, a woman with an apron gasping, her hand to her throat.

I scooped Maya up and she clung to my chest like a marsupial, as if she were a baby again and not a six year old. I could feel her heart thumping and as I lifted her into place her legs quivered against my stomach.

'The animal, the animal,' she said. 'It wanted to eat me. Mum!'

I looked around. It was too dark, I couldn't see anything, the tree canopy above us was so dense I couldn't even see the moon. I patted Maya on her back and my hand at once felt wet and I knew it was blood; I didn't have to see it to know that. And then I started running again through the bush with Maya on my chest like I had to get away from something, like if I kept on running my child would somehow be all right and the blood wouldn't be there.

Then I was back where I started and from inside the dining tent, the tent we were supposed to be in, happily having our meal, I could see four white faces staring out at us, like we were something dangerous.

'Thank God,' Tim said, running up from behind the dining tent. 'She OK?'

'No she's not OK!' I said, my jaw clenched. 'Get her in the light so we can see.'

The guests who were still in the dining tent stood up quickly as we came in, pushing back their chairs, and then they stood with their backs against the canvas walls and I could feel them watching as if we were some strange evening entertainment. I put Maya down on the edge of the table and I stood in front of her, her arms still round my neck.

'You OK, hon? What happened?' I pushed her hair back from her face, hardly daring to look at her and see what was wrong, but my eyes were already on her leg and I could see something white around her knee and it took me a while to realise it was bone. 'Oh Jesus,' I whispered, and I scooped her towards me again as she fainted. 'What have you got?' I shouted at Tim, who was clearing plates from the table and piling them to one side. I had a sudden vision of Craig MacKinnon making the exact same gesture all those years ago at the President's Hotel in Gaborone and I wanted to say, now is not the time for this. 'What can you get her?' I demanded.

'Lay her down,' said Tim.

'I'm not lying her on the *table*!' I hissed. I took a napkin, a big thick white apron that felt freshly starched, and put it gently against her leg, but unconscious as she was she jerked herself forward. 'You have to get us out of here. Look at that . . . She's got to see a doctor.'

'Well, there's a bit of a problem.' Tim had a bottle of red wine in his hand and I stared at him, wondering if he were going to pour himself a glass.

'Now!'

'There's no plane . . .'

'Well get a fucking plane.' I looked at Maya for a second, her eyelids quivered and briefly opened before closing again.

Then Phil appeared with Joe on his shoulders and when he saw Maya his face went white. 'What happened?

Maya ran off to find you. I've been searching everywhere!'

'I'll radio for help,' said Tim. 'I'll radio another camp, see what they can do. Craig might be able to help; he's just on Chief's Island. The important thing is not to panic. The boys are out there, they have guns and they'll make sure the hyenas don't come back.'

And I looked at Maya, at the splatter of blood on her face, at the way the bone protruded from her knee like some grotesque jellyfish, and I wanted to vomit.

We squashed ourselves in Tim's tent while he radioed for help and while the blood trickled down into my flip-flops, turning them crimson in the wavering light of the tent's paraffin lamp.

'Roger, roger,' said Tim. And I thought, oh for God's sake just talk normally.

'We need to stop the bleeding.'

I looked up to see a man in a guide's uniform bending over Maya. He took the edge of the table cloth where it hung over the table and began tearing off strips, making a terrible noise that was at once soft and jagged.

'What are you doing?' Tim asked. 'Electricity, do you know what you're doing?'

The man didn't reply, he just began to bandage Maya around the leg, pressing and bandaging, pressing and bandaging. 'She's lost a lot of blood,' he said when he was done. Then he stopped speaking, held his fingers on Maya's wrist and his lips moved as if he were counting.

And then we were in the plane and then we were in the clinic in Maun and everything became a blur. First we were in a green room where everyone seemed very busy. I saw a man set up a drip and a nurse squeezing on a plastic bag of fluid as if coaxing it down the tube.

'Is she OK?' I asked.

But the people were too busy rushing around to answer.

'Get her stabilised,' said a doctor to a nurse. 'Let's make sure she's got enough blood going round.'

Then they put us in a room of our own and to get to it we had to pass through an outside courtyard which for some reason had a fountain in the middle, and as we passed through it I could hear the water dripping down like a tap that had been left on. And I thought, what a waste of water, someone should turn that off.

I put Maya down on the bed and covered her with a sheet. Then I wondered where the boy from the tent was, the boy that Petra had helped onto the plane with us. There had been no room for Phil and Joe, not with the three of us. The boy had made no sound; he had just lain there across the back two seats while I sat in the front with Maya on my lap, my head right up against the window of the plane, and I had thought, if I just hold her, if I just keep her like this she'll be fine.

'Hello, my dear, how is our little patient?' I looked at the door as a nurse came bustling in. Maybe she had been asleep and our arrival had woken her and she'd been forced on duty, for her uniform looked awry, her hair uncombed.

'What's that for?' I asked. She had a needle in her hand and she was heading for Maya.

'Tetanus,' she said.

'Mum!' Maya yelled suddenly, and she yelled like she was having a nightmare, like she wasn't conscious of yelling at all, and I remembered reading that when people die they call for their mother.

'It's OK, hon,' I told her, and I squeezed my eyes and wished more than anything in the world that it was me and not her lying on the clinic bed. 'The nurse is just going to give you an injection.'

'But I don't want one!' Her voice sounded normal now, too normal.

'Yes, but listen, Maya, listen ...'

But Maya was getting too worked up to listen so I bent over the bed and took her face in my hands and made her eyes look at mine. 'It won't take a second, you just need to ...'

And then the nurse just jabbed in the needle without saying a word. And Maya sobbed and she looked at me like it was all my fault. And it was all my fault. I was the one who'd said, let's go to the camp. If we're here we may as well go on holiday, hey? Mum's fine, let's go to the Delta, let's see Isaac's camp. And then when I'd known it was my camp nothing could have stopped me. I hadn't listened when Isaac said kids shouldn't go, all I cared about was that it was mine.

And all that day I had been so irritated; I had so wanted to be on my own. Phil had irritated me, and so had Joe. And so had Maya. And I had let Petra Krause take me away from the fireplace, I hadn't even thought about leaving Maya behind. I hadn't even thought about whether she would be safe.

I looked at her where she lay on the bed, her feet poking out from under the sheet, her toes a deep brown from the sun, the remains of shiny pink nail varnish she'd put on days ago when we'd first left the UK. She'd been too impatient to let the varnish dry, she'd run off somewhere and the pink had smudged all over her nails.

It was all my fault, but it was Isaac's too because he was the one who'd called me home; he'd called me after a fifteen-year absence saying Mum had collapsed. If he hadn't called, I never would have come.

'What happens now?' I asked the nurse.

'Doctor will look at her again, he's coming just now. You may be flown down south. We have an agreement with a flying doctor.'

'South Africa?' I asked, and I thought of when I went to Bophuthatswana and of the photo shoot in a bikini next to the drugged elephant and I didn't want to go. I wanted them to say Maya is fine, she's absolutely fine and send us on our way. But she couldn't be absolutely fine if she was here in the clinic, if she'd been attacked by a hyena.

'I'm sorry,' said the nurse.

I panicked, what was she sorry for? Then I saw there was a man at the doorway and at first I thought it was the doctor, but then I knew it couldn't be because the nurse was trying to shut the door in his face.

'Kazi Muyendi!' the man managed to shout.

'Who's that?' I asked the nurse.

'Nobody.' The nurse sighed. 'Just a journalist. I don't know how he got in. He's been bothering us all evening.'

'A journalist? What, you mean he's looking for me?' And I thought, why would he want me? And then I realised, it wasn't me he was looking for, it was Maya. He had heard what had happened to Maya. He had heard about the hyena.

The doctor came and he was very gentle, he removed the sheet and he examined Maya.

'What do you think?' I asked anxiously.

He attempted a smile. 'I'm a little concerned about the puncture wounds, we wouldn't want them to get infected.'

I nodded furiously.

'It might be best to have some x-rays to see if anything is broken. But for now the wounds have been cleaned and dressed, so we'll wait and see if it heals.'

'*If* it heals?'

The doctor turned from the bed, ready to go.

'What about stitches?'

'Paper stitches are a possibility, that could hold the knee together, but infection is always a risk. The leg is badly damaged.'

I looked at him and I thought *the* leg? Like it's not her leg anymore, like when someone dies and people say *the* body, not her body or his body but *the* body.

After the doctor left Maya was delirious; she said she could see bunny rabbits on the walls and I looked at her and thought this can't be happening and it's all my fault.

During the night I heard the doctor and the nurse in the courtyard outside by the dripping fountain. I was at the doorway to the room when I first heard them and

I was looking out, out at the clear night sky and all the silver stars and thinking it was wrong that it could be so beautiful. Their voices were clear, I could hear the dripping and I could see the doctor and the nurse, see their outlines as they stood beside a heavy flowering bougainvillea tree in the corner of the courtyard.

'This is the fourth time he's rung,' said the nurse.

'Just don't answer,' sighed the doctor.

'You want me not to answer the phone? It's a clinic, how can I not answer the phone? They know it's her, I didn't say anything, but they know it's her. And of course they know it happened at the Muyendi camp.'

'She's not ready to talk to the media.'

Why would I want to talk to the media, I thought, as I stood in the doorway.

Maya was asleep; she was drunk on morphine. The nurse and the doctor had disappeared. I got gingerly onto Maya's bed and then I saw we couldn't both fit in the bed so I got out and got back in upside down so my head was next to Maya's feet, and I cuddled her toes and put my arm on her tummy and held my breath.

491

BOOK TEN
Nanthewa

Chapter Forty-Six

The morning I set off for Maun I could feel that my blood was high. The doctors at the clinic had said I should rest. 'Take it easy, Mrs Muyendi,' the foreign one with the misshapen face had said. As if a person can get anything done if they take it easy! Life is suffering, not something to be taken easy. These modern doctors know nothing, and anyway I couldn't stay where I was when my family was in trouble.

I told the maid to get my bags, I had packed them the night before and although I had hoped Grace would help me with this she was nowhere to be seen. I didn't know what was the matter with Grace, she was always at Gumare as if she had something important to attend to there. But as far as I knew, she did not. The maid failed to answer when I called for my bags, and when I found her the silly girl was weeping while she pretended to clean the kitchen. She is not able to see that she has been given a good opportunity by working for the Muyendi family. If she does well at our home then one day she may work in our general trading store.

I found I was shaking when I had finished scolding her. I was shaking because I was annoyed, but I was also shaking from thinking about all the things that were going wrong with our family and the way we had been cursed. I had been waiting for many years for my daughter Kazi to come home because I knew in my blood that one day she would. In the years she had been away Isaac had protected me well, he had worked hard in order to look after me, he had even thought he was protecting me by putting those letters of hers away. But still, I should have liked to have known she was writing to me. He should not have taken the money, God knows that, but he did not spend that money on himself, he used it to build up that camp of his so that we should all benefit from it. Kazi needs to realise that, things have been hard for us here. And she should not have gone to the camp angrily like that. Now I had to go to Maun, to make sure someone was looking after Maya properly.

The bus was very slow that day leaving the village. There are all manner of new buses these days but still they are not very comfortable. They have soft drinks and video screens, but the seats are too soft and not good for an old woman like me. I did not talk to my neighbours on the bus; if they knew who I was then I did not want any conversations about hyenas or any such thing. And if they did not know who I was then I did not want to begin any conversation in which they would soon find out.

If Isaac had not left in such a hurry then I could have travelled to Maun with him. For many years he had even wanted to buy me my own car. 'But who would drive it?' I had asked him. 'You would, Mama,' he had said. Imagine an old woman like me driving a car! In my day there were no cars, and once the vehicles did start coming in and out of Sehuba it never was a woman driving.

At last the bus stopped and we arrived in Maun. It stopped in a crowded part of the road, an area taken up with more taxis and buses and kombis than I had seen in my life. I got my stick and I put my bag on my head and set off at once, I had no idea where I was going, I just wanted to get away from the crowds. And I knew that Maun is dangerous these days, if people see you are a stranger then they might try to trick you in some way or rob you of your money. People don't look after strangers anymore; we have lost the traditional ways. *Motho ke motho ka motho ya mongwe*; a person is a person because of another person. That was what my aunty taught me, that was the way I was brought up. Now people think only of themselves and of how they can cheat others.

As luck would have it I had set off in the right direction, for when I came to the nearest crossroads I could see a large supermarket on the other side of the road and nearby a sign with a doctor's red cross. I knew my little English granddaughter Maya was at this clinic, that my son had organised for her to attend the private one and not the government hospital which is a terrible place and can make you quite ill.

I thought I would get myself a Coke. The doctors said I should not take Coke anymore but I had been sitting on that bus most of the day and my blood was weak and I need something to drink. I had some few pula in the strap of my dress and as I stood at the crossroads ready to cross I nudged myself with my arm to check the money was still there. And then right there in the road in front of me I saw a troubling sight.

A young man not much older than my son Isaac was standing in the middle of the road; he was having a conversation with someone who did not exist. First he nodded, then he shook his head, then he put out a hand and made as if to touch this person. Then he started shouting, and *Batho*! The language coming out of that man's mouth. If I could I would have stopped my ears from hearing it. I wondered if the man was drunk, but something about him told me he wasn't. He was dirty, his trousers were torn and they were stained, and when he turned I could see his buttocks were almost hanging out of the cloth. Where was his family? How could they leave him to behave like this?

Everyone was walking around the man; no one was bothered by him at all, so I knew he was a familiar sight in Maun, that he was here perhaps every day in this same spot with his imaginary friend.

Then as I crossed the road, careful not to step too near to the man, a little girl came up to me, all shy, her head down. I thought she wanted help, that she needed something from me, that perhaps she was lost.

'*Madi*,' she said, and she thrust her hand rudely in front of me just like that. She wanted money from me! And then two little boys came up to join her and they began to join in, and when I shook my head that no, I didn't have money to give them, one of the boys spat and another laughed.

This was it; this was the development my late husband Rweendo had talked about? A place so full of vehicles a person couldn't even cross the road, a place where men go crazy and stand in the street, a place where children were begging instead of going to school.

I reached the pavement outside the big supermarket and I was about to join the people at the wide glass doors when a white man hurrying past knocked into me so that I had to grab at my bag on my head before it toppled off.

'Watch where you're going,' said the man as if I were a stupid somebody.

I stopped at once. '*Rra?*' I asked.

The man had not been looking at me, he was in too much of a hurry, but now he did. He had dark glasses on his face and his chin had not been shaved for a very long time. I saw he wore khaki and I saw a company name written on the pocket above his chest.

'I said, watch it!' The man laughed, he was trying to get past me.

'It is you who should mind where you are going,' I said. But of course the man did not understand Setswana, he didn't know what I was saying. 'You mind where you're going because it's you who slammed into me. Didn't your parents teach you manners?'

The man shrugged and he got past me.

'*Ee!*' I shouted after him and waved my stick. 'This was our land you know, long before you people came.' I watched while the man jumped up into the front of a very large truck. The truck was open at the side and I could see a whole group of white people inside. The truck was very dirty; it looked as if it had been driving through the bush for weeks. I wondered for a second where the truck was from and where it was going, it could even be going to

499

Moremi; it was very likely that it was going to Moremi, and for all I knew these people might even be going to camp at Xuku itself. For these days there was a public campsite just near where our home had been before the chief game warden came and burnt it down.

I got my Coke without any further trouble and set off for the clinic. Only the pavements in Maun were too crowded for an old woman like me, crowded with flat-footed people walking nosily on concrete.

The clinic was a very grand building and I stood to one side for a moment to watch how people negotiated the doors that opened without anyone either pulling or pushing them. Then I steadied my bag on my head and went in. Nobody turned as I entered; the two young girls behind the desk paid me no attention at all because they have lost their respect for elders like town girls do.

'*Dumela Bomma*,' I said, and I rested my elbow on the counter.

'*Ee*,' said one of the girls, but she wasn't looking at me, instead she began pulling out little metal drawers and then closing them shut again.

'*Ke kopa thuso*,' I said at last.

'*Ee*,' said the girl, and now she got busy inspecting her fingers. 'What is it, *Mma*?'

'I'm looking for my granddaughter, her name is Maya, she was transferred here some three days ago.'

And then that made the girl pay me some attention. 'The Muyendi child? The one who the hyena . . .'

'*Ee*,' I cut in. What did she think she was doing, speaking people's private business out like that? 'Where is she?'

The girl looked at me quizzically then, as if trying to work something out. 'It's not visiting hours now.'

'Visitor hours? I'm not a visitor, I'm her grandmother!' I took my bag down off my head and laid it on the counter. I could see the girl didn't like this; she didn't like it that my bag was so dusty and old. But inside that bag I had everything I needed, I had the medicine that would help Maya to become strong again. 'I will wait here.'

The girl sighed and went back to her metal drawers.

I was left like that, waiting, for some time. The girls behind the desk left and were replaced with another two, and then finally I was told where to go.

'*Ko ko!*' I called at the door, which had a little metal sign in the middle. When there was no reply I knocked and went in and there was my little English grand-daughter lying on her bed, very still with her eyes closed. I was glad my daughter had given her first-born a Shiyeyi name; it showed that after all she had not forgotten where she came from.

It was very cold in the room, something like walking into a fridge freezer. It was not the sort of room a sick person should be in. Kazi was reading from a picture book, and as I saw her sitting there next to Maya in the bed I was reminded of how she did her schoolwork as a child, how those things had come easy to her. I thought how beautiful she had been then, how I had entered her for those contests so that she could feel proud of herself and that others would see her as beautiful as well. Now she was too thin, her face when it turned to me was worried and her hair looked like an abandoned nest.

'Mum!' Kazi said as she looked at me there in the doorway. She did not seem surprised, instead her voice sounded hopeful. She moved at once, as if to get up, but I patted her leg to show she should stay where she was. This was a serious business, I didn't want a fuss.

'How is my little English girl?' I asked, and as I went to stand by Maya, so Kazi went and stood on the other side of the bed. I looked at Maya, at her soft little face, and I saw she was red in the cheeks, unnaturally so.

'We're waiting for the doctor,' Kazi sighed.

Doctor! I got the medicine out of my bag and I took a handful of herbs and I rubbed them between my fingers for a while until the preparation was warm.

'What's that?' Kazi asked, and she leant over the bed to sniff it.

'Medicine,' I replied, and I lifted back the sheet and began to apply the herbs to Maya's leg.

'It smells so familiar,' said my daughter, and as she spoke her eyes were dreamy as if she was thinking of a long time ago.

'*Ee*,' I said. 'That is because I used to use some of this medicine on you.'

Then we were silent as I set to work and I applied the medicine gently, so gently that Maya was not disturbed and she didn't wake. But as I set to work I shivered a little in the coldness of the clinic room, and in the silence I could hear a noise something like a generator listened to from a distance.

And then there was a sharp knock on the door that startled both of us.

'Who's that?' Kazi asked.

I finished my work and as Maya stirred and her eyelids fluttered I patted her on the head; I didn't want her to wake and become distressed like her mother was. Then the door opened and that man walked in, that man who took my daughter off to the UK just like that.

He jiggled his hands as he came into the room and he had a crooked smile on his face that I remembered well. He looked like any other white working for *masafari*, only his clothes were particularly clean, particularly new and well ironed. Kazi saw him come in and she dropped the picture book she had been reading to Maya, she dropped it just like that on the floor.

'Hey, Kazi!' said the man.

'Craig,' she nodded, and I saw her fold her arms tight across her chest. I knew her husband had returned to these parts, for Lenny Krause had told me some years ago, but I had never seen him in person and he had never thought to pay a visit to my family, to the family whose daughter he had stolen all that time ago.

'Long time!' Craig smiled. 'Glad to see you got down here OK. And this must be your daughter!' He stopped halfway to the bed, and then he looked at Maya as if she were something he had lost.

'Who's he?' Maya opened her eyes at the sound of the man's loud voice and her eyes were staring as if she didn't know where she was.

'This is Craig,' said Kazi, 'Craig MacKinnon.'

'Who?' said Maya, and underneath the sheet I saw her feet fidget.

Craig laughed. 'Has your mother not told you about me?'

I looked at my daughter and I saw her scowl and I wondered just why she was so angry with this silly man when after all from what I had heard she was the one who had left him. I thought of the man she had come home with, the man Phil who I could see was a loving man, a loving man like Rweendo had been in the early days. He was a gentle somebody and I could see he loved my daughter very much, and that she in turn loved him although there were times when she was too sharp with him.

'Craig is someone I used to know,' said Kazi reluctantly.

'Used to know! For God's sake, Kazi, we were married!'

Maya stared at Craig and her forehead turned into a frown. 'Mum?' she asked.

'I guess we should thank you,' said Kazi coldly. 'For helping to get us out of there.'

'No problem!' Craig said. 'All in a day's work. Nothing too much in order to help a celebrity.'

I didn't know what this word celebrity was and as it was I was having to concentrate very hard to follow what they were saying. But it was not the words I was most concerned with; it was the way they were with each other. I thought that these two had hurt each other very much. There was something very angry between them and my daughter's body was stiff as she stood by the bed and so was her voice.

Kazi pulled at the sheet on Maya's bed, although it didn't need to be rearranged. 'So you're running a camp here?' she asked.

Craig smiled and I saw a funny little crease in his cheek that stayed there for some few moments even after he had stopped smiling.

'I thought you went to Zim?' said my daughter.

'Aye, I did. Then I came back here, back to where we met. I had some fond memories of Botswana, Kazi.' And he smiled at my daughter then.

'Mum?' asked Maya again, as if she was trying to remind her mother that she was there.

'Shshs,' Kazi said, and she looked at Craig, a look that said he wasn't wanted in this room.

'You just disappeared, Kazi,' he said, and still he spoke too loudly, he wasn't lowering his voice as a visitor to a sick person should. 'What was I supposed to do? You made me look like a right fool.'

My daughter smiled a little then and I knew what she was thinking, that he still was a fool.

'Off you went to London to make a name for yourself,' said Craig, and the look on his face made him ugly now.

Kazi didn't answer, she just went to a jug of water on the table by the bed and began to fill a glass.

'Didn't you?' asked Craig.

Still Kazi continued pouring the water. Then she handed it to Maya. 'You said I'd never make it,' she turned to him at last. 'Well, you know what, I did.'

Craig looked at me then, as if he thought I would have an opinion on this, but I busied myself putting away the medicine. My daughter had done well, I thought, she had realised her mistake in running away with this man and she had left him. And then I thought about how alone she must have been then, how far away and how alone.

I took my glasses off for my eyes were paining me; they were stinging from the coldness in the room. Perhaps these two would begin quarrelling, I thought, and there had been enough quarrels in our family for an old woman like me. I closed my eyes and then when I opened them again Craig had gone.

'We need to get you out of here,' I told Maya, getting up from my chair.

'We're still waiting for the doctor, Mum,' said Kazi. She seemed happier now; her arms were no longer folded against her chest, she had picked up the reading book from the floor.

'I'm moving you to the Kaunda household so I can look after Maya myself,' I said, and I retied my scarf on my head and I felt for my stick. I would go and make the arrangements and Isaac would help me. It was only as I left that clinic, as I got to the door that opened without being pushed or pulled, that I realised I had been so worried about my little English granddaughter that I had forgotten about the one who needed me even more; I had forgotten about Candy.

BOOK ELEVEN

Kazi

Chapter Forty-Seven

There is nothing like guilt to make you feel you can't move. That's what it felt like at the clinic, until Mum came storming in and moved us. Isaac appeared and did what he was told and drove us to someone's house. I didn't know whose it was, I took in only bits and pieces, like the fact you had to go down a driveway to get to it, the Doberman on a chain in the yard, the fake flowers on the living room table, a fluffy blue rug on the floor. There were real flowers too, in a glass vase in the middle of an old metal table, that Tim Loveless had sent. I thought of all the flowers I had the day Maya was born. Flowers were for births or deaths. I didn't want any now.

We were taken to a rondavel at the back of the main house, an old rondavel with slightly sunken walls, and there was an upright fan on the floor which whirred round its metal head like a camera. On the window were mosquito nets encrusted with dead insects. It took me a couple of days to work out why the rondavel made me so uncomfortable, and then I realised it was because it felt like a shrine. The bed had a tall white headboard and the whole thing trembled when you came near it. The mattress was laden with quilts and blankets and two pillows almost as big as Maya. It was as if the bed were waiting for someone to return.

Next to the bed, along the curve of the wall, was a cream-coloured dressing table with a large mirror and all along the mirror were photographs of a young girl. That's when I started to feel it was a shrine. It was only later I heard the rondavel used to belong to the first-born daughter of the family with whom we were staying and that she had died not long ago from Aids.

We spent several days in the rondavel until the haze began to lift, as it did the day Isaac came to talk to me. Mum was asleep under a tree outside and I had been leafing through one of Maya's school reading books when my brother came to the doorway.

'He he he!' he chuckled.

I turned and stared at him and for a second he looked like a young boy. Despite the suit he was wearing, despite the growth of beard on his face and his middle-aged belly, he looked like a young boy, like the boy who used to run after the tourist trucks through Sehuba shouting, 'Give me your money!' Like the boy the American Peace Corps took a picture of that day and made into a post-card. And I was about to tell him about the card when he said, 'I'm sorry, sis.'

I nodded and he came in.

'I'm sorry it had to happen to your daughter.'

'Or to anyone's daughter,' I said, enraged. 'Or to anyone's son.'

'Of course.' Isaac cracked on some gum in his mouth. I didn't know why he had to come visiting eating bubble gum. He was acting like this was just something that had happened. I was furious with him, and I was still furious

510

that we had had to ask Craig MacKinnon for help, that we had had to call on him and that he had the power to arrange our plane. I didn't want to be indebted to him; I didn't want him in any way involved with us. The way he had come to the clinic, walking in like he thought he was my saviour, I couldn't imagine what I'd ever seen in him.

'We're going to sort it out,' said Isaac.

'How?' I demanded. 'How are you going to sort it out?'

'Just stay calm, don't talk to the press, and we'll sort it out.'

'And how is Maya supposed to get over this?'

'Mum's here now,' said Isaac as he turned to go. 'She'll help.'

And I thought, help? Mum's not here to help, she's here to take over. She had got Maya and me out of the clinic because I'd been too exhausted to put up a fight. Now she was behaving as if she were a qualified doctor, applying poultices, telling Maya what to eat and what to drink, how to sit and when to sleep.

'Where's the boy?' Maya asked suddenly from the bed. I went over to her quickly and picked up a glass of water from next to the bed in case she was thirsty. I hadn't even realised she had been aware enough on the plane to know the boy was there. 'What's his name?'

'I don't know,' I said, feeling guilty. Maya took a sip of water and at once went back to sleep.

Then I heard Phil and Joe outside; it had taken them a while to get another flight down to Maun. They had only arrived the afternoon before. I could hear Joe saying he wasn't sleepy and Phil saying he was and I could tell he was trying to get him in the buggy. But Phil hadn't thought about how he was going to push the buggy through the deep sand in the yard. Ever since we got to Sehuba I'd been trying to show him you couldn't push a buggy in deep sand.

'OK?' Phil asked, appearing at the doorway to the roundavel.

'She's sleeping,' I said, nodding at Maya, at her body sandwiched between the two giant pillows on the bed.

'So is Joe. Where's your mum?'

'Outside, I guess. But she said she was leaving this morning.' I waited; I felt he wanted to say something more.

'I got a call.'

'Yes?'

'I got the job.'

'What?'

Phil pushed his glasses up with his thumb; he seemed nervous for some reason. 'The one I was going for, the one I've been talking about the whole time. Anyway, I got it.'

'Good, good, that's great.' I got up and went to the window and poked at the mosquito screen and at once dead insect wings came scattering down onto the floor like tiny broken autumn leaves.

'Kazi, I've been waiting for a break like this for years,' Phil said, and he sounded as if he were trying to persuade me of something. 'I just don't know why it has to come now.' He looked deflated. 'They want me back there next week.'

'You mean back in England? Well, we can't go.'

Again Phil pushed his glasses up with his thumb. 'When she's better.'

'When she's better,' I echoed, and I wondered when this would be. 'It's like we don't know each other anymore,' I blurted out, and I turned from the window to see Phil still standing in the same spot and I thought about the day I'd first met him in the green room at the BBC and how much he used to smile then.

'What,' he said, 'because we don't tell each other everything?'

'How do you mean?'

'Oh, like you being married for instance?'

I saw how rigidly he was standing and then I looked back to the window and I saw Isaac in the yard outside and he was standing next to Petra Krause. Where had she come from? Wherever I was, there she was too. They were deep in conversation and Petra had her hand on his shoulder. They looked as they did when they were children, when they were hatching some hunting expedition together, and Petra was looking right in Isaac's eyes and I realised then that she didn't normally do this. Were they going to have an affair right under my nose?

Phil has trapped me, I thought. I never told him I was married because in my head I wasn't. I had just tried to push Craig MacKinnon and that part of my life away, I thought none of it mattered once I met Phil. How was I going to explain that there was nothing underhand about this, that it was not a big secret, that it was just something I had chosen not to tell? And I didn't like the way he had saved this up; someone must have told him about the marriage, perhaps he had even seen Craig himself, but he'd been waiting until he could use it in an argument. Why couldn't he have just told me that he knew? What was wrong between us that we were fighting like this after what had happened to Maya?

'Hey!' Petra said, coming into the roundavel. '*Howzit?*'

Maya woke up again, and as Petra walked to the bed I could smell cigarette and a light, lemony smell. She handed Maya a little stuffed elephant. 'This is Nelly,' she said. 'She used to be mine.' And Maya held it very close so that the elephant bulged in her arms.

'So,' Petra said to me, and she raised her eyebrows because at that moment Phil turned and walked out. 'Am I interrupting something?'

'No,' I said sharply, too sharply because of what I had seen of her and my brother outside the window.

'The hyena was hungry,' said Maya from the bed, struggling to sit up, knocking one of the pillows to the floor. 'It thought I was food. But that's OK, isn't it, Mum? 'Cos he didn't eat me.'

I hurried over and sat on the bed and it trembled. 'Yes, it's OK now, you're going to be fine.'

'So,' said Petra. 'You know why this happened?'

'Oh God.' I put my head down and rubbed it with my hands. 'I can't think of anything else. I never should have left her alone, I never should have gone to the camp in the first place.'

Petra thrust her hands into her pockets impatiently. 'No, Kazi. Think about why the boy and Maya got attacked. It's because of lodges like Wilderness Camp. *Ja*. They've allowed things like this to happen. Things have changed because of the camps. Think about when we were young, Kazi, since when do hyenas attack people?'

'Perhaps they did ...'

'In their *tents*, Kazi! Not in their tents. We both knew that, we were always being told; if you're in a tent you're safe. *Yissus*! Have you ever heard of a lion getting inside someone's tent? No. But the hyenas have learnt to open the tents. Why? Because the tents are there. Think about the boy. Why was he attacked? Because he was there. Because we're building camps in the animals' backyard. Think how many deaths there are these days. The woman taken by the croc, the man killed by the hippos, people trampled by elephants. Just the day you arrived, you know what happened? Electricity saved two people from a hippo attack. *Ja*. And why did it attack? Because of all the boats. And now the hyenas. First they take a child from a tent, so they get a taste ...' Petra stopped and looked at Maya but she was asleep again with Nelly in her arms. 'They see people as prey, and we're close, we're all over the place. *Yissus*! We're easy to take. But that doesn't stop places like Wilderness Camp. Because that's what they're selling. Tim and my father and ...'

'And my brother?' I said.

'And your brother,' Petra sighed. 'That's what the tourists want. Excitement! Danger! Fear! So that's what they're selling. When the staff first told them about the hyenas, what did they do? Nothing. Because it was only the staff at risk. When the boy was attacked, what did they do? Cover it up. I talked with Electricity.'

'Who?'

'The man who helped Maya, who stopped the bleeding. Your cousin's son.'

'He is?' I felt disorientated, I was getting too much information and I couldn't sort it out.

'*Ja*. They hid the boy away and pretended it didn't happen and just kept on bringing the tourists in.'

I thought about telling Petra to lower her voice, I thought about telling her all this didn't matter, what mattered was getting Maya well.

'The press are onto this,' said Petra. 'Not just in South Africa. I've just had a call. There's a British film crew on standby in Jo'burg.'

I didn't answer. But I imagined someone in London opening their morning paper, propping it up next to a bowl of sugar puffs and reading a story all about how my child was mauled by a hyena. And I could see them digging out old modelling pictures of me to go with it. I could hear Diane on the phone, saying there were interviews lined up.

Petra leant up against the wall, her hands held out behind her.

'Are you writing something about this?' I asked.

'That's why I came here, Kazi. It was just supposed to be a travel feature. But you've seen what's wrong. The camps are only interested in making money. And the way they make money is by selling this idea of wilderness. But it's not just that, it's the way they're run. *Yissus*, these camps are corrupt, the whole system is corrupt. That's why things go wrong.'

'When you say they've learnt how to open the tents,' I began, still struggling to make sense, 'you mean the people at the camp *knew* this? When we got there, they already knew?'

'Of course they knew, think about the boy.'

'But how could they let us come?' I wailed. 'How could they let us stay there?' And I thought again how reluctant Isaac had been when I'd first suggested we visit his camp; how he'd said children under eight weren't allowed. So they'd known, both Isaac and Mum had known what had happened to Leapile's boy, that there was danger. And still they had let us come. But then could they have stopped me, would I have let them stop me?

'What's the boy's name?' I asked.

'What?'

'The boy, what's his name?'

'Kgosi,' said Petra.

'What does that mean, Mum?' Maya asked, waking up again.

I smiled at her and hurried over. 'It means King.'

BOOK TWELVE
Candy

Chapter Forty-Eight

I'm looking at the tree and the tree looks nice. It's dark, it's so dark out here but the tree is still green on top where the moon makes it light. I like the bark because it's like people's arms. It's like people made from clay all wrapped around each other and it's like they don't want to be around each other but they are.

There's been a lot of smoke coming from this tree. As soon as my grandmother left, when she forgot about me and went to Maun, it started smoking. I told the maid and I told MaNeo when she came looking for my father but they just laughed at me.

Petra Krause says this tree is an invader. It is invading us. She is the one who will tell those people in South Africa about the tree, then they will come and cut it down. If this tree is cut then those cuts won't heal, my grandmother said, it will just bleed and bleed and bleed.

When my grandmother was away I took my blanket outside and I stayed near the tree, all night long I stayed near the tree on the sand which was cool and held me in place. I brought some food out here, I brought the remains of my grandmother's birthday cake which is hard now like a biscuit, and I ate the cake under the tree and I looked at the people wrapped around each other.

No one bothered me under the tree; I just stayed there

in my nightie that smells of sleep and the tree was still in the night and so was I. My grandmother went to see Maya because the hyena took her by the face; she didn't care about me.

I'm looking at the tree and the tree looks nice. It's green on the top from the light of the moon and underneath it's all darkness. But it doesn't belong here. And they will come and cut it down. I look at the tree and I ask it:

Why did my Aunty Kazi have to come from England and spoil everything?

Why is my mother never around these days?

Why doesn't my grandmother love me best of all?

BOOK THIRTEEN
Kazi

Chapter Forty-Nine

'Are my friends going to school now?' Maya asked the morning after we returned to Sehuba. We were sitting outside under the mulberry tree, just as I had done as a child. And as we sat there I could see my eight-year-old self, the way I would sit under the tree so patiently, having my hair done, my mother getting me ready for a beauty contest, Isaac watching and playing on his imaginary canoe, Marianne Krause coming by and saying how beautiful I looked.

'Mum! I *said*, are my friends going to school now?'

I stopped dreaming and looked at her. She was almost back to her old self; she could walk properly again, although she still had some painkillers and her antibiotics, and she was talking as much as she ever did, as if to make up for lost time.

'You mean back in England?' I asked. 'Yeah, they're at school now.'

'But I'm not, am I, Mum?'

'No, you're not. Do you wish you were there?'

'No,' she said. 'I want to stay here,' and she blew a pink bubble.

So do I, I thought, so do I.

''Cos I really love Botswana, you know.'

'Where did you get that bubble gum from?' I asked.

Maya ignored the question. 'I'm really lucky, aren't I?' she asked when the bubble had burst. 'I'm blessed. The hyena didn't eat me, so I'm blessed.'

'Blessed?' It seemed like a strange word to use.

'That's what Gran says.'

And I thought, who's Gran? Maya called Phil's mother Grandma, so who was Gran? And then I realised that this was Gran, this elderly woman heading towards us from the house with a plate of biscuits in her hand. Mum used her stick to propel herself forward and when she reached us she heaved herself down with a sigh.

'The hyena wasn't a hyena,' Maya whispered in my ear. 'It was a witch!'

'It was?'

'Yes, Gran told me. And now I am protected for ever because it didn't get me.'

I looked at Maya. 'Who did your hair?' I asked, for I had only just noticed that it was in braids.

'Candy,' said Maya proudly. 'She's my cousin, isn't she, Mum? She said when I was away she missed me *so* much. She did my hair and I gave her my Barbie dolls.'

'You did?'

'Yes. That was kind of me, wasn't it, Mum?'

'Here, eat,' my mother said to Maya. She picked up one of the biscuits and she popped it into my daughter's open mouth. 'That's right,' she said with a smile, and she pulled Maya onto her lap, a second biscuit waiting in her hand. For a second I felt a stab of jealousy, that Maya was on my mother's lap.

'Here is your uncle,' Mum told Maya. I tensed myself

as Isaac appeared, thinking she would tell me to fetch my brother a chair. Instead she snapped at him, 'Where have you been?'

Isaac looked dishevelled; he wore an old t-shirt and trousers that were stained round the bottom. I wondered what had happened to the suit he'd been wearing when I saw him in Maun, when we left the clinic. His hair was uncombed and his face worried. Perhaps he had been to the camp. 'How is she now?' he asked.

'Why don't you ask her?' I said.

Isaac puffed up his lips like my mother. Then he turned towards the house as Grace came out. She was looking very smart, she had a new dress on, a swirly print of red and gold, and it fitted her well, the skin on her face was glowing. 'I'm going,' she said, and she lifted a suitcase onto her head. Then she took my hand and gave it a gentle shake. 'She will be fine,' she said. 'Won't you?' she asked Maya.

'*Ee*,' said Maya, and Grace and my mother roared with laughter.

Then Candy came out into the garden and sidled up close to her mother, pushing herself against her leg. 'I'm so tired,' she said, and I saw that she was, that although whatever had happened at the school was over, there was still something disturbed about her. Perhaps she was just totally exhausted. But then we all were.

'I'll come and get you,' said Grace, looking down on her daughter. 'Mama's baby,' she hugged her tight. 'I'll call for you when I'm settled.'

Then Isaac's mobile started to ring but he made no

move to answer it. Something had happened between my brother and Grace in the time since we'd been at the camp, in the time since Maya had been attacked, but I didn't know what.

I was the first to smell the fire. I woke in the dark in my old attic room, feeling that something was not quite right. I could sense Phil next to me, his breathing regular like a rumbling volcano, like Isaac's had been as a child, and I could hear Maya and Joe sleeping too, and it was like my whole family were breathing peacefully in unison like a family of frogs. So I lay there and tried to pinpoint what was wrong. Perhaps I had had a bad dream and that's why I woke, perhaps a mosquito had been bothering me. Then I heard a crackle and an enormous crashing sound like someone was hurtling a heavy object from a great height and it was splintering into tiny pieces. I jumped up and ran to the attic window and tore aside the piece of cloth and I looked down, down into the branches of the mulberry tree and I saw it was on fire.

Why hadn't anyone seen? All along while we were sleeping this had been going on, and the fire was too intense not to have been noticed, the insides of the tree were red hot, and as I looked down a branch fell and sparks flew off into the night air.

I watched for one more second, long enough to see a figure in a nightdress emerging from beneath the tree. Candy was gliding along on the grass, her feet bare, and I thought if someone didn't do something she would catch fire as well.

'Phil!' I screamed. 'Isaac!' and I was off like a flash down the attic stairs and running through the house.

For a second it took my breath away, the mulberry tree looked so beautiful on fire. Then Isaac was out with just his underpants on and Phil was with him. I picked up a bucket from the step, I did it without thinking because there had always been a bucket by the step, and I began to shovel in sand while Isaac ran back with the hosepipe. I almost wanted to laugh; how were we ever going to put out a fire like this? But I just kept on filling the bucket and Isaac kept on firing out water and we just all went on and on.

'She was sleepwalking,' I said to Mum the next day. We were sitting in the garden with Isaac. Phil had taken Maya and Joe to watch a football game in the village and they still hadn't come back. 'She had no idea what she was doing.'

My mother puffed out her lips, she wasn't convinced.

'I don't think she did it deliberately,' I said. 'I think she was sleepwalking, that's what it looked like when I saw her out the window. What I can't get is *how* she did it. I asked her if she had matches or something and she said no. She said she just looked at the tree and it burst into flames!' I laughed because this was so impossible. But then I saw I was the only one laughing.

'She's always been a little ...' Isaac hesitated and he sat down on the blanket next to me. 'Strange.'

'Strange?' I asked. 'How do you mean, strange?'

'It started when she was still small ...' and Isaac looked at Mum and Mum looked away.

'What started when she was still small?'

But Isaac didn't reply.

'It's so black,' I said, and we all looked at the tree, at the thick charred stump. I thought I could see it still smoking, but perhaps it was a trick of the light because the sun was fading now.

'It was always strong that tree,' said my mother. 'It was wind-resistant and drought-resistant, just like me.'

'But not fire-resistant,' I said.

My mother laughed and the setting sun caught her glasses and made them gleam. She seemed remarkably happy about the tree. She had even said we could make it into a table if Isaac could smooth off the branches that remained and then fix some wood on top.

And Candy was remarkably calm, considering. After I'd seen the tree on fire, after I'd tried to help put it out with buckets of sand, I'd taken Candy and put her to bed. She had slept soundly the rest of that night and late into the morning. Every time I checked on her she was asleep; even Bulldog and Joe yelling and playing outside her window didn't wake her up. I thought perhaps she would have forgotten what she'd done when she woke up, but when she did finally get out of bed she seemed refreshed and cheerful. Then she'd been very busy, making *motogo* for Maya and Joe, getting herself dressed. I gave her one of my nighties because hers was so old it was falling apart.

I could see her now inside the house on her knees doing the living room floor with big swishing movements of the cloth. Even from outside I could smell the paraffin and candles and melted plastic and it took me back to long ago when I was even smaller than her. And before beginning on the floor she had washed her school uniform and hung it on the line, all ready for tomorrow, for she said she was going back to school once more. I could see the uniform hanging there – the tunic and the shirt and the socks – like someone could just climb into them and put them on. Burning down the tree seemed to have decided something for Candy; it was as if she'd got rid of something that had troubled her. And although we all still sat near the tree, although we all kept on looking at it and discussing it, when Candy passed it it was like she didn't even see it.

I got up and went to make tea, for Mum wanted some and the maid had disappeared. No one knew when exactly, but she had taken various items from Mum's sideboard and run away with them. And things of mine were missing too, a pair of green espadrilles, a postcard from Sue, a pad of paper on which I'd been writing a letter to Abu who had her PhD now and would be on her way home. As I got to the house I nearly bumped into Bulldog and he beamed at me, showing a glimpse of a big new tooth in his mouth.

'What will happen at the camp?' my mother asked when I came back with the tea.

'How do you mean?' I set the tea things on the blanket, carefully placing Mum's best cups, except the two which the maid had stolen. We hadn't talked about the camp; we hadn't talked about what Petra had done. For days it was as if we had all been tiptoeing around each other.

'Well,' said Mum, 'with that newspaper article telling

everyone, everyone! About what has been going on there.'

'It was a good article,' I said, defensively. 'Petra writes well. It was fair.' It had caused quite a stir in Maun; everyone seemed to be talking about it there.

'I didn't like the photograph,' said my mother. 'Maya looked very dark skinned in that photograph.'

'Oh for God's sake,' I muttered.

'And that was family business,' said Mum. 'You shouldn't have allowed a picture of Maya in the newspaper for everyone to see.'

'But that's it, it's not family business, is it?' I asked, keeping my voice as level as I could. 'Petra wanted to write about why Maya, and Leapile's child, were attacked. That way it won't happen again.'

'The article told the truth,' said Isaac, and he stood up. 'It revealed what was going on.' I looked up at him with a smile because I could see it had taken him some effort to say this. Then I watched while he went to his car and came back with a bag.

'Where is the Coke?' Mum asked greedily, but Isaac didn't reply. He opened the bag and handed me a Lion beer. 'It's not right that you should be punished for what someone else did wrong,' said Mum. 'These journalists just like pointing fingers. It was Lenny Krause who should have done something about those hyenas, him and that white man. If they'd let you run that camp without interference, my son, well that would have been better. It's not right that you're the one to suffer.'

I gritted my teeth. Isaac was hardly suffering, not like

Kgosi or Maya had. I opened the beer and it fizzled.

'Lenny Krause is the one who is responsible,' continued Mum. 'He's the one who should be paying for this.'

'He has friends,' said Isaac, finishing his beer. 'He'll find a way out of this.'

'What do you mean, friends?' I drank from the beer and it felt heavy on my tongue.

'You wouldn't believe the people he has in his pocket.' Isaac threw down his can and began pacing. 'I'm talking police, I'm talking government . . . You have no idea, sis.'

'Are you *scared* of him?' I asked. Isaac lowered his eyes but I kept on staring at him and so did Mum so that I thought this was a question she had wanted to ask as well. 'He can't be that powerful, for God's sake, Isaac. He can't run a camp like that and get away with it. And what about the people he hired? That Tim Loveless isn't qualified to run a safari camp, is he? Petra told me all about him. She says someone was bribed, Isaac, that someone in immigration was bribed, that he doesn't even have a bloody work permit!'

'It wasn't me that appointed Tim Loveless,' said Isaac, and he squeezed his hands into his pockets and began rattling on his car keys.

'Your father would have been proud of the way you worked for that camp,' said Mum. She spoke as if she wanted to soothe Isaac, and as she spoke she patted the blanket next to her, encouraging him to sit down again. And I thought, she just won't move forward, she is still thinking of the past. 'I remember that one time I came to that camp of yours and how hard you were working.'

533

'It wasn't even his camp!' I objected. 'It was mine. Look, no one says he didn't work hard, Mum. Isaac always wanted Dad to be proud of him.'

'Although I don't know why,' said my mother, shifting her bottom, picking at a charred piece of stick that had fallen from the mulberry tree. I realised then that we were all sitting on Mum's old red blanket, a blanket she didn't usually let people use. It was so old, so faded, that I hadn't even realised this until now. 'I don't know why you cared what your father thought,' she said, throwing away the charred stick.

'What do you mean, you don't know why! Because you *made* us, Mum! You were always going on about how great Dad was, what a fine man he was, how respected, how hard working, how this, that and the other.'

'You were born in 1966, that was the first time your father got drunk.'

'What do you mean, he got drunk?'

'He was a drunkard and he died like a drunkard.'

I took another sip of my beer, even though I didn't want to because my head was getting muddier.

'I had to do something,' said Mum, and her voice sounded like a complaint. 'He fell into the mausoleum in the morning and that silly man, what was his name? Haldjimbo, he found him, and I was so ashamed for your father and for us that I told everyone he'd been attacked by a buffalo.'

'So you're saying you lied?' Goosebumps exploded along my arm. 'You lied about how he died?'

'I'm saying I didn't tell you what happened.'

'So you lied?' It seemed so important that she admit to this.

Mum puffed up her lips and looked defiant. 'I want some Coke; you have beer and this tea is too hot.'

That afternoon Phil came back from the football game and, as the kids ran off to play, I found him standing by the gate that led across to the Krauses' plot next door. He was wearing his moon t-shirt. His face was tanned but instead of looking relaxed he looked tense. For the past few days he had been looking tense; I had thought it was because of what had happened to Maya, or because of the drama with the tree, now I had a dull feeling that it was something else.

'We need to talk,' he said, and at first I thought he was joking, he sounded so formal.

'What is it? Did the kids enjoy the game?'

Phil frowned as if I was deliberately trying to distract him. 'If I'm going for this job then we need to leave. This is what I've been trying to tell you. I'm supposed to start this week, like I said. I'm going to have to go tomorrow.' Phil looked away; I could see him staring along the pathway that led into the Krauses' plot.

I didn't know what to say but my heart felt panicky, like he hadn't said what he really wanted to say, like something bad was coming next. 'Are you all packed and everything?'

'I'm all packed and everything.' Still Phil stared off down the pathway.

Look at me, I wanted to say, look at me.

Phil pushed his glasses abruptly up with his thumb. He

looked at me at last, but once he did I couldn't bear to see his eyes, I just focused on his mouth that I loved so much. 'You're glad we came now, aren't you, Kazi? You and your mum seem to be getting along fine. Even your brother . . . It's where you belong, isn't it?'

I nodded and tightened my hands on the gatepost.

'I came here because of you,' said Phil, 'you know that.'

'But you always said you wanted to come to Botswana, you said that the first time we met.'

'I only said that because of you.' Phil smiled. Then he turned away again. 'I've got to go. I'm going to have to go tomorrow. But you don't seem to be leaving, Kazi?'

I shook my head and I could feel the barbed wire at the top of the gatepost digging into the palms of my hands. How could I leave? I didn't want to go back to England; there was nothing for me there now. And I thought, I've lost him. That was it, that was what was wrong. He's going back to England and I've lost him. How did that happen? I've found my home again, I've found my family again, but I've lost Phil. In the distance by the house I heard a cockerel crow furiously.

'I'll be back,' he said. Then he put his arms out and I threw myself between them and smelt his smell and hugged him as hard as I could because I knew this was the last time and he wouldn't come back. He was going to England where he came from and where he belonged and where work was waiting for him. He wouldn't come back here; he wouldn't come back for me. And I didn't know if what I was losing outweighed what I had gained.

Then I felt his arms loosen and I felt him draw away.

And so I watched him go, waiting until he'd walked back along our pathway and disappeared into my mother's house. And as I watched him go I wanted to shout out: *I need you, don't go. If you leave now, you'll never come back. You never loved me, did you?*

What am I going to tell Maya and Joe, I thought, as I went round to the back garden where my mother still sat near the charred remains of the mulberry tree. What am I going to tell the kids about why their father has gone?

As I walked over I could see Isaac coming out of the house as well.

'Kazi *we*!' Mum called as she saw us both. 'What's wrong, my child?' Then she looked at Isaac and said, 'Get your sister a chair.'

BOOK FOURTEEN

Petra

Chapter Fifty

Yissus, this bakkie needs work. I don't know how I'm getting back to the Cape like this. It's in an even worse state than when I left for camp. Then I just needed a spare, now it's a wreck.

'Petra!' Dad shouts from where he is sitting on the stoep. I'm under the bakkie but I know what he's doing. He's sitting hunched on a packing crate drinking from a bottle of brandy. I need to get this thing fixed; I need to get out of here.

'Petra!' he shouts again.

It's hot under here. My fingers slide with grease. I've spent forty minutes on this. He's been drinking steadily since the piece came out. Says I know fokol. Says I'm the snake in the family.

'Where's Isaac?' Dad shouts.

As if I'm going to answer him.

'I'm waiting for him!'

This shouldn't take this long. I'm not working quick enough. I've got an hour before Electricity rocks up. If we're going to Linyanti before I head back to the Cape then I have to have this fixed. He'll make a good companion, Electricity; he doesn't talk much. If it wasn't for him that hippo attack would have been fatal. He helped Maya too. And he got his brother on the plane. He gets things done, I like that. And he doesn't show off about it. He's got time off now, and I want to know what will happen when it's just me and him. I want to see what will happen between us.

'Aunty Petra,' comes a little girl's voice. 'What are you doing under there?'

I look out from under the chassis. I can see Maya's shoes. They look like the school shoes my Aunty Antjie used to buy for me. And just like mine they are covered in muck.

'Come under and see,' I say to her.

There is silence. Maya is thinking this over. Then she scoots her little body down on the sand and joins me.

'I'm getting this fixed,' I say. 'See, here? This is where it's cracked.'

'Why?'

'Why what?'

'Why are you getting it fixed?'

'Because otherwise I can't drive it.'

'Where are you driving to?'

'The bush,' I grunt. I can't have a chat while I'm doing this.

'That's not fair! I want to come too! I went to the camp, you know, that's in the bush. I love it there. I really *really* love it there.'

'That's my girl,' I say. 'Here, hold this.'

Maya's gone, the bakkie's done. Dad's fallen off the packing case and he's right on the stoep. Stitches is lying next to him, farting.

I wipe my hands down my shorts. I need to get this thing packed up. I get the water container, the cool box, a spade, two blankets, the spare. I put two new notebooks and my tape recorder in the glove compartment. Then I'm ready and an hour's not yet up.

So there is time for one more thing.

Yissus, the Muyendi yard smells. The smoke from the fire is everywhere. You can't see it anymore, just smell it. It makes me realise the air in our place is actually fresh. Kazi's not here, Maya said she went to the cemetery with her mother. Phil's gone too, though Maya didn't seem to know where.

I walk up the pathway, squishing mulberries under my foot. I see Isaac as I come round the corner of the house just as I always did as a child. For a second it's like I'm calling on him to go hunting. I can see him from behind; he's bending over the tree. Perhaps he's writing something on the bark, using a penknife to carve out his name like he used to do. Man, that's crazy. He's an adult, he won't be doing that.

When I saw him in Maun he said it wasn't his fault, what happened at the camp. He said Lenny Krause knew fokol. And I said, it's you who knew fokol, Isaac.

I stop where I am. Isaac hasn't heard me; he doesn't know I'm here. He looks all alone. He is all alone. Grace has left; Dad told me, although I don't know how he knows. Seems Grace has a man, out in Gumare. And she's left Isaac for him. I don't think Isaac's taking it too well. It's going to be even worse if Grace sends for Candy and

Bulldog. But perhaps they won't go; perhaps they'll stay in Sehuba.

I go a few steps forward and I see he has a saw; he's not carving on the bark, he's sawing horizontally at the tree. I take a few steps to the side. The massive stump of a tree is nearly smooth. To one side I can see a chunk of fresh wood. Is he making a table?

'Petra!' Dad's voice comes from next door. His voice is faint, but I can still hear it. He wanted me to tell Isaac he was waiting for him, that he wants him over. He's been sending messages to Isaac for two days. And Isaac has just been ignoring him.

Dad's voice makes him turn. He sees I'm here. Then he looks at me and he lifts one hand, the hand with the saw. Isaac doesn't smile; he just gives me the thumbs up.

Epilogue

Day comes quickly to the Okavango Delta. There is a lull in the early hours when those that hunt rest and those who have been hunted die, when the night still encloses the world and when the trees are motionless and the rivers too. The land is black and solid then, until the lull breaks. Then down on the horizon the sky lightens into purple and the fronds of the palm trees come into focus like outstretched hands.

And then the sun begins to lift and mist pours over the delta channels like smoke, blurring the edges of the rivers where the papyrus stands. Only when the sun becomes a jagged ball, sliding over the trees and over the inland channels, does the water gain colour again. Then the mauve-soaked clouds break up, splattering across the sky, and the trees which moments ago looked joined become separate again. Hippos return from foraging and lumber back into the river, crocodiles soon slide from the water to bask in the sun.

Down at the jetty Leapile Muyendi was walking quietly, his shoes dampening in the dew. He had come to check the fishing nets. In front of him on the shore several mekoro were lined up like empty brown pea pods, each one slightly different in width and length and shape. The camp had sold its speedboat; the new manager said they weren't to be used anymore because they upset the hippos. And now there were mekoro made from fibreglass so the trees wouldn't have to be felled.

Leapile saw the fishing net was full and he bent down and released the fish, making one pile for the camp and taking two large barble fish for himself. He would cook them that night and his son Kgosi would get his favourite part, the crunchy marble-white eyes.

He finished gathering the fish and set off back along the wooden jetty which creaked a little, the wooden slats still tight from the night and only beginning to ease under the sun. His new trainers made him walk faster; they made his feet soft and bouncy as if he could walk all day.

He took the main path that led up to where the guests had their meals, passing the row of trees with new metal signs stapled onto their barks so that guests could learn their names: Wild Date Palm: *Tsaro*: *Phoenix reclinata*, Sycamore Fig Tree: *Mochaba*: *Ficus sycomorus*, Sausage Tree: *Moporoto*: *Kigelia africana*.

Leapile could hear two other guides at the bar area, drinking tea, planning an itinerary of the day's events. They were busy; the camp had suffered an empty few months after the newspaper reports but now, for the last few weeks of the season, it was full again. Last week half of the guests had been journalists.

Leapile passed the guides and the barman wiping down the rows of bottles lined up on the counter.

'Isaac Muyendi is coming tomorrow,' said one of the guides.

'Oh him!' said the barman dismissively.

Leapile frowned; there was no need to be disrespectful. In a cooperative, everyone had a part to play. Isaac had experience, he could still be respected for that, and people shouldn't forget those that had given them work.

He greeted the men and then made his way to the staff quarters. The old humps of canvas strung over simple metal frames had been replaced with sturdier structures and with doors that could be tightly secured. A new toilet had been erected close by. The empty cans and plastic bags and chicken bones were gone, and there was a dark green waste bin with a locked lid that even the baboons couldn't work out how to open.

Just before 11am the guests gathered for brunch: an American, a Swiss man, three South Africans and a Scottish couple. The table was laden with food, with scrambled eggs still steaming from the pan, flaky croissants with warm chocolate inside, bowls of golden melons and paw paws and mangoes, jugs of juice and jugs of filter coffee, crusty white bread with pumpkin seeds, little white porcelain jars of salted and unsalted butter.

Electricity sat at the head of the table, a South African guest on either side. It was an arrangement installed by the manager: the guides were to eat with the guests now, they no longer ate separately. He lifted up some motogo, holding the spoon away from his chest and from the new pale green shirt with epaulettes on the shoulder.

'What do you call this?' asked one of the guests, the Scottish woman who was always the first to be seated at brunch.

'Motogo, soft porridge,' said Electricity.

547

'Oh yes, that's right. It's lovely.'

'That's just what I said,' said the man next to her and he gave a little snort as he lifted his spoon.

'Julie,' said Electricity, speaking across the table to the woman opposite him. 'Here are the flyers for the cultural tour.'

'Oh!' she said brightly, trying to sound enthusiastic but failing. She had only two weeks to serve out of her notice and would then be gone.

'What's that?' asked one of the South Africans, leaning over to look at the flyer.

'We have started offering tours to Khwai,' Electricity explained to the people round the table.

'To where?' asked the Scottish woman.

'It's a village,' said Electricity, 'just near here. We are offering a tour for the new millennium, if you want to see how people live around here. Thank you,' he said to one of the waitresses as she handed him a pile of letters. Electricity flicked through them, stopping at a postcard with a foreign stamp. He turned it over and read, *Had a great trip! We'll be back next year. Klaus.*

He put the card down as his cell phone beeped. It was a message from Petra. She was back in Cape Town, a place he was looking forward to seeing.

'I just can't believe it's Halloween,' said the American woman, breaking open a croissant. 'I mean! It doesn't feel like Halloween. The kids back home will be trick or treating now. And look where we are!' and she waved the croissant at the brunch table set on the lawn, the small blue swimming pool off in the distance, the new observation platform built high in the tree for the guests to watch the wildlife. 'This is the end of the season, isn't it?' she asked Electricity.

'*Ee*. It is the end of the hunting season, we will close perhaps in a month or two.'

'That was something that leopard last night,' said the American woman, licking chocolate from the edge of her lips. 'My friends came last year and they were so disappointed not to have seen one. I mean that's why you come, isn't it? There was this guy, Tim, in charge and he promised them, but I guess he couldn't deliver.'

'No,' said Electricity.

'He still around?'

'No.'

'Moved on?'

'He has gone. To his home.' Electricity smiled, thinking about how the immigration men had come unannounced to the camp and asked for Tim and Julie, and how the staff had come up with any errand they could think of so as to be outside the manager's tent and hear what was said by the immigration men.

'We're off to Chief's Island next,' said the Scottish woman.

Her husband cleared his throat. 'Our nephew works there, Craig MacKinnon, he runs the place, do you know him?'

Electricity smiled but didn't reply; he knew immigration was planning another raid.

'Will you?' the woman asked Electricity, holding up her digital camera.

He stood and waited while the couple arranged themselves and then he took a picture. Above him white clouds hung low like mobiles in the sky.

Electricity sat back down as his walkie-talkie crackled and he spoke into it in rapid Setswana while the guests looked on expectantly. 'There are lions,' he said with a smile, and stood up. 'I'll meet you by the vehicles this afternoon.'

He left his guests and headed to the manager's tent, which stood alone not far from the observation platform. He started worrying again about his Kung Fu knife, he hadn't been able to find it that morning and he couldn't think who had taken it. He didn't want a dispute at the camp; the new manager didn't like disputes. It was probably his fault, he thought, he'd been thoughtless and left it somewhere. He stopped, hearing the sound of a truck up at the entrance to the camp and he wondered if it were the supplies truck that should have arrived the day before.

'*Ko ko*,' called Electricity as he walked up the three wooden steps to the porch of the manager's tent. Then he turned at the sound of children playing and his little brother Kgosi came running into view down one of the pathways, leaping in the air, running away from someone and enjoying it. Electricity watched as the others appeared, the little girl who went everywhere with his brother and the little boy who tried to follow them.

'It didn't get *you*,' said the little girl, waiting for her brother to catch up and then taunting him. 'It only got me because I'm special, I'm blessed. It got both of *us*,' and she pointed to Kgosi, 'but not you.'

The boy's face crumbled. 'It's not fair!' he shouted. 'I want to be special too.'

And then the girl relented and she went nearer to her brother and she whispered something in his ear and he laughed and threw both arms around his sister's legs.

'*Tsena!*' the manager called from inside her tent. Electricity could hear her and the Englishman Phil talking and their voices were soft and rumbling the way people sound when they are agreeing with each other, the way they sound when they are in love. Electricity wiped his boots on the side of the steps, approached the tent and went in.

Acknowledgements:

Many thanks to:

Dr Lydia Nyati-Ramahobo who gave me valuable
    background material on the Bayeyi in Moremi
Bonty Botumile, for her wealth of knowledge about the
    safari industry (any mistakes are mine)
Maitseo Bolaane, author of the DPhil thesis: 'Wildlife
    conservation and local management: the establishment
    of Moremi Park, Okavango, Botswana, in the
    1950s–1960s'
Glorious Bongani Gumbo, author of the MA thesis:
    'The political economy of development in the Chobe:
    peasants, fishermen and tourists, 1960–1995'
Neil Parsons, for answering questions and providing
    contacts
Kim, for casting a professional eye over the modelling
    chapters
Sue Dickie, for answering medical queries

I read the following books/publications while research-
ing this novel:

'Annual report of the Bechuanaland Protectorate for the
    year 1949', Commonwealth Relations Office

Country Houses of England, Scotland and Wales, Andrew
    Ginger
Cry of the Kalahari, Mark and Delia Owens
Desert Flower, Waris Dirie and Cathleen Miller
A Desert of Salt, K.R. Butler
Fabled Tribe, Clive Cowley
Fashion Babylon, Imogen Edwards-Jones
A History of Northern Botswana 1850–1910, J. Mutero
    Chirenje
Married Life in an African Tribe and *The Tswana*, both by
    Isaac Schapera
No Lifeguard on Duty, Janice Dickinson
Okavango, Jewel of the Kalahari, Karen Ross
Starlings Laughing, June Vendall Clark
The Tragedy of Supermodel Gia, Stephen Fried

Many of the places in this novel are real; others are fictional, for example Wilderness Camp, Sehuba, Xuku (as used in the book) and the castle on Mull. The chapters concerning the birth of Moremi Game Reserve are based on historical (if disputed) evidence. All the characters portrayed in the novel are entirely fictitious.